RAVE REVIEWS FOR BRETT KING'S
THE RADIX!

"*The Radix* brims with rich detail, in a story fraught with action, suspense, and intrigue. The reader is in highly capable hands with Brett King—a fresh, exciting voice in the international suspense genre. Settle back, enjoy the ride, and savor this debut."
> —*New York Times* bestselling author Steve Berry

"Brett King's *The Radix* is a gem of a novel, a thrilling blend of historical mystery and modern intrigue. Lightning paced and expertly told, here is a debut not to be missed!"
> —*New York Times* bestselling author James Rollins

"A topnotch thriller! Part *Da Vinci Code*, part *24*, *The Radix* is roller-coaster storytelling at its best."
> —*New York Times* bestselling author Jeffery Deaver

"*The Radix* is a relentless, plot-twisting, labyrinthine quest to decipher the medieval mystery of the 'Voynich Manuscript'—a very real tome that still conceals an arcane code that no secret service agency—including the CIA and KGB—has been able to crack in the past five hundred years."
> —*New York Times* bestselling author
> Katherine Neville

"*The Radix* is a pulse-pounding thrill ride of a book."
> —Jason Pinter, bestselling author of
> *The Fury* and *The Mark*

CRASH LANDING

With the copter's blades spinning on the way down, Brynstone braced for a hard landing. His eyes widened. The copter was hurtling toward a restaurant. Perched on Aspen Mountain's summit, the Sundeck Restaurant boasted a dazzling view of the Roaring Fork Valley. He could see people inside. If he hit the building, everyone could die.

Without hesitating, he dropped the Agusta Bell, missing the restaurant. Sundeck staff pressed against the windows, staring in disbelief as the helicopter blasted into the mountainside beneath them. The impact rocked him in his seat. The skids hit the snow and snapped off as blinding powder sprayed the helicopter.

He braced as the helicopter rolled down the steep mountain face. The upright mast split off, sending rotor blades flying into the air. He glanced through the shattered window above the pilot's seat and couldn't believe what he was seeing. Still attached to the stabilizer bar and swash plate, the rotor blades whirled skyward, heading toward the suspended gondola. . . .

THE
RADIX

Brett King

LEISURE BOOKS NEW YORK CITY

For Cheri, Brady, Devin, and Tylyn,
the four people who know me better than I know myself,
and who teach and inspire me,
with their love,
to be a better man.

A LEISURE BOOK®

May 2010

Published by

Dorchester Publishing Co., Inc.
200 Madison Avenue
New York, NY 10016

ISBN 10: 0-8439-6382-4
ISBN 13: 978-0-8439-6382-3
E-ISBN: 978-1-4285-0854-5

Visit us online at www.dorchesterpub.com.

THE
RADIX

Acknowledgments

The story of *The Radix* has been alive inside my mind for more than seven years. Although other projects consumed me during that time, the Radix legend always returned to enchant my imagination. It is with thanks and heartfelt gratitude that I acknowledge the people who helped bring this story to life.

From beginning to end, my wife, Cheri, acted as muse and mentor, editor and accomplice, critic and cheerleader. She never let me lose focus while remaining—always—the love of my life. With Cheri as my wife and best friend, I consider myself to be the luckiest man alive. My beloved children, Devin, Brady, and Tylyn, bless me every day with never-ending laughter, hugs, and inspiration. Although they often mistake me for playground equipment, words can never capture the profound joy they bring to my life. My parents, Dee and Don King, taught me the value of enthusiasm, determination, and hard work. No matter how rambling my dreams and schemes, they have always been there to support me.

My tireless agent, Pamela Ahearn, far exceeded my every expectation and did so with dedication, wisdom, enthusiasm, and a sparkling sense of humor. Thank you, Pam, for never giving up! I am indebted to Don D'Auria—a man every bit as colorful as his office—for taking a chance on me. As executive editor at Dorchester Publishing, he welcomed me with charm, warmth, and patience while helping me navigate the publication process. I also want to thank everyone at Dorchester for their efforts on my behalf. As a team, their talents in editing, artistry, and publicity helped me realize this dream.

A special thanks goes out to my buddy, Troy Barmore, for his candid opinions about this book, all shared with intelligence and splashes of acid wit. His breadth and expertise proved to be an inspired help. I owe a huge debt to my amazing mates, Kyler Storm—a true-to-life superhero—and Candice Storm, a wellspring of inspiration. You both kept me fired up, time after time, while proving that extreme and challenging dreams can come true with faith and perseverance. A special thanks to Dr. Wayne Viney, my cherished friend and mentor, for his faith in me and for bleeding all over my early work with his red pen. Under his guidance, I learned the value of editing and scholarship while discovering a love for the history of ideas. Wayne and his lovely wife, Noni, have taught me more than they will ever know. A boy wonder from the old days, Nathan Clay has been a co-conspirator and fellow cinemaphile. It was a delight corrupting you during your formative years. Like Nate, Ryan Christie has read every shred of fiction I have ever written, yet still chooses to speak to me. I am indebted to you, Rhino, for your positive spirit and for pulling off that black op on foreign soil. My brother, Dennis, and my sister, Gayla, and their families have always been a critical force in my life. For years, Penny Morton, LuAnn Harrah, and Connie Strommenger have expressed interest in my writing, and I'm grateful for their encouragement. After enduring marathon phone calls with me, Gabriel Porras and Trisha Maas at Blue Jay Technologies designed my website with uncompromising creativity and dedication, leaving me awestruck with their talent and vision. Of course, I have to thank Joe, my favorite nemesis and raconteur, for never taking himself—or me—too seriously. You'll always be my hero for rescuing that mysterious one-eyed cat (RIP O-EDC).

I also owe a huge thanks to the people who have shared

comments after reading early drafts of this book or have offered support and encouragement that sustained me over the years, including Kristen Hnida, Ashlee Tripp, Jenn Shaw, Amanda Molencamp, Anne Bliss, Courtney Davis, Kristen Richards, Patty Berger, Dr. Tom Pazik and Leanne Pazik, Alicia Pazik, Laura Kinde, Alex Sward and Ashley Sward, Lauren O'Mara, Laura Mangum-Childers, Aaron Clay, Amanda Clay, Kirsten Orcutt, Kim Shepard, Lisa Kurthy, Vickey and Tom VanParys, Mary Ann Tucker, Dick Hayes, Dr. Andri Bjornsson, Maggie Tillquist, Dr. Don Cooper, Dr. Tim Koeltzow, Holly Greenberg, Adam Cohen, Jenn Elliot, Natalie Pitts, Emily Hennrich, Carl and Alice Hennrich, Amanda Carroll, Lauren Phillips, Erin Christiansen, Megan Gromelski, Elisebeth Hare, David Scott, Aaron Bothner, Julie Giarratano, Bridget Carey, Linda Ensley, Timea Schrantz, Dr. Frank Vattano, Dr. Henry Cross, Dr. Michael Wertheimer and Marilyn Wertheimer, Dr. Diana Hill, Elly Cushman, Leslie Brick, Mike Viney, Kevin Crochetière, Dr. Debbie Clawson, Dr. Doug Schwartzsmith, Jaymie Thorne, Meredith Karol, Renea Nilsson, Chloe Wheeler, Roman Aleksejev, Nancy Grabowski, Jude Cass deLaubenfels, Brittany Yakobson, Julianne Wilson, Kelly Murphy, Dan Gustavson, Erica Merrill, Lindsey Bullard, Christine Gebbia, Renee Foster, Amy Woolridge, Terri S. Thompson, the Prinster family, Kathryn Keller, Cassie Jahn, Katie Kingsley, the Heyse family, and my old friends, Kevin Lucy and Scott Doughty. Finally, I am grateful to Frank Hinchion and Joe Rowsell for technical and medical advice.

Let me add that any errors of fact or content in the following pages or any liberties taken in the name of fiction belong to me alone. I hope you enjoy reading the first book in the Radix series.

B.K.
August 2009

Prologue: The Dying Hour

Cathedral of Notre-Dame de Paris
Christmas Eve, 1502

> *I know that there are numberless people who would, to satisfy a whim, destroy God and all the universe.*
> —Leonardo da Vinci

Nothing could save him now.

Father Raphael della Rovere crept toward a gargoyle and took refuge behind its wings. He whispered a sacred verse before peering around the stone brute. Thunderheads rolled above Paris, corrupting the night with anvil gray clouds. Beyond the bell tower, rain danced a dark ballet on the River Seine.

Riding three days without sleep, he had arrived at Notre-Dame before twilight. It offered sanctuary now, but for how long? Stomach tight with dread, the hooded priest leaned over the ledge. Beneath him, a limestone dragon belched rainwater down the cathedral's southern face. Not a soul down there. Della Rovere darted behind another grotesque, bracing for a look from the western facade. Fright caught in his throat as he gazed down.

His greatest fear awaited him.

The Holy Guard had tracked him to Notre-Dame. Amid flickering torches, the eighty mounted warriors resembled an assembly of phantoms. Dressed in chain mail, they were armed with swords and lances and iron maces. They would not rest until della Rovere revealed his secret. Could he endure their torture? The priest feared he was unsuited for martyrdom. He wiped his eyes, clinging to some mad hope of escape.

Down on the plaza, papal warhorses blasted mist into the drizzling night. A spirited black charger strutted before the cavalry, its golden cuirass and headdress shimmering in torchlight. The tail, woven in a net studded with pearls and rubies, slapped against its hide. Hooves shod in gold stamped the cobblestone. He had recognized this horse from countless military pageants. But where was the rider? The bloodthirsty Duke of Valentinois was not among his cavalry.

Footfalls pounded on the wet balcony behind della Rovere.

Clumsy with panic, he twisted back, raising a bull's-horn lantern.

Cesare Borgia emerged from the bell tower. The tall duke was draped in a velvet cloak with gold brocade over black armor. Across his breastplate, a medallion of diamonds blazed in the lantern light. Tangled auburn hair framed his bloodred mask.

"How did you find me?" della Rovere asked, frozen in terror.

"Providence," he answered from behind his mask. "God directed me to find you."

"That is a lie."

A peal of laughter. "You made a grave mistake stealing the Radix from the Vatican."

"I had no choice but to seize it from your father, the Pope."

"You have no choice now but to surrender it to me."

"First," the priest stammered, "I ask to look you in the face."

Borgia cocked his head, considering it. "Very well, behold me."

Reaching behind his neck, he unbuckled two leather straps, then slid off the mask. Della Rovere couldn't unlock his gaze. Cesare Borgia had once been considered the most handsome man of his age. Countless artists had used his face as a model when painting portraits of Jesus Christ. But now, Borgia resembled a demon more than a savior. Disease had stripped his beauty, scoring his face with angry pustules and blemishes. The French pox had chewed his nose down to an obsidian cavity. He was more hideous than the priest had imagined. More grotesque than three years ago when their cousins, Francesco della Rovere and Angela Borgia, had been joined in marriage.

"Does the disease bring you misery?"

"Can you not see the answer carved into my face? At times, the pain is extraordinary."

Della Rovere whispered, "Good."

"Obey the Holy Father. Hand over the Radix."

The priest dropped his gaze to the balcony's stone floor, pitted like Borgia's face. "Your father locked me in the Vatican Library to study the Radix. When I discovered its power, I swore your family would never possess it."

"You have forgotten," Borgia sneered. "The Radix *is* our possession."

"Only because you plundered it from the Knights of Rhodes," the priest answered, his voice rising. "You cannot comprehend its power. The Radix is the unfathomable mystery of God. The Secret of Secrets."

He did not trust Pope Alexander VI, and for good reason. Born Rodrigo Borgia, he was rumored to have committed his first murder at age twelve. As a cardinal, Borgia had bribed his way into the papacy with silver and villas. He had fathered ten illegitimate children in a time already known as the Golden Age of Bastards. Hushed stories told about the Pope sleeping with his own daughter, Lucrezia. Della Rovere would never surrender the Radix to a man who poisoned enemies and corrupted the Church. It would give unfettered power to Pope Alexander VI and his son. And then nothing could curb their wickedness.

"You've hidden it at Notre-Dame, haven't you?" Borgia asked. "I'll tear apart this old church stone by stone."

"On my word as a Franciscan, I promise the Radix is not here."

"I believe you, Father. You are a thief, not a liar. But know that I shall find it."

In the distance, lightning glinted over the Abbaye de Saint-Germain. Watching the sky, the priest said, "No one shall ever find it. The Radix is lost to history."

Borgia ran his tongue across his small white teeth. "You judge me and the Holy Father, but you have your own demons."

"Of what are you speaking?"

"Your wife," Borgia answered, his eyes cold and complicated. "I'm speaking about how you killed her."

"I did not mean for that to happen."

"That's what you say in confession. Still, you killed Isabella."

"After Isabella's death, I took the vows of priesthood. God has forgiven me."

Borgia offered a grim smile. "Has your dead wife forgiven you?"

Angry at reliving the memory, della Rovere squeezed the crucifix around his neck. "Evil has poisoned your soul."

"And foolishness has clouded your mind. Perhaps you need the counsel of an old friend." Borgia waved at the tower. "Niccolò, come."

A lean thirty-three-year-old man stepped out of the shadows. Della Rovere recognized his owlish face. Wide, curious eyes and sharp cheekbones melded around his pointed nose. And the lips, thin and perpetually amused. His childhood friend, Machiavelli.

"Niccolò," he cried. "Why are you here?"

Machiavelli bowed, looking small beside Borgia. "I serve as his Florentine secretary."

"You dare work for Cesare Borgia? I know you wish to write a book about him. I thought hatred motivated you, not admiration."

"Raphael, you do not understand."

"I understand Borgia. *You* are seduced by him." Gritting his teeth, della Rovere asked, "Did you tell him about Isabella's death?"

"Like you, I had no choice. If it is his pleasure, he can make and unmake a man."

"You see?" Borgia grinned before sliding on the red mask. "He does understand me."

· "Obey him, Raphael. You know his power over men."

"I do," della Rovere said, turning to the duke. "Your oppressive will has broken Maestro Leonardo of Florence. As your engineer in chief, da Vinci has laid down his paintbrush to design bottles of poison gas and revolving scythes that can shred men like grain."

Borgia cut him off. "Does Leonardo know where to find the Radix?"

"He knows a great many secrets, but nothing about where I've hidden it."

"Better for him," the duke said. "Before me, cities tremble. Kings and artists prostrate themselves in the dust. Why do you not fear me?"

Thunder rattled the stained-glass windows. Winter rain teemed down, pelting the cathedral with a volley of silvery droplets.

"I do fear you. But I fear God's wrath more than the Devil's strength."

Borgia barked a humorless laugh. "Have you witnessed my strength?"

"I have seen you twist a horseshoe with your bare hands. I have seen you slay six wild bulls, the last beheaded with a single stroke of your broadsword."

"Indeed. With this very sword." Borgia pulled the gleaming weapon from its scabbard. Lightning cleaved the sky, glowing brilliant on the broadsword. Borgia grabbed Machiavelli's hair, then pressed the blade to the man's throat. "Tell me where to find the Radix or I'll behead Niccolò as easily as that bull."

Machiavelli's eyes sparkled with fear.

"Save your friend," Borgia shouted over the downpour. "Tell me where you've hidden the Radix."

Della Rovere removed his hood. He faced the heavens, then closed his eyes. Thunder roared like cannon fire. Rain trickled down his face in icy rivulets, plastering blond hair against his cheek. Turning sideways, he clutched a gargoyle. He raised his boot, stepping onto the slick ledge. His legs trembled.

"Taking your life is a mortal sin," Borgia warned. "Have you forgotten the bitter lessons from Dante's *Inferno*?"

"Suicide would prove a better fate than betraying the Holy Secret."

"Raphael," Machiavelli pleaded, with the blade creasing his throat. "Listen to reason."

"I have," della Rovere rasped. He hung his lantern on the gargoyle's wing. "Farewell, my friend." He blessed the two men, then made the sign of the cross over himself. Feeling his body teeter, he stepped backward off the ledge.

Shoving aside Machiavelli, Borgia charged at the priest. With leonine grace, Borgia slashed his broadsword through della Rovere's ankle. The pain felt raw and bright, but he didn't cry out. Notre-Dame's rose window blurred past as he plummeted, the wind howling in his ears.

Cesare Borgia locked his gaze on Father della Rovere. A mask of calm slipped over the priest's face before he crashed onto the plaza. Blood seeped onto the wet stone, forming a crimson halo around his head. Papal soldiers dismounted their steeds. They gathered in a circle around della Rovere's broken body.

"I must ask," Machiavelli said, looking up at him. "Why did you sever his foot?"

"I had in my mind a saying from Emperor Caligula: 'Strike so that he may feel he is dying.'" Borgia ran his gloved hand across the blood-splattered gargoyle. "Niccolò, you must tell no one that della Rovere came to Notre-Dame. Not a soul." Borgia caressed the man's chin, then lowered his finger. He made a slashing gesture across Machiavelli's throat, leaving a line of della Rovere's wet blood.

"You can trust my silence," Machiavelli assured him. He peered over the ledge, wiping blood from his neck. "I never conceived he'd take his life."

"He was a desperate man. A disgrace to the House of Borgia. A Judas willing to rob the Vatican of its greatest treasure."

"And now," Machiavelli sighed, "that treasure has died with him."

Part One
The Close and Holy Darkness

None knows the secret of God.
—Sikh scripture

Chapter One

It all came down to tonight. Months of planning had led John Brynstone to this moment. He had to find the Radix, no matter what the cost.

He never imagined a two-year quest would bring him here, breaking into a residence in Aspen's exclusive Starwood Estate subdivision. At fifty-six thousand square feet, the mansion was larger than the White House. The thirty-year-old agent had prepped day and night for this assignment, studying blueprints and surveillance parameters. He belonged to an elite force charged with blackbag ops for the most secretive intelligence agency on the planet. He wasn't a thief.

Tonight, he had no choice.

"Jordan," he said, touching the throat microphone. "I'm inside. Copy?"

"Roger that, Dr. Brynstone." A quiet edge crept into her voice. "Be careful. Over."

"Copy that."

"You dig this, don't you?" Jordan Rayne marveled. "The thrill of it all."

"Think you have me figured, huh?" He smiled. "Heading to the library. Brynstone out."

He darted in the shadows above the ballroom. A Rocky Mountain blizzard raged outside the mansion's wraparound windows. Holding his breath, he peered over the railing. Dressed in checkered kaffiyehs, two men lingered near a marble pillar. They worked security for Prince Zaki bin Abdelaziz, the ambassador to the United States on behalf of the Kingdom of Saudi Arabia. Additional guards prowled Zaki's ninety-five-acre estate. It had been a challenge breaking into Hala Ranch. Maybe the biggest of Brynstone's storied career.

Darkness could not conceal the ballroom's grandeur. Cast in reddish gold glass, Arabic chandeliers decorated the gold-leaf ceiling. A stone entryway and mountain-view windows framed the parquet floor. Prince Zaki had romanced power and privilege in this room, hosting gilded parties for presidents and kings and celebrities. Tonight was different. Guards carrying assault rifles patrolled the grand hall. Buzzing in Arabic, the shorter guard kissed the barrel of his MP5 submachine gun, joking about his girlfriend. His buddy roared with laughter. The aroma from their clove cigarettes drifted to the balcony, tickling Brynstone's nose.

As the guards joked about American excess and stupidity, he adjusted his backpack and night-vision goggles. Keeping it quiet, he crept toward the end of the balcony. He turned a corner, then paused before the double doors of Zaki's library. He unzipped his black coat, wet with snow, revealing a black shirt over his Kevlar vest.

The pit of his stomach swirled with butterflies. He liked that sensation. Sometimes his covert missions didn't inspire a nervous edge. That was a dangerous sign. It meant overconfidence or complacency. Not tonight. If Brynstone's research proved accurate, Prince Zaki had collected a relic that had vanished from the earth five hundred years ago.

For centuries, the Radix existed in rumor and secrecy. Saints whispered its legend. Alchemists craved its power. Papal leaders feared its threat to biblical doctrine.

Sucking in a breath, he swiped a smart card through the metal reader. The library doors glided open. Another wave of anxiety tickled his consciousness. So much could go wrong tonight, but Brynstone sensed he was close to discovering the truth about the Radix legend.

In the emerald fog of night-vision goggles, Brynstone glanced around the room, wondering where to start. At three thousand square feet, Zaki's library was bigger than most people's homes. Along with ancient Egyptian arti-facts, the prince collected Arabic and Islamic artwork from the Seljuk period and the Mamluk Empire. Priceless antiquities congregated with sculptures posed on marble pedestals. Floor-to-ceiling bookshelves adorned the walls.

The prophet could be hiding anywhere in here.

Built into the east wall, a 440-gallon aquarium bathed the room in arctic light. Six lionfish drifted inside the tank, their dorsal spines seething with venom. A blue-ringed octopus lurked beneath a shelf of purple live rock. Only four inches long, the Australian cephalopod's bite could kill ten men.

A twin tank dominated the opposite wall. Shadows darted inside, triggering motion sensors to activate ultra-violet lighting. Like stars spilling across the heavens, scorpions glowed whitish green in the black light. The terrarium seemed to pulsate as the fluorescing creatures scrambled over rocks. Zaki favored lionfish, a killer octo-pus, and scorpions. *Turns out it's true*, Brynstone thought. *People do buy pets that match their own personalities.*

Beside an Egyptian sarcophagus, he discovered an ob-ject that chilled him. Encased in a glass cube, an Arabic dagger pierced a human skull. He moved a step closer. With a hilt cut from a rhino's horn, the jambiya's curved blade was wedged near the coronal suture.

Brynstone caught his chiseled reflection in the display glass. He squinted, intensity sizzling in his ice blue eyes. He pushed up night-vision goggles onto his thick black hair. Pinching the skin at the bridge of his nose, he closed his eyes. How many years had it been? His mind flashed to a childhood memory of a stormy Nantucket evening when he had rolled his wheelchair into his father's study. The most terrible night of his life.

Jordan Rayne's voice crackled inside his earpiece. "Have you found the prophet?"

His head snapped around. He blinked as he scolded himself for losing focus.

"Dr. Brynstone? Do you copy? We have word Zaki has returned to Aspen. Over."

Ugliness churned inside his gut. Security languished when diplomatic business called away Ambassador Zaki. That's why Brynstone had chosen tonight to break into the main residence of Hala Ranch.

"I thought Zaki was in Washington with the president."

"Their meeting turned into a screaming match. Prince Zaki stormed out of the Oval Office," she answered. "He's back in Colorado. His Airbus landed at Aspen County Airport."

"In this snowstorm?"

"He's heading to Hala Ranch in a helicopter. We should abort Operation Overshadow."

"I can't. We've come too far. Is Zaki's State Department security detail with him?"

"Affirmative," she answered. "His guards will secure the main residence before Zaki arrives. You can expect company any minute."

"Then I better shut up and find the prophet. Brynstone out."

He slid on the goggles, then searched the library for an image of a prophet. Find it and he'd discover the passage to the secret chamber.

The Koran mentioned twenty-five prophets, including Mohammed as well as Jesus, Adam, Noah, Abraham, Moses, and Solomon. He didn't expect to find a likeness of Mohammed, given the Islamic ban against portraying his image. But none of the paintings and sculptures here featured anything resembling other prophets. Had he received compromised intelligence about the entrance to Zaki's secret chamber?

Outside, a rhythmic sound slashed through the wind.

His heart slammed in his chest as he peeked out the window. A helicopter roared above the foothill a half mile behind the mansion. Snow swirled around the heliport as a greenish yellow beacon summoned the Agusta Bell 139. The chopper touched down in a halo of floodlights. Zaki was home. His arrival with a State Department security escort would make Brynstone's escape more challenging. Zaki also traveled with a roster of former British Special Air Service men. Hala Ranch's security far outnumbered the local sheriff's department.

Time was running out to find the prophet. Brynstone felt the dizzy tingle of adrenalin. A challenge like this sharpened his thinking and heightened his vigilance. Made him feel alive.

He noticed an oil painting depicting a seated woman dressed in lavender robes. A young man kneeled beside the throne, absorbing her wisdom. Painted in the neo-classic style, it clashed with the Islamic artwork. He wondered if the woman was a sibyl. Maybe even the Delphic oracle counseling Oedipus? If so, she might be the prophet who would guide him to Zaki's secret chamber. *No,* he decided. *It doesn't make sense.* Although Ibn Hazen had suggested that Mary, the mother of Jesus, was a prophetess, most Islamic scholars believed that Allah had never chosen a female prophet.

He jolted at the sound of footsteps. Light sliced beneath the doors. Outside the library, a card activated the swipe reader. As Jordan Rayne had predicted, Zaki's guards were running a last-minute check throughout the main residence of Hala Ranch.

He scrambled across the library.

The door unlocked with a soft click.

Brynstone opened the standing Egyptian sarcophagus, hoping it was empty.

Not the best hiding place, he told himself. *Still, Scooby-Doo would be proud.*

Chapter Two

Aspen
5:06 P.M.

Brynstone had crammed his body and backpack inside the sarcophagus in Prince Zaki's library. The lights came on before he'd closed the lid all the way. He froze, not surrendering a breath. Peeking through the inch-wide aperture, he strained to see the guard. Brynstone glanced at the mahogany floor. A smart card rested ten feet from Zaki's desk. It must've fallen from his belt. He cursed himself. On his way in here, he'd taken out a guard named Tareef to get that card. It offered hope of escape without attracting attention.

The guard's walkie-talkie crackled in the silence. "This is Imad. Library is clear."

Brynstone hushed a sigh of relief.

Reaching for the light switch, Imad glanced back, casting a final look at the room. Brynstone held his breath, waiting to hear the door close. Nothing. He stiffened. Imad walked toward the desk. Cradling his submachine gun, he picked up the smart card. Speaking into his two-way, he said, "Faysal, tell Tareef I found his card. He dropped it in the library."

"I have not seen Tareef."

"And why would Tareef's card be up here? He never patrols the library." Suspicion playing on his face, the guard hurried toward the desk.

Brynstone strained to see him.

"Prince Zaki walks in as we speak," Faysal growled. "Get down here, Imad."

The guard pocketed the card. He flipped off the light, then bolted from the library.

Brynstone emerged from the sarcophagus and rushed to the spot where Imad had been standing. He made a sweeping glance at the desk. A book of pre-Islamic poetry. A foot-tall sculpture of a praying mantis. Hand-written notes scrawled in a clean *dizaani* script. A black scorpion trapped inside a Lucite paperweight. Six Arabic journals arranged in a uniform stack.

He shot another look at the mantis. Perched on green-ish bronze hind legs, the statue's oversized forelegs were folded in prayerful reverence. It came to him in a flash. He remembered that *mantis* originated from an ancient Greek word meaning "prophet." Some Arabic cultures be-lieved the mantis bowed in a praying fashion as it faced Mecca. A smile. With a little help from Imad, he had found the prophet. Now he needed to figure out how the mantis would lead him into the secret room.

As he grabbed the sculpture, he noticed that the man-tis's clawed forelimbs were moveable. He coaxed them apart. As they opened, the statue's triangular head tilted. The thing moved like a real mantis, the only insect able to peer over its shoulder. The praying mantis turned its creepy gaze toward the terrarium. Moving with a whoosh, the tank glided three feet to the right. Scorpions clam-bered across the rocky landscape. Their venomous tails jabbed at the air as the terrarium slid away to reveal a metal door.

Now we're getting somewhere.

He hurried to the door. The keypad featured an alphanumeric display, like on a phone. He removed a tracing device from his backpack, then clipped it to the keypad.

"Work your magic, Jordan," he whispered. "But make it fast."

"I'm on it," she purred. "I'm bypassing the tamper-protection hierarchy."

He trained his gaze on the door. Zaki's security team was circulating the grounds. The prince would visit his library any minute now. It was his second-favorite room at Hala Ranch.

"How's it going, Jordan?" he asked, stripping urgency from his voice.

"I'm running a rotating algorithm now. Narrowing it down."

"I need it now," he muttered.

A shadow passed in the hallway, breaking up light from beneath the door.

"Check the monitor," she said. "Let me know if it does the trick."

A series of numbers appeared on the small screen. He punched the eight-digit PIN into the keypad. The door unlocked. He opened it, then ducked inside the secret chamber. Looking back, he pressed a red button. The terrarium rumbled across the floor, sealing him inside.

"I'm inside the chamber. Commencing phase two of Operation Overshadow."

"Good luck."

"Thanks for your help. Brynstone out."

Carved into the wall, Arabic letters spelled out the secret chamber's name: ASSEMBLY OF THE DEAD. The hexagonal room featured thirty marble compartments, each with glass doors, separate humidity sensors, and recessed lighting. Inside the booths, upright mummies guarded the room like battle-hardened sentries. Many in the collection had been stolen from museums and smuggled into this country.

He passed from one mummy to the next, marveling at their preservation. Some looked gray and paper-thin, with withered faces. Others appeared almost alive, with serene expressions. A diet of old mummy movies had fed his childhood. The ones with Boris Karloff and Christopher Lee had scared the crap out of him, but also inspired his fascination with paleopathology.

Mummies filled every compartment except one. Prince Zaki's collection boasted desiccated specimens from different eras and cultures: the ancient Egyptians, the Jivaros, the Sauras, the Alaskan Aleuts, and the Chachapoya cloud people. Bog mummies stood side by side with catacomb mummies and "mound people" recovered from tree coffins going back to Denmark's Bronze Age. The corpses had been embalmed using everything from sugar, lime, and salt to frankincense, mercury, and alcohol. Zaki even owned a drooping Old West outlaw, preserved with arsenic. He moved past each mummy's booth until one captured his attention. He caught his breath after reading the Arabic inscription above the glass door.

ALEXANDER THE GREAT

He leaned in, taking a look at the corpse mounted on a stainless-steel post. Was this for real?

Mummified in Babylon, Alexander's body disappeared around the first century CE. The Macedonian leader's will had demanded his corpse be submerged in a golden coffin filled with white honey. Outside of a textbook, Brynstone had never seen a "honey mummy." God knows, he'd always loved the name.

He hadn't come here to find Alexander the Great's mummy, but he couldn't tear himself away. Alexander's body was in decent condition. His face was another matter. The nose was missing, thanks to a famous royal blunder. Three centuries after Alexander's death, Caesar Augustus had inspected the mummy, brushing his hand across the face. Bad idea. Caesar had snapped off Alexander's nose.

The noseless mummy posed one of the greatest mysteries in paleopathology. Speculation about Alexander's passing ranged from malaria to West Nile fever to a poison conspiracy. If Brynstone analyzed the mummy, he could solve the ancient mystery. Not tonight. He needed to find the mummy of Lorenzo Zanchetti. He suspected it held a greater secret.

He found the Renaissance mummy four compartments down from Alexander the Great. The soft-tissue preservation was the best Brynstone had seen. Friar Zanchetti had eyebrows and eyelids. Even a black curly beard. And he had a nose, more than his Macedonian neighbor could say. The Italian monk appeared asleep, not mummified. Zanchetti looked good for a five-hundred-year-old mummy. Come to think of it, he looked good for a mummy from any period.

Brynstone pulled a small monitor from his backpack. Using suction backing, he attached the high-resolution screen to the inside wall of the booth. At the monitor's base, he plugged in an endoscope designed to explore the tissues and organs separating the lungs. The slender probe contained a miniature camera composed of hundreds of ten-micron glass fibers. Using the fiber-optic instrument, he could grab a crystal-clear visual of the mummy's bodily canals.

If Brynstone's painstaking research over the last two years was correct, a priest named Raphael della Rovere had found a curious hiding place for his stolen treasure. Before Cesare Borgia could track him, della Rovere had stashed a priceless relic inside Friar Zanchetti's corpse.

According to legend, a small stone box called the *cista mystica*, or mystic coffin, contained the Radix. He wanted it, but wouldn't risk unnecessary damage to the mummy. After slipping on latex gloves, he eased two fingers inside the mummy's shriveled mouth, then inserted the endoscope's lighted tip. He could search here without leaving a clue Zaki might notice.

Watching the monitor, he angled the flexible tube into the larynx and down the trachea. He jumped when a spider appeared on the screen. He chuckled in relief. The creature had crawled inside the mummy's throat and never found its way out. From the look of it, the spider had been trapped inside Zanchetti for two or three centuries.

He probed farther, but didn't see anything. Growing impatient, he removed the endoscope from the mouth. That's when he noticed Zanchetti's missing finger. The ring finger on the mummy's left hand had been severed. Did della Rovere intend it as a clue that the *cista mystica* was lodged near the heart?

Long before it was known as the ring finger, the third finger on the left hand was called the heart finger. Medieval scholars believed that a special nerve ran from the heart to the third finger. This belief inspired the matrimonial tradition of placing a ring on the third finger because it was connected to the heart, the center of love and fidelity. The tradition persisted, although most people wearing wedding rings had no idea that ancient medicine had inspired the practice.

A post inside the booth held the mummy upright. Grabbing a scalpel, Brynstone made an incision in the chest as if he were performing laparoscopic surgery. He inserted the endoscope's glowing tip into the opening, then fed the tube inside the chest cavity. Moving between the ribs, the probe snaked deeper into Zanchetti's body. *Better be right*, he thought. *No time for mistakes.* On the monitor, the edge of a small box came into view. Could it be the *cista mystica*? Flushed with adrenalin, he rotated the endoscope toward the box.

The monitor went black.

He'd lost the image. He knew from experience it could be several things. An internal calibration problem could result in poor image transmission. Or maybe a defect produced by misalignment in the apparent field of view.

Brynstone removed the endoscope from Zanchetti's mummified chest and almost dropped it in shock. He rolled back on his feet, breathing and swallowing, ears ringing.

The endoscope was coated in blood.

Chapter Three

Washington, D.C.
7:10 P.M.

"We cannot discuss this at the White House," Deena Riverside whispered to the president's brother, backing up her words with a glare.

"I'll discuss it wherever I damn well please," Dillon Armstrong answered. "Especially given the substantial amount of money I'm pouring into this deal."

"This could be dangerous for us. We have to keep it quiet."

She glanced around the Blue Room, making sure no one was within earshot. The French Empire décor and sapphire blue furnishings sparkled with holiday adornment. Near the door to the South Portico, a string quartet played "Silent Night." Dressed in cocktail attire, the other White House guests were absorbed in conversation.

"I promise, this will be worth it," she said. "But you need to be patient."

"Patient?" he snorted. "I didn't become a billionaire by being patient. You know what really bothers me, Deena? We don't have any guarantees that Pantera can deliver."

"It's a complicated process," she assured. "Trust me, it will pay off."

"It better." He checked his cell. "I need to take this call. When I get back, I want hard details."

Dillon Armstrong stormed across the Blue Room, heading for the Cross Hall. Dressed in a black suit, he looked like a shorter, younger version of the president. Deena had never enjoyed an easy relationship with the man. More than anyone else, he controlled her corporate fate. The pressure was on. If she didn't close this deal, she could be fired from her chief-executive-officer position.

President Alexander Armstrong watched the dark-haired child from across the Blue Room. At least half of his fifty guests attending the Christmas Eve party were household names. Didn't matter. He focused his attention on the little girl in the center of the room.

Four-year-old Andrea Starr dropped her head back, staring at a crystalline angel dangling from the eighteen-foot Christmas tree. Her small mouth lowered in awe as she pivoted on her leg brace for a better look. Her father, Isaac Starr, was the vice president of the United States. Although Armstrong and Starr had once been political rivals, they had settled their differences before coming to the White House. Armstrong had been with the Starr family on the day Andrea was diagnosed with spastic cerebral palsy.

Armstrong marched toward the Christmas tree. Coming up beside her, he said, "Close your eyes, Andrea, and hold out your hands." At fifty-five, he was tall and barrel-chested with a full head of hair going gray. Armstrong reached up and plucked an ornament from the mammoth noble fir. He placed the silver angel in her open palm. Her eyes fluttered open.

The child's face glowed. "Thank you, Mr. President," she giggled.

After kissing the top of her head, he watched as she

showed the ornament to the vice president. A finger tapped Armstrong's shoulder.

"You're good. Anyone ever tell you that?" Deena Riverside smiled. Five years younger than the president, she looked elegant in a knee-length designer dress. Her cinnamon brown hair was pulled into a knot at the top of her head, a single strand curving around her cheek. An electric smile and warm eyes added radiance to her otherwise-simple face.

"How do you do it?" she asked, sliding her hand around his arm. "You're able to enchant little girls and little old ladies and everyone in between."

"I took a correspondence course." He flashed a smile. "Presidential Schmoozing 101."

He had known Deena for years, going back to when she had masterminded his successful New York gubernatorial campaign. That was before she became CEO at Taft-Ryder Pharmaceuticals. Today she was one of only twelve women running a Fortune 500 company.

"Where's the First Lady?"

"Migraine. Helena has hosted more than twenty Christmas and Hanukkah receptions at the White House. Guess it caught up to her."

"Sorry to hear that."

Was she? Deena and the First Lady shared a bitter relationship. For years, he had concealed his brief but intense affair with Deena. Poisoned with guilt, he had confessed to his wife. Since then, Helena couldn't tolerate sharing any room with her.

"Heard about your meeting with the Saudi ambassador," Deena said as they passed a lighted topiary tree near the Monroe sofa. "Dillon said you had a screaming match with Zaki."

"I'd rather not talk about that," the president said, watching Dillon Armstrong return from the Cross Hall. A smart-looking woman in a navy designer gown intercepted him near a holiday urn brimming with greenery, limes, and pineapples. The woman appeared helpless to resist the legendary Armstrong charm.

"Do you know her?" Deena asked.

"Society columnist. Helena invited her."

"Terrific," she answered in a lukewarm tone.

Dillon Armstrong dipped into the crowd, working his way toward them. Four years younger than the president, he had dueled in a friendly rivalry with his brother since childhood. Maybe it was some kind of middle-child syndrome, but Dillon was obsessed with one-upping his brother. Known as a brilliant investor, he had hit a milestone at age thirty-three when he cleared his first billion. The president's little brother was worth twenty billion dollars now, give or take a few billion. Two years ago, Alexander Armstrong had found a way to go one better, when he became president of the United States. Take that, Dillon.

"Merry Christmas, little brother," the president said. "You look stressed."

"Not at all," Dillon answered with a characteristic swagger. He turned to Deena. "We need to talk." He grabbed her hand, leading her toward a door to the South Portico. She glanced back, looking helpless.

The president had never seen that expression on her face. His brother's relationship with Deena stirred ambivalence in him. Following the president's advice, Dillon had recruited her to run Taft-Ryder Pharmaceuticals. In less than five years, they had transformed an anemic company into a corporate powerhouse. As far as he knew, they shared a positive work relationship. This conversation looked different.

A White House aide intercepted him. "Mr. President, the prime minister of the United Kingdom is calling from his Christmas holiday in Barbados."

"I'll take it in the Oval." He followed the aide, glancing back at the windows facing the South Portico. He had to know what was going on out there.

* * *

Deena breathed in chill air as she and Dillon walked across the South Portico's semicircular walkway. Snow cloaked the southern magnolia tree Andrew Jackson had planted as a tribute to his deceased wife, Rachel. Since that time, every president, including Alexander Armstrong, had planted trees at the executive mansion.

"I didn't see Brooke at the party," Deena said.

"She's in Manhattan." His eyes flickered. "We separated two months ago."

She stepped back, concealing her shock. She had no idea their marriage was troubled.

A Secret Service agent named Natalie Hutchinson hurried up the stairs that hugged the portico. Dressed in a black uniform, she looked more like a police officer than a member of the security detail that shadowed the president. "Mr. Armstrong, we prefer you not spend time on the South Portico. For security reasons."

"Deena and I need a little privacy to discuss business."

The agent gave a resigned look. "Please keep it short."

Watching her walk away, Dillon braced his hand against a pillar. He turned to Deena. "I'm concerned about Taft-Ryder. You're on the verge of destroying everything we worked to build."

She sighed, wishing she had grabbed a drink before he had dragged her out here.

Her corporation had hit hard times during the past two quarters. Before she had joined the pharmaceutical giant, his holding company had invested in Taft-Ryder, rescuing it from bankruptcy. As a value investor, he was a master at spotting undervalued companies with high growth potential. Trade magazines had christened him the Market Alchemist based on his skill for transforming corporate underachievers into Wall Street gold.

"Like I said before, Dillon, we have several promising drugs in our pipeline. We're hoping Taft-Ryder can deliver new drugs to offset the old ones coming off patent."

He glanced at Agent Hutchinson near the entrance to the Blue Room. "I don't share your optimism, but we'll discuss that later. I want to talk about the Radix. Can you assure me that Pantera will find it and deliver it to us?"

She stared at the wintry night. "I have faith in Pantera. It looks promising."

"I've offered top dollar to own the Radix, but if you don't control this deal, it could turn into a public-relations nightmare."

"I'm sorry," Agent Hutchinson cut in. "Could you move inside now?"

Deena jolted around, surprised to see her. In truth, she was relieved the Secret Service agent had interrupted their conversation.

"We're finished," he answered.

As they walked across the South Portico, he grumbled, "Expect a call from me in the morning. You better have the deal worked out."

Deena Riverside nodded, dreading the potential consequences of not delivering the Radix to the president's brother.

Chapter Four

Aspen
5:16 P.M.

Blood oozed from the Renaissance mummy.

John Brynstone leaned closer to examine the incision. He wondered if he was hallucinating. A crimson line trickled down Friar Zanchetti's withered chest. Snapping to his senses, he unrolled gauze, then wiped the endoscope. He placed it on the monitor, with the glowing tip facing the mummy chamber.

The endoscope's camera filmed an image from over his shoulder. A blurry figure darted across the screen, coming toward him. He spun around. The man had appeared from nowhere. At six five, he had three inches on Brynstone. Seemed like twice that.

The guy worked State Department security detail, though one wouldn't guess it from his clothes. State loved the Hala Ranch assignment because they could ditch the suits and neckties. In a mountain ski town, dressing in sweaters, jeans, and cowboy boots was like wearing camouflage. Especially in Aspen, where wealthy tourists paraded around in tight neon pink ski suits laced with fur collars.

Looking like a warrior in a reindeer-themed sweater, the State agent brandished an Arabic saber.

"Didn't realize the State Department replaced your guns with swords," Brynstone taunted. "Looks like President Armstrong's budget cuts hit you guys hard."

"Zaki doesn't permit firearms in his Assembly of the Dead."

"Know how to use that thing, Agent Cregger?"

"How'd you know my name?"

"I do my homework."

His eyes looked severe. "Tell me your name."

"John Robie," Brynstone lied.

Cregger smirked. "Okay, you might pass for Cary Grant's son if he had one. And I believe you're a cat burglar."

"Guess you've seen *To Catch a Thief*."

"Twenty times. I'm a huge Hitchcock fan."

"My luck."

"Zaki's men never search the mummy room," Cregger muttered. "Good thing I did."

"My luck again."

"Whoever you are," he said, reaching for his two-way, "I'm calling this in."

Brynstone crossed his arms. "Can't take care of me yourself?"

"Okay," the agent fumed. "You want me? You got me."

Cregger wielded the saber as he rushed him. Brynstone grabbed the agent's meaty wrists, twisting away from the weapon. The curved blade brushed past his shoulder, then sliced into Friar Zanchetti's chest.

"What the hell?" the agent squawked. "That mummy's bleeding."

That was all the distraction Brynstone needed. He slammed his fist into Cregger's chin, knocking him backward. The bloody sword clattered to the floor. The agent recovered and blasted into him, sending them crashing into the booth. Zanchetti's corpse burst like a piñata under their weight. The mummy's head snapped off, rolling onto the marble floor. Brynstone absorbed the impact. His chest burned. Spasms climbed from his left hand to his shoulder.

Cregger staggered to his feet. He stumbled back, looking for his saber.

From the floor of the booth, Brynstone glanced up at the mummy. It was smashed but still upright. A stone box about the size of a computer mouse rested inside the bloody chest.

The cista mystica. *Is that it?* Rubbing his head, he sat up. *I can't let Cregger see it.*

He rolled out, clutching his arm. The agent staggered toward his sword. Brynstone grabbed the scalpel. He hurtled it through the air, stabbing Cregger's hand. Pain darkened the agent's face. Gritting his teeth, he ripped out the scalpel. The big man lunged.

Brynstone coiled into a kick, smashing his foot into the man's wrist. The scalpel spiraled away. No more weapon, but Cregger had the momentum. He charged like a bull, forcing Brynstone back into the booth. As they toppled, the agent rolled on him and punched him in the ribs. Wheezing, Brynstone saw the endoscope cord and ripped it out. He wrapped the cord around Cregger's throat, then yanked hard, making the man's neck muscles flare. Cregger's face turned red as he clawed at the cord. In desperation, he reached for Brynstone, grabbing his throat and squeezing. Brynstone's pulse thundered inside his neck. Red spots pierced his vision like meteors puncturing the night sky.

He had to take out Cregger. Looking up, he saw the *cista mystica* peek out of the mummy's chest. The box seemed poised to fall. Drawing remaining strength, he shifted to the right, rocking the mummy. The stone box plummeted from Zanchetti's chest, striking the State agent's head. He recoiled in surprise. Brynstone grabbed him, then smashed his head against the marble wall. Blood rained down Cregger's face. His eyes closed.

And he dropped.

Stillness came over the mummy chamber. The brawl had reduced the Zanchetti mummy to a bloody pulp. Stepping over Cregger, Brynstone picked up the *cista mystica*. The box was small, with a sliding lid. After all this time, he'd found it. He thought about his father, knowing that Jayson Brynstone had dreamed about this moment a hundred times.

Now the big question, he thought. *Is the Radix inside?*

An engraved plant decorated the lid. He'd seen this plant symbol once before. Right there, he knew the search wasn't over.

A voice came from behind, rough and tinged with anger. "We have a problem."

He turned, not seeing anyone.

"The Washington meeting did not go well. President Armstrong angers me."

Glancing toward the door, Brynstone realized the terrarium glass served as a one-way observational window. From inside the Assembly of the Dead, looking through the terrarium, he could see into the library. He didn't like what he saw. Prince Zaki sat behind his desk, talking on the phone. His voice came in through a ceiling speaker.

Brynstone didn't like being in the same place as this guy.

Beginning with the Reagan administration, Zaki's distant relative Bandar bin Sultan had served as the senior Saudi ambassador to the United States. As dean of Embassy Row, Prince Bandar had hosted parties in his Colorado mansion with a guest list that read like a who's who of Beltway insiders. Aspen had been his favorite home—if a place with fifteen bedrooms and even more bathrooms could be called simply a home. Under Prince Bandar's patronage, Hala Ranch—from an Arabic word meaning "welcome"—lived up to its name. After Prince Bandar's retirement, Prince Turki al Faisal was given the job. When he stepped down due to health concerns, the House of Saud named a surprising choice for their new ambassador.

Prince Zaki had proven a formidable businessman in negotiating with American defense contractors and oil companies. The secretary of state adored him. The president called Zaki a trusted ally. Unlike Prince Bandar, Zaki had a more controversial reputation outside the boardroom. Three years ago, he was rumored to have murdered Wayne Kissner, a U.S. guest worker in Saudi Arabia. The State Department brushed aside the call for an investigation and ruled Kissner's death a suicide. Despite outrage from human-rights groups, the State Department deleted Prince Zaki's involvement in Kissner's homicide from its annual human-rights report.

Emerging from the scandal, Zaki assumed the ambassador title and later purchased Bandar's ninety-five-acre mountaintop estate. He was the only ambassador with his own State security detail. The State Department justified it based on death threats and his status as a prince.

Brynstone knew otherwise.

He looked around, wondering how Cregger had magically appeared in here. The chamber housed thirty mummy compartments, all occupied except one. He peeked inside the empty booth. Pushing on the back wall, he found it opened to a spiral staircase leading to the ground floor. He'd researched Hala Ranch's blueprints, but hadn't seen anything about this route. It offered the perfect escape.

As the prince ranted in the background, Brynstone looted Cregger's access card and keys. He removed a specimen bag from his backpack, then crouched beside Zanchetti's corpse. Now that it was split open, the mummy showed recognizable tissue change. He collected bloody tissue chunks and dropped them into the bag.

Cregger was crumpled on the floor. Out cold. Brynstone started to open the stone box.

"Turn around, buddy," a voice growled.

He swallowed. Hearing the man behind him, he slipped the *cista mystica* into his belt pack. He'd have to wait to see if the Radix was inside the box.

"Raise your hands," the man demanded.

Brynstone turned to face him. Not a State agent, but an American private contractor hired by Zaki. He was armed with a Glock.

"Don't you know?" Brynstone asked. "Guns aren't allowed in here. House rules."

"I don't sweat the rules."

"You're my kind of guy, Anderson."

A surprised look. "Who are you?"

"John Robie."

He seemed impressed to find Cregger on the floor. "You did that, huh, Mr. Robie?"

"With a little help from a mummy. And an endoscope cord."

"Hands behind your head. Come with me."

The man punched the button, triggering the terrarium to slide across the floor. Anderson motioned for him to step into the library. Brynstone thought about ducking into the empty booth, but decided against it. The guy could squeeze off several shots before Brynstone made it down the staircase.

Anderson shoved him through the door leading into the library. Two State Department agents were talking to Zaki.

"Mr. Ambassador," Anderson said. "I found this intruder in your mummy chamber."

Dressed in a conservative suit, Zaki strutted over. A bead of sweat curved around his chubby face. "Who is this man?" he demanded in flawless English.

"John Robie. He took out Cregger, if you can believe that."

"Did he destroy any mummies?"

"One is smashed open. The Italian mummy, I think."

Zaki's eyes widened. "Please say Alexander the Great is intact."

"Alex is fine," Brynstone assured. "Although he could stand a nose job."

"Silence," Zaki hissed.

A guard rushed into the library. With broad shoulders and a square black beard, Tareef looked more intimidating than earlier in the night, when Brynstone had bashed him over the head. The guard aimed a Skorpion Model 61 submachine gun. Brynstone hadn't seen one since he'd infiltrated a Czech security facility.

"That man," Tareef said. "He stole my smart card."

"Notify Aspen police," Zaki growled.

"Oh, you don't want to have me arrested," Brynstone advised. "I know things. Important things."

"What things do you know, Mr. Robie?"

"Things that would unsettle the State Department. Perhaps I should tell the agents."

"Perhaps I should slice out your tongue," Zaki snapped, before regaining composure. Walking to his desk, he waved at the State agents. "Please go. You, too, Mr. Anderson."

The agents started to leave. Anderson cocked his head. "You certain, Mr. Ambassador?"

Zaki nodded. "I am most certain."

The man glared at Brynstone, then turned for the door.

Chapter Five

Everyone here thinks I'm crazy. Cori Cassidy knew that's what the doctors and nurses thought about her. Even the ward attendants. She had been admitted to the Amherst Psychiatric Hospital five days ago. Since then, she had talked to a numbing parade of clinicians, all probing her mind for clues. But she wasn't crazy. Not at all. It was her little secret.

She glanced around Amherst's Psychotic Disorders Unit. Was there a more depressing place to spend the holidays? Across the dayroom, an African-American woman named Delsy slammed her pajama-draped body against a steel-reinforced window, cursing her private demons in a shrill Southern cadence. Near Delsy, a gray old woman clamped hands over her mouth as drool trickled between her weathered knuckles. Wasted lives, drowning in madness.

Stuffing hands into the pockets of her powder blue pajamas, Cori walked to a patient standing bolt upright, dressed in jeans and a tattered sweatshirt. She circled him. Deep in a catatonic stupor, he did not blink, twitch a muscle, or even seem to breathe. His outstretched hand appeared stiff and waxy. Immobility had reduced his bare feet to swollen bluish purple lumps. He looked like a statue in the dayroom, a monument to the tragedy of schizophrenia.

As she reached to touch his hand, a rumbling voice stopped her. "I wouldn't do that."

She jolted around to see a man dressed in hospital-issue white shirt, black belt, and white pants. Tall and athletic, he was a striking figure on the psych ward. "Name's Mack Shaw. I'm a psychological technician, not to mention your new case manager. You must be Cori."

She nodded. Looking at the patient, she said, "Can he hear us?"

"Not sure Harley wants to."

"He hasn't moved for hours. Why is his hand raised?"

"The forces of good and evil are waging war on his fingertips. If he tilts one finger, it shifts the balance in favor of evil. I hope for Harley's sake, good kicks evil's butt real soon."

The young man stared ahead, his face an expressionless mask.

"We'll let Harley get back to his private crusade," Mack said, taking her arm in a gentle escort. At five three, she felt like a little kid, walking beside him. "I got called in to work on Christmas Eve," he grinned. "Just like Santa Claus."

"I don't expect Santa makes any stops here."

He shook his head. "Too bad, huh? This place could use a visit from ol' Saint Nick."

"Why don't you do it?"

"Dress like Santa?" Mack chuckled. "Y'all think these folks want a black Santa?"

"Why not? You'd be great."

"Don't have the body." He rubbed his belly. "Santa would kill to have abs like mine."

"Ever hear of pillows? Stick two up your shirt and you're ready to go."

"And do what? Have these people sit on my lap and tell me all their Christmas wishes? What they want, I can't deliver. Santa don't know how to take away madness and replace it with sunshine."

A doctor stared at her from across the dayroom. His white lab coat provided a stiff cover for his hunched frame. Hooded dark eyes and tousled brown hair gave a sinister cast to his face. Realizing she had caught him staring, the peculiar man turned his attention to a nurse.

Mack looked over. "You know Doc Usher? He's bright, but a little strange. Maybe it's the company he keeps. Unlike the other psychiatrists, he works with only one patient."

"Which one?"

"Sorry. That's a big secret."

"I like big secrets," she said. "Do you know Usher's patient?"

"Don't know the guy's real name, but I've met him."

Dr. Usher shot another look at her. He walked with the nurse into an office.

"Tell me about him. Is the patient here in the dayroom?"

"Didn't you catch the part about it being a secret?" He grinned, shaking her hand. "Nice meeting you. Happy holidays." Mack took four steps, then stopped. He looked back and stared into her sparkling blue eyes. "Cori Cassidy, huh? And how old are you?"

"Twenty-two," she answered, running fingers through her short blonde hair.

"You have schizophrenia?"

"That's what they say."

"Good answer." Mack looked around. "Get this. Unlike everyone else in here, I had a nice conversation with you. We're two regular people talking here."

Oh my God, she thought. *He figured it out.*

"Ever hear of Nellie Bly?" he asked.

Cori shook her head.

"She was a reporter in the 1880s. Back in the day, mental hospitals treated people like animals. Nellie Bly went undercover as a patient to investigate Blackwell's Island insane asylum in New York City. After her editor freed her, she exposed the hospital in a book called *Ten Days in a Mad-House.*"

"Why are you telling me this, Mack? You think I'm a journalist?"

"Are ya?"

"Promise you. I'm not a reporter."

"Scout's honor?"

"I was never in Girl Scouts."

"Not even Brownies?"

"I look awful in brown. It was a fashion choice."

He waved his finger. "I got my eye on you, girl. You hear?"

She made a soft nervous laugh. *That was too close.* He almost found out the truth.

Cori spied Mack Shaw working the floor fifteen minutes later. She closed her diary as he ambled toward her. Built like a linebacker, he seemed as gentle as a kitten. Although not a kitten you'd want to piss off.

"Hey, Cori." He glanced around the pink-tiled day-room. "Remember when I said Doc Usher sees only one patient?"

She arched a blonde eyebrow. "Thought that was a big secret."

"Mm-hmm. You tell me your secret, I'll tell you Doc Usher's secret."

"I don't have a secret."

"Sure you do. You're not crazy. Why are you in a psych hospital?"

"Let me get this straight." She flicked her short hair. "If I tell you why I'm here, you'll tell me about Usher's patient?"

"I'll do better," he vowed. "I'll show you his patient. C'mon. Let's talk."

Mack led her to a quiet corner of the dayroom. She curled her legs on a battered sofa. He straddled a chair, crossing his massive arms over its back.

He caught her tucking blonde hair behind her ear. "Used to have long hair, didn't ya?"

"Until last Tuesday." She made a sweeping motion across her arm. "Chopped off thirteen inches. Made my head feel lighter." She glanced down. "My mom passed away from leukemia. I donated my ponytail to Locks of Love in her memory. They make wigs for kids suffering hair loss from chemotherapy, alopecia, and burns."

"Nice tribute." He rested his chin on his arms. "You go first, Cori. Spill your secret."

"Okay, here goes. I'm a first-year grad student at Johns Hopkins. I want to be a psychologist. Or at least I did a week ago."

"This place change your mind?"

"Don't know," she confessed, suddenly interested in her French manicure. "Maybe." She took a breath. "This fall, I had a cool psychology professor named Joe Berta."

Mack nodded. "Been on the floor a couple times. Good guy."

"One day after class, Berta invited me to join a research project. Sounded crazy at first. He wanted to replicate a famous study by Stanford psychologist David Rosenhan." She looked around. "Back in 1973, Rosenhan sent eight 'pseudopatients' to mental hospitals. None had a psychiatric disorder. After being admitted for schizophrenic-like symptoms, each pseudopatient acted normal. They stayed in hospitals anywhere from seven to fifty-two days."

"Why lock up sane people?"

"To see if the staff could tell the difference between pseudopatients and real patients. Get this: not one staff member figured out that the pseudopatients were normal. The label of schizophrenia blinded everyone. Well, *almost* everyone. The real patients could tell the fake ones. How ironic is that?" She laughed. "One guy came up and said, 'Why are you here? You're not crazy.' Another patient accused a pseudopatient of conducting an experiment."

He grinned. "I can hear the fake patient saying, 'Yeah, I am, but don't tell anybody.'"

"Exactly. Rosenhan's study embarrassed the psychiatric community. It proved the context of mental symptoms could make a bigger impression than the symptoms themselves."

"Yeah, but that was in seventy-three. You think the same thing would happen today?"

"That's what Berta wants to find out. He admitted me and seven other pseudopatients to different mental-health centers. We got to pick where we wanted to stay. I picked this place."

His eyes narrowed. "You've been here five days. What's the verdict?"

"Even though I acted normal, everyone has treated me like I'm psychotic. Until tonight."

"Your secret's safe with me. One question, though. Why'd you pick Amherst?"

"Ever hear of Simon Guthrie?"

"'Course," he chuckled. "Famous psychiatrist. There's a painting of Dr. Guthrie in the lobby. He founded this hospital."

"He was my grandfather. He died when I was four. When I saw Amherst on Berta's list, I decided to come here."

"I wonder if Albert Usher could tell you're a fake patient."

"Speaking of him," she said, "it's your turn. Tell me about Usher's secret patient."

"I'll do better. When my break comes up, I'll introduce you to his patient. I promise it's the craziest shit you've ever seen."

Chapter Six

Erich Metzger existed as a nonentity. It was the story of his life.

An Interpol agent had described him as "the most feared assassin on the planet." *Certainly the most expensive,* Metzger thought. *Certainly the best.*

At seventeen, he had joined a skinhead gang that dabbled in hate crimes. Boredom more than anger motivated him to carve a swastika into the forehead of an old man in a wheelchair. After his arrest, he didn't serve jail time. Instead, the judge assigned him to the German military. As a soldier, Metzger demonstrated unusual skill as a marksman. After his parole ended, two former KGB operatives hired him as an assassin. He found their money easy to accept. The assignment proved more difficult, not from a technical standpoint but from a psychological one.

He was hired to assassinate his mother.

He understood why the men wished for Truda Metzger's demise. In the years after the Berlin Wall crumbled, she became a cunning politician who opposed black-market operations. Her enemies vowed to kill her. The only question was, who would be the assassin?

He took the assignment because he could provide a humane death.

He made certain Truda Metzger did not suffer.

After assassinating his mother, he found he could kill without anguish. All fear and apprehension vanished with her death. A liberating feeling. It wasn't that he enjoyed killing. It was that he excelled at it. But this one, tonight, he would enjoy. How could he not?

He awaited General Santiago Rojas in an eighteenth-century villa nestled along the Italian Alps. Basking in the hospitality of admirers, the old man took refuge in a sleepy fishing village hugging Lake Como. Few people knew Rojas hid among the Italians. He moved often. It was a matter of survival.

Named after the capital city of Santiago, General Rojas had ruled his native Chile with an iron fist. After master-minding the bloodiest coup in his country's history, his dictatorship crushed anyone who dared oppose him. Rojas supervised the torture and execution of political prisoners and suspected leftists of every stripe—farmers, politicians, schoolteachers, bankers, factory workers. A gleeful sadist, his torture sessions made Uday Hussein's cruelties seem like the work of a child plucking an insect's wings.

Metzger remembered one case that surpassed all others. When a British journalist interviewed a single mother on the street, she had chastised the general's regime. That night, Verónica Piñera was arrested and taken from her children. Police imprisoned her in a coffin at La Moneda, the Chilean presidential palace.

Days later, she was brought before Rojas and beaten with a rubber truncheon. Electrical shock was delivered three times a day, continuing until Verónica lapsed into convulsions. He summoned her two small boys to witness their mother's torture. As they watched, General Rojas sprinkled flesh-eating beetles across her exposed body. Verónica Piñera shrieked as the greedy parasites tore into her skin. Death came, slowly and painfully, hours later.

If torture ever became an Olympic event, Metzger mused, gold medals would strangle the general's neck. Scores of people around the globe wanted him brought to justice, but not American intelligence. The CIA had cataloged his abuses, but ignored them because General Rojas had been an ally once against Communism's threat in South America.

Now in his eighties, the general was in failing health. Nonetheless, he had escaped arrest in London after an attempt to extradite him. There would be no trial. Neither the general's wealthy friends nor the CIA could stop Metzger. He didn't care about human-rights violations. In a curious way, he admired the man's ability to elude execution. In the last decade alone, fourteen assassins had tried to kill Rojas. That streak of failure would end tonight.

Metzger moved to the window. The Italian Alps glowed in ghostly moonlight. What occupied Rojas's mind when he stared at the snow-flecked mountains? Did northern Italy's operatic countryside conjure bittersweet memories of the Chilean Andes?

Voices drifted from outside the bedroom suite. He moved behind the drapes.

Two men stood silhouetted in the doorway, chattering in Spanish. Lights brightened the spacious bedroom as a man named Cristóbal searched it. Breathing with silk pressed against his face, Metzger watched the bodyguard check the window. He didn't look behind the drapes. Cristóbal declared the rooms secure and assured the general he would stand guard. Rojas bid him good night and closed the door. Metzger was alone with General Rojas. *At last.*

Distant church bells serenaded the new hour as he waited to assassinate the old dictator. Now ten feet away, Rojas wrapped his plump body in a bathrobe. Moving to a chair, he smoked a cigar and enjoyed a snifter of fine brandy. Metzger shook his head. *Enough waiting.* He emerged from the drapes.

"*Buenos noches, Señor General,*" he greeted in passable Spanish.

Rojas jumped to his feet, dropping the cigar. Metzger motioned with the gun for him to sit. The general looked small and pathetic. Not at all like a monster.

"Who are you?" the general demanded.

"For you, I am Death."

Rojas chortled. "You are mistaken. I am Death."

"For weaker men, yes." Metzger walked around the chair. "Do you remember me?"

"Your face means nothing to me."

"Your son-in-law knew me." He picked up the smoldering cigar, studying it. "Your aide hired me to assassinate Vicente eight years ago. I'm sure your daughter has not forgotten. Is she still angry with you?"

Worry glazed Rojas's face. "Metzger? Is it you?"

"Fresh from hell."

The old man pointed to the door. "I have a bodyguard. Cristóbal has served me well for years. Others wished to kill me. Cristóbal stopped them all."

"Cristóbal does not frighten me."

"Make a sound and he will."

"If you insist." He aimed his pistol at the television and fired. The bullet pierced the screen, bursting light and glass. The general turned toward the door.

"You see? He is gone," Metzger explained. "I arranged for Donata to visit Cristóbal."

"Who is Donata?"

"A whore." Metzger smiled. "But a beautiful whore. I understand this man, Cristóbal. Courage is in his heart, loyalty is in his brain, but another organ commands him when he sees a beautiful woman." He flipped the cigar into Rojas's lap. The general batted it to the floor. Cursing, he examined the burn on his flabby thigh.

Metzger began tying him to the chair.

"I have great wealth." Rojas looked up with sad eyes, affecting the look of a wounded dog. "How much to leave me alone? Name your price."

"I've named a price. Someone paid it. They will be disappointed if I do not kill you."

"Whatever they paid, I'll double it. Triple it."

"The price you pay tonight is to die. Nothing more."

"I cannot honor your request, Señor Metzger."

"And I cannot take time to torture you properly. I must board a plane for the United States to kill another man."

"Who is he?"

"I suppose there is no harm in telling a dead man. I have been contracted to kill John Brynstone."

"Is he important?"

"Yes, although he doesn't realize it. He is a man who knows too much. That kind is always dangerous."

"A politician?"

"A scientist."

"Why kill scientists? They are not important," Rojas chortled. "Who is paying you to murder Brynstone?"

"A powerful man. He calls himself the Knight."

Rojas narrowed one eye. "Is the Knight paying you to kill me?"

"Do you remember Verónica Piñera?" Metzger asked, tightening the final knot. "On a balmy Chilean night long ago you beat her. You electrocuted her. Then you invited her sons to witness her murder."

The general laughed. "She learned a lesson that night."

"So did her sons. They escaped your country. A British family adopted them. Today, the sons of Verónica Piñera are wealthy. And they hunger for revenge."

Rojas's lip quivered.

"As I said, I cannot torture you in a more deserving manner. For that, I apologize to your countless victims. But be assured I have studied your methods. You were a master of torture—sleep deprivation, noise, and isolation. Even hypnosis. It takes time. And that I do not have."

Rojas sneered. "Then what do you have?"

"I have these." Metzger pulled out a jar brimming with flesh-eating beetles. "Remember how you sprinkled these hungry creatures over Verónica Piñera's naked flesh?" He lowered the jar before the general's eyes. Beetles swarmed inside, their armored shells resembling polished obsidian. Color drained from Santiago Rojas's face as Metzger unscrewed the lid.

Chapter Seven

Aspen
5:29 P.M.

Brynstone stood near the oversized globe, his face registering no emotion, as the Saudi ambassador worked into a controlled rage. Zaki planted both hands on his desk.

"You must speak, Mr. Robie. Tell me how you discovered my mummy chamber."

In truth, Brynstone was a Special Collection Service agent who did this kind of thing for a living. No chance he'd give that answer. Stretching his neck, he kept it vague.

"The prophet showed me the way. Took me a while to figure it out." He motioned with his head. "At first, I looked for the answer in your Delphic-oracle painting."

"A gift from your President Armstrong. I keep it for the occasions when he visits Aspen. After tonight, it goes in the garbage."

Tareef walked past the terrarium and spoke to Zaki in Arabic. "This man claims to have information. Perhaps it is a trick."

Brynstone feigned a blank look, as if he couldn't understand their conversation.

"Still, I believe him," Zaki said. "I see it in his eyes. However, I do not think he will tell us without encouragement. Resolve this situation for me. Imad will assist you. Search him. Then employ your 'sharing methods.' Do whatever is necessary to make him talk."

"And if he dies without sharing?"

"Then let his wisdom die with him. Do not allow the American agents to see your work."

Brynstone had heard enough. He ripped the submachine gun from Tareef, then kicked the man's chest. The guard smashed into the globe. Ducking behind his desk, Zaki pressed a button, triggering an alarm.

The weapon in Brynstone's hands gave him an idea. He opened fire with the Skorpion submachine gun, unloading the twenty-round magazine. The 7.65 millimeter slugs blasted the terrarium glass. Scorpions clambered out of their home and poured into the library. The nimble creatures streamed over Tareef's body, plunging stingers into his flesh. Rolling onto his knees, the guard slapped at his face. Zaki scurried onto his desk, not noticing a scorpion on his back. The three-inch arachnid darted across his cheek before clutching Zaki's nose. The scorpion's stinger curled into striking position. Eyes bulging, Zaki held still, paralyzed by fear.

"Get it off," he whispered.

Darting closer, Brynstone slammed the Skorpion's wire butt at Zaki's face. There was a sharp crack as he thumped the scorpion from Zaki's nose.

"Problem solved," Brynstone said.

Zaki collapsed on top of his desk, cursing in Arabic as he held his broken nose. He reached for the praying-mantis sculpture. He slapped the claws, triggering the terrarium to close the passageway. Six men burst into the room. With blood streaming from his nose, Zaki demanded, "Kill him."

In a hail of gunfire, Brynstone dove into the chamber before the terrarium moved into place, shutting off the library. A wave of scorpions darted beneath the door. He grabbed his coat and backpack, then raced toward the empty booth.

From the library, Zaki separated the mantis claws. The terrarium opened an inch, then jammed. He screamed at his guards, "Go through the terrarium."

Scorpions greeted the two men as they crawled into the tank. Pulling back, they opened fire inside the Assembly of the Dead, shattering glass and blasting mummies.

"Stop your fire," Zaki screamed, waving his hands. "You'll ruin my collection."

Brynstone rushed down the spiral staircase. He didn't know where it would lead, but he had no other option. Dropping from above, scorpions rained around him like hailstones. Wiping one from his hair, he checked his belt pack. The *cista mystica* hadn't fallen out.

On the bottom step, his boot crunched a dazed scorpion. Opening the door, he bolted into the chill air. He had stashed cross-country skis on the other side of the main residence, but he saw a faster way out. Lined with pine trees, a winding road led to the heliport, a quarter mile from the mansion. He sprinted up the foothill, feeling the punishing effects of thin air at this altitude. Despite snowfall from the fading blizzard, the road was dry. Underground grids circulated heat beneath the concrete, melting snowflakes the second they hit.

Time was running out.

A veneer of fresh snow covered the half bubble that housed the helicopter, making the heliport look like an enormous igloo. He swiped Cregger's card through the reader posted on a metal box. The bubble shuddered, then parted from the center, each side retracting in an opposite direction. Snow slid off and toppled around the heliport.

From down the hill, snowmobiles roared to life from the mansion's auto bay. Brynstone stepped inside the retractable bubble, then climbed into Zaki's helicopter. He fired up the engine.

State Department agents and Zaki's men raced on snowmobiles. Everyone was taking shots at the Agusta

Bell. Having escaped the mummy chamber, State agent Steve Cregger seemed to have a different plan. As the helicopter was getting lift, he gunned the sled's Polaris engine up the hill. His snowmobile hurtled beneath the copter as it turned into the wind.

Bursting through whirling snow, Cregger jumped off the airborne machine. Brynstone didn't think he could make it. Wrong. It seemed personal for this guy. Cregger wrapped his arms around the Bell's landing skids, then tried to swing his legs around the cross tube.

Sorry, buddy, Brynstone thought. *You're not hitching a ride.*

Lifting at an angled incline, he directed the copter over pine trees. Cregger struggled for a better hold on the cross tube. Brynstone dipped the Agusta Bell, letting branches rip at the agent's legs, peeling him off the skids. Cregger brought out his handgun. He squeezed off two shots before dropping into a cushion of forest.

Brynstone climbed to a high hover, but didn't want to risk cutting out the engine in dangerous wind conditions. The copter started to speed-climb, buzzing away from Hala Ranch.

The whole time, one thought haunted him. *What if the Radix isn't in the* cista mystica?

Moonlight sparkled on frosted mountaintops as Brynstone buzzed away in the helicopter, leaving behind Zaki's Colorado retreat. He had escaped the Saudi ambassador's security force, flushing him with a sense of victory. Right now, that feeling alarmed him. Something could still go wrong. And it did. He glanced at the instrument panel. The chopper was puking fuel. He peered over his shoulder. Smoke boiled out of the tail boom. Turned out Agent Cregger was a decent shot. Brynstone needed to ditch the bird. Somewhere that wouldn't put civilians at risk, but not too isolated. He had an unmarked vehicle waiting for him.

Aspen spread out beneath him. Old and new blended in architectural harmony. Victorian buildings, modern retail, and condo developments mingled with multimillion-dollar trophy homes on Aspen's outskirts. People weren't skiing, but they weren't asleep, either. In the aura of twinkling Christmas lights, downtown Aspen buzzed with revelers. The legendary nightlife drew the glitterati to high-end boutiques and cafés, while powder hounds lingered at boots-on après-ski taverns. Not a good place to set down a copter.

Aspen Mountain loomed ahead with its formidable 3,267-foot vertical. Rising above the town, the mountain—called Ajax by out-of-towners—had narrow ridges with steep terrain falling in both directions. The chopper was running low on fuel, forcing an emergency landing. Even without dangerous wind conditions, landing on mountainous terrain was treacherous. That wasn't the only problem. Armed with torches, skiers twisted down the mountain like fireflies. Above them, a suspended Silver Queen Gondola dangled over Aspen Mountain's slopes.

He had a guess as to why the skiers were down there after dark. Every January, Aspen paid tribute to winter with a four-day festival called the Wintersköl Carnival. Like a frozen Mardi Gras, Wintersköl boasted a fireworks extravaganza and a torchlight descent down Aspen Mountain. He guessed the Aspen Skiing Company took advantage of holiday hours to run a closed torchlight practice before Wintersköl. He couldn't risk endangering lives.

He gripped the lever to the left of his seat. Moving the collective control up, he created pitch change in the rotor, causing the helicopter to climb. Aspen Mountain was coming up fast. Fighting damage to the helicopter and fierce crosswinds, he couldn't clear the mountain. With his right hand on the cyclic, he eased back on the stick to bleed off any remaining momentum. He kept the parking brake armed and reduced all power. With blades spinning on the way down, he braced for a hard landing. His eyes widened. The copter was hurtling toward a restaurant. Perched on Aspen Mountain's summit, the Sundeck Restaurant boasted a dazzling view of the Roaring Fork Valley. The lights were dimmed as if the place was closing for the evening, but he could see people inside. If he hit the building, everyone could die.

Without hesitating, he dropped the Agusta Bell, missing the restaurant. Sundeck staff pressed against the windows, staring in disbelief as the helicopter blasted into the mountainside beneath them. The impact rocked him in his seat. The skids hit the snow and snapped off as blinding powder sprayed the helicopter. It burst through a white swell, then into midair before striking the mountain again, carving a trench in the slope. A wall of snow cracked loose. Thundering down the mountain, the wave threatened to crush the torchlight skiers. He hoped they had abandoned their formations and raced to safety before the avalanche caught them.

He braced as the helicopter rolled down the steep mountain face. The bird busted apart as it flipped upside down. The upright mast split off, sending rotor blades flying into the air. He glanced through the shattered greenhouse window above the pilot's seat. He couldn't believe what he was seeing. Still attached to the stabilizer bar and swash plate, the rotor blades whirled skyward, heading toward the suspended gondola.

A blond-haired man peered out of the Silver Queen Gondola. Brynstone gaped in horror as the spinning blades slashed the gondola's cable. The chopper punched through powder, hurling him upside down as if he were strapped inside some psychotic carnival ride. The Agusta Bell's tail boom snapped free, then flipped into the air. The cowling ripped off the top, smashing the windows. As it cracked apart, he unbuckled his seat belt, then jumped onto the overturned cowling. Shrapnel from the broken window sliced beneath his bulletproof vest, leaving a gash across his hip. No time to contemplate the pain. With the avalanche roaring behind, he rode the engine cover like an enormous toboggan. In seconds, the wave would crush him.

The red gondola plummeted from above. Still attached to the free-swinging cable, it swung down on its tether like a small bus strapped to a bungee cord. The car must have already hit once, bashing the front end, before sailing back into the sky. The man dangled out the door.

Banking hard, Brynstone steered the cowling underneath the gondola car as it swung toward him. Ugly choices. If the gondola came too close, he'd be crushed. If his timing was off, the avalanche would shred him. He jumped for the gondola, diving into a wall of white. He cracked into something hard, but managed to find a hold. The car rocketed away from the mountain, this time with him hanging on. As his legs dangled, he felt someone tug at his arms. The blond man pulled him inside the gondola.

"That's a beaut," the man cried in an Australian accent. "Good on ya, mate!"

"We invented an extreme sport," he laughed. "Hope we survive to claim credit for it."

The gondola shuddered as it dropped again. Brynstone looked out the shattered window. The roar thundered like Niagara Falls. The car plunged into the avalanche's crest. The force ripped apart the front end. Snow flooded through the windows. The sides buckled, then popped open, tearing the floor. He shoved open a trapdoor in the ceiling. Fueled by adrenaline, Brynstone climbed through the hatch and reached down. The man grabbed his hand as the gondola's bottom half disappeared below them.

Both men grabbed the gondola's suspension bracket, hanging on. With the avalanche rumbling around them, the roof dug into the snow, nearly flipping them into the air. Tension overwhelmed the cable. The roof snapped free. Kicking up a mist, they cruised down the mountain on the crumpled gondola roof. He stared down the avalanche's backside as snow blasted his face. He hoped the *cista mystica* in his belt would survive the ride.

"Over there," the Australian shouted. They leaned to the side, swerving the gondola roof toward an evergreen grove. The roof flipped, flinging them into powder.

A bitter stillness settled over the mountain. Buried in snow, Brynstone groaned as he raised his head. He caught his breath and rolled over before reaching down. He found the box in his belt pack. Was the Radix inside? He had to check. Digging himself out, he opened the *cista mystica*. Relief rushed over him. The Radix was inside the box. It was mesmerizing, unlike anything he'd ever seen. Simple yet beautiful. He wanted to hold it. Study it.

A few feet away, the guy brushed away snow.

Brynstone didn't want to close the lid, but he couldn't risk the man seeing the Radix. Sticking it in his belt pack, he squinted at the path of destruction carved into the mountain.

"Did it hit the skiers?" he asked, his face cold and stinging.

"Nah," the blond man said, staggering in waist-deep snow. "It'll break up in the Dumps." He squinted. "Is that blood on the snow?"

Brynstone looked down. "Took shrapnel to the hip."

"Name's Cooper Hollingworth. Let me drive you into town. Aspen Ski Co keeps a snowcat to shuttle skiers up the slopes. It's Chrissie Eve and we're freezin' our balls out here. I owe you. You saved my life."

"Saved your life?" He coughed. "I almost killed you with that helicopter."

"Maybe it was my wake-up call," he grinned. "I came to work for Aspen Ski Co to score free passes, but I miss my girl. Raelene's back in Canberra. Surviving this makes me think I should go home. I love these spiffy hills, but I am sick of this town's rich Figjams."

"*Figjams?*"

"Fuck I'm good—just ask me. That's what we call 'em where I come from."

"I'd appreciate a ride." In the moonlight, Brynstone opened his wallet, then held out cash. "I need you to forget that you helped me. Will this do the trick?"

Hollingworth gaped at the bills. "For that kind of money, mate, I can forget anything."

Chapter Eight

Washington, D.C.
7:33 P.M.

President Alexander Armstrong was taking a call when Secret Service agent Natalie Hutchinson entered the Oval Office. He motioned for her to take a seat on a chenille sofa poised near the fireplace. She obliged, staring at the blazing fire as she clutched her black cap. She was a dedicated agent, serving with distinction for the Service's Uniformed Division. He had summoned Hutchinson from her post outside the first floor of the Executive Residence.

After sending holiday wishes to British prime minister James Gray and his wife, Ann, Armstrong ended the call. As he came around the ornate *Resolute* desk, Agent Hutchinson rose to her feet.

"Take a seat," he said. "Please."

She complied, glancing at the enormous eagle stitched in the blue presidential rug. He eased into an accent chair. "I need your help, Natalie."

That brought the stony gaze he associated with Secret Service agents. He owed his life to these people, but their detached style unnerved him. He prided himself on his ability to read people. But the Service? No chance. They were Vulcans in sunglasses.

"Earlier tonight, my brother and Deena Riverside were on the South Portico. What were they talking about?"

"I didn't listen to their conversation, sir. I advised them to return to the Blue Room."

No expression. Like a talking corpse. He leaned forward.

"Natalie, I'm concerned about my brother. I know you can relate to that." He paused. "I need to know what they were discussing. It's critical."

She swallowed. A sign of life. "Didn't make sense, sir."

"Tell me anyway."

She cleared her throat, fighting her stoic instincts. "I overheard Fortune—I mean, Mr. Armstrong—mention something about the Radix," she said, pronouncing it *RAY-dix*. "He planned to pay a great deal of money to purchase it."

"How much?"

"I believe he said top dollar. He expressed concern about it turning into a public-relations nightmare. That's all I heard, sir."

Armstrong headed to the fireplace. He drummed his fingers on the white marble mantel. "This thing they talked about. What did you call it?"

"The Radix. I have no idea what it means, sir. Their conversation was brief. They returned to the Christmas Eve party in the Blue Room."

He rubbed his eyes. "Thank you, Agent Hutchinson. You may go."

She opened the door on the curved wall and headed into the corridor outside the Oval Office. He stared at the Christmas tree near the window, thinking about his brother. Dillon was a smart businessman who wasn't afraid of risk. He'd been burned a few times, but this seemed different. If he messed up, the blowback would hit the White House. Armstrong had a vision for his reelection strategy. There was no room for damage control for his little brother's mistakes.

He had to learn more about the Radix.

He needed to know what Dillon was planning with Deena.

Baltimore
7:55 P.M.

Cori Cassidy had revealed her secret. Now, it was Mack's turn.

Twenty doors surrounded the Amherst dayroom, each leading to patient bedrooms. Staff locked the private quarters during the day, forcing patients into the dayroom until bedtime. Cori had wondered about the twenty-first door. The staff acted as if it didn't exist. Now Mack held a security pass card in front of a metal proximity reader. The door clicked open. They descended a white stairwell. Tiny hairs bristled on Cori's arms. Dr. Usher had a single patient.

Why do they keep him down here? Is the guy dangerous?

At the landing, Mack swiped his card, then led her into an elevator. He hit a button. The elevator rattled down a few floors. He had a somber look on his face.

"We're going down to the secret ward. Hang back after we step out of the elevator."

The doors parted. They entered an observation room. She peeked around the corner. An attendant hunched over a metal table, stuffing chocolate cake into his mouth. He was dressed in a white shirt and pants.

"Evening, Perez," Mack greeted, heading to the table. "Today your birthday?"

"Nah," he answered. "I bought this for two bucks. Sometimes people order a cake but never pick it up. The bakery doesn't want the cake, so they practically give 'em away."

"Big cake," Mack said, leaning in to read the words

spelled in blue frosting. " 'Happy Ninety-first Birthday Uncle Fred.' That what that says?"

"I'm thinking Uncle Freddie never made it to the big day." Perez grinned. "Poor bastard. His loss is my gain."

"You're a sick man. You understand this, don't you?"

Perez dropped his fork. "Who's that? You can't bring a patient down here."

"She's not a patient."

Wiping frosting from his mouth, Perez noticed the pajamas. "Looks like one to me. Doc Usher will go ballistic if he finds out."

"Don't tell him."

"You idiot. Only a few people know about this ward. Why'd you bring her down here?"

"Easy now. She's undercover, reviewing our hospital," Mack lied. "Amherst wants a glowing report. She promises to not mention this ward. Right?"

She nodded, coming over. "I understand the need for confidentiality, Mr. Perez."

"Get this. Cori's grandfather was Simon Guthrie. The guy who founded Amherst."

Perez huffed, moving to the console. "Guess you came to see Leo. You'll have to search for him down there."

She walked to a picture window. The darkened ward was the size of a basketball court, with walls reaching fifty feet. They stood in an observation room built high into the south wall like a stadium suite. "I've never seen anyone come down here."

" 'Cause we're not supposed to use that door in the dayroom." Perez shot a look at Mack. "We use the one below this window. We slip in and out without other staff knowing."

From her vantage point in the booth, she saw thousands of books stacked atop each other forming seven-foot-tall walls. A labyrinth made from books.

"Look over there," Mack said, pointing at the shadowy walls beyond the maze.

She squinted. Letters and symbols painted in different colors decorated the west and north walls from floor to ceiling. An obsessive and disciplined mind had poured itself onto the canvas of the hospital walls. It was beautiful, but in a way she couldn't fully comprehend.

Outside the labyrinth, a man crouched near the northeast corner, surrounded by paint buckets. Gray hair drifted down his shoulders and mingled with his beard. His face conjured the look of a Greek philosopher, but his body suggested the rugged dimensions of a mountain man. He wore a paint-flecked sweatshirt, jeans, and ragged Converse tennis shoes. Facing the east wall with a brush in each hand, he painted with his right hand while tracing the mirror image with his left.

Mack grinned. "Blows your mind, huh?"

"How does he do that?"

"His brain works differently than ours."

"That's for sure," Perez snorted.

"What's he painting?"

"Italian and Latin words. Probably something about the Void."

"What's the void?"

"One of his crazy ideas. The Void refers to the moment you realize you're losing your mind. Leo also calls it the Revelation of Madness. He fell into the Void eighteen months ago."

"I'd love to talk to him," she said. "Dig into his mind."

"That's one place you don't wanna dig," Perez said. "Leo doesn't talk. He'll say a little to Doc Usher about the Void, but that's it. He blows me off. I talk anyway. I'm his babysitter. No one knows who he is. Well, people at the top know, but they're not talking. Officially, Leo doesn't exist."

"Why not?"

"Don't know. Wouldn't tell you if I did. Whoever he is, he has important friends. We have orders to do whatever he wants. Leo writes it down and we do it. Including setting up scaffolding to reach the highest walls."

"You called him Leo."

"That's our nickname. Guy thinks he's Leonardo da Vinci. Part of his delusion. He has a personality only a psychologist could love."

"Turn up the lights," Mack urged. "Show her the other walls. Then we'll go. Promise."

Annoyed, Perez reached for a dimmer switch. The room awakened in the glow. Her jaw dropped. She moved to the window and pressed her hands against the glass.

From this distance, with the lights up, the words and symbols painted on the north wall formed a composite image of Jesus with disciples surrounding him. A forty-foot replica of da Vinci's famous painting *The Last Supper*.

The west wall featured another da Vinci replica. Here again, words and symbols melded together to create a giant composite image of the Madonna clustered with an angel and the infants Jesus and John the Baptist in a foliage-laced grotto. During a trip to London with her mom, Cori had seen Leonardo's *The Virgin of the Rocks* at the National Gallery.

"How'd he do that?" she asked. "I've seen composites where images combine to form a photomosaic picture, but the ones I've seen are computer generated."

"It's a mystery," Perez confessed. "Dude has lots of free time. Sometimes he'll sit down there cross-legged, staring at the wall for days. Then he'll jump up and start painting like a wild man. Doc Usher said da Vinci did the same thing when he painted *The Last Supper*."

"Uh, guys," Mack interrupted. "Look down there. Check him out."

Leonardo stood beneath the observation booth, staring right up at them. He had navigated through the book maze to the south wall. Eighteen months of exile in the clandestine ward had bleached his flesh as white as the stairwell. Madness sparkled in his coal-rimmed eyes.

He pointed up at the observation booth.

"I must speak to you," he said in a bottom-octave rasp. "Come down here."

Perez grabbed the microphone, his voice booming through speakers. "Yo, Leo, man. Be cool, okay? I'll come down and talk—"

"Not you," Leonardo answered. "The girl."

She stared at the disquieting figure, frozen in his gaze. *Why does he want to talk to me?*

"You know him?" Mack asked.

"Never seen him before."

He stood without moving, his finger poised in her direction. "Come down here," Leonardo said, his words deliberate and commanding. "Alone."

"Ah, man," Perez moaned. "I don't wanna piss you off, but that ain't happening. Understand, Leo? The girl stays up here."

"This guy's hardly spoken," she cut in. "Now he wants to talk. I'm going down there."

"No way," Perez said. "Ain't safe. Shaw, get her outta here."

"*Stop,*" Leonardo growled. "Come down here now. I must speak to you, Cori Cassidy."

Part Two
Synchronicity

There is no good that cannot produce evil and no evil that cannot produce good.
—Carl Jung

Chapter Nine

Cori peered through the window on the ward's south wall. She stared down at Leonardo, surprise frozen on her face. The mental patient hardened his gaze as he pointed at her.

"How'd Leonardo know your name?" Mack asked.

"The microphone," Perez said, switching it off.

"I never told you my name," she protested. "He must know me somehow. I could talk to him. Could be a big breakthrough."

"Yeah?" Perez gave a bitter laugh. "Only thing that'll get broken is your neck."

"Is he dangerous?"

"Before coming here, he killed three people. Including a woman."

She looked down, staring into Leonardo's eyes. He hadn't moved, still pointing up. Frozen like the catatonic man in the dayroom.

"I'll be okay."

"Let her go," Mack said. "I'll be responsible."

"Oh, you will, huh?" Perez shoved her aside and got up in the big man's face. "Can't tell you how great that makes me feel."

"Back off, Perez."

He didn't budge. "Okay, your girl goes down there and the crazy man tears her apart. Now we got us a fake patient murdered by a patient who isn't supposed to exist. Baltimore police are gonna love that story."

As they argued, she eased open the door to the ward, then slipped out. She hurried down the stairs, fueled with exhilaration. Leonardo waited at the bottom. She lingered on the last step. The eerie man was bigger than she'd realized. Despite his age, he looked intimidating, with broad shoulders and well-muscled arms. Maybe this was a bad idea.

Little too late for that, Cori, she told herself.

A faint smile raised Leonardo's lips. "Follow me."

He ducked inside the book labyrinth. She hesitated before going in. She looked back toward the observation room.

Perez hurried down the stairs. "Don't go in there. You hear me, girl?"

Leonardo yanked on her wrist. Her head jerked as they moved inside the labyrinth. Perez chased after them. Inside the maze, they took a left turn, then a right, then another left. After two more corners, Leonardo released her hand. She bit her lip and staggered backward, inching against a wall of books.

"I won't hurt you," he said in a composed voice.

She glanced at the seven-foot walls. Each book was stacked with precision, forming seamless multicolored partitions. She noticed the book spines. *Gulliver's Travels. The Decameron.* Theophrastus's *Historia Plantarum. Amazonia.* Machiavelli's *The Prince.* Collected Shakespeare. Al-Dinawari's *Kitab al-Nabat.* Leonardo had crafted his maze with the same meticulous artistry as that on the walls surrounding them.

"I'll find you," Perez shouted, his voice sounding distant. "You know how many times I've sat up in that booth, tracing my way through this stupid book maze?"

"I know your mom," Leonardo whispered. "She's brilliant. Read all her books."

"Have you seen her latest? It was published a month ago."

"Her best yet. You helped her research it." He tugged at his beard. "Are you familiar with the Swiss psychiatrist Carl Jung?"

She nodded. Jung had studied with Sigmund Freud before rejecting orthodox psychoanalysis to start his own school of analytical psychology. Defying conventional methodology, Jung had explored the depths of the unconscious mind through the analysis of dreams, mythology, art, philosophy, religion, and alchemy.

Leonardo clamped his big hand on her shoulder. "Jung is at the heart of understanding our puzzle. We must learn his secrets."

"What puzzle? What secrets?"

"We'll discuss it later. Synchronicity brought you here, you know? Our families share a bond, going back to Simon Guthrie."

"You knew my grandfather?"

"My father had a nervous breakdown thirty years ago. He was diagnosed with bipolar disorder. Your grandfather was my father's psychiatrist. Dr. Guthrie helped my father. I felt a connection to this hospital. After I fell into the Void, I came here."

"Don't remember much about my grandfather," she said. "I'm glad he helped your dad."

"One day, I came to this place to visit my father. Dr. Guthrie stopped in. He introduced me to his daughter, Ariel. Beautiful girl. You look a great deal like your mother."

"That's how you recognized me?"

"I saw the photograph of you with your mother on her book jacket. We met years ago, when you were little. You wouldn't remember. I came out to Princeton. You were playing in your mother's office. I wrote her a while back. Haven't heard from her."

"You don't know about Mom?"

Perez interrupted, yelling, "I want you two outta the maze."

They both jumped as books toppled several rows away. Perez had pushed over a wall. He did it again, knocking over wall after wall like massive book dominos.

Leonardo frowned. "Let's go before that idiot injures himself."

He directed her toward a route different than the one they had taken in here. After a few turns, they stepped outside the labyrinth near the stairs where Mack waited.

"See you soon, Cori." Leonardo winked. "Remember this: the Tree of Life blossoms in the Land of the Dead."

"Why did you say that?" she asked, shocked.

Leonardo didn't answer as he ambled back to his brushes and paint cans. Mack escorted her up the stairs. She saw Perez cursing and kicking a wall across the chamber. Books tipped forward—almost in slow motion—before thundering around him. He stepped over the rubble, slipping on a book cover as he slammed into another book wall.

"Perez. Up here." Mack waved from the top step. "Hey, brother, thanks for an interesting evening."

Astonished, Perez looked across the overturned books. Leonardo dipped brushes into paint as if nothing had happened. Cori followed Mack to the elevator, knowing she'd better get back to her room before staff reported her missing.

Chapter Ten

Brynstone was supposed to enjoy this moment. So why didn't it feel right?

After getting a ride from Cooper Hollingworth, he had climbed into a GMC Yukon and burned his way out of Aspen. Heading eastbound on a ribbon of winding canyon road, he punched a number into his cell and waited for his operation supervisor. He cleared his throat, then said into the phone, "I have the Radix."

"Are you certain?" Lieutenant General James Delgado asked. "You verified it?"

The director of the National Security Agency caught people off guard with his serene voice. Delgado didn't sound military, no brusque growl or barking commands. His composed speech hinted that nothing ever bothered him. Maybe nothing did.

"It's difficult to verify, given our limited knowledge." Brynstone went easy on the brake to avoid sliding on the icy road. "We need sophisticated testing to determine its authenticity, but I believe it is the Radix."

"I'm proud of you, son. Your father would be proud too. Call the minute you touch down in Baltimore. I'll be waiting at Fort Meade."

The Aspen blizzard had trudged southeast, leaving glacial roads in its wake as Brynstone headed through Glenwood Canyon. Clouds dipped low, giving the look of ghostly smoke between the three-thousand-foot canyon walls. Even at night, illuminated in flashes of halogen, the canyon vista was breathtaking. Forged in the Pleistocene era, dramatic slabs of rock loomed over a dozen miles of I-70. The Colorado River raged through the gorge, carving a serpentine chasm in the ancient stone. From time to time, he'd steal a glimpse out the window, looking over the cliff at rapids coursing around ice floes.

Snowpack covered the icy roadway. The good thing? Traffic was sparse as the blizzard and the holiday conspired to keep people off the road. Feathery snowflakes swirled along the windshield, riding the passing storm.

Brynstone's cell vibrated on his belt. He was surprised to pull a signal inside the canyon. He checked the caller ID, expecting Jordan Rayne, but finding his wife's number.

Kaylyn Brynstone knew he pulled dangerous government assignments, but she had no idea that tonight's mission had brought him to Colorado. His superiors had ordered him to conceal his covert fieldwork. Expecting an emergency, he flipped open his phone.

"You said you didn't want to miss this, John. Listen, okay?" Kaylyn cooed to their daughter, "Tell Daddy. Can you say it?"

As a first-time father, he had hungered for this moment. Countless times, he had tried to imagine Shayna's first words.

"She'll say it," his wife assured. "I swear she said it twice already."

He glanced in the rearview mirror. Swerving headlights on the interstate caught his attention. In a reckless maneuver on the ice-streaked road, a vehicle darted around a Mitsubishi Galant. He could see the black Mercedes-Benz SUV now as it cruised into place behind an aging red Ford Windstar.

"Come on, sweetie," Kaylyn begged in the voice of a desperate parent whose child refused to perform on demand. "Tell Daddy."

"Shay, it's me," he added. "Can you talk? How's my sweet baby girl?"

"Okay, let's try this. I'm putting her on camera."

He glanced at the road, then pulled back the phone. Curled on her mother's lap, Shay's bright eyes made his world halt. She tugged on her Pooh hat. Nothing made him smile like a baby in a hat. Any hat. Baseball caps, beanies, berets, straw hats, bonnets. You could stick it on his headstone: JOHN BRYNSTONE LOVED BABIES IN HATS.

He gave another quick look at the interstate before returning his gaze to Shay. Her hair had grown—honey blonde like her mother's—and wisps poked out beneath her hat. He swallowed hard. She had grown so much. His daughter. His only child. Her eyebrows arched in concentration. Her small lips puffed. Then she said something like "Daa-da."

He sank back. He was an expert at controlling his emotions. Not now. Tears stood in his eyes, blurring the image of his child. He blinked them away.

"We miss you, John." Despair crinkled in Kaylyn's voice. "It's Christmas Eve. When are you coming home?"

"Soon," he answered, training his gaze on the road. "I'm trying my best here, Kay."

Only he wasn't. This was a raw issue. Ever since his stint as an Army Ranger, he prided himself on doing his best. Not this time. Not with his family. He hated it when giving his best at work conflicted with giving his best at home.

He glanced at the mirror. The Mercedes took a chance on an opening. It zipped around the minivan, coming up behind, the driver invisible in the halo of headlights. It took a hard sweep around his Yukon, speeding past. The SUV swerved back in the lane, moving in front of him. Not a good idea, driving like that on frozen roads. The driver managed to keep it steady, staying two or three car lengths ahead.

Kaylyn added, "We've only seen you once since Thanksgiving."

Biting his lip, he realized his relationship with his wife had never been more strained. Headlights flared in the rearview mirror. He glanced into it, seeing a dark blue Ford Explorer closing in from behind. Red light illuminated his windshield as the Mercedes-Benz in front hit the brakes. Back in game mode, he sensed that the two SUVs were setting a trap.

"Listen, Kay, I need to go. I promise I'll be with you and Shay soon."

Her fragile voice dipped. "Promises don't cut it anymore, John. Our marriage is falling apart. Are we headed for a divorce?"

"Kaylyn, I can't—"

"Hear that?" she interrupted, a sudden lightness in her words. "Shay said it again."

He couldn't tell Kaylyn that his life might be in danger. He didn't want to scare her, but this felt like bad timing. The Mercedes ahead hit the brakes again as the Explorer moved closer.

"John, listen to her. She said it perfect this time."

"Honey, I gotta go. Love you." He ended the call.

And maybe his marriage.

A figure emerged from the Mercedes's moonroof. Tareef bin Al-Khasib had survived the scorpion attack back at Zaki's mansion. He didn't look happy. He brought out a Steyr AUG assault rifle, wind whipping his beard as he aimed. Definitely not happy.

Brynstone hit the high beams, blasting light at Tareef. The man pulled back, shielding his face with his hand. That was the distraction Brynstone needed. He punched the accelerator, bursting past Tareef's Mercedes, then diving back into the right lane. The road was open now, with no one ahead. That's when he heard gunfire. Tareef had pivoted around, facing front now. More gunfire, this time cracking the glass of his rear window.

The speed limit was posted at something like fifty through the winding canyon, but he took it up to eighty. Both SUVs raced to keep up with him on the slick roads.

He squinted. Up ahead, two separate two-lane tunnel portals were chiseled into the south wall of the canyon. He punched it, sliding as he zipped toward the eastbound bore. Dry pavement waited inside Hanging Lake Tunnel, and he couldn't wait to hit it. Behind him, both vehicles matched his pace. He wasn't losing them.

Inside the tunnel's entrance, a variable message sign announced, LEFT LANE CLOSED, with a green arrow above his lane and a red X in the parallel one. Beyond it, an overhead smart sign used radar to detect vehicle speed, displaying a message in flashing red letters: YOUR SPEED IS 97 MPH. It blurred by along with another one advising, 45 MPH CURVE AHEAD. *Good advice*. Taking the tight curve at this speed pulled the Yukon close to the tunnel wall. His brake lights splashed a red glow on the curved walls around him.

Behind him, the Explorer swerved into the left lane.

Tareef ducked inside the Mercedes as it surged alongside the Yukon. Behind the wheel, Imad slammed into Brynstone's vehicle. Metal squealed against concrete as the Yukon crunched against the tunnel wall. Orange sparks showered the passenger window. Brynstone jerked on the wheel, pulling away from the wall. From behind, the Explorer smashed into his SUV, sending the Yukon into a fishtail. Imad came in hard again, pinning him against the tunnel wall as the Explorer stayed in position behind, engaging him bumper to bumper.

The four-thousand-foot tunnel was nearing its end. He had to solve this headache before they moved back outside to snowy roads. He unbuckled the seat belt, then hit the button for the power-tailgate window. It lowered with a hum, the breeze stirring his black hair. The Explorer crammed against him from behind while Imad pinned him from the side. With two SUVs trapping him against the tunnel's right wall, he didn't worry about steering the Yukon. He whipped out the Glock from his holster, then pulled a second sidearm from the console. He spun around, facing the back seats. Looking out the open tailgate window, he had a clear view of the Explorer. More familiar faces. Anderson was driving, with Faysal beside him. Both men shouted. Brynstone seemed to be pissing off everybody tonight.

He took aim out the tailgate window. Anderson's eyes widened, and he hit the brake, falling back. Too late. Deciding against a headshot, Brynstone opened fire with both guns blazing. The Explorer's windshield shattered as bullets peppered the glass. The SUV sideswiped the tunnel wall at a high speed. Anderson overcorrected and turned too sharp, triggering a rollover. The Explorer landed hard on the passenger side, coming to rest across both lanes.

The Yukon lurched back without the Explorer pushing it. He flipped around and holstered the Glock before grabbing the steering wheel. In the Mercedes, Imad and Tareef had pulled away, waiting out Brynstone's standoff with Anderson. He caught up a few hundred feet from the tunnel's exit. Like a deranged jack-in-the-box with an assault rifle, Tareef popped out the moonroof again, taking wobbly aim as Brynstone surged alongside their vehicle.

Bullets bombarded the rear door and shattered the window.

Catching a rapid breath, he gambled on a PIT maneuver. It had been years since he'd forced another car into a spinout. He aligned his front tires with the Mercedes's rear tires, then banked hard to the right, steering into the SUV at the tunnel's exit. The Mercedes lost traction, then glided into a skid. Imad couldn't control the vehicle. With his upper body exposed, Tareef was clinging to the roof until the spinning force pulled him inside. The Mercedes slid hard into the guardrail, popping rivets as it burst through the metal barrier. The SUV flipped over the edge, dropping off the viaduct. Screaming, Tareef and Imad plunged toward the Colorado River.

At the tunnel's exit, the Yukon hit an icy patch, sending Brynstone into a spinout. He skidded over the emergency crossover, a brief strip of concrete connecting the eastbound and westbound lanes. Beyond the crossover, the icy roadway stretched into two viaducts separated by cantilevered pavement slabs. Fighting for control, he avoided the slabs, but slid onto the westbound bridge of the divided highway, going the wrong way. The good news? He didn't see cars heading toward him. Despite the efforts of snowplows and sand spreaders, the road was slicker than the eastbound lanes. Construction had closed off the right lane, blocked with orange and white barrels weighted with sandbags. Missing one construction drum, he brought the Yukon to a dead stop, facing the wrong direction on the quiet road.

He blew out a quick sigh. Made a hushed laugh. Then, from the corner of his eye, he saw headlights. A semi-trailer truck rolled around the rocky corner, lights blazing as it headed for him in the left lane. With the big rig bearing down on him, he had to act fast.

Sweat breaking on his face, he tried a moonshiner's turn, hoping he could execute it on the slick road. Placing the Yukon in reverse gear, he punched the accelerator, then drove backward for a five count. Heading in reverse with the truck coming at him, he steered hard to the left while hitting the brake. The Yukon flashed into a 180-degree turn, facing west now. Releasing the brake, he shifted into drive, then hit the accelerator again.

He glanced in the rearview mirror. Showing no mercy, the driver of the eighteen wheeler came at him with a blaring horn. Brynstone stayed ahead of the rig, speeding back toward the twin portals. Needing to go east instead of west, he decided against entering the westbound bore. Swerving to the left, he raced over the median crossover, missing the pavement slabs as he returned to the eastbound lanes. He slid into the eastbound entrance of the Hanging Lake Tunnel, facing the wrong direction again before grinding to a stop.

This time, it didn't matter.

Inside the tunnel, the overturned Explorer straddled both lanes, blocking traffic. Behind the bullet-riddled windshield, Faysal held his head, braced against an airbag cushion. And Anderson? He had climbed out of the rolled SUV, sliding down its chassis to the pavement.

A middle-aged man parked his red minivan behind the rolled Explorer. He jumped out, looking to help. Two college students, a kid wearing a wool cap and his malnourished girlfriend, joined the Good Samaritan. Anderson held his head, as if he had a concussion.

Brynstone walked toward them. He brought out his handgun. Anderson saw it first, the weapon registering in his dazed eyes. The woman noticed him coming. She yelped, then sprinted back to her car.

The college kid pointed at the Glock. "Dude, put that thing away, okay?"

Brynstone kept walking, pulsing with adrenalin as he came at them like a gunslinger. He growled, "Get out of here."

The college student hustled back to the Galant as the middle-aged man ducked behind his van. Anderson stayed on his feet. Fighting to stay tough, he balled his fingers into a weak fist.

"My baby daughter said her first word tonight," Brynstone said with a calm menace. "You had to go and ruin that moment. Makes me downright unhappy."

He slammed his boot into Anderson's chest. The force rocked the man backward, and he struck his head against the Explorer's crumpled fender. Anderson collapsed on the road. Blood dribbled from his nostril.

Brynstone turned, then headed back to the Yukon.

"Next time, stay in Aspen," he called, "with the damned scorpions."

Chapter Eleven

Christmas Eve was tranquil in the Rocky Mountains. That was, Brynstone had decided, if he didn't count tonight's drama in Aspen and Glenwood Canyon. Turning off picturesque I-70, he drove the battered Yukon to the Eagle County Airport. Although Zaki's Hala Ranch was back in Aspen, Brynstone had opted to fly out of Eagle County. Renowned for its altitude and location, the airfield operated even when adverse weather forced other mountain towns to ground their flights. Blessed by what the local Ute Indians had called a hole in the sky, Eagle enjoyed more visual-flight-rule days than any airport in the region.

He drove into a private hangar tucked inside the airport's Vail Valley Jet Center. He pulled to a stop near a government-chartered Bombardier Learjet. As he climbed out, Jordan Rayne hurried down the foldout ramp. She was dressed in an olive green sweater, black Gucci skirt, and pointy-toe boots. Wind slapped long red hair against her cheek. She was tall, with bold green eyes. A beauty mark enhanced her seductive smile.

"Good evening, Dr. Brynstone."

"Told you before. Call me John."

She noticed blood on his forehead, then glanced at the shattered glass and bullet holes defacing the Yukon. "Rough night. Huh, John?"

"You missed one hell of an adventure." He followed

her up the stairs. Inside the cabin, she pulled in the ramp and signaled the pilot for takeoff.

"Where's Banshee?" he asked.

"Conference room." Jordan rolled her eyes. "She got so angry at me tonight."

"Why can't you two get along?"

"We're both green-eyed divas. Better go. You don't want to keep her waiting."

He headed toward the back of the jet. He opened the door of the conference room, then stepped inside, looking around. A sleek black cat napped on the center of the mahogany table. Brynstone smiled. He leaned over the table and scooped up the cat.

"Good news, Banshee. I made it back in one piece."

Her black head nuzzled against his hand. Making a low chirp, she stared up at him with her solitary green eye.

He ditched his clothes, then cleaned off the blood and sterilized the gash on his hip. After the Learjet cruised into the air, he changed into Levi's and headed for a leather club chair with Banshee curled against his bare chest. The cat watched as he opened a medic kit, then removed a needle and nylon string. Banshee jumped down and sprinted away.

Shrapnel had grazed above his waistline on the right side. Twisting, he sucked in a breath, then poked the curved needle into his laceration. His skin jiggled with each pull as he stitched the jagged wound. Rotating his wrist, he watched the needle dive in and out of his flesh, making a trail of sixteen simple interrupted sutures. He tied a knot and finished the job.

Still bare chested after dressing the wound, he thought again about Zaki's library. He pictured the Arabic dagger jammed inside the skull. Seeing the weapon had evoked an old memory. His mind flashed to when he was a ten-year-old boy, wheeling into his father's study. Clinging to the doorknob, he had gaped at papers strewn across the floor. His gaze had drifted to his father's desk. Jayson Brynstone was sprawled on his back across the desktop, his bloodied arm dangling off the corner. Reliving the moment, he could see the jambiya dagger plunged deep into his father's chest. He recalled his father's best friend, collapsed on the floor, the man raising his hand in a warning.

In his twenty-year-old memory, the man's voice sounded choked and desperate.

Get out of here before he comes back. Hurry, Johnny.

Brynstone remembered turning the push rims on his wheelchair as he backed out of the room, thinking he had no place to hide. He remembered wheeling down the hallway of their Nantucket summer home, heading toward his bedroom. At the landing, he had heard footsteps closing in from behind. The man had grabbed the handles and shoved the wheelchair toward the top step. Brynstone remembered struggling to brake as he looked down the dark stairs, thinking he was about to die.

He shook off the memory.

His lips tightened as he looked up.

Jordan emerged from the galley. "Ready for a dirty martini?"

"You must be a mind reader."

She gave him a pretty smile as she placed his drink on the table, glancing at the muscled contours of his stomach. "Why the sutures?"

"I sparred with a chunk of shrapnel after my bird slammed into the mountain."

"Nice job stitching yourself up."

Pulling on his cadet-blue roll-neck sweater, he said, "Been doing it since I was a kid."

"Didn't you sew up Banshee when she lost her eye?"

"It was the least I could do after she saved my life. Banshee wouldn't let anyone else near her that night." Recognizing her name, the cat sauntered over and rubbed against his leg.

"Why all this do-it-yourself suturing?" Jordan asked, reaching in the medic kit. "Is it because you have an aversion to physicians?"

"I was in and out of hospitals until I was eleven. Vowed to never go back."

"You can trust me. I went to Vanderbilt med school before I got bored and quit. I'll fix that nasty cut on your forehead." Leaning over, Jordan's breast nudged his shoulder as she cleaned the wound. "You made quite an impression on Ajax Mountain. I picked up a local feed. A lift operator named Cooper Hollingworth may have died in the avalanche. Your helicopter shredded his gondola."

"He survived. I gave him some cash. He's moving back to Australia with his girlfriend."

"Nice. A happy ending."

"Not for everybody. Zaki's men tracked me to Glenwood Canyon. Turned ugly."

"I know," she said, smoothing a bandage across his forehead. "The Colorado Department of Transportation runs a command center deep inside the tunnel. I patched into a feed from their cameras at the Hanging Lake Traffic Control Center. Wanna see the highlight reel?"

"Once was enough."

"No stitches after all. At least not on your head." She looked down at him. "I still miss the goatee. Why'd you lose it?"

"My daughter refused to kiss me unless I shaved."

She traced her hand along his defined jaw. "Smart kid."

"Have you talked to DIRNSA?" he asked, pronouncing the official abbreviation of Director of the National Security Agency, *DERN-zuh*.

"Twice." She sat across from him. "You made General Delgado's day."

"He won't be happy about Glenwood Canyon. I'll tell him after I talk to my wife."

Jordan cocked her head. "Haven't you already called her?"

"Our daughter was crying." He stared out the window. "Kaylyn said she'd call back."

* * *

Kaylyn Brynstone was slender and blonde, with crisp eyes and a face that radiated good humor. Even on a night like tonight. Her daughter had two teeth breaking through her gums. Cutting an incisor and a molar at the same time brought out Shayna's fussy side. In full sob only minutes before, she was finally relaxing.

Kaylyn offered a cold teething ring. Her daughter gummed it. By the time she carried her toddler downstairs, the ring's magic had faded. Curling on the sofa, Kaylyn sang Brahms's lullaby. Wasn't working. She stood and moved the child to her chest, patting her back. Shay rested her chin on her mother's shoulder. Lilting around the room, she turned from the Christmas tree so her daughter could gaze at the twinkling lights.

Christmastime made her nostalgic for New York City. When she'd first moved to Los Angeles, the Hancock Park neighborhood had captivated her, especially the hint of citrus in the spring air. December was different. The weather was too sun drenched and balmy to seduce her into the holiday spirit. More than anything, John's absence made this Christmas unbearable.

Before moving out west, she had had what seemed like a dream job. For several years, she had been a buyer for Barneys New York. The job paid well, but too many designers made crazy demands. A phone call had inspired a career change. When she'd graduated from Duke University a decade earlier, the art department asked to keep two sculptures. Flattered, she had agreed. One day, her former art professor called. Dr. Diane Levine explained that during a Duke alumni exhibit, someone had broken into the Nasher Museum of Art and stolen Kaylyn's sculptures. The thieves had ignored the other work. They just wanted her sculptures.

"Aren't you furious?" Levine had asked.

She wasn't. In a weird way, it was a compliment. She had an epiphany that night: *If people like my work enough to steal it, they might like it enough to buy it*. She moved from her loft in SoHo and drove to California to jump-start her bohemian fantasy of becoming an artist. It worked out. The Museum of Contemporary Art in Los Angeles purchased two sculptures for its permanent collection. She created an outdoor piece for the Olympic Sculpture Park on Seattle's waterfront and was preparing for a solo show at a San Francisco gallery.

She had met John Brynstone at an artist reception during a West Coast exhibition. Desperate for money, she had sold her favorite piece, a sculpture named *Eclipse*. He bought it and broke her heart. Two weeks later at the Grove, she recognized the handsome black-haired man at a trendy restaurant. He bought her a drink. She told him she missed *Eclipse*. He promised visitation rights. The rest was history. She loved him but hated his secrets, especially about his intelligence work. For all she knew, he could be having an affair.

She prayed that wasn't the case.

Chapter Twelve

Washington, D.C.
10:51 P.M.

Growing up on a hardscrabble South Carolina farm, Deena Riverside never imagined she'd visit the White House, let alone spend the night in the Lincoln Bedroom. Now a successful pharmaceutical executive, she had stayed here four times. Like other presidents, Alexander Armstrong favored his affluent donors with sleepovers in the famous bedroom.

This place had served as Lincoln's cabinet room during the Civil War, but never his bedroom. Decorated with rich fabrics, it was small but handsome, with a beaded globe chandelier presiding over Victorian parlor decor. Her favorite piece was the rosewood bed with its six-foot-tall carved headboard. Framed by a crown-shaped canopy, the bed was draped in flowing satin over white lace, reaching to the floor.

The part Deena never told her friends was that the mattress was lumpy as hell.

She moved to the sitting room east of the Lincoln Bedroom. Curling on the Victorian medallion sofa with her notebook computer, she stared at the marble fireplace in the northeast corner. Her mind drifted to her conversation with Dillon Armstrong earlier in the evening at the Christmas party. She acted like it didn't upset her. The truth was, she didn't want to lose her job. As CEO of Taft-Ryder Pharmaceuticals, she ran one of the world's premiere pharmaceutical companies. Some stockholders grumbled that she was running it into the ground.

Civil War surgeon Zachary Taft, a relative of William Howard Taft, had founded the company in 1870. A year later, it became the first pharmaceutical company to hire a full-time chemist, Dr. Leland Ryder. Taft-Ryder's biggest success came from cough syrup marketed as Dr. Ryder's Miracle Discovery for Coughs and Colds. Sold by Victorian physicians and sideshow hucksters alike, the syrup tripled company profits.

In reality, Dr. Ryder's "miracle discovery" was actually a cocaine extract.

Taft-Ryder flourished until the Great Depression crushed profits. In the decades following World War II, the company fell behind pharmaceutical powerhouses like Pfizer, GlaxoSmithKline, and Merck. Taft-Ryder's

Returns

fortunes changed when Dillon became an investor. After bringing Deena on board, they became unstoppable. As CEO, she had gambled on an antidepressant drug known as Romzar. The drug became Taft-Ryder's "bread-and-butter molecule" and profits blasted through the ceiling. Management uncorked the champagne when *Fortune* magazine named Taft-Ryder "America's Most Admired Pharmaceutical Company."

Then all hell broke loose.

Patent and other market exclusivity expirations hit Taft-Ryder hard. When generic equivalents for their top two drugs hit the market, branded product sales dropped 90 percent. If things didn't change soon, the drug giant would need to lay off ten thousand workers and shut down several manufacturing and research sites.

The pressure was on. If she couldn't turn around Taft-Ryder Pharmaceuticals, she would lose her job. She needed a miracle.

She needed the Radix.

10:55 P.M.

President Alexander Armstrong placed *The Night Before Christmas* on the nightstand, then tucked his children into bed. The First Lady lingered at the door. Their two children shared a bedroom suite in the southwest corner of the Executive Residence's third floor.

He read to his children every night. That surprised Helena, because he'd never made time for it during his years as governor of New York at the Executive Mansion in Albany. With greater demands on his schedule now, reading to his children counted among his few simple pleasures at the White House.

Curled on her pillow, Alysha was asleep. Not Justin. At three, he was already a chronic insomniac like his old man.

"Give me a scratchback, Daddy. Pleeeeease." He raised

his Batman pajama top and rolled over, hugging his pillow.

"Not tonight, Justin," Helena said, her hand poised at her forehead. The migraine had passed like an earthquake. Now she was dealing with the aftershock.

"I'll scratch your back, tiger. Let me talk to Mom first."

Armstrong came over and kissed his wife. "I promise Justin will be working on visions of sugarplums in no time. You've had a rough day, Helena. Get your rest."

She nodded and yawned. Lean and regal, with sable brown hair, Helena Armstrong had become one of the more fashionable first ladies in history. "Sorry I missed the party."

"Everyone sent you warm wishes."

"Even Deena Riverside?"

"Even Deena."

"You've had a rough Christmas Eve too. Have you talked to Ambassador Zaki since he stormed out of here?"

"I'll call tomorrow. We'll work it out."

"Can you get some sleep?"

"I have a love-hate relationship with sleep. Lately, it's been hate."

"Why don't you watch a movie?" she suggested, running her finger along his pebbled black tie. "It always helps you relax and focus. It'll take your mind off things."

"I'll think about it."

They kissed again. He watched her move to the hallway. Returning to the bed, he was ready to scratch Justin's back. Little guy was conked.

"Some kind of a miracle," Armstrong whispered.

He pulled down Justin's shirt before tucking in the sheets. After the heated exchange with Ambassador Zaki, he was hoping for a peaceful holiday.

Chapter Thirteen

Airborne over Colorado
9:05 P.M.

Brynstone cupped Banshee's face. She issued a deep purr. The cat's one green eye formed a slit, disappearing in silky black fur.

Last July, he had traveled to Ireland to meet a Radix scholar named Reece Griffin, a historian at University College Cork. When he arrived at the man's flat, he heard gunfire. Kicking in the door, he found Griffin facedown, with an exit wound in his back. A rangy young man had stepped into the room, aiming a gun. Griffin's cat squealed from the kitchen, as if crying at the sight of her dead master. In surprise, the man fired at the kitten. Brynstone slammed into him and sent the guy crashing through a third-story window. He had peeked out the shattered window, finding the man sprawled on the dented hood of a white car. Waiting for the police to arrive, he grabbed his medic kit, then cleaned and stitched the cat's swollen eye.

The kitten's cry had distracted the gunman and saved Brynstone's life. In choosing the cat's name, he had found inspiration in the Irish myth of the banshee, a female spirit who wails when someone is about to die. Whenever he headed out on a mission, his one-eyed companion joined him. Kaylyn called them soul mates, sharing a fearless streak and a craving for adventure.

Lowering the cat to the floor, he grabbed his belt pack. Jordan Rayne moved into the seat facing him. She crossed her long legs. Jordan was beautiful without even trying. And she wasn't used to men ignoring her.

He dug inside the belt, then placed the stone box on the table. He ran his finger across the engraved lid.

Jordan met his eyes. "Is that—?"

"The *cista mystica*."

"Is the Radix inside?"

He nodded.

"Wonderful," she purred. "I'll deliver it to DIRNSA."

Before he could answer, his cell vibrated. He checked the number. "It's Kaylyn."

Jordan nodded. He tucked away the box as she walked to the galley. He put the phone to his ear and paced the Learjet's aisle. His wife didn't waste time.

"We need to work on so many issues, John. I'm frustrated. I just wish you could be here. Is that too much to ask?"

"I know, Kaylyn. I know you want Christmas to be special for Shay." He closed his eyes. "Look, I can't make Christmas Eve, but I'll make sure I'm home tomorrow."

"Are you serious?"

"I need some more time on this assignment. After I wrap things up, I'll fly to LA."

"You promise?"

"Promise." He laughed softly. "Seems like our life's turning into an Elvis song. You know, 'If I Get Home On Christmas Day.' "

"Yeah?" she asked. "I'll take that over 'Blue Christmas' anytime."

They talked a little more, the conversation playing smoother than Brynstone had expected when he'd first answered her call. After hanging up, he contacted a microbiologist named Bill Nosaka, asking him to analyze a soft-tissue sample from the Zanchetti mummy.

Jordan peeked from the galley. She walked to his seat with another Grey Goose martini.

"Not your style to eavesdrop on people," he told her.

"You're kidding, right? I work for the United States Special Collection Service." She handed him a drink. "Why so paranoid?"

"Because I work for the Special Collection Service."

"We're a lot alike," she said, relaxing in the seat beside him. "We'll both put our lives on the line if the SCS demands it."

She was right. Brynstone thought about the time he had bugged the Moscow home of the director of the Federal Security Service of the Russian Federation, the successor to the Soviet KGB. He'd barely escaped with his life. And then, last summer on the Philippine island of Jolo, he'd used his surgical skill to implant a nanotech bug inside the mouth of a World Islamic Brotherhood leader. Brynstone had sedated the terrorist as he slept, then installed the microscopic recording device in his upper gum line. Unaware that the American government could monitor his conversations, the terrorist had provided invaluable intelligence on the Brotherhood's activities. Brynstone thrived on those assignments.

"The SCS is notorious for destroying marriages," Jordan continued. "How is Kaylyn?"

His voice softened. "Lonely."

"I know that feeling."

"Your parents divorced when you were a kid, right?"

She nodded. "They still don't talk."

"Your dad's a scientist?"

"Stephan Rayne. A Nobel laureate in chemistry." The cat batted at the lacing on her boots. Jordan reached down to pet her, but Banshee shot back her ears, then skittered up the aisle. "They had nothing in common. Mom was a fashion model."

"Why'd they marry?"

She made a face. "Dad's family had money. Simple as that."

"Are you more like your mom or your dad?"

"Dad, no question. He raised me. Mom always said I

got her body and his brains. My older brother, Robert? He got dad's body and mom's brains."

"You got the better deal."

"Thanks." She giggled again, brushing back red hair. "Why the questions?"

He took a drink. "My wife hinted at divorce earlier tonight."

"Is that what you want?"

"No. I don't think Kaylyn does, either. She's torn, feeling like she can't go on like this."

"That's no surprise, given the danger and secrecy of our work," Jordan added. "Like I said, the divorce rate among Special Collection Service agents is astronomical."

A glance, still guarded. "I'll do everything I can to save my marriage. I don't want my daughter to deal with divorce."

"Sometimes that's better than parents who fight all the time."

"We're not together enough to do that." He shook his head. "Wanna know one strange part? General Delgado has been giving me marriage advice."

"Doesn't surprise me. DIRNSA acts like you're the son he never had."

"James Delgado saved my life," he said, dropping his gaze.

"When you were an Army Ranger?"

"Long before that. He and my father were best friends. My dad was a high-ranking intelligence official. One night when I was ten years old, Delgado visited our vacation home. He caught an intruder attacking my dad. Delgado warned me to get out. He stopped the intruder, but the guy stabbed Delgado. My dad died that night. Delgado came close."

"Is that why DIRNSA has that jagged scar down the side of his face?"

He nodded.

"I've wondered, but nobody talks about it." She sipped

the martini. "Didn't you say your father was interested in finding the Radix?"

"I didn't learn about that until a couple years ago. From what Mom told me, he didn't discuss stuff like that."

"A man of secrets, huh? Guess it runs in the family. No wonder your dad and General Delgado were buddies."

"Jordan, we need to discuss Operation Overshadow. Something about tonight's mission at Hala Ranch is eating at me." He sunk back in his seat. "And I may need your help."

Los Angeles
8:15 P.M.

Little more than a year old, Shayna Brynstone wobbled toward the Christmas tree. The toddler gurgled, holding a conversation with her fish-eye reflection in a glass ornament. For Kaylyn, the tender moment brought a smile. And a tear. She wished John could be here.

Earlier in the evening, she had blurted the word *divorce* while talking to her husband. As much as she despised saying that, maybe it had inspired John to head home tomorrow. She knew almost nothing about her husband's intelligence work, but she understood that he thrived on it. He was addicted to taking risks.

His childhood had been riddled with Perthes disease. The illness brought avascular necrosis, sapping blood supply to his hipbone. He was subjected to multiple surgeries. Bedridden and in traction for months, John was forced into a body cast. Even a wheelchair at times. After his body had betrayed him, he developed his mind. His father encouraged John to read everything he could get his hands on.

His illness hadn't been the only challenge. His father, Jayson Brynstone, had been murdered one night in their Nantucket summer home. Fortunately, his father's best friend, James Delgado, had stopped the intruder from

attacking John. Since that night, Delgado had become a
substitute father for her husband.

John had hit a turning point at age eleven, dealing
with the disease, if not his father's death. He left behind
the wheelchair and body casts and returned to school.
The disease had run its course. Children who had teased
him for being small and frail were astonished to find that
John was bigger and stronger than his classmates.

After that, John never looked back. Sometimes that
was a good thing. Sometimes bad.

He refused to talk about his disease or his father's
passing. She'd never had the chance to meet Jayson Brynstone, but her mother-in-law claimed that John and his
father had shared a close bond. The basic architecture of
John's face bore a resemblance to his father's, all chiseled
lines and tanned features. The similarities persisted over
generations. Shay's cool blue eyes matched perfectly the
eyes of her father and grandfather.

John had confessed that coping with disease had taught
him to live without fear. She sensed that the only time her
husband lowered his guard was when he was with his
family. After his bedridden childhood, he craved risk because it made him feel alive. That's why he'd followed his
father's career path as an intelligence field agent.

John thrived on chaos and danger. She needed safety
and stability. They made it work until Shay came along.
Kaylyn had always dreamed about sharing holidays with
her own family. Raised by her grandparents, she had never
celebrated Christmas during her childhood. She had
vowed to make the holiday special for her child. She
couldn't wait to have John home.

She scooted off the sofa and moved to her daughter. She
reached under the tree, then placed a package at Shay's
feet. The child's eyes brightened as she tugged on the ribbon. Kaylyn helped her daughter tear the paper. She and
John had bought this gift back in October.

Shay squealed when she saw the stuffed pink bunny

inside the box. Grabbing it, she plopped her face into its fluffy back. She raised her head, seeming to talk with her eyes. Kaylyn wished she could read her daughter's mind. She couldn't wait to hear Shay's next words.

Airborne over Colorado
9:20 P.M.

Brynstone could read the bewilderment on Jordan's face. He drummed his fingers on the armrest. "Something tonight didn't feel right."

"Hala Ranch was an unusual op for us. The SCS doesn't go around stealing relics."

"Exactly. What is your understanding about the goal of Operation Overshadow?"

"Here's what I know," she said. "You were tapped to break into Hala Ranch and steal the Radix. Ambassador Zaki will do anything to get it back."

"That's where I have a problem. The intelligence was correct about Zaki locking a valued possession inside his mummy room. Turns out that his prized possession was the mummified remains of Alexander the Great, not the Radix. Zaki went bat-shit crazy when his men fired in the direction of Alexander's mummy. He never mentioned the Zanchetti mummy."

"Maybe he was acting."

"Don't think so. I'm starting to believe Zaki doesn't know the Radix even exists."

"We were briefed that he has ties to the World Islamic Brotherhood. We were ordered to retrieve the Radix as leverage, so we could pressure him into sharing intelligence."

"Maybe General Delgado gave the green light to Operation Overshadow based on corrupted intel. Someone claimed that Zaki valued the Radix, then took it a step further. Maybe they falsified a link between Zaki and the WIB."

"DIRNSA isn't going to be happy to hear that someone gave him corrupt intel."

"He's not going to hear it."

Her mouth curled in surprise. "You're kidding. We have to tell Delgado."

"Not until I can figure out who gave Delgado faulty intelligence about Zaki. A dozen people had their fingerprints on this mission. Telling DIRNSA might tip them off."

"You think so?"

"If Delgado knows, he'll initiate an investigation to find the source. By then, it could be too late. If we deliver the relic to General Delgado and the source hears about an investigation, we run the risk of the Radix falling into the wrong hands." Brynstone fought a disquieting feeling. He didn't have all the answers, but something felt wrong. Until he discovered the truth, he had to take action. "Jordan, do you trust me?"

"More than anyone I know. What's your plan?"

"We'll land in Baltimore, but we're not taking the Radix to Delgado's NSA office at Fort Meade. I need to consult a colleague. He worked for the NSA before you transferred over."

"What if your colleague is the one who gave compromised intel?"

"He knows about the Radix, but nothing about Zaki. We need to go dark after we land so I can talk to him. We can't let Delgado know what we're doing. Trust me on that."

Chapter Fourteen

Deena slipped on a white robe bearing the White House emblem, then moved to the adjacent Lincoln Sitting Room. She curled on an overstuffed Victorian sofa. With a view of the roaring fireplace, she checked e-mail on her Black-Berry. A journalist had contacted her for an interview for *BioPharm International* magazine. A Merck colleague sent gossip that the FDA had denied Pfizer fast-track status on a new cholesterol drug. Then she came across an e-mail from Pantera. Deena never guessed she'd put this kind of faith in a stranger, but Pantera was impressive. Call it intuition, but she trusted her contact.

Pantera had e-mailed Deena a text message from a cell phone. Although brief, it was what she had been waiting to hear.

> *We think the scientist found Radix. Will get it from him soon. Have funds avail to secure sale of Radix. ttys*

She jumped when a knock came at the door. She scrambled off the sofa, then headed back into the Lincoln Bedroom to answer it.

Leaning against the doorframe, Dillon Armstrong gave a sneaky smile. "Mind if I come in?" He peeked back at the Secret Service agent in the East Sitting Hall before stepping inside.

"Does your brother know you're here?"

"Last I knew, he was busy reading bedtime stories." Dillon tossed his coat over the back of a Victorian slipper chair. "You might not believe this, Deena, but I want to apologize. I was a little biting out on the South Portico."

"I know how much Taft-Ryder means to you. It was your first big success in the pharmaceutical industry. You want to see it succeed."

"I've always been good about keeping my personal life and my corporate life separate. Doesn't seem to be the case anymore. The separation with Brooke has been eating on me."

"Maybe this will help." She read aloud the text message from Pantera.

"Good. When do we make the exchange?"

"In a matter of hours, I hope."

"Look, Deena, if you're comfortable with this acquisition process, that's good enough for me. I've placed funds in an account in a Luxembourg bank." Dillon grabbed his coat. "Let's go to my place. I'll give you the account number."

"You won't regret this," she answered. "I promise."

11:35 P.M.

The Knight pressed binoculars to his face as he peered through the Mercedes's windshield. Along with his assistant and two security operators, he scanned the area around the National Cathedral. He'd spotted the sinner here four nights ago.

Floodlights splashed ethereal light on the cobblestone square. A figure emerged on the snowy sidewalk outside the Gothic cathedral.

"There's the homeless man," the Knight said, his mouth curling into a smile. "He looks cold."

"The guy in the long coat?" Max Cress asked, staring through night-vision binoculars.

"That's him. He's perfect."

The man ambled down Wisconsin Avenue. Dressed in an oversized coat and grimy sweatpants, he wore a knit cap over long greasy hair. His fingers peeked through tattered gloves as he pushed a rusty shopping cart crammed with garbage bags and aluminum cans.

"Here's the plan," the Knight said. "Cress and Weber, I want you to keep an eye on him. He stays close to the Bishop's Garden this time of night. You'll need to wait until after the midnight candlelight service is over. If it looks clear, send the team to pick him up. I don't care if you wait half the night. And be certain we don't have an eyewitness."

"Want him delivered to the house?" Cress asked.

"Of course. Get him a shower. Trim his beard into a forked shape at the chin, but not too close. After that, feed him."

"What will you do to him?"

"He is a sinner begging for redemption," the Knight said. "I have been sent to save him."

Baltimore
Midnight

Alone in her darkened hospital room, Cori Cassidy snapped open her eyes. She listened for a moment, hearing a staff person outside her bedroom. Relaxing again, she snuggled inside her blanket, basking in a cocoon of warmth. She diverted her thoughts to Tessa Richardson. Cori's roommate couldn't fly home for the holidays because she was writing her doctoral dissertation. At least Tessa wasn't stuck in a psych hospital.

Cori replayed her conversation with the patient known as Leonardo. Gave her chills when she thought about his words: *the Tree of Life blossoms in the Land of the Dead*. She worried that her conversation with the man would trigger a recurring dream.

Her nightmare played out the same way every time. In

the dream, Ariel Cassidy explained from her deathbed that she was about to die. In the next blurry second, Cori found herself inside the Princeton University Chapel, peering into her mother's casket. The coffin was always empty. She spied her dead mother watching from beneath the chapel's stained glass science window. She glided to Cori, then whispered in her ear. After that, Ariel Cassidy climbed into her casket. The lid closed. The dream ended. It always happened that way.

She could count on the dream whenever bad things happened. If she was having relationship trouble, she had the dream. Or if someone was sick or dying. Or when her father started dating Yvette. Ethan Cassidy had met her at his law firm. Half his age, Yvette was a brunette with huge fake boobs who seemed obsessed with his money. Her father had to move on with his life. She just wished he had waited more than three months after her mother's passing.

Everything had soured during a family vacation. After her dad had gone to bed, she caught Yvette dancing with younger guys at a club. Big turnoff. The next morning, Cori called her on it. Yvette stopped speaking to her. At Thanksgiving, her dad had announced a Christmas trip to the Fiji Islands with Yvette and Jared, Cori's younger brother. The catch? She wasn't invited. That was totally fine, except Cori missed spending the holidays with Jared.

The next day, she signed up for Professor Berta's experiment.

Cori didn't want to dream about her mother in this place, but she sensed the nightmare would come anyway. And as always, Ariel Cassidy would whisper the same words before climbing into her casket: *the Tree of Life blossoms in the Land of the Dead.*

Chapter Fifteen

Brynstone was ready to take a chance. He needed to go dark after landing in Baltimore. Would the risk pay off?

Talking to Jordan, his voice lowered. "The Radix has power. I saw that firsthand tonight. That's why the House of Borgia wants it."

She frowned. "It's hard to believe they're still out there."

"Believe it," he answered. "They hunger for the Radix."

The Borgias' obsession with the Radix stretched back more than five centuries. Before Cesare Borgia died in 1507, he made his oldest child, Domenico, take a blood oath to reclaim the lost Radix. Domenico Borgia's mother was a Ferrarese nun who had died giving birth to her son in 1495. Raised in secrecy by Cesare's sister, Lucrezia, the illegitimate child was nurtured on stories about the relic that had once belonged to his grandfather, Pope Alexander VI. Along with two of Lucrezia's surviving children, Domenico had dedicated himself to regaining the relic. Domenico's children and several cousins had inherited the clan's passion.

Their quest sparked tension with skeptical family members, including Francis Borgia, later canonized in 1671. Despite the rift, Domenico Borgia's descendents continued their search. Over centuries, their obsession for the Radix bordered on fanaticism. The latest generation had even returned to Cesare Borgia's ruthless and bloodthirsty ways.

Brynstone placed the stone box on the table. He pointed to the image engraved on the *cista mystica*'s lid. "See that? It matches a plant symbol in the Voynich manuscript. It tells me our work isn't over." He leaned back. "We can't understand the power of the Radix until we consult an expert on the Voynich manuscript."

"Explain that," Jordan said. "How does it fit in?"

"In 1912," he began, "an American book dealer and collector named Wilfrid Voynich visited a Jesuit college at the Villa Mondragone in Frascati, Italy. While searching the monastery's antique manuscripts, he discovered a book written in an unknown language. The pages were filled with a bizarre enciphered script and cryptic watercolors of unfamiliar plants, unknown astronomical constellations, and naked women immersed in tubs of green liquid."

"Back up a sec," she interrupted. "Did you say, 'naked women in tubs'?"

"Mm-hmm."

"Pretty strange."

"Everything about it is strange. It has been called the most mysterious manuscript in the world. It's in the Beinecke Rare Book and Manuscript Library at Yale University."

"When was it written?"

"It's not clear. Past speculation placed it anywhere between 1450 and 1600. For more than a century, people have tried to decipher its meaning. It's cryptology's Holy Grail. No one could crack it. Until recently."

"Someone figured it out?"

He nodded. "The VMS consists of five sections in an alphabetic script of nineteen to twenty-eight letters, none bearing a relationship to any known letter system. Computer analysis of the VMS revealed two distinct 'languages' or 'dialects' of Voynichese, called Voynich A and Voynich B. Most of it is nonsensical, designed to throw off cryptologists."

She tilted her head. "This is wild."

"A British cognitive scientist thinks it was written using a sixteenth-century device called the Cardan grille. It's a card cut with window slits you place over a text table containing suffixes, infixes, and prefixes. You can create an endless constellation of syllables to design new words. Some think it contains meaningless words. The colleague I mentioned earlier? He's a Voynich expert. He deciphered clues embedded in the rule-based language in the fourth section and parts of the first and third sections."

"Who wrote the VMS?"

"It's been attributed to everyone from Leonardo da Vinci to the English scholar Roger Bacon." He stretched his legs. "My colleague has a different idea."

"Who does he think wrote it?"

"Raphael della Rovere."

Her green eyes sparkled with realization. "Serious? The priest who mummified Friar Zanchetti more than five hundred years ago?"

Trained as a physician, Raphael della Rovere became a priest in 1496. A Franciscan from Florence, he became a respected medical historian and scholar of Hebraic classics. He was also a thief. In 1502, della Rovere smuggled the Radix out of the Vatican. Months before his theft, Cesare Borgia had stolen the relic from an aging cardinal named Pierre d'Aubusson. Known as the Shield of the Church, d'Aubusson was the grand master of the Sovereign Military Order of Saint John of Jerusalem, a group originally known as the Knights Hospitaller. In a secret 1476 ceremony, the knights had appointed d'Aubusson as the Keeper of the Radix.

A quarter century later, Cesare Borgia learned about the relic, traveled to Rhodes, and attacked d'Aubusson. As Pope Alexander VI's son, Borgia drew on Vatican favors to escape with the Radix before the Knights of Saint John captured him. Borgia returned to the Vatican and delivered the Radix to his father. The delighted Pope commissioned scholars to study the relic, but none could decipher its secret. The Pope knew the Radix was valuable, but he could not unlock its power. In desperation, the Vatican summoned della Rovere, who was regarded as an eccentric but brilliant thinker. It was a bitter decision for the Pope. Raphael della Rovere was the nephew of Borgia's most aggressive rival, Cardinal Giuliano della Rovere.

After months locked in a Vatican library, della Rovere discovered the true meaning of the *Radix ipsius*. He feared if he shared the secrets of the Radix with the Vatican, the Pope would abuse its power for personal gain. Following the death of his wife, della Rovere was more willing to take chances. Under cover of darkness, the priest stole the relic from the Vatican Library. A furious Pope Alexander VI sent his bloodthirsty son to find him. At the time, Cesare Borgia was the Duke of Valentinois and captain general of the papal army.

Della Rovere considered returning the Radix to the Order of Saint John, but decided that Borgia might steal it again. With the Pope's militia closing in, he concealed the relic in a secure place. Although Borgia never revealed where he found the priest, he returned without the Radix. Borgia didn't know della Rovere had hidden it inside Lorenzo Zanchetti's mummy.

After his mummification in 1502, Zanchetti was buried beneath the Church of San Sebastiano in the Italian village of Navelli. His corpse was forgotten until the church floor collapsed, revealing catacombs containing more than two hundred mummies. When Brynstone learned Friar Zanchetti was among the uncovered mummies, he took the next flight to central Italy. He'd arrived in the Tuscany highlands to learn that the mummy had been stolen the previous day and vanished on the black market. A member from the House of Saud purchased the Italian monk in July. Three months later, Brynstone learned Prince Zaki had transported the mummy to Aspen. Since then, he'd been planning for this night.

"After decoding the Voynich manuscript, my friend

learned the *cista mystica* was concealed inside the Zanchetti mummy."

"Della Rovere mentioned that in the Voynich manuscript?"

"Alluded to it in code. We filled in the gaps." He pointed to the engraved image on the box. "That mystery plant appears in section one of the VMS."

"John, I shared that I trusted you. Do you trust me?"

"Of course."

"Then can I see the Radix?"

"I should warn you," he said, pushing the stone box across the table. "It may not contain what you expect."

"Can you be any more cryptic?" Jordan joked, running a hand through her hair as she stared at the *cista mystica*.

"Go ahead," he urged. "Open it."

After shooting a quick glance at him, she opened the lid, then peeked inside the stone box. She yelped, slapping the lid closed as she jumped back in revulsion.

"My God," she gasped. "Is that a human finger?"

"Belongs to Friar Zanchetti."

"That's impossible," she said, flipping the lid open again. The muscles around her mouth curled in disgust. "Zanchetti died five hundred years ago. That finger looks pink, like it was severed from a living person."

"Surprised me too," he admitted. "I had no idea what the Radix could do until I saw Zanchetti's mummy."

"I don't get it. The finger is the Radix?"

"The Radix is beneath it." He opened the medic kit and found latex gloves. Stretching them over his hands, he reached inside the stone box. He placed Zanchetti's ring finger on a specimen bag. The fingertip was wrapped in aging brown cloth. "Look inside the box."

She peeked in. A look of awe came over her face as she studied the Radix. "It's amazing," she whispered. "I've never seen anything like it. But what's with the finger? Why'd della Rovere store it in the mystic coffin?"

"Good question." He examined the finger, then unraveled

the cloth. Finding a scalpel in the medic kit, he wedged the blade beneath the fingernail.

"Geez," Jordan groaned. "You're not seriously ripping off the nail?"

"Now I know why you dropped out of med school." He wiggled the scalpel, then lifted the fingernail from the skin.

She rolled her eyes. "Truly gross."

"Paleopathology isn't always pretty." Brynstone squinted at the nail. "Della Rovere scratched a message beneath Zanchetti's fingernail. He placed the nail back on the finger, then wrapped it. After five centuries, it adhered."

Jordan scrunched her nose. "Why would he do that?"

"He wanted to hide it where people wouldn't think to look."

"Those are symbols," she said, squinting at the fingernail's underside.

"A Voynich B cipher," he added. "Hopefully, my friend will know what it means."

Chapter Sixteen

Washington, D.C.
12:46 A.M.

"I have a question," Deena said, riding with Dillon in the back of his limousine. "Aren't you and the president a little old for sibling rivalry?"

"You say that like it's a bad thing."

She laughed, glancing out the window at the Dupont Circle neighborhood in Washington, D.C.'s northwest section. "Where's your penthouse?"

"On Seventeenth and P. I'm staying here during the

separation." He looked at her. "Alex and I haven't lived in the same town since high school. Even back in Sag Harbor, I realized we needed distance."

"Why are you staying here?"

"An investment deal. Plus, I'm logging time with lobbyists on K Street." He pointed out the window. "We're here."

The Lafayette was a majestic old redbrick building with brick stairs leading to a bright green door. Deena knew this neighborhood. She loved the area's trendy restaurants, custom shops, coffeehouses, and small boutiques. As the limo driver pulled curbside, Dillon leaned in. "You need to open a Christmas present."

"Dillon, a present? I didn't get you anything."

"You found the Radix," he smiled. "It's going to save my investment in Taft-Ryder."

1:00 A.M.

Alexander Armstrong headed for the East Wing as Secret Service Agent Kevin Quick shadowed his every step. Like most modern presidents, he found refuge in the White House's family theater. A night at the movies allowed escape without Secret Service hanging on him. Cinema came in a close second to golf as the president's favorite way to unwind. He walked down the East Colonnade, a white corridor adorned with a wreath on each window, before entering a narrow room. The place had served as a White House cloakroom until it was converted into a screening room during FDR's administration. Armstrong had spent countless hours in here, sometimes using it to rehearse his State of the Union address. Willie Cohen, the White House projectionist, waited outside his booth.

"I hate asking you to do this so late, Willie."

"Not a problem, Mr. President." He motioned to the seats. "We don't want to keep Mr. Cooper waiting. Just give me a couple minutes to get it ready."

As Armstrong headed down the theater's red velvet

stairs, he said, "Didn't you tell me this movie has been screened more than any other at the White House?"

"That's what the records show. My predecessor, Paul Fischer, kept notes all the way back to Eisenhower. Enjoy, Mr. President."

Passing seven rows of chairs, he plopped down on a red overstuffed armchair in the front row. Buttered popcorn waited on the matching red ottoman. Digging in, he reflected on *High Noon*'s popularity for Oval Office leaders. Gary Cooper's unflinching portrayal of Marshal Kane resonated with American presidents. They understood the pressure of making decisions against the clock. Especially when you had to go it alone, sometimes with the world against you.

He glanced over as the vice president slid into the chair beside him. Isaac Starr's face conveyed a sense of quiet authority. He resembled baseball legend Jackie Robinson in his later years—all calm resolve and salt-and-pepper hair—when he had taken up the cause of civil rights.

"I thought you hated Westerns," Armstrong said.

"Not this one. It's an existential morality play in a cowboy hat." Starr looked over with dark, restless eyes. "Nice party, Alex. You made Andrea's night with that angel ornament."

"Glad she liked it. How's she feeling?"

"We started a new program at Children's National. It's making a difference with her cerebral palsy." Starr glanced over. "Had any more thoughts about our reelection strategy?"

"Our latest approval ratings look solid. If we stay on track, we'll crush them."

Starr gave a roguish grin. "I just said the same thing to your brother in the Palm Room. I was leaving the press-corps office when I saw him with Deena. Mind passing the popcorn?"

Armstrong handed him the bucket. "When did you see them?"

"Maybe thirty minutes ago. Everything okay, Alex?"

He brought out his cell phone and called for a status update on Dillon.

An agent reported that Fortune—the Secret Service codename for his brother—and Deena had departed the White House at twelve thirty-five in the morning.

"Deena was supposed to spend the night in the Lincoln Bedroom," he fumed. "They were arguing at the party. Dillon was concerned about spending a lot of money on something called the Radix. I'm concerned he's planning something rash."

Starr thought it over. "I'm sure it's on the level. Your brother is an investment genius."

"If Dillon pulls a stupid stunt, it could haunt us next November. Maybe he suffers from Nixonburger Syndrome. It's a condition marked by excessive greed, poor decision-making, and profound stupidity. It afflicts the siblings of the president of the United States."

"Including Nixon's brother, I take it?" Starr asked, handing back the popcorn.

"Back when his brother was vice president, Donald Nixon opened a chain of hamburger stands. He sold Nixonburgers in California, including one near Disneyland."

"Sounds like a plan suited for Fantasyland."

"Don was a lousy businessman. In 1957, Howard Hughes loaned Don Nixon more than two hundred thousand dollars to rescue him from bankruptcy. It was a bombshell that damaged Dick Nixon's 1960 presidential bid and his run for governor of California two years later. After Nixon became president, he had Secret Service wiretap his brother's phone."

"Wow," Starr chuckled. "What are the chances of Nixon doing that?"

"We've had a near epidemic of Nixonburger Syndrome. Billy Carter and Sam Houston Johnson. Roger Clinton. Neil Bush." He frowned as the house lights faded. "Someday, you'll be in charge of this office, Isaac. When that happens, you'll be glad you're an only child."

"Your brother's not like those guys. Dillon isn't a political risk."

"My brother screwed up before. Not that he'd admit it. We kept it under wraps."

"Can you excuse me, Alex? I should tell my wife I'm staying for the show."

"Hurry." He pointed at the screen as Lee Van Cleef and his henchmen rode down Hadleyville's dusty street. "You're gonna miss the best part."

"What's the best part?" Starr asked, standing.

"All of it."

1:30 A.M.

As the fireplace blazed behind her, Deena curled on the mahogany floor and sipped wine.

Dillon's Lafayette penthouse projected a sleek urban look. It had a more casual spirit than his place with Brooke in the Lenox Hill neighborhood on Manhattan's Upper East Side. After they arrived at his penthouse, he had given her the Luxembourg account information for purchasing the Radix.

He came over, joining her beside the fire. "I need to ask you something." His eyes sparkled. "Were you ever intimate with Alex?"

"No," Deena lied. "We came close. Or maybe it was my imagination."

"I don't think so. I saw it tonight at the party. Alex has a thing for you."

Her face burned. "You're imagining things."

He reached inside his suit pocket. He handed her a small white box tied with a sapphire ribbon. As he reached for his Chardonnay, she opened the box and found a pear-shaped diamond necklace. She clamped her hand over her mouth, making a hushed sound of surprise. "I love it."

"You better. I flew to the Brisbane salon to purchase it from Stefano Canturi."

She felt stupid not recognizing the designer's name. He unclasped the necklace, then brought it around her neck as she raised her cinnamon brown hair. The diamond slid into place, finding a home at her neckline. "It's gorgeous. I hope you didn't spend too much on it."

He laughed. "If you hope that, then there's something wrong with you."

Hearing the alert tone, she grabbed her cell from the coffee table. "It's a text from Pantera." Her eyes widened. "It's confirmed. The Radix has been found."

Washington, D.C.
2:00 A.M.

President Alexander Armstrong relaxed as Gary Cooper's stoic marshal faced down his past in *High Noon*. He appreciated Isaac Starr joining him. Despite an omnipresent army of staff and advisors, the White House was one of the loneliest places on the planet. Armstrong heard whispering at the back of the theater. He craned his neck. His national security advisor, Wendy Hefner, talked with Secret Service Agent Kevin Quick.

He and Starr stood as the black-and-white image of Coop's face wrapped around them. The president raised his hand. "Hold up, Willie. I need to confer with Ms. Hefner."

The projector stopped. The house lights brightened. She hurried down the stairs. Dressed in a dark suit, she wore her ash blonde hair pulled back in a ponytail.

"Sorry to interrupt, Mr. President," she said, catching her breath. "The Saudi ambassador wants to speak on the phone. Prince Zaki wouldn't share details, but it's clear he's not happy."

* * *

Back in the Oval Office a few minutes later, Armstrong put Zaki bin Abdelaziz on speaker. The vice president stood beside the desk.

The ambassador sounded terse. "Mr. President, we have enjoyed a cordial partnership until yesterday afternoon. Given our past alliance, I must ask for an end to your harassment."

"I don't understand."

"I am speaking about the man who broke into my Hala Ranch home last night."

He barked a laugh. "If someone broke in, Mr. Ambassador, you should notify Aspen police. Not the president of the United States."

"This goes beyond a police matter. I have a state-of-the-art security system, Mr. President. This man used advanced technology to bypass it. He disabled my camera equipment. He immobilized my security team. He crashed one of my helicopters. Five members of my security team were sent to the emergency room. Two had to be fished out of the Colorado River. This man is not a common intruder. He is nothing less than a sophisticated vandal."

"Sounds impressive. I still don't see why you called me."

"I believe the break-in was a retaliation for my troubled meeting with you yesterday."

Isaac Starr shook his head.

"With all due respect, do you realize how ridiculous that sounds, Mr. Ambassador?"

"The intruder disabled all but one camera. I have sent pictures of him."

Wendy Hefner hustled into the Oval with photographs. She spread them across his desk.

"I was handed the pictures, Mr. Ambassador. My people will look into this situation."

"He called himself John Robie, but I suspect he lied. He escaped in my helicopter. A heliport camera took the pictures you are looking at. Please find someone to identify this man."

Zaki ended the call.

"Wendy," Armstrong told his national security advisor, "get the CIA director and the NSA director in here for an immediate meeting." He moved to the south-facing windows behind his desk, then stared at the December night. "I want to get to the bottom of this fast."

Chapter Seventeen

Baltimore
2:12 A.M.

Sleep had been merciful. Much to her surprise, Cori didn't dream about her mother. Something else jolted her awake. A sound.

"You in here?" a man asked, stumbling into her darkened room. "Cori?"

She recognized the voice. *Leonardo.* How had the mental patient escaped his secret ward? He staggered to her bed. Blankets cascaded off the mattress as she scooted against the headboard. She twisted a sheet across her chest.

"Don't have much time," he rasped. "The Borgias want to kill me." He coughed, switching on a flashlight. Blood speckled his cheek. Leonardo placed her mother's book on the bed, then brought out a business card. "My name's Edgar Wurm. Contact the man on this card. Tell him, 'The Tree of Life can kill as well as heal.' Got it?"

"I guess," she stuttered.

"Tell him to get inside the mind of Carl Jung. Learn his secrets." He gave her the card. "This is critical. It could affect the lives of millions."

"But Leo—Edgar. Let's call Mack Shaw. Or the police."

"Do *not* call the police. If the Borgias discover we talked, they'll kill you." Wurm turned off the flashlight, then glanced out the hallway. "They're coming. I must go." Looking back, he whispered, "Sorry to get you involved, Cori. Good luck."

Then he was gone.

It was confusing. Who were the Borgias? Tonight had been one of those Alice-in-Wonderland moments in her life, situations where curiosity led her into discovery and danger.

She flipped over the business card. Wurm had scrawled a series of numbers on the back:

157:13:08–09/14:05:02–03/316:01:01/07:07:07
98:28:01/03:05:13/64:02:16/63:25:07/404:30:04–05/84:08:06

She had no idea what it meant. She slid the card inside her mother's book. This night seemed surreal, like a new nightmare. And it was getting worse. Muffled voices came from outside her room. Was it Leonardo—Wurm—talking to someone? She rolled off the bed, then slid her mother's book under the mattress. She hurried to the doorway.

A flashlight blinded her. She shielded her eyes.

"Stop right there," a woman hissed. Dressed in a white lab coat, she was in her late twenties, tall and athletic. Sleek black hair halted above her shoulders. She had gray eyes with flawless lips and skin—a fusion of coldness and beauty.

"Who are you?" Cori asked, catching her breath as she looked up. Her head came an inch below the woman's shoulder.

"Dr. Elizabeth Reese." She swept a penlight's beam down Cori's face to the name sewn on her lab coat. "We have a problem."

She caught herself shivering. "What's wrong?"

"An escaped patient."

"I didn't see him."

The woman smiled. "I never said the patient was a man." A soft laugh. "Climb back in bed."

She ordered another person—maybe a man—to search the other rooms.

Cori crawled onto her bed, then pulled up covers and watched the door. Wurm had warned about the Borgias. *Is that them? He said they'd kill me.* She listened for a sound.

The woman darted into the room, stopping at the bed. She dropped the penlight into her lab coat, then leaned down. "Tell me," she cooed, running her fingers through Cori's blonde hair. "Did this madman visit your bedroom?"

She thought it over. Perez claimed Edgar Wurm had killed three people. She remembered blood smeared on his cheek.

"You have beautiful hair, dear. Did you have it cut?"

She nodded.

"On the hospital ward?" The woman's eyes narrowed. "We don't allow patients to get haircuts. Nothing sharp, you know. Bad things happen when dangerous patients handle sharp objects. But you don't seem dangerous. In fact, you don't seem crazy at all."

Following Berta's orders, Cori hadn't acted psychotic during her hospital stay. Now seemed like the time to feign madness. She tapped into a conversation she'd had with Delsy.

"I did get a haircut," she said in a conspiratorial whisper, as if someone were listening. "Jesus cut it."

"What?" the woman asked.

"Jesus slips into my room every night with golden scissors. The Ten Commandments are engraved on the handle. All seventeen of them. An angel gave them to Christ for his birthday. He cuts my hair, then checks my teeth for sin. Jesus wants me to take my meds like a good girl, then kisses my forehead and tells a bedtime story. Promise you won't tell or the whole floor will want Jesus to cut their hair. Promise?" Cori breathed hard. *Is she buying it?*

The woman sneered. "You crazy bitch."

"Excuse me, lady," Mack Shaw's rumbling voice broke in. "What're you doing in this patient's room?"

Cori hugged herself. *Thank God he's here.*

The woman was as tall as Mack. "I'm a psychiatrist. Dr. Elizabeth Reese."

"No, you're not. Liz Reese is a foot shorter. Now, who are you?"

She ripped off the lab coat, then pitched it at his feet. "Didn't fit anyway."

"How'd you get this?" he asked, bending to pick up the coat.

She grabbed Mack's arm and yanked it behind his back. She shoved him on the bed, pinning Cori beneath them. The woman raised a knife. She sliced Mack's neck. Cori screamed. Blood sprayed the sheets. His body convulsed. Cori couldn't catch her breath. She couldn't believe this was happening.

A man called from the door. "Adriana, I found Wurm."

"Good," she answered. "Take him to the Hartlove Slaughterhouse."

The woman glanced back, then disappeared into the hallway.

Blood dripped from Mack's severed neck onto Cori's arm. Awash in grief and fear, she struggled to free herself, squeezing out from under him. Wiping tears, she crawled off the bed and scooted against the wall. Sliding to the floor, she curled into a fetal position.

Not Mack. Not Mack.

She was scared, unsure about whom to trust. Wurm said she shouldn't call the police. Confusion settled in, but one thing was clear: she needed out. Mack's body straddled the bed, his fingers pointing to the floor. Then it hit her. *Mack knew the truth about me. Everyone else in here thinks I'm crazy. They'll think I killed Mack.*

She saw a security pass card dangling from his belt. It was her ticket out.

"Sorry, Mack," she whispered, unlatching the pass card. She slid on the lab coat. It fit her better than it had Adriana. Cori snatched her mother's book from the mattress.

Sneaking into the dayroom, she inched along the wall, then sprinted toward the door leading to the secret ward. She swiped Mack's card before hurrying down the white stairs.

The elevator took her down to Edgar Wurm's room. Perez had mentioned an exit beneath the observation window. The card could unlock it. She reached in Liz Reese's coat and found Adriana's penlight. Was the woman a Borgia?

And what if she's waiting outside the elevator?

The elevator hummed to a stop. The doors parted.

She peeked out. *Dark down here.*

She switched on the penlight, then searched the observation room. Perez slouched in his chair, sleeping with a newspaper on his lap. Sneaking around him, she moved to the window. Wurm's room was dark too. She debated bringing up the lights, but didn't want to wake Perez. She slipped on something wet. Catching herself, she glanced down, shining the light on her bare foot. Blood dripped off her toes. She shined the flashlight on Perez's face. His head was almost severed from his neck. She cupped her mouth, stifling the urge to vomit.

Looking to wipe blood from her foot, she spied hospital uniforms hanging inside a closet. After cleaning up, she traded her bloody pajamas for blue scrubs, then slid on Reese's coat. She pushed open the door, then rushed down the stairs. Only half of Wurm's book maze stood upright after Perez's rampage last night. She hurried around the books to the exit.

She raised Mack's card, ready to swipe it.

A gun barrel nuzzled the back of her head.

"Step away from the door," a cool voice ordered from behind.

She froze, not recognizing the man.

"Do it," he barked.

Cori took a step back.

"Who are you?" he demanded.

"A psychiatrist," she answered, borrowing Adriana's lie. "Dr. Elizabeth Reese." She sighed, thinking she'd messed up. What if the guy was security? He'd know the staff.

"Turn around."

She moved slowly. Her hand was shaking.

The man's dark features framed piercing eyes. Dressed in a long black coat, he didn't look like security. *Is this guy a Borgia? Was he the one talking to Adriana outside my bedroom?*

"All the docs go barefoot around here?" the man asked.

"Didn't get a chance to grab my shoes. While I was on break, a patient escaped."

"The patient who stays down here?"

"Yeah."

"What happened?" he asked. "Place is torn apart. And you have a dead man up in that observation room."

She stayed with the bluff. "It's been a long night. Now if you'll excuse me, I need to notify the police." She started to turn, keeping it tough. "I'm sure they'll want to question you. I'd advise you to stay here."

"You're not going anywhere." He pointed a handgun at her forehead.

She swallowed hard, losing her composure. Her mother's book dropped and hit the floor.

"Move to the wall."

She didn't argue.

The man picked up the book. Turning it over, he studied the jacket photograph. He made the connection. "Guess what, Dr. Reese? This book says your name is Cori Cassidy." The business card peeked out from the book. He glanced at it, then flipped it over. He examined the back of the card. "What does this number sequence mean?"

"Swear I don't know."

"Where'd you get this card?" he asked with blazing eyes. "I'm not in a good mood. Tell the truth this time."

"A man named Edgar Wurm gave it to me. Told me to contact the guy on the card."

"John Brynstone?" he asked, reading it again.

"Yeah."

"What did Wurm want you to tell Brynstone?"

She didn't answer.

"Tell me," he snarled.

"It didn't make sense."

"Tell me anyway."

Cori considered what had happened to Mack Shaw and Perez. And she remembered Edgar Wurm's warning. Something clicked for her.

"Forget it," she said, surprised by her own defiance. "I'll only talk to Brynstone."

"Then you better start talking." The dark-haired man brought out his ID card. "Because I'm John Brynstone."

Chapter Eighteen

Surprise played on the woman's face. Brynstone sensed fear in her voice.

"You know Edgar Wurm?" Cori Cassidy asked.

"I worked with him before he lost his mind." He glanced at Wurm's ravaged hospital ward. "I haven't seen Edgar in eighteen months. We stayed in touch while he was in this place."

"Can you get me out? Please?"

He thought it over. "Are you a patient?"

"No," she answered. "Actually, yes. But not really."

He arched a dark eyebrow.

"Edgar Wurm warned me about the Borgias. That Adriana chick killed Mack. She nearly killed me."

He believed her. The last time Brynstone confronted the Borgias, he'd barely escaped with his life. This girl wouldn't stand a chance. "Why didn't Adriana Borgia kill you?"

"She ran off when a guy said they captured Wurm." Cori met his eyes. "Get me out and I'll tell you where they took him." She jumped as elevator doors opened in the observation booth. "Someone's coming," she warned. "Stop wasting—"

He clamped his hand over her mouth. A peculiar-looking man peered down from the booth's window. Not Wurm or a Borgia. The guy didn't see them.

"Know him?" Brynstone whispered, taking away his hand.

She nodded. "A psychiatrist. His name's Dr. Usher."

Brynstone didn't want the staff seeing him, but he wasn't sure what to do with this girl. Maybe she could help find Wurm. Usher pushed a dimmer switch.

The ward brightened as waves of light moved closer.

Gotta get out of here.

Brynstone grabbed her hand, swiping the card across the reader. The door unlocked.

He holstered his gun while escorting Cori into a tunnel beneath the hospital. A service door led outside to the snowy hospital grounds. He wrapped his coat around her. Glancing at her bare feet, he offered to carry her. She accepted. That surprised him.

She tightened her arms around his neck as they hurried to the street.

A Cadillac Escalade hybrid blazed across the lot. Headlights flashed over them as the SUV swerved to a stop. Jordan Rayne leaned over, opening the passenger door. Brynstone dipped Cori into the front. She curled up, basking on the heated leather seats. He climbed in behind with Banshee. As he petted the cat, her tail twisted into a question-mark shape.

"Let's go," he told Jordan.

Cori turned to her. "Who are you?"

"Don't ask," Jordan advised as she drove away from the hospital.

"She's right, Cori," he said, leaning between the seats. "Don't ask questions. I kept my end of the deal. You're out of the hospital. Now, tell me where the Borgias took Wurm."

"Adriana mentioned a slaughterhouse. Hartlove Slaughterhouse."

"Think you can find it?" he asked Jordan.

"I'll drop you at your vehicle, then I'll get on it."

Cori's hands clenched. "I need to call about Mack Shaw. You should have seen what they did to him."

"I know how the Borgias operate," Brynstone said. "I've seen their work."

"I hate leaving Mack."

Jordan looked over. "Nothing you could do."

"You said Wurm had a message." Intensity flickered in his eyes. "What did he say?"

"It was strange," she started. "Leonardo—excuse me, Wurm—said to tell you the Tree of Life can kill as well as heal."

That puzzled Brynstone.

"Look, while Jordan searches for Wurm, I'll take you home. Where do you live?"

Cori gave directions to her home in the north Baltimore neighborhood of Hampden. She added that Wurm was interested in Ariel Cassidy's research. "My mother was a medieval-history professor at Princeton. I didn't get a chance to tell him about a notebook my mom gave me, but it might help. It's at my place."

"Here we are," Jordan said, pulling behind a parked black Escalade. "I'll deliver the mummy tissue sample to Nosaka and track down Wurm."

"I appreciate you sticking out your neck for me."

"I'll do whatever it takes to help you, John."

With his cat tucked under his arm, Brynstone and Cori hurried to the SUV. In the distance, Jordan's vehicle disappeared around the corner, driving at high speed.

"She's in a hurry," Cori said, climbing inside the SUV.

Brynstone slid his key into the ignition, but didn't start the engine. Banshee hopped onto Cori's lap. He took advantage of the distraction to check his stitches.

She scratched the cat behind her ears. Banshee pressed her head against Cori's arm.

"What happened to her eye?"

"A bullet grazed her eye. She saved my life, so I adopted her. Truth is, she adopted me."

"What a funny kitten you are," she said, rubbing Banshee's neck. "All the cats I know attack the pedals when you put them in a car."

"She's a good traveler. Better than most kids. Probably better than most adults."

"Thanks for getting me out of that hospital. You said you knew Edgar Wurm before he lost his mind?"

He nodded. "He's a cryptanalyst. He tried to break code on something called the Voynich manuscript. It pushed him over the edge. He became paranoid. Wurm claimed he was getting messages from Leonardo da Vinci."

Cori made a face. "What sort of messages?"

"He had human skulls from an anatomy lab in his basement. He'd chiseled the base of each to widen the opening. Edgar painted da Vinci's messages inside each skull."

"What kind of messages?"

"Some strange code. Couldn't decipher it. Later, Wurm claimed he was da Vinci. He knew too much and was too valuable to lose, so they hospitalized him at Amherst. The whole time, Edgar believed people were out to get him."

"That's not a paranoid delusion. The Borgias kidnapped him tonight."

"What else did he say at the hospital?"

"When we met, Wurm said, 'The Tree of Life blossoms in the Land of the Dead.'" She coughed. "Mom studied the Tree of Life. That 'Land of the Dead' quote? It's in her book about alchemy. It's an early form of chemistry. Know about it?"

"The alchemists were guys in the Middle Ages who tried to transform lead into gold."

"That's a cover-up. It wasn't about making gold. Some kings executed alchemists if they couldn't change base metals into precious ones. Driven by fear, some looked for a formula for gold. Greed motivated others, but that's like saying all lawyers are ambulance chasers."

"If alchemists weren't converting lead into gold, what were they looking for?"

"A secret medicine. They tried to find a universal cure for disease. The 'elixir of life' was a life-prolonging medicine that could heal and transform people."

"Transform them?" he repeated. "How?"

"Make them immortal. If you knew the formula, you could do more than cure a person. You could give them eternal life. That's why Mom called her book *The Perfect Medicine*."

"I want to talk to your mom," he said, starting the engine.

"So did Wurm." Cori rubbed her crossed arms. "She died earlier this year. Leukemia."

"Sorry to hear that." He glanced at her. "What did she write about the Tree of Life?"

She brightened. "A root from this mythical tree grew until two thousand years ago. Then it vanished. Alchemists called it the *Radix ipsius*, meaning 'root of itself.' It was independent of any other class of plants. Separate even from God."

"You know about the Radix?"

"It goes by many names. The Healing Root. The Prime Material. The Hidden Treasure. The Secret of Secrets. An alchemist named Paracelsus called it the *increatum*. That means 'uncreated.' He thought it was uncreated, like a deity. The Radix was said to be equal to God."

He had heard that last part, but the stuff about alchemy was new.

"Ever hear of the philosopher's stone?" she asked. "It's an alchemical code name for a substance that could transform anything—including people—into a more perfect creation."

"Is the Radix the same as the philosopher's stone?"

"The Radix is the Prime Material," she said, looking down at Banshee, who napped on her lap. "The main ingredient used to create the philosopher's stone or the elixir of life."

"So, if someone found the Radix—"

"Finding the Radix wouldn't be enough. You'd need the Scintilla."

She explained that *scintilla* came from a word meaning "spark." In alchemical circles, it was a recipe or formula used to create the elixir of life. Alone, the Radix could heal, but to maximize its effects and potential, you needed a spark to ignite the transformation.

You needed the Scintilla.

"Why'd the alchemists use obscure names like *Scintilla* and *philosopher's stone*?"

"They wanted to keep their work secret, so they invented codes and cover names to disguise their ideas. They did it for security. Or maybe it was flat-out paranoia." Her eyes narrowed. "You can still see their work today, but you have to know where to look. Of course, there's a familiar symbol for the Radix. One that's in every pharmacy in the country."

"The *Rx* symbol?"

She nodded. "Even many pharmacists don't realize that *Rx* is an abbreviation based on the first and last letters of *Radix*."

They drove down Hampden's Thirty-fourth Street, passing town houses adorned with holiday decorations. Twinkling green and red lights splashed across the windshield.

"Talking with you reminds me of conversations I had with Mom when I helped with her book. Too bad it's all just a legend," Cori said. "Here we go. Turn on this street."

"Let's say someone found the Radix. Sounds like it would be the most powerful medicine of all time."

"Don't take this stuff seriously, Dr. Brynstone. The Radix legend is a fairy tale for historians and archeologists."

"Yeah? Did your mom believe in it?"

"There's my house. The one with the lopsided Christmas lights hanging off the roof."

He parked the Escalade beside the snowy sidewalk.

"Sounds like your mother did a lot of work on the Radix. It's a weird circumstance, but my father also studied it."

"Maybe, like Wurm said, it's synchronicity."

"What's that?"

"In Jungian psychology, synchronicity is a meaningful coincidence between two things that aren't linked in a causal way. Like when you pick up the phone to call a friend and she's already on the line. Or when you dream about someone dying and that person passes away."

"You experienced that with your mom, didn't you?"

She smiled. "You're a good psychologist, Dr. Brynstone."

"So are you. Not many people can reach Wurm. Sounds like you managed to do that."

"Back to your question," she said. "Mom believed in the Radix. She talked about writing a book on it, but never had the chance. There was a time when I wanted to believe. If I'd had the Radix, I could've saved her. Too bad it's all a myth."

"Cori," he said, staring into her blue eyes, "it's not a myth."

Cori wondered if the guy was crazy. Or was he serious? "Let me understand," she said, studying this man she barely knew. "You think the *Radix ipsius* is more than a myth?"

"I'm a skeptic by nature," Brynstone said. "In the case of the Radix, I'm a believer."

She shook her head. "Even if it existed, the plant disappeared two thousand years ago."

"One root survived," he said. "In 1502, a man named Raphael della Rovere concealed it inside a mummy. No one has laid eyes on the Radix until last night. That's when I found it."

She shot him a look. He wasn't joking. "Where'd you find it?"

"Can't tell you."

"Show it to me."

"Can't do that."

"Okay, let's say you did find the Radix. If Mom was right, it couldn't achieve its full power without the Scintilla. You'd need other ingredients to create the perfect medicine." She stared into his eyes. "I remember Wurm mentioned something in his book maze. He said Carl Jung was at the heart of understanding the puzzle."

"The psychiatrist?" he asked. "That Carl Jung?"

"Wurm mentioned him. Something about learning Jung's secrets." She tickled Banshee's ear. "My mother found a link between Jung and the Scintilla. She had boxes of notes that were never published. After her passing, Princeton stored the archives. A fire burned part of Dickinson Hall. All that's left is the one notebook in my house. I'll show you."

She climbed down from the SUV. Walking barefoot up her slick driveway, she noticed her Volkswagen bug hiding beneath snow. She pulled a key from a hiding spot on the porch.

"Three in the morning," he said, noticing a light in her town house. "Someone's awake?"

"My roommate, Tessa. Nocturnal grad student."

She unlocked the door, then rubbed her cold feet on the carpet. Cori stiffened. Her living room was trashed. An overturned lamp rested beside the coffee table. Papers were strewn across the room. The Christmas tree had been knocked over. Shattered ornaments cluttered the floor.

"Oh, God," she said in a small voice. "What happened?"

"Borgias," Brynstone whispered, moving around her. He handed over his keys and brought out a handgun. "Wait in the Escalade. It's not safe here."

He ducked into the kitchen. After taking a quick look at the first floor, he moved upstairs. She followed up the stairs toward her bedroom. Keeping a safe distance, she waited until he checked it. He moved down the hallway. She peeked in her room.

He turned. "Why are you here? Get out."

"I need the notebook." She moved into her bedroom and stepped over books. Her Mac was smashed, inside the closet. Every drawer had been pulled out. She checked the desk.

"Mom's notebook. It's gone."

"Stay here. I'll clear the other rooms." He disappeared down the hallway.

She stared at the chaos, then changed into low-slung jeans and a sweater. She slid on running shoes, then grabbed her phone and a navy peacoat. She noticed a golden necklace trapped beneath a spill of DVDs. A gift from her late mother. She wrapped the locket around her hand, then darted into the hallway. Brynstone stood in Tessa's doorway.

She joined him. Cori rose on tiptoes and peeked around his broad shoulder.

She spied a ripped nightgown over Tessa's blood-speckled leg. "Oh, no. Is she dead?"

"She's alive." He moved her toward the stairs. "I used her phone to call 911."

"I need to help her," Cori sobbed.

"Jordan texted me. Baltimore police are looking for you in connection with the homicides of two Amherst Hospital staff. Someone reported you as an escaped mental patient."

Cori was dazed. "I didn't kill Mack or Perez. I can explain to the police." Her mind flashed back to Wurm in her hospital room. He had warned against calling the authorities.

"We have to go," Brynstone said, turning at the sound of a distant siren. *"Now."*

Chapter Nineteen

"Sorry to summon you so early on this Christmas morning," Alexander Armstrong said from behind his Oval Office desk. "We have a matter concerning Ambassador Zaki."

"What's the situation, Mr. President?" Lieutenant General Jim Delgado asked. At fifty-six, the National Security Agency director was square jawed, with a steel gray buzz cut. He looked tough, with an old scar cutting his left eyebrow down to his cheek. DIRNSA had bulbous pale blue eyes and spoke in a detached voice. Delgado didn't talk like brass Armstrong had known, the man sounding more like that damned computer from *2001: A Space Odyssey*.

Vice President Isaac Starr stood beside Central Intelligence Agency director Mark McKibbon, a lanky man with sandy hair swirled over his receding hairline. Usually a cheerful warrior, he seemed grim this morning.

Armstrong spread photos across his desk. "This man broke into Zaki's home."

"Do we know his identity?" Starr asked.

"I didn't tell Zaki," the president said, "but I know the man. His name is John Brynstone. I presented a medal to him. He's a Special Collection Service agent."

In 1978, the Central Intelligence Agency and the National Security Agency formed a joint intelligence organization that drew on the best of both agencies. The Special

Collection Service combined stealthy CIA operations with NSA technology. As far as the government was concerned, the SCS didn't officially exist. Neither did its secluded three-hundred-acre campus in Beltsville, Maryland. Little wonder it was the most secretive intelligence agency on the planet.

The Special Collection Service's colorless name made it sound like an organization better suited to librarians than cyberspooks. SCS agents employed intrusive methods that included breaking into targeted facilities to steal information and installing hidden listening devices, as well as swiping computer passwords and spreading software viruses in enemy databases.

"I met Dr. Brynstone and his wife and baby daughter at the award ceremony. Anyone here know why he was breaking into Hala Ranch?"

Delgado licked his lip. "We intercepted a hot signal linking Ambassador Zaki with Islamic separatists known as the World Islamic Brotherhood. As a top SCS agent, Brynstone was sent to infiltrate the Saudi ambassador's home last night."

"Did he plant eavesdropping equipment in Zaki's home?"

"Actually," the CIA director said, "Brynstone was there to retrieve a relic."

"You're kidding."

"Not at all. Historians and archeologists have been interested in this relic for centuries."

"But not intelligence experts."

"Let me back up, Mr. President," Delgado said. "For years, Edgar Wurm was a top NSA cryptanalyst. His project supervisor complained that Wurm had a hobby that interfered with his NSA work at Crypto City. For the last thirty years, Wurm has studied the Voynich manuscript. It's an obscure document riddled with ciphers and mysteries. They say it drives cryptologists crazy. That proved true in Wurm's case."

"But it paid off," McKibbon added. "Wurm determined that the Voynich manuscript held clues about where to find this relic. That's where Brynstone comes in."

"Tell me about him," Starr said.

"His father was a top NSA administrator. Before following in Jayson Brynstone's footsteps, John became an army captain at age twenty-five, assigned to the Eighty-second Airborne. He distinguished himself at Fort Bragg and became an Army Ranger. Brynstone was tapped to serve as a long-range-surveillance team leader. He headed up an elite LRS force charged with clandestine reconnaissance for intelligence gathering deep in hostile territories."

"He's mentally tough," McKibbon said. "Outscored everybody on military-intelligence tests. This soldier can outthink anybody in the room. He holds a doctorate in paleopathology."

"Hold up," Starr said. "He has a degree in paleo-*what*?"

"Paleopathology. The study of ancient diseases. He specializes in mummy research. Brynstone's a risk-taker. The man never gives up. We couldn't have designed a more perfect special operator for this mission."

"Brynstone offered the best chance to find it," Delgado agreed. "He's our only agent with paleopathology experience. Wurm's obsession rubbed off on Brynstone. They worked together until Wurm was hospitalized. At that time, an NSA agent named Jordan Rayne joined Brynstone's team. Rayne and Brynstone ran a black op tonight called Operation Overshadow. It involved breaking into Zaki's home to steal the relic."

"Explain something. Why do we want this relic?"

"We believe the ambassador values this relic more than any other possession," McKibbon said. "And we believe he will do anything to get it back."

Delgado nodded. "Including sharing information on the World Islamic Brotherhood."

"Brynstone takes the relic and Zaki sells out the Brotherhood to get it back. What kind of relic are we talking about?"

"Mr. President, the relic is called the Radix."

Armstrong and Starr exchanged looks. The vice president made an expression, showing he remembered discussing Dillon's interest in the Radix. The president flashed back to his conversation with Secret Service agent Natalie Hutchinson. He had to find out how his brother was involved.

Wrapping one hand around his fist, he asked, "Did Brynstone find it?"

McKibbon coughed. "That's where we have a problem, sir."

"They landed in Baltimore, but Brynstone and Rayne failed to report in. We've had no contact with them. We have reason to believe our OPSEC was compromised."

"Let me get this straight. Two high-level intelligence agents are missing, and the NSA has no idea what happened?"

"That's correct, sir," General Delgado admitted.

"You think someone got to them?" Starr asked.

"That possibility is on the table," McKibbon said. "We haven't been able to track them."

"The Department of Defense can't track them?" Armstrong snapped. "We have satellites orbiting twelve thousand miles above the earth that can find an ant on a sidewalk in Cincinnati."

"We're working on search coordinates, but let's play with an idea. What if they decided to go off the grid? If anyone knows how to be invisible to our satellites, it's John Brynstone."

"Can't agree, Mark," Delgado said. "John would never go dark without authorization."

"We have to consider every alternative," Armstrong said. "Can't we use the military's Precise Positioning Service to track them if they make a phone call or an Internet search?"

"Brynstone and Rayne are equipped with our best technology. They can block signal broadcasts on both military and civil-use frequencies."

"That's just great," the president said, rubbing his stiff neck.

"We'll find them," General Delgado assured. "John Brynstone is like a son to me. I'm confident he'll turn up soon."

Baltimore
3:02 A.M.

Brynstone drove the Escalade along a tree-lined strip of neighborhood, heading toward an industrial complex. After Jordan's warning about the Baltimore police, Cori needed to be a safe distance from her home. After Jordan located the Hartlove Slaughterhouse to free Wurm, he planned to draw upon government connections to clear Cori with the authorities. He couldn't risk doing that now. Not as long as he was off the grid.

Cori stared out the window. He decided to get her talking.

"Tell me about that necklace."

She wiped her eye, then held out the locket. "Mom gave it to me before she died."

"What's that symbol engraved on the front?"

She traced her finger around it. "Some plant," she sniffed.

The symbol matched the Voynich plant symbol on the *cista mystica*'s lid. He decided against telling her. Maybe he'd said too much about the Radix. Still, he sensed he could trust her. A little.

She looked at him with red eyes. "Tell me about Edgar Wurm."

"Guy's brilliant. Two doctorates and an IQ of one ninety-six. We met while working for a government intelligence agency."

"Which one?"

"Can't discuss it. I picked up the pieces after Wurm lost his mind eighteen months ago."

"You're saying the government wants the Radix?"

"I never said that. The Radix was an obsession that my father and Edgar Wurm shared."

"Sounds like Wurm has been researching it for years. I saw his books."

A burning realization came into his mind. Why hadn't he thought of it before?

"A book code," he said. "That's what it is."

He noticed a police cruiser heading in the opposite direction. Reaching in his pocket, he brought out the business card Wurm had given Cori back at the mental hospital. He glanced at the numbers scrawled on the back of his card.

157:13:08–09/14:05:02–03/316:01:01/07:07:07
98:28:01/03:05:13/64:02:16/63:25:07/404:30:04–05/84:08:06

He handed the card to her. "See the number sequence? Wurm wrote his message in the 'traitor's code.' Benedict Arnold used it back in 1779 when he conspired with the British to betray American interests. It's a basic key-book method of encipherment."

"Why would Wurm leave his message in code?"

"Edgar couldn't write a grocery list without putting it into a cipher." He looked over. "I bet Wurm used your mother's book as an encipherment key."

Without hesitation, Cori grabbed Ariel Cassidy's *The Perfect Medicine.*

"What's the first number string on the card?" he asked.

"Um, 157:13:08–09."

"Turn to page one fifty-seven in your mother's book."

She opened it and started flipping pages. "Got it."

"Go down to the thirteenth line. Count over to the eighth and ninth words."

She traced the page with her finger. "It reads, 'The general principle of alchemy—'"

He handed her a pen. "Write down the first two words on the card."

She jotted "The general" on the back of his business card.

He frowned, spotting a Chevy Cavalier behind them. Was it an unmarked Baltimore PD vehicle? He kept driving.

"Mind deciphering the other numbers?"

"I'm on it," she reported, flipping to page fourteen. "Two words. It reads, 'deceived and,'" she said, jotting down both on the card.

"Keep going," he answered, glancing at the rearview mirror as Cori searched the remaining number sequences in her mother's book. After a few minutes, the Cavalier turned, then sped away, heading west. She positioned the pen in her mouth as she flipped pages. A couple blocks to the south, he stopped at a streetlight.

"Here ya go," she announced, handing him the card. "It's a strange message."

He glanced at Cori's flowing script. Wurm's message chilled him.

The general deceived and betrayed you your father never searched for the Radix

Was it true? He swallowed, his eyes going blank for a minute.

He was fighting a growing sense of bewilderment. And he was a little pissed off. He had trusted General Delgado. The man claimed Jayson Brynstone had dedicated his life to finding the Radix. Was it all a lie? Why would Delgado do that? Until Brynstone discovered the truth, he had to take action, even if it threatened his relationship with his NSA mentor. All at once, Wurm's message took on a new meaning. He had used the traitor's code, drawing a parallel between the betrayals of General Benedict Arnold and General James Delgado.

Brynstone dropped his head, thinking over Wurm's twisted irony. The light changed. He hit the accelerator.

"Is that true?" Cori asked. "That part about your dad. Is Edgar right about that?"

"We need to find Wurm," he said. "I need to know the truth."

Washington, D.C.
3:20 A.M.

President Armstrong had asked Isaac Starr to wait after their meeting with NSA director James Delgado and CIA director Mark McKibbon. After excusing the Service agents, he said, "Remember in the theater, when I told you my brother planned to purchase the Radix?"

Starr nodded. "Now we hear about it from the NSA and CIA directors. You think your brother is involved with Brynstone? Maybe he went dark to deliver it to Dillon."

"I wondered the same thing."

"You still worried the Radix might be a Nixonburger?"

"I'm not sure. But I'm more concerned than ever."

Starr frowned. "I wonder what Dillon is planning."

"There's one way to find out." He grabbed the phone, then speed-dialed a number, waiting for his brother's voice.

"Alex? Is something wrong?"

"I want to speak to you," he said in a flat voice. "In person."

"How about in the morning?"

"How about now, Dillon?"

A yawn. "This better be important."

"Oh, it is important," he growled. "One more thing. Is Deena with you right now?"

A long pause. "Alex, that's none of your business."

"Get over here now. I'm waiting." He hung up, then glanced at the vice president. "You want to leave before I meet with my brother?"

"And miss the fireworks?" Starr grinned. "The Service would have to kick me out before I'd miss seeing another battle between you two."

3:27 *A.M.*

Deena sensed a wildfire of attraction growing between her and Dillon. He had convinced her to stay at the penthouse while he met with the president. Coming down to see him off, she emerged from the elevator. The Lafayette's spacious lobby had an art deco theme, featuring a grand marble entrance and twin elevator banks. Two big men waited in the lobby. She wasn't comfortable around Dillon's bodyguards.

"Why does the president want to see you in the middle of the night?"

"He didn't tell me. But Alex did ask if we were together."

"I need to tell you something," she said, bringing her hand to her chest. "You said you thought Alex was attracted to me."

His face darkened. "You slept with my brother. Didn't you?"

"It was a long time ago, Dillon. Look, I don't know where this relationship will go, but I won't start it off lying to you. You need to know about Alex and me. It was brief and it's over. I don't love him. That's all there is to it." She reached around his neck, pulling in close for a kiss. "You know, I think I'm falling for you."

He pulled back. "I'll talk to my brother. See what's on

his mind. When I get back to the penthouse, we'll arrange to secure the Radix. Then we'll celebrate."

He marched toward the door. She craned her neck, then looked out the lobby window. His limousine was parked at curbside in front of a Honda Civic. Dillon stepped into the brisk night air. He wore a dark wool overcoat and clutched an umbrella. One bodyguard, a white guy, walked in front of him. One trailed—a smaller, African-American man.

She turned away, texting Pantera as she headed back to the elevator.

A deafening explosion rocked the lobby.

Coming from the street, the blast toppled her. As she plummeted, beveled opaque windows shattered behind her. Glass shards burst into the lobby. Heat seared her back and hands. Bewildered, she looked down at her reflection in the polished marble floor. Hair sprayed around her face. She groaned, sitting up and brushing away hair. She grabbed her head. Her lip was bleeding where her face had slammed into the floor.

Back at the desk, the concierge called 911. His voice sputtered with urgency. The man lurched past without making eye contact. Glass crunched beneath his shoes.

A terrible realization hit as she watched the concierge hurry toward the door. Dillon was out there. Someone had tried to kill him. Taking a clumsy step, Deena climbed to her feet and staggered toward the door, screaming as she rushed to the sidewalk.

Part Three
The Secret Church

Submit to the present evil, lest a greater one befall you.
—Phaedrus

Chapter Twenty

Sirens wailed in the night as Deena Riverside stepped through the crumpled green door swaying from warped hinges. Not noticing the glass embedded in her feet, she stumbled down the brick stairs onto the sidewalk outside the Lafayette apartment building. A dull ringing sounded in her ears, almost as if her head were submerged under water.

Dillon's limousine was rolled onto its side, straddling the sidewalk. The open door pointed toward the sky. She rushed to the sedan, then peered inside. The driver's face was pressed against the window, his cheek forming a pink oval on the shattered windshield. Spidery lines of blood trickled down the dead man's forehead.

Eyes stinging with tears, she searched for Dillon and found a trail of shattered glass. She spied a man curled on the sidewalk, his arm missing. His shredded coat covered his head like a funeral sheath. She pulled back the coat to find a face bloodied and burned. It wasn't Dillon. It was a bodyguard, the first out the door of the Lafayette building.

Onlookers scrambled from their Dupont-neighborhood homes. An Arab man crouched over the second bodyguard, hoping to resuscitate him. Her shock began to thaw as she took in the spectacle of destruction. The explosion had flipped a Honda Civic and slammed it onto the sidewalk. Wandering around the block of smoldering metal, she found Dillon trapped beneath the Civic. The car had crushed his legs. She cradled his bloodied head. His eyes were rolled back in his head. His hair reeked of smoke. All at once, she lost the cool reserve that had helped her weather boardroom warfare.

An ambulance and four Metropolitan Police squad cars arrived, bathing the sidewalk in red and blue light. First responders spiraled around the victims, pushing back the crowd. She looked up as a fire engine squealed to a stop. A female firefighter sprinted over.

"Help him," Deena cried. "He's Dillon Armstrong. The president's brother."

"We'll do what we can," she assured. Clutching Deena's hand, the woman pulled her to her feet. Deena stumbled, leaning on the firefighter for support.

The crowd chattered behind her. One bystander mentioned a car bomb. Another man agreed, guessing that an explosive had detonated inside the Honda Civic. A woman murmured Dillon's name, then took a picture with her phone. He looked broken, pinned beneath the car. All she wanted was to hold him and hear his voice again and to know he'd be all right.

3:44 A.M.

"You sure you don't mind me being here when your brother arrives?" Isaac Starr asked. "Maybe I shouldn't involve myself in a family squabble."

Armstrong adjusted a picture of a sailboat on the wall of his private study, a room adjacent to the Oval Office. "Your presence will send a message to Dillon—"

His chief of staff, Alan Drake, opened the door and interrupted the conversation. His face was ashen. "Mr. President, I have bad news about your brother."

Before Drake could finish, Secret Service agents burst into the private study.

"Sir, come with us," Agent Quick barked.

Three agents surrounded Armstrong. Additional agents grabbed the vice president before hustling them both out the door. They hurried through the Oval Office dining room to a hallway on the first floor of the West Wing.

"What happened to my brother?"

"We'll brief you on Fortune later, sir," Agent Quick said. "Our threat level was just elevated from yellow to orange. We're relocating you to PEOC."

"Do you have Helena and the children?"

"Affirmative, sir."

Secret Service escorted Armstrong and Starr down to the White House basement, where additional agents waited. They scrambled through a long tunnel, heading toward a bunker beneath the East Wing. Armstrong knew better than to ask questions now, but he couldn't ignore a sinking feeling in the pit of his stomach.

Outside the Lafayette, a firefighter darted over to Dillon Armstrong. He stuffed high-pressure airbags beneath the Civic's smoldering frame. It didn't look as though they could lift a vehicle, but as the rubber airbags began to inflate, the car rose from the sidewalk. Firefighters positioned cribbing two-by-fours beneath the Civic, stabilizing it as the twisted vehicle rose. Two firefighters pulled Dillon from beneath the car.

As Deena watched, a pudgy EMT studied her. "You have glass in your back."

Deena blinked. She had faced away when the explosion shattered the Lafayette's windows. Like shrapnel, shards had embedded in her shoulder. Adrenaline had muted the pain until now. She winced as the EMT made a small cut in her blouse to treat her lacerations. Bright pain sliced her shoulder. She recoiled, groaning as the man removed glass.

"Talk to me," a Metropolitan police officer said. Taller

than Deena, he was husky, with a pallid complexion. "What happened tonight?"

Catching her breath, she replayed her conversation with Dillon in the Lafayette's lobby. She peered around the officer and saw EMTs wheeling Dillon on a gurney toward an ambulance.

"Can I go with him?"

"Not yet," the cop said. "We'll make sure you get there."

Clutching the diamond pendant around her neck, she watched the ambulance race away. Her world had shuddered, tilting from elation to despair in the space of a few terrible minutes.

The Presidential Emergency Operations Center was sequestered far beneath the East Wing of the White House. Designed to withstand blast overpressure from a nuclear detonation, PEOC offered refuge in the circumstance of a direct threat to the White House.

Armstrong and Starr emerged from the tunnel with their Service detail as they headed for the executive briefing room, adjacent to PEOC. Helena and the children had been taken to a nearby room. He hoped to visit them after getting an update from his national-security advisor. A minute later, Wendy Hefner came over from the Situation Room. She walked in with a White House physician, a slender woman with long strawberry blonde hair. Dr. Jenn Shaw wore a white lab coat emblazoned with the presidential seal.

"Mr. President, your brother was targeted by a car bomb less than a half hour ago." Hefner explained about the explosion outside Dillon's apartment in the Dupont Circle neighborhood. He was pinned beneath a vehicle until rescue workers could free him.

Armstrong stepped back, rocked by the information.

"What's Dillon's condition, Jenn?" Starr asked.

"He's in an ambulance on its way to George Washington

University Hospital. He'll be rushed into the GW Surgery Center upon arrival. His driver and one of his bodyguards didn't survive the blast. Another bodyguard is also en route to the hospital."

"Who is responsible for this?" Armstrong blurted.

"Unknown at this time, sir," Hefner said. "The FBI believes twenty kilograms of A-4 plastic explosives were used in the bombing. That's an eyeball estimate. The explosives were planted in a Honda Civic. The device was detonated by remote control. The blast shattered windows in buildings and flipped the Civic onto your brother."

He winced, taking in the thought. "No one has claimed responsibility?"

"Still early, but we're mapping every contingency. There's a chance the same organization may target you and the first family, as well as the vice president. That's why Secret Service relocated you to PEOC."

Armstrong opened a cabinet, reaching for a snifter and a bottle of bourbon. He removed the cap and poured himself a drink. "Anyone else?"

No one answered.

"When can I see him?" he said, before tasting the bourbon.

"Not until we get an all clear, sir. The hospital poses a substantial security risk."

"I know the surgeons at George Washington," Dr. Shaw assured, patting his arm. "Your brother is in good hands, Alex."

He nodded, finishing his drink. "Stay in touch, Jenn. Meantime, I want to find out why this happened to Dillon."

4:05 A.M.

Deena answered an endless round of questions. Glancing at the fence of yellow crime-scene tape, she saw bomb experts examining the ruined car. Crime-scene investi-

gators busied themselves, taking photographs and collecting evidence. Two men in dark suits rushed to them.
One flashed his badge.

"United States Secret Service," the agent announced.
"We'll take it from here."

The cop sputtered as they escorted Deena to a black
sedan. One agent ordered the EMT to follow, then called
in an alert to the police.

"I want to see Dillon."

"Time for that later, ma'am. Don't worry. Mr. Armstrong will be fine."

Deena nodded, wishing she could believe it.

4:09 A.M.

President Armstrong slipped into a room in the PEOC
facility beneath the East Wing. His wife and two children
slept on cots. Under different circumstances, Helena
would be a bundle of frenzied energy, stressing over the
security threat that had forced them into the bunker. Despite her migraine, she seemed at peace in her sleep.

Three-year-old Justin had turned sideways on the cot,
his arm dangling as if he might tumble to the floor. Armstrong scooped up the fidgety child and returned his head
to the pillow. Justin smacked his lips but didn't wake up.
Armstrong knelt beside his daughter's cot and dragged
the blanket to Alysha's chin. He fumbled it, waking her.

"Um, Daddy?" she asked, rubbing her eyes. "Has Santa
Claus come yet?"

"Not yet. I'm sure he'll visit after you go back to sleep,"
he said, working the time-honored tradition of holiday
manipulation.

"I'm sad about Santa Claus. He can't get past Secret
Service to come into the bunker."

He chuckled. "We issued him special security clearance. Right, Kevin?"

At the door, Agent Quick nodded. "Yes, sir. Mr. Claus

has been cleared for priority clearance. We'll escort him into the residence the minute he arrives."

Alysha pressed it. "But the White House has a no-fly zone. What if the air force sends heat-seeking missiles and shoots down his sleigh and reindeers?"

"Daddy won't let that happen. Go back to sleep, sweetie."

She made a hard yawn, then rolled on her pillow.

He lingered at her bedside, running fingers through her sun-washed blonde hair. As she dropped off to sleep, he thought about his brother. He wondered about that secretive purchase Dillon and Deena had discussed during the Christmas party. Did it have anything to do with what had happened to his brother tonight?

Chapter Twenty-one

Los Angeles
1:14 A.M.

Kaylyn Brynstone heard the ringing phone in her dream. Divorcing herself from sleep, she tracked the sound to her bedroom phone. Still groggy, she moved to her nightstand and checked the caller ID. Blocked number. She answered it, expecting her husband. A woman's voice surprised her.

"Please hold for a call from the president of the United States."

"What?" she asked, wondering if she was still dreaming. She heard Alexander Armstrong's warm baritone on the line.

"Mrs. Brynstone, this is the president. We met in March when I presented a medal to your husband."

"Of course, I remember."

"I'd like to talk to John."

"I'm sorry, he's not here."

"Is there any chance I could get his number?"

She gave him the number of a phone her husband had purchased before leaving. He bought a new one before every assignment.

"How is your beautiful daughter? What was her name? Shayna?"

"Yeah," she laughed. "Shayna. Good memory."

She glanced at the baby monitor as her daughter gave a distressed cry from inside the crib. Despite cutting a tooth, Shay hadn't made a peep in hours. President Armstrong thanked Kaylyn, then apologized for the late call.

After hanging up, she hurried to the nursery.

She flipped on the Pooh lamp, bathing the nursery in soft light. Leaning over the crib, she met Shay's blue eyes. Sometimes it gave her goose bumps. Seeing her was like looking into John's eyes. Shay whimpered and clutched her pink bunny. Kaylyn ran teething gel across her daughter's sore gums, then fitted the child with a fresh diaper. Kaylyn went to her bedroom, then cuddled beneath the blankets with Shay.

Minutes later, mother and daughter were asleep.

Maryland
4:17 A.M.

Snow danced in the Escalade's headlights as Brynstone headed south on I-95. Cori had fallen silent again. Maybe she was thinking over the trauma that the Borgias had inspired, from the two murdered hospital attendants to the assault on her roommate. Poor kid.

Banshee cuddled against her, working some feline therapy.

A call came in, but not on his smart phone. It was the phone with a number he had given only to Kaylyn. He took the call, surprised to find that it wasn't his wife.

"Good morning, Dr. Brynstone. This is the president." Armstrong's voice sounded weary but resolute.

"Can you hold a moment, sir? I need a secure place to talk."

He pulled onto a shoulder, then hit the brakes. As Cori watched, he grabbed the keys and jumped out the Escalade's door. The interstate was dark and desolate on this early holiday morning. Walking behind the SUV, he cleared his throat, still shaken from Wurm's message.

"Sorry for the delay, Mr. President. Is this a secure line?"

"Of course. Where are you?"

"I'd rather not say, sir."

"I'm told you made an uninvited visit to Hala Ranch last evening."

"That's correct, sir."

"Prince Zaki is furious. He thinks that I ordered a break-in."

"I'm sorry, sir. That's not—"

"Dr. Brynstone," Armstrong interrupted. "Did you find the Radix?"

"If I may ask, sir, how do you know about that?"

"General Delgado briefed me on Operation Overshadow. He explained about using the Radix as a bargaining chip to compel Zaki to come clean on the World Islamic Brotherhood."

"I don't buy that story," Brynstone said, his breath visible in the frosty air. "Not anymore. I believe Operation Overshadow was initiated under false pretenses."

"Explain."

"Prince Zaki purchased a Renaissance mummy on the black market," he continued, looking around. "After tonight, I'm convinced Zaki had no idea the Radix was hidden inside. I believe Operation Overshadow has nothing to do with Zaki or the Brotherhood. It's possible that Delgado used NSA resources to fabricate a link between

Zaki and the WIB. I'm starting to suspect that Delgado wants the Radix for himself."

"Any evidence to back up your suspicions?"

"I'm trying to prove it now, sir. I need to stay dark to accomplish that."

"Back to my question. Did you recover the Radix?"

"Affirmative, sir."

"Good. Stay in touch. I have an interest in seeing how this plays out."

After the president gave him a secure number, Brynstone glanced back. From inside the Escalade, Cori watched him. A minute later, he ended the call, then climbed inside the vehicle.

"That looked like an intense little conversation," she said. "Who called?"

"President of the United States," he answered, starting the engine.

"Okay, fine," Cori sighed. "Don't tell me."

Near Washington, D.C.
4:34 A.M.

Preparation. Stealth. Intuition. Infiltrating a high-tech facility was artistry as much as procedure. The same basic principles applied to a residential break and enter. For the second time in ten hours, Brynstone had stolen inside a home. It helped that he knew the place.

He waited and watched.

In the adjoining room, the homeowner exercised on a recumbent bicycle. He switched his television from *The Longest Day* to the feed from surveillance cameras around his property. A closed-circuit image showed a security person sprawled facedown near the pool. In surprise, the homeowner yanked his feet from the pedals and straddled the bike.

As expected, the man scurried into the billiard room.

As he turned the corner, Brynstone moved into action. The syringe came fast, stabbing the man's arm. Lieutenant General James Delgado flipped on the lights. He gaped in disbelief, as if awakening from a nightmare.

Wincing, he ripped out the syringe.

He spied Brynstone near the billiard table.

"Good lord, soldier. Why did you stick me with that needle?"

"Remember my Beijing op last year? You gave me security clearance to use bichloromethate toxins."

"You injected me with BT-17?" Hostility colored his words. "Why would you hit me with a classified toxin?"

Brynstone glanced at his watch. "We have a one-hour window. After that, the antidote won't reverse the effects." In a low voice, he said, "I'm here because you lied to me."

"And you lied to me, John. You promised to deliver the Radix after touching down in Baltimore. Why didn't I see you then?"

"I didn't want to be seen."

"Glad you came to your senses."

"I didn't come here to bring you the Radix."

"Then you made a critical mistake." Delgado stepped behind the bar and reached beneath the counter. He brought out a service pistol. "Give me the antidote."

"Answer my questions first."

"Let's try this again." Racking the slide, Delgado pointed the Beretta M9 in the direction of Brynstone's head. "Give me the antidote. Now."

"Forget it."

Delgado glared and lowered the handgun to aim at Brynstone's right leg. Without hesitation, he pulled the trigger. A dull clicking sound. The magazine was empty. He stared at the gun. In a resigned voice, he said, "You thought of everything. Didn't you, John?"

"Zaki didn't know the Radix was inside the Zanchetti mummy. You lied about the purpose of Operation Overshadow. Why?"

"Obvious, isn't it?" Delgado placed the empty Beretta on the counter. He moved to a barstool. "I want the Radix. You and Edgar Wurm gave me the best shot at finding it."

"You said that my father wanted to find the Radix. How could you lie about that?"

"I suspected Wurm might tell you the truth someday. Fear and intimidation only last so long." Delgado's eyes brightened with intensity. "You're the son I never had, John."

In the yard lights beyond the window, a stand of birch trees cast flickering shadows on the wall. Brynstone growled, "You're wasting precious time."

"I saved your life when that intruder killed your father. You could have been stabbed like I was, but I stopped him." He touched the scar trailing from his eyebrow. "I've tried to help you throughout your career. Do you know why, John? Because there's no one else like you."

"Did my father even know about the Radix?"

"Years ago, I was the deputy director for intelligence for the Joint Chiefs of Staff. Back then, your father told me about a young NSA cryptanalyst named Edgar Wurm. Your father called him a 'water walker,' the kind of analyst who finds the best path to a solution. Wurm wanted to be the first crippy to crack the Voynich manuscript. It became an obsession."

"That hasn't changed."

"Rather than reprimanding him for wasting time, your father encouraged him," Delgado said. "It worked. The more Jayson feigned interest in the Voynich discoveries, the more Wurm committed to his NSA duties. He idolized your father. And then, one day, Jayson told me Wurm believed the Voynich manuscript could lead to the Radix."

"My dad never had an interest in finding it?"

A thin smile. "He never admitted it, but I think he did. At the time, Jayson had a son who was stricken with Perthes disease. A boy who might never leave his wheelchair. Your father taught you to expand your mind. Still, Jayson feared the disease would cripple your life."

"He never mentioned that to me," Brynstone said in a hushed voice.

"You represented his greatest hope and his greatest fear. Too bad Jayson didn't live to see you climb out of that wheelchair."

"You set me up like a pawn. You used me to get what you wanted."

"You're looking at this all wrong. How tragic you can't see the importance of your mission." Delgado licked his lip. "You called last night from Glenwood Canyon. You said you had the Radix. Tell me, John, did you witness its power? Did it make you a believer?"

Brynstone sensed movement outside the door. He pivoted, reaching for his gun. The footfalls were measured and quiet. His eyes darted left, keeping Delgado in his gaze. Sweeping the Glock, Brynstone saw a figure in the shadowy hallway.

Cori Cassidy caught her breath, her expression radiating fear.

Seizing the interruption, Delgado rose off the stool. Brynstone pointed the gun.

"Sit down," he said between gritted teeth. He turned toward Cori. "I told you to stay in the study."

"I know, but you have to see this." She held up a folder stuffed with papers.

"You brought a guest," Delgado said, turning to her. "Welcome, Miss Cassidy."

"How do you know her?" Brynstone demanded.

"He knows me through my mother's work," she answered. "Remember how Mom's papers burned at Princeton? Well, they didn't. I found two of her folders on his desk."

Delgado shrugged. "I needed Ariel's archives, so I planned a fire at Dickinson Hall."

"Where are the rest of Mom's archives?"

"Sorry, Cori, that's all I have."

Unconvinced, she looked at Brynstone. He cocked his head, keeping the handgun trained on Delgado. "You're handing over those archives. Let's go."

Cori followed Brynstone down the basement stairs. His gun was trained on Delgado as he led the way. She puzzled over the complicated relationship between the men. Wurm claimed that Delgado had lied to Brynstone about his father. It tore him up, though John tried to hide it.

At the landing, they entered a narrow corridor. A hint of redwood tickled her nose.

The cellar boasted row after row of wine bottles stacked in wooden racks. Each bottle had been placed on its side, label up, and had a tag on the neck. Moving around a wine rack, Cori found the men at the far end of the cellar.

"Open it," Brynstone ordered.

Delgado moved to his knees and pulled a recessed handle that blended with the wooden floor. He opened a hatch, revealing a ladder leading down to a room.

"Go," Brynstone told him, pointing the gun.

Delgado slid into the opening, climbing down the wooden ladder. Brynstone followed. Cori remembered John saying that he had been a guest at this home. He knew the place.

Climbing down, she saw him inspecting a stack of document boxes. Delgado's face flashed hot annoyance. Stacked in careful rows, five white boxes were labeled in her mother's handwriting. She almost couldn't handle this moment, believing for so long that Ariel Cassidy's archives had been consigned to fire. "It's all here," she muttered. "Mom's Radix archives."

Brynstone looked at Delgado. "Let's get this upstairs."

Chapter Twenty-two

Stuffed bookshelves lined every wall in General James Delgado's study. His "ego wall" featured framed photographs and military commendations alongside diplomas from the Naval Postgraduate School, the National Defense University, and the United States Military Academy at West Point. An oversized NSA symbol emblazoned with an eagle clutching a key was centered behind the desk.

Delgado sat ramrod straight, handcuffed in an armchair.

Seated behind the cherrywood desk, Brynstone studied notes that Ariel Cassidy had written after a visit to the Kristine Mann Library at the C. G. Jung Center in Manhattan. Cori leaned forward on a leather divan, reading another notebook. He knew that she had given up any hope of seeing the archives again. It must have seemed surreal for her, sitting in the home of the director of the National Security Agency, reading her mother's "lost" papers.

"It's gratifying to see your interest in the Radix," the general said, interrupting their work. "I've been studying it since you were a child."

Brynstone ignored him. He kept his gaze trained on the notebook.

"Ariel Cassidy was critical in solidifying the role of alchemy in understanding the Radix and the Scintilla,"

Delgado added. "After her book came out, I learned about her unpublished work. I had hoped to consult her, but she had the poor judgment to go and die."

Cori shot an angry expression at the man.

Brynstone gave her a look, as if saying, *Don't let him get to you.*

He dropped his head, then continued scanning Ariel's archives. He examined a photograph of a broad-shouldered man with a pipe fixed in his beefy hand. His thinning white hair was cropped like that of a Prussian soldier. Small wire glasses perched on his aquiline nose.

"That's Carl Jung," Cori said. "Freud called Jung his 'crown prince' of psychoanalysis, but treated him like an inferior son. Jung thought Freud was obsessed with sexuality. They shared a volatile friendship for years. In time, they stopped speaking."

Delgado cut in. "Jung was a leader, not a follower. He was intelligent and charismatic, and people were drawn to him."

He explained that Jung counted among his disciples Edith Rockefeller McCormick, the daughter of John D. Rockefeller. She had been married to Harold McCormick, the heir to the farm-equipment fortune. The McCormicks proved critical in founding the Psychological Club, a gathering of Jung's circle for lectures and social events. Mary Mellon and her husband, financier Paul Mellon, were also followers of Jung. The Rockefellers, the Mellons, and the McCormicks were among America's wealthiest families. Delgado added, "Without their financial backing, Jung wouldn't be as well known today. Some claim he created a cult and they funded it."

"What kind of cult?"

"A secret society inspired by pagan mystery cults from the Hellenistic world. It has been suggested that some of Jung's followers used his work as the foundation for a quasi-religious sect. A kind of 'hidden Church.'"

"Why that name?"

Delgado shuffled in his chair. "Historically, there has been the visible Church and the hidden Church. The visible Church refers to the public face of Christianity, the one you see with crosses and stained-glass windows and ceremonies. But scholars like Franz Cumont claim that centuries ago, beneath the visible Church, secluded underground chambers hosted initiations. Gathering in secrecy, members participated in mystical traditions that included everything from Hellenistic mystery cults, alchemy, and Grail sects to Rosicrucianism and Freemasonry."

"You're saying Jung's analytical psychology represented the visible Church?" Brynstone asked. "He attracted a cultlike following—a sort of exclusive society—that could be likened to a secret Church?"

"That's what some people believe," Delgado answered. "Maybe only his closest followers knew the truth. Many in his inner circle were 'Valkyries.' That's the name given to Jung's female followers. In Norse mythology, Valkyries were the twelve handmaidens of Odin."

"I don't know," Cori argued, running her fingers through her hair. "Jung doesn't seem like a cult leader."

Delgado winked. "Think about how Jung's beloved alchemists guarded their secrets. To learn their beliefs, you had to prove yourself to their inner circle."

"But alchemy was more of a spiritual quest," she protested.

"I believe Jung was on a spiritual quest to study the mysteries of the unconscious," Delgado countered. "Alchemy inspired his psychotherapy. Both involved transformation from something imperfect into something far better. In Jung's therapy, a person must undergo a psychological and spiritual transformation to become an individuated or whole person."

"It is true that alchemy inspired Jung's work," Cori added.

"It inspired his paternal grandfather too," Delgado said. "He was also named Carl Gustav Jung. The elder

Jung was a Freemason and grand master of the Swiss lodge. According to Masonic legend, the first Freemasons built the Temple of Solomon in Jerusalem. In the following centuries, alchemy dovetailed with some Masonic ideals. That was true in the Jung family. His grandfather changed the family crest to reflect his appreciation of alchemy. Carl Jung wrote about the 'fateful links' to his grandfather and other ancestors."

Brynstone's phone rang. Stepping into the hallway, he answered it. Jordan Rayne was calling from the road after getting a lead on the Borgias. Once he'd gotten directions, he ended the call. He motioned for Cori to join him, then spoke in a whisper.

"Jordan found the Hartlove Slaughterhouse. Hopefully, Wurm's there."

"Let's go."

"I like your spirit, Cori, but this could be dangerous."

"More dangerous than facing the Borgias in the hospital or nearly running into them after they almost killed my roommate? Or breaking into the home of the NSA director?"

"Actually, yes."

"I need to go with you, John. I need answers as much as you and Wurm do."

He got it. Her unquenchable curiosity overruled her need for safety. He nodded. "Let's load up your mother's archives."

"What about General Delgado?"

"I'll take care of him."

They returned to the study. Brynstone placed a lid on a box, sensing Delgado's hypnotic gaze. No doubt about it, he was in the mood to play mind games.

"You've always been the empiricist, John. Needing to see to believe. Despite your risk-taking personality, you've never been one to take a leap of faith. Time to stop clinging to scientific skepticism. Together we can capitalize on the power of the Radix. Join me, son."

Brynstone placed the handcuff key on the desk. He removed a syringe and vial from a black pouch. Plunging the needle into the vial's stopper, he flipped the bottle and extracted the chemical into the syringe. He pulled the needle from the stopper and tapped the syringe.

"That better be the BT-17 antidote," Delgado said.

"I don't have an antidote."

"*What?* You sonuvabitch."

"You don't need an antidote for saline solution."

"You injected me with saline? Then what's in that syringe?"

"A tranquilizer." He pinched a fold of Delgado's skin on his arm, bringing in the needle.

"A tranq, John? All that special ops training and that's the best you have? A needle?"

He raised an eyebrow. "Hmm. Good point."

Brynstone placed the syringe on the desk. Reaching in his holster, he brought out a Glock. He turned to the general.

"You're going to shoot me, John?"

"I don't believe in wasting bullets."

He flipped the gun around, then raised it in the air. Delgado tried to duck as the butt slammed against his head. Eyes rolling back, the man slumped against the chair.

Brynstone stood over him. "Trust me. You would have preferred the syringe."

Chapter Twenty-three

Edgar Wurm batted open his eyes. He felt as if he were floating. Glancing down, he realized he was suspended ten feet above a bloodstained floor. A rope binding his wrists together was looped over a meat hook. Pressure ripped at his arms, nearly dislocating his shoulders.

"Ah, you're awake."

Adriana Borgia marched across the slaughterhouse and stopped beneath him.

White hair clung to his sweaty face. His sweatshirt was streaked with blood. He remembered the torture now. He faked a serene expression, hoping it would piss off Adriana.

Beneath a snakeskin trench coat, she wore a wool sweater, tattoo-tight leather pants, and knee-high boots with stiletto heels. Her black hair shimmered in the arctic blue light. She grabbed a metal box, then pressed a button. Releasing a mechanical whine, the cable rolled the pulley block, lowering him. As he touched down, Santo Borgia joined his sister.

Tall and intimidating, she placed her hands on her hips. "Where is the Radix?"

Wurm frowned. "No one knows, Adriana. Especially your people. Remember, it was Cesare Borgia who lost it five hundred years ago."

Ignoring the dig at her ancestor, she said, "John Brynstone knows."

He peered into her gray eyes. "Haven't spoken to him in eighteen months."

"The time for lies has passed." She turned to her brother. "Santo, the cattle prod."

Taking it, she gave a frosty grin, then switched on the prod. His eyes widened at the crackling purple light. Adriana jammed the prod into his neck. Wurm's heart hammered, sending his body into convulsions as the meat hook held him upright. Pain streaked down his chest. She grabbed his beard, jerking his face close to hers.

"Speak, old man. Where is it?"

"Go to hell," he choked.

Santo flipped the rope and released Wurm's tied hands from the meat hook, then restrained him from behind. Weakened from the torture, he couldn't put up a fight.

Adriana reached for pliers, then seized his slack hand.

"After kidnapping you from the psych hospital, we administered sodium pentothal. You mumbled something about 'removing the fingernail.' That gave me an idea." She grabbed his index finger. "Anything you care to tell us, Dr. Wurm?"

In a daze, all he could mutter was "Don't."

She squeezed the pliers around the nail on his index finger, threatening to rip it off.

She won't do it, he told himself. *She won't.*

"Last chance," she cooed. "Where is the Radix?"

Caught in Santo's grip, he stared with defiance. "Lost to history."

She yanked off the fingernail. Blistering pain flooded his hand.

"I thought the Voynich manuscript held the answer," he choked. "I was wrong."

"I see." She moved the pliers to his ring finger. "Give me a reason to stop."

"I know you." His words slurred. "Nothing will make you stop."

Adriana cursed before tearing out the second fingernail. He yelled, trying to pull away. He was too weak to break Santo's iron-tight grip.

She centered the pliers on his pinky finger. "Tell me."

He spat in her face. She wore a cold smile as she dropped the pliers. She wiped spittle from her nose. "I'll take that as a no," she said. "Time for the salt."

She grabbed a blue container, then opened the spout. He swallowed. She sprinkled salt onto his fingertips. His head dropped. Without fingernails to protect the vulnerable skin, his hand turned red and began twitching. It felt like he'd reached into flames.

Santo released him to answer his phone. Wurm slumped, fighting the pain.

"Adriana," Santo interrupted, handing over his cell. "It's Lucrezia. She has a question about the notebook. Something about the tower."

She talked for a minute, then closed the phone. She turned to her brother. "I need to take off. Stay here and watch Wurm."

"Can I kill him?" Santo asked, looping Wurm's bound hands over the meat hook. He pressed the button. Suspended from the meat hook, Wurm's limp body rose into the air.

"In time." Adriana tossed him the phone. "We'll kill both Wurm and Brynstone."

Maryland
5:35 A.M.

Cori sequestered herself in the backseat with her mother's archives as Brynstone headed north on I-95. During the long drive to the slaughterhouse, she found a folder marked "Radix ipsius." It was empty. In another box, she found notes on the Scintilla. Two boxes later, she found answers in a folder marked "Philemon."

Early in his career, Carl Jung had felt pushed to the brink of psychosis and even suicide. In 1913, Jung began practicing what he called "active imagination," a kind of conscious dreaming. During one trancelike meditation, he encountered a wise old man named Philemon. Dressed in robes and held aloft by colorful kingfisher wings, Philemon became Jung's spiritual guide, opening his eyes to the power of the unconscious. After ending his relationship with Sigmund Freud, Jung delved deeper into his mystical journeys. He related his experiences to those who had won his trust. He gathered a group of disciples and shared his *Seven Sermons to the Dead*. Some had suggested that Jung and his followers hoped to create a spiritual rebirth for humanity. It reminded Cori of the promise of knowledge and rejuvenation that had inspired earlier quests for the Holy Grail.

"Learning interesting stuff?" Brynstone asked.

"Yeah, but there's a lot of material here."

"Keep reading. I'm making good time. We'll be at the slaughterhouse soon."

She pulled back, drawing another folder from her mother's archive box. She tried to focus, wishing she could banish Adriana Borgia from her mind.

Potomac, Maryland
5:45 A.M.

The man who called himself the Knight lived in a secluded mansion in the Bradley Farms neighborhood of Potomac, an affluent suburb in the Washington, D.C., area. His book-lined study inside the three-level Colonial was cultured, like the man himself. His only vice came in small white tablets scored with a cross. Amphetamines helped him maintain his rigorous schedule. As Cress entered the study, the Knight swallowed a Dexedrine.

"We picked up the homeless man," Cress reported. "He's showering now."

"Finally, some good news. Buzz me when he's ready.

And tell Dante to prepare whatever the man desires for breakfast. I'll join him later."

Alone now in his study, the Knight brought up the surveillance feed from his private jet. Hidden cameras had recorded Erich Metzger since the jet's departure from Italy. During the first hour of his flight to the United States, the assassin had read about Brynstone. After that, Metzger had indulged in a bottle of Romanée Conti. After consuming the French Burgundy, he had lapsed into sleep for a few hours. When it was time to wake him, the Knight dialed the jet. The phone rang on a table near the assassin. With lightning reflexes, he grabbed it.

"Herr Metzger?" the Knight asked in a cool voice. "I hired you to kill John Brynstone. I have another request. He has something I want. I need you to retrieve it."

"It will cost you."

"And I am ready to pay. Brynstone has a relic. It is known as the Radix. Acquire it before you kill him."

"What does this Radix look like?"

"You'll know when you see it. I'll double your payment if you find it."

"If he has this Radix, I will seize it."

"Don't disappoint me," the Knight urged.

"I am incapable of that."

Metzger hung up. Stretching, he headed down the aisle. He entered the jet's lavatory, holding his phone. The Knight brought up the camera feed as the assassin leaned over the sink and flipped on the fan. The noise masked his call, but the Knight could read lips. The man dialed a number, then turned out the lights. The Knight growled. He guessed Metzger was calling his Berlin associate, Franka. No doubt he was asking her to research the Radix.

Chapter Twenty-four

Nestled on the Delaware River, Lambertville had enjoyed prosperity in the 1800s as a sleepy factory town, pumping out everything from rubber bands to underwear. After the next century brought hard times, the New Jersey town transformed itself into a tourist destination, famous for antiques and artists. Nine violent crimes had marred Lambertville last year. None were homicides. Brynstone knew the Borgias wouldn't mind increasing the murder rate.

On the outskirts of town, he turned down a road spoiled with muddy ruts. As the storm crawled north, he parked the Escalade near a chain-link fence. A faded sign announced the Hartlove Slaughterhouse.

He glanced at Cori. "I need you to stay here. Promise you'll do it this time?"

She nodded, climbing up front. The cat joined her.

"I know why you and Banshee became friends. You both ignore me when I try to keep you out of danger."

Cori gave a sheepish grin.

"I borrowed a little something from General Delgado's collection." He handed her a Ruger Single Six .22-caliber revolver and explained how to use it. He could read anxiety in her eyes. "The Single Six is a good choice, since you're new to firearms. Easy to operate and reliable."

"Maybe I should stick with you."

"Safer out here. You'll be fine, Cori." He handed over a pair of keys. "Good luck."

Outside the SUV, he brought out his Glock. After checking the clip, he pulled back the slide and chambered a round. He spotted movement near a tree. He aimed the gun.

Jordan stepped from behind a century-old sycamore. "You found it."

"Yeah." He shot out a breath, lowering the Glock. "Hey, I meant to ask on the phone. Did you deliver the Zanchetti tissue sample to Bill Nosaka?"

"Affirmative. He's started the analysis." She glanced at the SUV. "You brought Cori? Is that a good idea?"

"She's tougher than she realizes," he said, checking the battery on a heat sensor. "Give me the sitrep."

Jordan gave a tactical report, describing layout, exits, and potential threats. They discussed protocol for room-clearing. Ready to move in, they bypassed the padlocked gate for an opening in the fence. Emerging beneath a corrugated metal lean-to, Jordan pointed to disturbed mud. Fresh tire tracks. Someone had been here this morning.

Brynstone stretched his arm, prepping himself. Getting his mind set for the big moment. He hungered for a chance to face Adriana again. He owed the bitch after last year in Dresden.

He moved to the back door, peering into the slaughterhouse's filthy windows. He reached for the doorknob.

"I got your six," Jordan whispered.

He nodded, then opened the door. The air inside the slaughterhouse reeked with decay. Above the rusted door, a cage restrained a blue light. They passed sausage and hot-dog boilers before arriving at a gloomy hallway. He stopped at a cooling locker. A lever, like on the back of a beer truck, locked the door. He opened it, then checked inside. The cooling locker ran about ten by thirty feet. Rows of bins, like airport lockers, lined both walls.

Refrigeration had vanished from this room, but water dripped from the ceiling. The heat scanner showed body markers twenty feet away. He signaled to Jordan that two people were in the next room.

Inside the SUV, Cori's hand was hot with sweat as she held the revolver. Banshee curled on the driver's seat, deep in a nap. She told the cat, "At least one of us isn't freaking out."

Her mind flashed to childhood memories of visiting her mother at Princeton University. She remembered a fascination with the gargoyles lurking around campus architecture. Back then, Ariel Cassidy had told bedtime stories about them coming to life in the moonlight. She claimed they prowled the campus, smashing windows in Wu Hall and assaulting other modern buildings that violated the Collegiate Gothic style. Harmless mischief for such creatures, but it became the stuff of childhood nightmares. Always wanting to appear strong, Cori had never confessed to her mom that the stories frightened her.

She glanced at the Ruger now, the revolver looking like a weapon suited for a movie sheriff. Cori twisted around, looking at the slaughterhouse.

"Come on, John," she whispered. "Hurry up."

Brynstone peered into the kill shed. He caught a whiff of rancid meat that would've nauseated a USDA inspector. Years of urine, blood and feces had splattered this floor. That crossed his mind when he stepped on something sticky. *Don't even think about looking at your shoe.* He glanced at the high ceiling. Dangling in dead air, meat hooks waited like raptor talons, eager to slice into flesh.

"Watch out," a voice called from across the kill shed. Edgar Wurm hung by his arms from a meat hook. "Behind you," he shouted.

Too late. A man blasted into them. Jordan hit the floor first, losing her SIG Sauer and groaning as the two men rolled over her. Santo Borgia, big and fierce, scrambled to his feet. He threw a cross-body block that sent Brynstone rolling across the floor. The Glock spiraled out of sight. Jordan pounced on the big man. She landed two solid hits on Santo's face before he flipped her over a table. She turned on her side, clutching her arm.

The man stood over her, holding a livestock prod.

When fighting Borgias, it was always a good idea to make it short. Brynstone grabbed a solid metal device from the table, a tool used to remove spinal cords from cattle. He busted it over Santo's head, snapping the device in half. The man hit the sticky floor, landing facedown.

"That your new weapon of choice?" Jordan panted, finding her SIG. "What is it?"

"Trust me," he replied. "You don't want to know."

"Excuse me," a voice called overhead. "Could you get me down from here?"

Brynstone ran over and grabbed the control box. The meat hook descended, bringing Wurm to the floor. He looked older than his fifty-five years. His shoulder-length hair was longer than in his NSA days. Craggy wrinkles and a slate gray beard gave him the look of a Civil War veteran. He was still powerfully built, but Brynstone wouldn't have recognized the weathered face under different circumstances.

He had stayed in communication with Wurm during his hospitalization. As an expert cryptanalyst, Wurm had devised a super-encipherment code containing layers of transposition. He'd printed that code on paint-can labels to conceal messages for Brynstone. A staffer named Perez brought Wurm's paint cans out of the hospital without realizing he was transporting information.

"Good heavens," he rasped as his feet touched down. "Is that you, John Brynstone?"

"You okay, Edgar?" he asked, pulling the rope from the meat hook.

"Been better." He rubbed his wrists. "Have you talked to Cori Cassidy? She's a revelation. Her mother is an expert—"

"I know."

"Who's the woman?"

"Jordan Rayne. She's with the Special Collection Service." Brynstone noticed the bloodied fingers. "Is that Adriana's work?"

"Afraid so," he said, cradling his hand. "Could use a bandage."

"Sure thing, Edgar."

"Glad to see you, John. I didn't expect we'd meet again until after you found the Radix."

Jordan and Brynstone exchanged a quick glance. Wurm picked up on it.

"What are you not telling me?"

Brynstone glanced down at Santo Borgia, making sure he was out.

"Edgar, we found the Radix."

Wurm's eyes cast a manic gleam. "The Voynich paid off, didn't it?" he cackled.

"What do we do with him?" Jordan asked, standing over Borgia's fallen body.

"Let Adriana deal with him," Wurm said.

Brynstone nodded. "We'll see if Santo can survive her wrath."

Chapter Twenty-five

Los Angeles
4:37 A.M.

Kaylyn Brynstone rolled off her pillow, listening for that sound again in the stillness of her home. Had it been a dream? *No.* She heard the rattling noise downstairs. She couldn't believe it. *John's home.* She eased out of bed without disturbing Shay. Kaylyn pulled on a silk kimono robe. She rushed down the winding staircase, calling for her husband.

"John. Hey, Johnny B. Where are you?"

No lights on down here. Going room to room, she searched for him. Her stomach muscles bunched up. *What if it's not John?* She tried to dismiss the thought. *Security system would've sounded if someone broke in.*

She remembered Shay upstairs, alone.

Kaylyn hurried up the steps, then ducked into her bedroom. Reaching in the darkness, she patted the mattress. Shay was gone. Panicked, she ran her hands over the king-size bed. She found the stuffed bunny, but not Shay. Heart slamming in her chest, she climbed onto the mattress but found twisted sheets. Moving across the bed, her fingers brushed a small leg. In her sleep, Shay had scooted against the headboard. She scooped up her daughter. Shay awakened. Kaylyn handed her the bunny, then darted to the room next to her studio. It was aglow in moonlight. Draped in sheets, her sculptures congregated like phantoms in a graveyard.

Was John hiding under a sheet, waiting to surprise her? He'd done that last Halloween.

Pulling aside the curtain, she peeked at the outdoor sculpture garden. She'd half-expected to see someone there, lurking on the cobblestone terrace or standing beside the tiled pool. Nothing but an eerie stillness. She exposed her face to the window, pressing her cheek against the glass as she strained to see the back door.

"Mrs. Brynstone?"

She yelped, clutching Shayna as she spun around. A man in a suit watched from the doorway. He'd turned on the hallway light. Shay sensed her mother's fear. Her lip puckered before she cried. Kaylyn backed against the wall.

"Wh-who are you?"

"FBI." He stepped inside, then flipped a switch. Spotlights positioned on overhead tracks brightened the display room. The stranger held out a badge. "Agent Daniel Lowe," he answered in a Savannah-sweet drawl. "Need to ask you a few questions, ma'am."

"Daaa-da," Shay blurted.

"Shh, sweetie," Kaylyn said, not taking her gaze off the man. "Why are you in my house?"

He gave a sheepish look. "We had a report about an assassination job on your husband. LA field office sent me to run surveillance on your house. I found the front door wide open."

"When?"

"Just now."

"I heard a noise. A few minutes ago. It wasn't you?"

"No, ma'am. I just got here. You think someone else is in the house?"

"I thought it was my husband."

"I'll look around." The agent tucked his ID badge inside his coat, revealing his black stealth holster. He pointed to her kidney-shaped desk. "You and the baby crawl under there." He turned off the lights. "Do it."

She ducked under the desk. A moment later, she reached in the darkness and found the phone. She brought it close and dialed John. Dead. The line had been cut. She dropped the phone, then huddled with Shay beneath the desk. Beginning with a whimper, the toddler worked into full-blast sobbing. Kaylyn raised her shirt, pulled down her bra, and directed the child's mouth to her breast. It worked. Shay's tear-stained face softened as she suckled, still holding the bunny.

She had planned to stop nursing by Shay's first birthday. The weaning process hadn't gone as planned. Turned out Shay hated cow's milk. Right now, she was grateful her thirteen-month-old was still nursing.

Staying low, she reached up, then ran her fingers across the desk, finding a sculptor's knife. Converted from a power-hacksaw blade, it was perfect for carving soapstone. Maybe the knife could protect them.

Where is Agent Lowe?

She wanted to call John, but her cell was in her purse.

She heard muffled voices. Two men argued downstairs, their words cut off by the discordant crash of piano keys. Shay pulled away from the nipple, her head turned, listening. Kaylyn coaxed her daughter back to her breast.

Someone rushed into the room.

Holding her breath, she prayed the child would keep nursing. She was running low on milk on her left side, but she didn't dare switch Shay to her right breast.

"All clear," the man announced, breaking the silence. "Let's go, Mrs. Brynstone."

"Agent Lowe?" she asked, pulling down her shirt and climbing out from beneath the desk. Shay nestled against her mother's neck. "What happened downstairs? I heard voices."

"Later. We need to move you to a secure location. Follow me."

Sliding the knife into her robe, she trailed as he peeked into the hallway. Blood was splattered across the agent's neck. She clutched her child, thinking, *God, what's happening to us? John, we need you.*

Sweeping the gun, the FBI agent headed into her bedroom. Finding it safe, he waited outside the door as she changed into a black rib-knit turtleneck and jeans. She grabbed the diaper bag before the agent ushered her to the stairs.

"*Gaaah?*" Shay gurgled. "Bwwaaah-beee."

"Keep that kid quiet," the agent hissed.

Running her hand across the child's soft head, she kissed Shay's cheek.

Halfway down the staircase, she glanced at the darkened living area and saw a body near the grand piano. She couldn't see a face, but it looked like a man.

"Oh, dear God," she gasped, covering her mouth.

The agent looked back. "Keep it together, Mrs. Brynstone. It's just a dead body."

Chapter Twenty-six

•

Lambertville
7:41 A.M.

Sitting in the Escalade, Cori flipped a page in her mother's notebook. She had bypassed this journal because it contained only a single page of handwriting. Giving it a second look, she realized that Ariel Cassidy had written an entry a short time before her death. In a rush of insight, she realized that this notebook was the successor to the one stolen from her apartment.

Two paragraphs speculated on the Scintilla's ingredients, followed by Ariel Cassidy's final entry:

> *I am convinced that Jung was unaware of the location of the Rx. Like CGJ, I have concluded that the Rx has vanished forever into the winds of time. Given that staggering loss, much can be learned by finding the Sc. I have an unswerving faith that CGJ knew where to find it (perhaps he even possessed it). Despite two trips to the Shrine of Philemon, I cannot find the Sc. After every trip, I dedicate hours at the Firestone Library to translating Jung's symbols. I believe the Sc is at the Shrine of Philemon, but leukemia has sapped my energy. I hope to visit in the autumn.*

Cori believed the undated entry was the final one her mother had put to paper. But where was the Shrine of Philemon?

She heard voices. She snapped her head around, glancing out the window. A sense of elation spiraled inside her. John Brynstone, Jordan Rayne, and a disheveled Edgar Wurm walked toward the vehicle. Anxious to get rid of the gun, she placed it inside the console between the seats.

Brynstone and Wurm stopped to talk to each other. Jordan headed for the Escalade.

Climbing inside, she said, "Hiya, kid. You've had a rough Christmas."

Cori nodded, turning her gaze toward the windshield. "What are they talking about?"

"No idea. John looked a little intense. I could tell he didn't want me hanging around."

"You know the truth about my dad," Brynstone said in a determined voice. "Tell me everything."

"Your father was a great man." Wurm's gaze softened. "Jayson supported me when others refused to understand my passion for the Radix. I would not be here without your father. Or without you, for that matter."

"Then why did you let James Delgado manipulate me?"

"He manipulated me too, you know," Wurm muttered. "I tolerated it because I was looking at the bigger picture. Delgado and I both thought you were the best candidate to find the Radix. For Delgado, it was a sin of commission. For me, it was a sin of omission. I couldn't risk sharing the truth. You busted your ass to find that precious root because you wanted to fulfill your father's mission."

Brynstone's eyes blazed. "It wasn't Dad's mission."

"You would have stopped had you known that. But we can't stop. We have to find the Scintilla."

"That's another thing. Why didn't you tell me about the Scintilla?"

"I just learned about it. Ariel Cassidy's scholarship enlightened me. You and I communicated over the past eighteen months through encrypted paint cans. It's not easy to convey Professor Cassidy's ideas under a paint-can label."

"Now you've drawn Cori into this mess," Brynstone said. "And so have I."

"She wants to be drawn in. She may not know it, but that desire burns deep within her."

Brynstone ran fingers through black hair. "Not sure I agree with you."

"Don't you see the irony, John? You searched for the Radix because it satisfied Jayson Brynstone's dream. Now that you know the truth, you feel betrayed and empty inside. On the other hand, Cori abandoned her mother's quest to find it. She felt betrayed that Ariel Cassidy studied the Radix at the expense of her daughter. Now that she knows the legend is authentic, she'll help find the Scintilla."

Brynstone looked down.

"I understand your sense of betrayal, John, but we need you. We have the Radix. Now we need the Scintilla. We need to maximize the root's power." He placed his big hand on Brynstone's shoulder. "This is bigger than us. Or even Delgado. Can I count on you, John?"

Brynstone looked at Cori inside the vehicle. "We've come too far to give up now."

Cori watched as the two men returned to the vehicle. Seeing Wurm for the first time since the hospital, Cori jumped out and hugged him.

"Good to see you again, Edgar." She pulled back, looking at his blood-streaked shirt. "What happened?"

"Borgias." Wurm made a face. Narrowed his eyes. "Who brought the cat?"

Cori chirped, "That's Banshee Brynstone."

"Terrific," Wurm said. "I'm allergic to cats."

"Since when?" Brynstone asked.

"Since about four seconds ago." He frowned. "You know black cats bring bad luck."

"Isn't it great news about the Radix?" Cori said, changing the conversation. "Can you believe it?"

"I wondered if I would live to see the day. Show it to me."

"Later. Let's go before we have to deal with the Borgias again. I'll drive to Jordan's vehicle." Brynstone looked at Jordan. "You mind taking a look at his fingers? Adriana did a number on them."

"I'm on it," she answered, grabbing the medic kit.

Cori rode shotgun with Brynstone as the Escalade blazed down the mud-streaked road. In back, Jordan taped gauze around Wurm's bloodied fingers. He winced as she applied pressure. "Not a good day for fingernails," she sighed.

As Jordan treated his hand, they briefed him on finding the *cista mystica* in the Zanchetti mummy. Wurm seemed thrilled that Ariel Cassidy's notes had not been destroyed in the Princeton fire. Cori explained Delgado's involvement in the arson and told about removing the archives from the general's house.

"You broke into DIRNSA's home? That takes cojones, doesn't it?" Wurm chortled. "So, Ms. Cassidy, have you gleaned anything helpful from your mother's journals?"

She nodded, holding up the last entry. "Mom thought Jung might have found the Scintilla. She hinted it might be hidden at some place called the Shrine of Philemon. Only problem? Her notes don't mention where to find that shrine."

"I know where to find it," Wurm answered. "You all up for a trip overseas?"

Cori spun around. "Where?"

"Switzerland. Carl Jung built a castle there. He nicknamed it his Shrine of Philemon."

Jordan stabbed her finger at the windshield. "Pull over," she insisted. "Right there."

Brynstone hit the brakes. She opened the door and

jumped out. She turned with a wave of long crimson hair, looking around.

"What's wrong?" he called, climbing out.

"What's wrong is I parked behind those trees. My vehicle is gone."

She headed for a grove of evergreens, taking out her gun. He brought out his Glock, covering her. Wurm joined them outside the Escalade.

Jordan followed tire tracks to a ravine. She peeked over. "That bitch. She rammed my SUV and sent it rolling down there."

"Adriana did that?" Wurm asked.

She glared, as if it were a stupid question. She kicked a stone over the hill. "I need to get my stuff." She side-stepped down the hillside.

Wurm whispered to Brynstone. "She's gorgeous, but edgy."

"You have no idea."

After watching her, Wurm faced him. "In the interest of dragging skeletons from closets, I need to come clean with you about the night your father died."

"I'd like to hear it."

"Twenty years ago, Jayson invited me to your summer home. Rumor had it he planned to restrict my Voynich studies."

"Delgado said my father encouraged your work."

"True, but I strained his patience." Wurm cradled his bandaged fingers. "I still remember driving down that unmarked dirt road leading to your home."

Brynstone flashed to that childhood summer in Nantucket. He could see the gray shingled cottage decked with window boxes. A cutting garden bordered it with tall grass waving in the wind.

Wurm tugged on his beard. "Your father had left the door unlocked for me. I heard a creaking sound and moved toward the stairs. I saw a boy in a wheelchair near the top landing."

"You saw me?"

He nodded. "I saw the silhouette of a man behind you, raising a dagger. I shouted and started racing up the stairs."

"All I remember is being pushed from behind."

"The intruder shoved you off the landing. Your wheelchair flipped over and dumped you onto the stairs. Metal clattered against the wooden steps. The chair smashed hard against me and sliced my leg. I scooped you up in my arms and rushed you down to the living room. It looked like you had a concussion. At least you were breathing."

"Did you look for the assailant?"

"I searched your bedroom. The window was open. In the distance, I heard a car's engine. I couldn't see headlights."

Brynstone shoved his hands in his jeans pockets. This version was different from the one Delgado had told decades ago.

"I checked room to room," Wurm said. "At the hallway opposite your bedroom, I heard a gurgling sound. I peeked inside the study and found your father on the desk with a dagger in his chest. His best friend, Jim Delgado, was slumped on the floor in a pool of blood. He had multiple lacerations, including that slash down his face. But no sign of the assailant."

"I can't remember you at the house that night."

"Delgado didn't want you to know. I went to call an ambulance, but he stopped me. He told me to leave the house, get on the ferry, and ride back to Hyannis. It would look bad if police found me at your house. Jim convinced me that dark things from my past could return to haunt me. He was protecting me, but that meant he had to lie to you and take credit for saving your life. Never mind that he couldn't have saved you without my help."

"Authorities never found the man who murdered my father."

"Afraid not. I didn't exactly lie to you before, John, but I

lied to myself. It was one reason I took refuge in the Amherst hospital. To his credit, Jim funded my hospitalization as long as I researched the Radix. I kept the truth
from you until this morning, when I thought the Borgias
might kill me. That's why I wrote the book-key code on
the back of your business card. If anything happened to
me, I wanted you to know the truth."

"Guess I should thank you for saving my life."

"I know a good way to do that. Come to Zurich and
help us find the Scintilla."

"Promised Kaylyn I'd fly home today to see her and
Shay for Christmas."

"Is that necessary?"

"Yeah, it is," Brynstone glared. "But as soon I can, I'll
catch a flight to Europe."

"You have to, John. It will prove worthy of your time."

Chapter Twenty-seven

Los Angeles
4:55 A.M.

As Shay slumbered on the bed, Kaylyn stepped from the
bathroom and found Daniel Lowe digging in a briefcase.
For their safety, the FBI agent had brought them to the
Ramada Plaza Hotel in West Hollywood, about fifteen
minutes from her mid-Wilshire home. The room was
bright and had an art deco theme.

"Kid's out cold," Lowe grinned. "She sure loves that
stuffed rabbit."

"Who was that man in my home?" Kaylyn asked,
twisting her blonde hair into a ponytail.

"The dead guy? An assassin. He would've killed you and your baby."

She stared in disbelief. "Are you serious?"

"His name's Metzger. It's German for 'butcher.' Name fits."

"He wanted to kill us?"

"He wanted to kill your husband." Lowe's phone interrupted. "Excuse me, ma'am. It's the special agent in charge. My boss." He stepped into the bathroom, then closed the door.

That's when tears came. She wanted to talk to her husband. Jabbing her hand in her purse, she fished around for her phone. She couldn't find it. She looked at the bathroom door. *Did Agent Lowe take it?* She wiped a tear. *That's ridiculous. Why would he take my phone?*

She kissed her sleeping child, then walked to the bathroom. She cupped her hand around her ear, pressing it against the door. Despite the muffled voice, she made out words. The man inside the bathroom didn't sound like Agent Lowe. A growling German accent had replaced his southern drawl. She closed her eyes, concentrating. The FBI agent spoke again. His words came through the bathroom door in one burning moment.

"Rest assured, I will kill Dr. Brynstone," the man said, "but first I may need to kill his wife and child."

"I operate by my own methods," Erich Metzger said into the phone as he paced around the cramped bathroom. "If you want the Radix, it will take time."

"I don't have time," the Knight said. "Kill him and seize the Radix."

"I have researched John Brynstone. He is a man of intelligence and dedication. I must toy with him. I must frustrate him. Brynstone will not hand over the Radix unless desperation forces him. I will make him desperate."

"As an assassin, you are without rival. But others want the Radix. I must have it."

"Then you must wait. Remain patient and don't interrupt me again." As Metzger ended their phone conversation, he spat, "You don't want me as your enemy."

He rubbed his stiff neck, returning his thoughts to Kaylyn Brynstone. He'd brought her here under the guise of an FBI agent. He'd conjured a Southern accent, the better to temper the menace in his own voice. Returning to Agent Lowe's mind-set, he opened the bathroom door.

"Sorry 'bout that, ma'am. My SAC is an old-school G-man, and he's a pain—" Metzger looked around, unbelieving, at the hotel room.

Kaylyn Brynstone was gone. And she'd taken her baby.

Kaylyn punched the button for the hotel elevator, but didn't waste time waiting. She took the stairs instead. Shay awakened and began crying.

"It's okay, honey," she pleaded, hurrying down each step.

Shay plugged her thumb into her mouth. Kaylyn eased open the door. Two women emerged from an elevator along with a man in a suit. He was the same height as her kidnapper. She couldn't see his face. Was it the German man?

Metzger had underestimated Brynstone's wife. And this made him smile. Bless her little soul, she'd turned it into a game. The unexpected pleasure of hunting her would heighten the joy of killing her.

Abandoning his FBI disguise, he pulled the brown wig from his close-cropped hair. He peeled prosthetic appliances from his nose and around his eyes. After removing false teeth, he wiped makeup from his face. No time for another disguise. He'd risk appearing in public as himself. He hadn't been in this country in years and the Americans weren't expecting him. He wouldn't be recognized.

He kicked off his shoes and removed his suit. He

pulled on Mickey Mouse cargo shorts he'd purchased at LAX along with a sweatshirt emblazoned with the words *California Cool* in garish orange letters. Lifts in his running shoes made him taller. He completed his new look with a Dodgers cap.

He studied his reflection. Was there anything less threatening than a tourist?

Kaylyn hurried down a long hallway. Turning the corner, she collided with a stocky man. Holding her child, she couldn't brace for the fall. Wrapping her arms around Shay, she protected her daughter as they hit the floor.

The man turned, poised for a fight. "All right, I've had enough." He took a step toward her, crunching the glasses that had fallen from his face.

She reached for the sculptor's knife in her coat, ready for anything. When the man saw Shay, the angry look in his eyes melted into concern. He grabbed his twisted glasses, then offered his dark hand to Kaylyn.

"Sorry, thought you were someone else. Couple punks in the parking garage tried to mug me. They broke the clay sculpture my son made for me last night. Some people can't help but ruin the holiday spirit." He studied her. "You okay, lady?"

"Could you take me to the police? Fast. A guy—a stranger—is chasing me."

"Sure, I'll drive you," he said, bending his glasses back into shape. "Name's Frank Muller." He grabbed the bunny, then offered it to her daughter. "Let's go."

She forced a smile. "Thanks, Mr. Muller."

Clinging to her daughter, she followed the man to the Ramada's parking structure. She glanced around. The German was nowhere in sight. She heaved a sigh of relief.

"My ex invited me over for Christmas Eve. I'm heading back to Fresno to open gifts with my stepkids," Muller said as he unlocked his Saturn. "Sorry, I don't have a baby seat."

"I'll just hold her." She crawled inside the backseat with Shay.

Muller ran his hand across the passenger headrest as he backed out. A crashing sound came from behind the car. Muller slammed the brakes. Kaylyn turned. A crumpled body rolled off the trunk, then disappeared behind the car.

"Guy came out of nowhere," Muller spat as he jumped out.

Shay seemed okay, just startled. Kaylyn climbed out, embracing her daughter. The man lay facedown on the cement.

"Hey, buddy," Muller said, rolling him over. "You okay? I didn't see you." He kneeled and pressed his ear against the man's chest. She reached down for the guy's baseball cap. He looked like a tourist, with Mickey Mouse shorts and a sweatshirt that read "California Cool."

His eyes shot open.

"Frank, he's awake."

"Thank God." Muller jumped to his feet. "Mister, I'm sorry."

The tourist reached in his coat, bringing out a gun with a silencer. Kaylyn heard a muffled sound like a burst of air. Eyes wide with surprise, Frank Muller staggered against the car. Blood seeped across his shirt as he slumped to the concrete floor. Turning Shay away, Kaylyn screamed in disbelief. The tourist vaulted up, pointing his gun. He looked different from the FBI agent, but she recognized the eyes. Dead and black.

"Your friend's wound isn't fatal," he teased. "But I can make it that way."

The man holstered his gun, then grabbed her left arm. As she held Shay, Kaylyn reached in her coat pocket with her right hand. She brought out the sculptor's knife, ready to stab him. As she swung it, the man seized her wrist, then squeezed. Pain spiraled inside her hand. He stepped in closer, his breath hot and acrid on her cheek.

With one sweeping motion, he directed her hand, moving the knife beneath Shay's chin. The child squirmed. Kaylyn tried to pull away her daughter, but he pressed the blade to Shay's soft neck.

"Resist me again," he hissed, "and the baby suffers for your stupidity."

Chapter Twenty-eight

Outside Lambertville
8:06 A.M.

Cori scratched Banshee's ear and darted a glance at Jordan. The woman was smoldering in the front seat next to Brynstone. It wasn't that her SUV had been trashed, Cori decided, but more that the Borgias had made Jordan look vulnerable.

Edgar Wurm, in contrast, seemed overjoyed, a real change from the man Cori had encountered at the hospital.

"Show Edgar the fingernail," Brynstone said, driving on Old York Road.

Jordan slid on gloves, then handed a pair to Wurm. Twisting around in the passenger seat, she held out her hand. "This belonged to Zanchetti. We found it inside the *cista mystica*."

Cori leaned in, her chin brushing Wurm's shoulder as he picked the human fingernail from Jordan's palm. Brynstone had told her about the priest on the drive to New Jersey. Studying the nail, Wurm turned it. Symbols were scratched on the inside surface.

"The work of della Rovere, I presume. Looks like Voynich B symbols."

She glanced at him, absorbing the deep grooves in his forehead. A web of wrinkles flared around his eyes. Wurm's face brought to mind a Rembrandt painting of an imposing old man with a beard, hands clasped before him, lost in introspection.

"It's a warning. A cautionary message for whoever finds the relic. It claims the Radix can be dangerous, especially when combined with certain ingredients."

"You're talking about the Scintilla," Cori added.

The napping cat rolled on her leg, making a deep humming sound.

"You mentioned it earlier," Jordan said. "What's the Scintilla?"

"It means 'little spark,'" Wurm explained. "Think of it as a recipe that creates the perfect medicine. Alone, the ingredients do nothing. Add the Radix and ordinary ingredients transform into a consecrated ointment called a chrism. If you know the Scintilla's ingredient list, you can use the Radix to create two chrisms. The White Chrism can heal, the black can kill."

"Kill how?"

"Before falling into della Rovere's hands, the Radix was once used for destructive purposes. A skeptical knight in the fourteenth century tested the Black Chrism."

"Using the Radix?"

"A sliver," Wurm nodded. "According to legend, the knight traveled to Central Asia and mixed a compound to create the Black Chrism. He fed it to gutter rats. Didn't harm them. Later, trading ships transported the infected rodents west to the Mediterranean Sea. The vector-borne plague caused a pandemic in Europe, killing twenty to thirty million people."

"The Black Death," Jordan whispered. "Are you serious?"

"That's what the legend says. Together, the Radix and Scintilla can deliver the greatest good *or* the greatest evil. Della Rovere possessed the recipe, written by the original authors. He wished he'd had the Scintilla before his wife died."

"The story is that he killed her," Brynstone said.

"He did, while attempting to save her. She had been bitten by a *zanzara*. That's Italian for 'mosquito.' Like many malaria victims, she vomited and suffered chills. Della Rovere immersed her in ice water to reduce the fever. In desperation, he bled her, a common practice five hundred years ago. He'd been without sleep for five days, caring for her."

"He overbled her?" Cori asked.

"Afraid so. After mourning her death, he joined the priesthood. Of course, Cesare Borgia wanted the chrism to heal his syphilis. The disease had disfigured his face. Borgia wore a variety of masks to hide the scars."

"Borgia's father also had syphilis," Brynstone added.

"Can't believe the pope had sex," Jordan said. "Not to mention syphilis."

"At times, certain church leaders were more licentious than the sinners they condemned," Wurm answered. "Their moral lapses disturbed many of the faithful, including della Rovere."

"Did syphilis kill the pope?"

"In August 1503, Cesare Borgia and his father contracted malaria from *zanzare*. Pope Alexander VI never recovered. Ironically, the new pope was the late della Rovere's uncle. Giuliano della Rovere was one of Borgia's greatest rivals. He became Pope Julius II. You know, the guy who commissioned Michelangelo to paint the Sistine Chapel ceiling."

"You said Raphael della Rovere had the Scintilla?" Cori asked.

"He was the last known person to possess both the Radix and the Scintilla. First, he stuffed the Radix inside Zanchetti's mummy. As Borgia's militia approached the Italian village of Navelli, he escaped with the formula. The Scintilla was missing when Borgia tracked

him down. Borgia's descendents have been searching for
it ever since."

"The Radix is useless without the Scintilla?" Jordan
asked.

"Not useless," Brynstone said. "I've seen its power.
Over time, it can regenerate necrotic tissue in a mummy."

Washington, D.C.
8:09 A.M.

Dillon Armstrong was undergoing another round of surgery. More than anything, the president wanted to visit
his brother. Sequestered in PEOC, Armstrong resolved
instead to confront General Delgado. He remained seated
as the man marched into the briefing room. Armstrong
steeled himself, ready to go toe-to-toe with DIRNSA.

"Sorry to hear about your brother," Delgado said. "We
have not detected chatter suggesting terrorist factions
were involved with the car bomb. Rest assured, we're doing all we can to determine the cause of your brother's
tragedy."

"Appreciate that, General," Armstrong said as the Service agents left them alone. "Give me an update on John
Brynstone."

"He paid a visit to my home just after oh-four-hundred
hours. He injected me with a BT-17 toxin."

"Are you serious?"

"Under pressure, he admitted he'd lied about the whole
thing. Thought he could bully me into sharing classified
information." Delgado cleared his throat. "I believe John
Brynstone is a rogue agent."

"That's an abrupt turnaround. Earlier, you regarded
him as a son."

"Not anymore. He went dark without authorization.
He broke into my home, then threatened me."

Armstrong frowned. He trusted Brynstone's claim that
Delgado had lied to instigate a mission. Brynstone al-

most had a sixth sense when it came to collecting intelligence data. He could cut through technical sources and find answers. Star agents like Brynstone had restored credibility to the intelligence community.

"Let me be clear, Mr. President. Even though the SCS is a joint organization, Brynstone is one of my men. As soon as we track him, I'm sending a TAC team to apprehend him."

Armstrong gave a stone-cold stare. "He stays in the field. That's an order, General."

"With all due respect, sir, I don't—"

"What's the real reason you want Brynstone? Is it because he knows you fabricated a link between the World Islamic Brotherhood and Ambassador Zaki? You designed false intel that has nothing to do with terrorism and everything to do with getting your hands on the Radix."

"Where'd you hear that?"

"Brynstone. I called on an untraceable line, so your NSA wiretap boys can't search it."

Delgado shook his head. "He's playing you for a fool."

"I believe you're the one doing that." Armstrong rapped his fist on the table. "You falsified connections between the Saudi ambassador and terrorists. You compromised relations with a foreign government for personal gain. Clean up this mess. And do it quietly."

"It's more complicated than my wanting a relic. I'm trying to accomplish something that surpasses politics. I need Brynstone to hand over the Radix."

"This Radix sounds like a lot more than just a relic. What makes it important?"

"Perhaps it's best if you don't ask that question, Mr. President."

"Perhaps it's best if you don't abuse your position, Jim. You can't manipulate me."

"Really? J. Edgar Hoover manipulated every president from Coolidge to Nixon, and they named the FBI building after him." Delgado headed for the door before calling, "Merry Christmas, Mr. President."

New Jersey
8:20 A.M.

Christmas morning arrived without a dawn. A fitful sun lurked behind iron gray clouds as Brynstone drove the Escalade across a joyless stretch of Highway 202, making their way to the airport. Jordan tapped away on her computer. From the backseat, Cori studied the landscape. With bandaged fingers interlaced on his chest, Wurm snoozed beside her. Banshee was tucked beside him, a clump of black fur.

Brynstone felt an easy camaraderie with them. Jordan was a tough-minded pragmatist, smart and dependable. Both bright, Wurm and Cori had bonded over the shared terror of confronting the Borgias. Maybe some haunting synchronicity had bound all their fates together.

He wasn't a man given to introspection, but there was little he could do to escape it now. He couldn't say what his three friends might discover in Switzerland. Right now, he focused on a flight to California to spend time with his family. He had tried contacting Kaylyn, but she was ignoring his calls. He sensed his marriage slipping away.

"Hear that?" Jordan asked. "Someone's calling you."

He snapped open his cell and found a call from Kaylyn. He was anxious to tell her he'd booked a flight out of Newark. His jaw tightened when he saw Kaylyn's face on the phone's screen. A hand pressed a knife beneath her chin.

"John," she said, her eyes wide with terror. "Come to LA. *Now.*"

"Kaylyn, who's doing this?" He pulled onto the shoulder, then slammed the brakes.

"He'll call in a few hours and tell you where to meet." A tear streamed down her cheek and dripped onto the blade. "Hurry, John. He has Shay too." The screen went black.

He couldn't believe what he had seen. His mind raced, dizzy with colliding thoughts. Who had kidnapped his wife and daughter? And how could he get them back?

Cori leaned in from the backseat. "What happened, John?"

"Someone abducted my wife," he said in a low voice. "And my daughter."

"Think it was the Borgias?" Jordan asked.

"Don't know," he answered, pulling back onto the interstate. "I need to find out."

"Anything I can do?" Cori asked in a wavering voice.

"Go to Switzerland with Edgar and Jordan. Find the Scintilla."

His LAX flight didn't leave until two. He needed an earlier departure. He grabbed the phone and called the one person who could help. Alex Armstrong picked up after the first ring.

"Mr. President, I'm sorry to bother you."

Jordan's head snapped around, looking at him.

"Good to hear from you, Dr. Brynstone. I spoke to General Delgado. He said you visited his home. Sounds like you had a rather animated discussion."

"That's one way of putting it. I have a problem, sir. Any chance I could ask a favor?"

"Name it."

"I need a flight to LA. Immediately. I'm taking Edgar Wurm and Jordan Rayne to Newark International, but the flights are all late times. They're headed to Switzerland with a research associate. Hopefully, they can find a missing link to the Radix's power."

"I can help," Armstrong answered. "But skip Newark. Dillon and I share ownership of several private aircraft at Teterboro Airport. It's a Jersey airfield about fifteen miles northeast of Newark. I'll have a crew ready when you arrive."

"I owe you, Mr. President," he said, heading north.

"I need to warn you. Delgado plans to send a TAC team to bring you in. You know too much for his liking, Dr. Brynstone."

Chapter Twenty-nine

Near Teterboro, New Jersey
8:56 A.M.

Streaks of amber slashed the cold morning sky over the New Jersey Turnpike. Cori stared out the window, thinking over the tragedy that had befallen Brynstone's wife and child. She knew it had to be tearing John up inside, but he gave no hint of it. A state trooper in a white Crown Victoria pulled alongside the Escalade. Tinted windows prevented the officer from seeing her, but Cori scrunched in her chair. Banshee watched her, puzzled.

Her whole world had turned upside down in the last twelve hours. She believed she could convince authorities that she hadn't killed Mack Shaw and Perez, but John had advised her to wait until they returned from Europe. She peeked out the window again. The trooper was still there. A refinery in the distance brought to mind an old Bruce Springsteen song. Like the fugitive in "State Trooper," Cori prayed she wouldn't get pulled over on the Jersey Turnpike.

Brynstone headed for the exit ramp. She sighed when the officer didn't follow.

"You look troubled," Jordan said.

She forced a smile. "I'm fine."

Jordan returned to her laptop. Cori looked forward to getting to know the woman on the flight to Switzerland.

She wished her mother could've met Jordan Rayne and John Brynstone. Would they succeed where Ariel Cassidy had failed?

She listened as Jordan took an incoming call from a microbiologist named Bill Nosaka. She put him on speaker. "Billy, did you analyze the soft-tissue sample I delivered?"

"That's why I'm calling," Nosaka said. "You got your holidays mixed up, Jordan. It's Christmas, not April Fool's Day."

"What are you talking about?"

"You asked me to analyze a sample from a Renaissance mummy, but the one you delivered shows no sign of microbiological destruction. No spore-forming bacteria."

"You're sure?"

"Without a doubt, Jordan," Nosaka answered. "I need to do further testing, but I can assure you this sample is not from a desiccated corpse. Especially not five-hundred-year-old mummy tissue."

"Thanks, Billy," Jordan said. "Sorry to drag you into the lab during the holidays."

After he hung up, Brynstone said, "Nosaka couldn't tell that Zanchetti's tissue sample was five centuries old. Even locked in a stone box, the Radix regenerated necrotic tissue."

Wurm tugged at his beard. "Imagine its power when you mix it with the Scintilla."

Teterboro
9:04 A.M.

Not far from Manhattan, Teterboro Airport was built in Bergen County as a reliever airport for northern New Jersey and the New York metropolitan area. But it was better known for attracting private and corporate aircraft, inspiring its nickname, the Heathrow of Bizjets.

After arriving at Teterboro, Jordan offered to buy a shirt so Wurm could dump the bloodstained one he was wearing. Brynstone parked at the Aviation Hall of Fame located on the airport grounds. As Jordan closed her computer, Wurm jumped out, then opened the door for her. He smiled, watching her walk into the building. He moved up front, riding shotgun.

"I want you to see this before you leave for Switzerland," Brynstone said, facing them. He pulled a stone box from his pocket. Wurm leaned closer.

"My God," he whispered. "The *cista mystica*."

Cori craned her neck from the backseat. The carving on the lid looked familiar. She reached for the necklace from her mother and stared at it. The plant engraved on the box matched the one on her locket.

Brynstone lifted the lid. Inside the box, an airtight vial contained a green stalk the size of a lipstick tube. He held up the vial. A blackish purple bloom crowned the tip of the Radix.

"I've never seen anything like it," she said, marveling at a plant species that had turned extinct two thousand years ago. "It's beautiful. Still alive after so many centuries."

"I've waited a lifetime for this moment," Wurm said, taking the vial. He cradled it inside his large hand and ran his finger along the glass. "Do you realize the authority contained in this little stalk? It holds supremacy beyond words. The Keeper of the Radix could well become the most powerful person in the world."

"That's why I couldn't give it to Delgado." Brynstone removed another vial from his pocket. It contained a different stalk, lighter green in color and less vibrant. "Remember this, Edgar? It's the replica you made."

"A decent facsimile. The design is based on della Rovere's drawings in the Voynich manuscript. I created this mock-up so John would have an idea how it might look."

"Once you've seen the Radix, you know it's impossible to fake it. Still, it helps that no one has seen the root in five hundred years."

He placed the counterfeit root in the box, then slid it inside his pocket.

"Too bad Jordan isn't here."

"She saw the actual Radix," Brynstone answered. "I showed it to her when we flew back from Colorado."

"What will you do with it?" Cori asked.

"I'm giving the Radix to you."

"Oh, John," she said. "We're not ready."

"Take it. The Radix belongs with the Scintilla."

Wurm unscrewed the lid. The stalk slid out onto his palm.

Cori's eyes closed as the fragrance played sweet in her nostrils. A mesmerizing scent, potent but soothing. Like nothing she'd smelled before.

"How many great people dreamed about holding this?" Wurm wondered. "Galen obsessed over it. Paracelsus would've sacrificed everything to serve as Keeper of the Radix. Avicenna and Averroës both dreamed of studying its legendary powers. Isaac Newton might have abandoned physics and optics to make the Radix the centerpiece of his alchemical studies. Descartes hungered for it, believing it would bring glory to his beloved Catholicism. And long before his conversion, Augustine busted a man's nose who said the Radix didn't exist."

"Did da Vinci know about it?" Cori asked.

"Like others, Leonardo kept his obsession with the Radix a secret," Wurm answered. "He learned about it in 1472 when he joined the Company of Saint Luke, a guild of artists, apothecaries, and physicians. Sometime around 1483, he began searching for it. Leonardo was still obsessing over the Radix in 1502 when he told Cesare Borgia about it."

"Never understood how da Vinci could work for a guy like that," Brynstone said.

"Borgia could seduce even a Renaissance genius. Remember, he was the model for Machiavelli's *The Prince*.

He was an expert at combining the cunning of the fox with the violence of the lion."

"Sounds like everything Borgia learned, he picked up from his old man," Brynstone said.

"You remember Mario Puzo?" Wurm asked. "The guy who wrote *The Godfather*? He called the Borgias the original crime family. He regarded Pope Alexander VI as the greatest Mafia don of them all."

She nodded. "Now Borgia's descendants are carrying on the family tradition."

Wurm studied the root. "I hold what da Vinci could possess only in his formidable imagination. When I think of the things that could be accomplished . . . ," his voice trailed. He placed the Radix in the vial, capped it, and shook his head. "I can't, John. I'm sorry."

He looked over. "Can't what?"

Wurm handed the vial to him. "Can't take it."

Brynstone glanced at the backseat. He handed the vial to Cori. "Guess that makes you the Keeper of the Radix. Take it, Cori."

Apprehension creased her face. She took the vial, then unscrewed the lid, tipping the end. The Radix slid down the glass tube toward her hand. She raised the vial, stopping it from coming out. She didn't want to touch it.

Not yet.

Many times she'd doubted the truth behind the Radix legend. Ariel Cassidy had never convinced her. Neither had John Brynstone. In this solitary moment, her skepticism washed away. Even without touching it, she sensed the ancient root's hypnotic power. She indulged a fantasy in which her mother had never died but instead worked in her study. She visualized herself placing the Radix in her mother's hand. She flirted with that image, watching Ariel Cassidy's face brighten. She wished her mother were alive to experience this moment.

Cori glanced up. Wurm was staring at the Radix. The burning look in his charcoal eyes troubled her. He wanted it back. She slid the vial into her jeans pocket. Their eyes locked in a fierce gaze. Wurm's face twisted into a weird mix of relief and bitterness. He turned around, leaving her to stare at his long gray hair. She glanced down at her trembling hands.

Cori was still shaken, minutes later, as she waited inside the private hangar at Teterboro. She looked up as Jordan walked over.

"Our jet's almost ready, John," she announced. "Cori and Edgar better go soon. Ariel Cassidy's archives are already on board."

Brynstone looked puzzled. "Aren't you're going with them to Europe?"

Jordan shook her head. "I'm going with you, John. I want to help you find Kaylyn and your daughter. After that, we'll reunite and help them look for the Scintilla."

"It's dangerous."

"I've made up my mind," Jordan interrupted, closing his lips with a press of her slender finger. "I want to help you. Don't waste time trying to change my mind."

"I'm disappointed with your decision, Jordan," Wurm cut in, "but I now have a reason to do this." He pulled her in and kissed her. Her eyes widened in surprise before she pushed away.

"Always wanted to kiss a woman with a beauty mark. What did you think?"

She wiped her mouth. "I think you need a shave."

"It's my way of thanking you for the new shirt," he said. "Reminds me. I need to ditch my bloody sweatshirt."

"C'mon," Jordan said. "I saw a men's room. I'll point it out to you."

As they walked away, Cori stepped closer to Brynstone. "I'm glad Jordan is going with you to Cali. It'll be nice to have someone you can trust."

As Banshee curled around their legs, Cori wondered if Brynstone was thinking about taking back the Radix, his mind playing the alternatives. She reached in her pocket, then pulled out the vial, holding it in her hand. "I don't know if I should take this."

He shook his head, closing fingers around hers. "You keep it, but don't tell anyone you have it. And don't let Wurm bully you. He'll try to dismantle your mind. Pick apart your brain, neuron by neuron. Don't let him."

"Gee, thanks. I'm not scared at all now." She unchained the heart-shaped locket from behind her neck and handed it to Brynstone. "This belonged to my mother. Can you hang on to it while I'm in Switzerland?"

He studied the golden locket. "You don't want to take it?"

"I saw Wurm staring at the plant symbol engraved on front. You know that crazy look he gets? Kind of freaked me," she said, rising on her toes and wrapping her arms around his neck. "Good luck finding your wife and daughter."

He kissed her cheek. "Good luck finding the Scintilla."

Brynstone looked up as Wurm ambled over with Jordan. The big man looked better in his new black shirt.

"It's time for your flight," Jordan told Cori.

He hugged her again. She held tighter this time, as if she were siphoning his strength. He shook Wurm's hand as Jordan embraced Cori, who stooped and petted the cat.

"Let's go," Jordan said. "I'll show you where to find the jet."

"Go ahead, Cori. I'll catch up." Watching them walk away, Wurm lowered his arm across Brynstone's shoulder. "I want you to take the Radix, John."

"I'm not taking it back."

"I told you I can't keep it."

"I understand. That's why Cori has it."

"But she shouldn't have the Radix," Wurm growled. "You know how much is at stake."

"Don't you trust her?"

"She is bright like her mother. A good kid, but she can't be the Keeper. She doesn't comprehend its power."

"That's why she's the best person to keep it."

"John, listen to me—"

"You listen to me." Brynstone stabbed his finger into Wurm's chest. "Do all you can to help Cori. And you sure as hell better not hurt her. Understand?"

Wurm drew in a hard breath and nodded.

Brynstone softened his voice. "Good luck, Edgar. God knows you'll need it."

Chapter Thirty

Potomac
9:30 A.M.

The Knight slid into a chair at his dining table. Seated opposite him, the homeless man was dressed in a silk designer robe. A ponytail restrained his clean brown hair. After a fresh bath and shave, he looked like a new man. His weathered face brimmed with character. The homeless man attacked the sumptuous meal with the appetite of a beast.

"I instructed Dante to prepare any dish you requested," the Knight said, amused. "I assumed you wanted breakfast."

"I wanted a real meal," the homeless man said. "Got ketchup?"

"For what purpose?"

"For this." He pointed at the filet mignon.

The Knight sighed and turned to Cress. "Bring the man ketchup."

"Sure appreciate this, mister." The man gulped his wine, leaving droplets on his beard. "But why'd you invite me?"

"Credit the holiday spirit. What is your name?"

"Andy."

"That's perfect."

"Sure is a big place you have here," Andy said, looking around as he placed foie gras on bread. "You famous or something?"

"I am a knight."

"Don't mean to be insulting, sir," the man said, as Cress placed ketchup on the table. "But the way I see it, the world don't need knights no more."

"Many share your misguided opinion, Andy. But we can't be blind to the truth. More than ever, our world is lapsing into dark times. My fraternal order offers hope and salvation."

Andy dumped ketchup on his steak. "Don't follow, mister."

"The world teeters on the edge of apocalypse. Sinners must be eradicated to make way for forward-looking ideas."

"Sinners?" Andy asked. "Like the church—"

"The Church has lost its way, like everyone else," the Knight interrupted. "The Church begs for my renaissance. It needs an avenging angel."

"A knight needs a sword," Andy said, changing the subject. "You got one?"

With a stiff formality, the Knight flicked his hand. Cress nodded, then moved to an adjoining room. With eyes like dark glass, he stared at his guest. "You're going to enjoy this."

Cress returned with an oblong box. He moved Italian black truffles, then placed it on the table. Sliding on white gloves, he opened the box and removed a sword.

"Sure is a beauty. Can I hold it?"

The Knight nodded.

"Gotta be strong to use this thing." Andy raised the golden handle with both hands, studying an eight-pointed cross in the hilt. "What is that?"

"The Maltese cross. The symbol of the Sovereign Order of the Knights of Malta."

Cress took the sword and returned it to the case. He removed it from the table.

"Eat. You'll need your strength." The Knight studied him. "I must ask you something, Andy. Are you a sinner?"

"Who isn't?" he smiled, revealing a mouthful of decayed teeth.

"What would you do for redemption? For immortality?"

"Haven't given it much thought."

"What do you think, sir?" Cress looked at his watch. "Does he meet with your approval?"

"I'm not happy about the teeth, but I can correct that. He'll do."

At Cress's signal, two men in dark suits marched into the room. One pulled back the chair. The other grabbed Andy's arm. The homeless man lunged forward, clamping his hands on the chair, struggling to stay seated.

"Hey, why you doin' this?" he protested. "I'm not done eating."

"Yes, you are," the Knight said. "Take him."

Andy reached for a table knife, but his hand was batted away. He kicked his feet and tried to fight, but proved too frail to resist. The men dragged him from the dining room.

"Begin the procedure," the Knight told Cress. "Call me when the anesthesia wears off. Andy must be lucid during my work. I want him to experience everything I do to him."

Part Four
Land of the Dead

*It is by going down into the abyss that we recover
the treasures of life.*
—Joseph Campbell

Chapter Thirty-one

Brynstone peeked out the jet's window, glancing at the snow-streaked Appalachian Mountains. He had expected exhaustion to hit after boarding the Gulfstream luxury jetliner back in Jersey. Instead, adrenaline burned inside whenever he thought about Kaylyn and Shay. Had Adriana's family kidnapped his wife and child? The House of Borgia would do anything to get the Radix. But did they know he'd found it?

Banshee played in the aisle, kneading her paws.

He pulled out the *cista mystica*, containing Wurm's replica of the root. His hunt for the Radix felt incomplete without the Scintilla. That had to wait until he had his family back.

Jordan noticed the stone box. She cleared her throat, then pointed at the flat-screen TV.

"John, check this out."

A cheerful anchorman stared into the camera. "Maryland authorities describe the woman as an escaped mental patient from the Amherst Psychiatric Hospital in Baltimore. Police are calling her a person of interest in the homicides of two hospital employees. She is also linked to the assault of her roommate." A picture from Cori's Facebook profile appeared on the screen, showing her with long blonde hair. "Cori Cassidy's whereabouts are unknown. Now let's return to our top story."

Brynstone rubbed his face, relieved that Cori and Wurm had made it out of the country. Their transatlantic flight had taken off almost an hour ago this Christmas morning.

"I knew about the hospital staff," Jordan said. "I hadn't heard about Cori's roommate."

"Tessa Richardson. The Borgias broke into Cori's home, searching for Ariel Cassidy's notebook. I'm guessing Tessa got in their way."

"Seems like the Borgias are always one step ahead," she said.

"I know what you mean. How did they know to find Wurm at Amherst or about the notebook at Cori's house?"

"John, look," she pointed at the television. "It's the president."

A cable news network was airing highlights from President Armstrong's press conference. The banner at the bottom of the screen reported, BREAKING NEWS: PRESIDENT'S BROTHER TARGET OF CAR BOMB. The network cut to footage showing Dillon Armstrong trapped beneath a twisted car. While addressing the media, the president's stony temper cracked when he discussed Dillon Armstrong's situation.

"A car bomb," Jordan said. "Who would do that to the president's brother?"

Brynstone didn't answer.

Television crews captured Armstrong's grimace as he walked from the news conference without taking questions. Outside George Washington University Hospital, a female reporter added, "We're told Dillon Armstrong is in surgery. According to our sources, President Armstrong has not visited the hospital because a heightened alert was issued at the White House. We have no word on any leads about who planted the car bomb."

Brynstone shook his head. Everything was going to hell today.

Airborne over the Atlantic Ocean

On the flight to Switzerland, Cori explored the Airbus Corporate Jetliner, finding it crowded with amenities more lavish than at any hotel she'd stayed in. The Armstrong luxury jet boasted an exercise room, conference center, and wine alcove. She tried to imagine the first family flying on this plane. She couldn't help but be impressed.

She wanted to check on Tessa, but Brynstone had advised her to wait. She thought about his cat and realized she missed Banshee. Wurm had crashed on the couch in the front cabin. To escape his snoring, she grabbed her mother's journals and a bowl of fresh fruit, then headed to the jet's bedroom. Peeling open a banana, she curled on the bed and started reading.

Ariel Cassidy had dedicated several journal pages to Carl Jung's paternal grandfather and namesake. The elder Jung had been a German-born medical student when his radical political beliefs led to his arrest in his early twenties. After serving his prison term, the elder Jung moved to Paris in 1821. A short time later, he moved to Switzerland to become a professor of surgery at the University of Basel. A staunch Freemason, Jung's grandfather became the grand master of the Swiss Lodge. During this time, he developed a deep appreciation for alchemy. In later years, that heritage helped to inspire his grandson to create a kind of spiritual alchemy.

Cori's mother noted that alchemists had used *Decknamen* or cover names to disguise and protect their secret craft from outsiders. In fact, alchemists had coined the word *arcanum* to describe secrets revealed to loyal followers. It had been suggested that Carl Jung cloaked his concepts with psychiatric code words like *collective unconsciousness* and *archetype*. Whatever secrets he might have coveted, Jung did refer to the unconscious mind as the Land of the Dead. Coming from her dead mother, those same words had haunted Cori's nightmares.

In his autobiography, Jung described having a "frightening dream" in January of 1923. His nightmare involved the German god Wotan, who appeared in a primeval forest and ordered a gigantic wolfhound to carry away a human soul. The next morning, Jung learned that his mother had died. The experience inspired him to build his Swiss retreat, a castlelike complex in Bollingen, Switzerland. Two months later, he began constructing a stone tower beside the shallow upper end of Lake Zurich. Over the next dozen years, he worked on the complex. He had dedicated it as the Shrine of Philemon, but it was better known as Bollingen Tower. In her journal, Ariel Cassidy wrote that Jung's "dream castle was a stone personification of his unconscious mind."

Cori had to figure out what Jung knew about the Radix and the Scintilla. What better place to crawl inside Jung's mind than at his Bollingen retreat?

Chapter Thirty-two

Washington, D.C.
11:42 A.M.

The United States Secret Service had transported Deena Riverside to a nondescript office space three blocks from the White House. Between interviews, she found a new text message from Pantera:

The DA tragedy adds a wrinkle to our deal. Multiple parties are interested in the Rx. Do you have sufficient funds to complete the deal in time?

She replied that she had the money. She made plans to have a contact meet Pantera to collect the Radix. Pantera had never mentioned additional parties before, but it didn't bother Deena. She had locked in the price. Business as usual. Taft-Ryder's future rested on acquiring the Radix. With Dillon in a coma, she was more anxious than ever to get her hands on it.

A man in a blue suit approached her. "Ms. Riverside, I'm Special Agent Antonio Casañas with the United States Secret Service."

"Sorry, Agent Casañas. I already told your investigators everything I know."

"We have a few more questions," he said. "Then the president wants to meet with you."

Potomac
12:05 P.M.

"What's the latest on Brynstone?" the Knight asked, pressing the phone against his ear. Standing in his study, he looked out the window as afternoon light filtered over the scenic riches of Montgomery County.

"I'm setting a trap for him," Metzger reported.

"Your cat-and-mouse games tire me. You need to understand the urgency of this matter."

The assassin chortled into the phone. "I've never heard you sound frustrated before," Metzger said. "It's refreshing."

"It is my destiny to become Keeper of the Radix. Find it." He slammed down the phone.

Cress knocked on the door, then entered the study. "The procedure was successful. You won't notice the incision. Andy is ready for you."

"Good," the Knight answered. "I am ready for him."

* * *

Washington, D.C.
12:47 P.M.

Deena had taken an elevator deep beneath the White House. After Secret Service Agent Casañas drove her through a long tunnel, she arrived at the Presidential Emergency Operations Center beneath the East Wing. Alex was waiting in a conference room. He hugged her, then pulled back a chair for her.

"Last night, you talked to my brother on the South Portico. Mind telling me what you discussed?"

"A confidential business deal."

"Involving the Radix," the president added.

"How do you know about that?"

He leaned back in the chair. "Tell me what it is and why Dillon wanted it."

She interlaced her fingers, staring at the presidential symbol emblazoned on the table. "The Radix is a medicinal plant that went extinct. The last remaining stalk disappeared centuries ago, but was rediscovered. Taft-Ryder is interested because of its pharmaceutical potential. We plan to identify the genetic markers of the plant genome. Analyze its biochemical properties."

"You could do that?"

"It's already been done with another plant. Ancient healers used the date palm of Judea to create medicine. The date palm is a powerful symbol of Israel, showing up on ancient coins and modern Israeli currency. The Bible and the Koran praised the plant for its medicinal properties. In ancient times, it represented the Tree of Life. Crusaders destroyed this Judean date species during the Middle Ages."

He nodded. "Another plant with healing properties that disappeared centuries ago."

"But listen to this. While excavating King Herod's palace at Masada, archeologists uncovered seeds from this ancient date palm. Radiocarbon dating placed the seeds at around two thousand years old. Back in 2005, a botanist named Elaine Solowey at the Arava Institute for Environmental Studies in Israel took one seed—she nicknamed it Methuselah, after the 969-year-old grandfather of Noah—and fertilized it."

"What happened?"

"The Methuselah seed sprouted. After about six months, it was a foot-tall plant with six leaves. Last I heard, it was four feet tall. If the tree is female, it could bear fruit some day. Solowey believes the ancient plant could be useful as a modern medicine."

The president considered the possibilities.

"Think about it," she continued. "Researchers succeeded in germinating a two-thousand-year-old seed. Imagine what we could do with the Radix sample. We could manufacture the ultimate drug. Maybe it could cure diabetes, Alzheimer's, depression, or cancer. Taft-Ryder would crush the other pharmaceutical houses."

A knock came on the door to the briefing room. An attractive woman in a white lab coat peeked inside. "Sorry to interrupt, Mr. President, but I have an update on your brother."

"Deena, this is Dr. Jenn Shaw. She's a White House doctor." He moved around the table. "Any word on Dillon?"

"I talked to the ER clinical ops director," Dr. Shaw explained. "Shattered glass and shrapnel caused injuries and burns. Metal fragments punctured two organs, so it's touch and go. They rolled your brother into recovery. We'll see how he progresses from there."

"How bad is he, Jenn?"

"Right now, I'd say your brother has a fifty-fifty chance of pulling through."

Deena closed her eyes, absorbing the information.

President Armstrong looked at his watch. "Secret Service can try to stop me from going to that hospital, but it won't do them any good."

Chapter Thirty-three

On the Gulfstream, Brynstone started to call Cori. Before he could dial her number, a call came in. It wasn't Kaylyn.

"*Guten Morgen,* Herr Doktor," the man soothed. "You have a beautiful family."

"Who are you?"

"Let me assure you, I am not your enemy. Not yet."

"First things first. You need to prove that my family is alive and you need to do it now."

"As you wish."

A muffled sound. In a crackling voice, Kaylyn said, "John, please hurry—"

"Satisfied?" the man asked, coming back on.

"I'll be satisfied when I put a bullet in your head."

"Remember, Herr Doktor, I'm the one in charge."

"I want my wife and daughter," Brynstone growled.

"That's a possible outcome. Are you in the air?"

"I should land at LAX a little after one thirty."

"Excellent. I will contact you then."

"Wait. Tell me who you are."

"A fair request," he said. "I am known as Erich Metzger." He ended the call.

Shaking his head, Brynstone tossed the phone into the seat beside him.

Jordan studied him. "John? Are you okay?"

"That was the man who abducted Kaylyn and Shay. He claims he's Erich Metzger."

"The assassin? *That* Metzger? Did the Borgias hire him to target your family?"

"Maybe." He watched Banshee jump from the top of one chair to the next.

"John, I know people on the West Coast who can help. I took point on a few jobs with them before I came over to the SCS. All three are former Emergency Reaction Team agents from the Special Operations Unit."

"I don't need NSA's Men in Black. I can handle Metzger."

"He's a machine, John. A butcher. You are a formidable thinker and a resourceful warrior. But you're no match for that psychopath. Mind if I call them?"

He looked out the window. After a pause, he answered, "Make sure they're good."

Airborne over the Atlantic Ocean

Time had disappeared during the flight to Switzerland. Cori immersed herself in the world of her mother's scholarship. After a good three hours of intensive study, she wandered out of the bedroom. Journals and stacks of papers surrounded Wurm at the oval table.

"Nice nap, sleepyhead?" she asked, patting his shoulder. "I see you found coffee."

Wurm raised a black mug. "I've consumed enough caffeine to kill a small child."

She laughed nervously. She wasn't sure she wanted this guy wired on coffee.

"What happened to your locket? The one with the plant engraving?"

"Decided to not bring it." She pointed to his notebook. Wurm had scrawled the word *Wotan* beneath *Jung*.

"Jung had a dream about Wotan taking away his mother on the night she died," Cori said. "What do you know about Wotan?"

"The Vikings called him Odin. The god of gods in

Northern Europe. The chief divinity of Norse mythology. Early Germans called him Wotan. Sometimes Wodan or Woden."

"Never heard of Wotan."

"Sure you have. You honor his memory every week."

She gave a puzzled look as she took a chair across the table.

He shoved aside journals. "Wednesday is named after him. It means 'Wotan's day.'"

"Guess I never knew that."

He gave her an amused look. "Wotan's not the only one. Thursday is named after Odin's son. You know, Thor, the thunder god?"

She laughed at Wurm's exuberance. He was caffeinated and totally engrossed in his ideas.

"It doesn't stop there," he said. "Wotan's wife gets a day of celebration too. Frigga was a love goddess in Germanic paganism. That's where we get Friday."

She pursed her lips. "Is every day named after a deity?"

"Crazy, isn't it? You know Saturday? Best day of the week, right?" Wurm said, rambling. "It was named after the Roman god of agriculture and harvest. It's an Old English translation of the Latin *Saturni dies*, or day of Saturn. Tuesday honors the Germanic god Tiu. He's like the Roman god, Mars."

"Edgar."

"Some people think Mars inspired Monday, but they're wrong. Monday comes from an Old English corruption of the Latin *lunae dies*, or day of the moon. Monday means 'moon day.' Ancient pagan societies set aside a day for ritual moon worship."

"Edgar. Slow down, buddy."

"But the big one is Sunday. A pagan cult of Mithras worshiped the Roman sun god Sol Invictus on his special sun day. It was a big thing. Now, you might know the Jewish Sabbath day is the period from Friday sunset to Saturday nightfall. But what you didn't know is that Constantine changed everything in 321, when he moved the Roman day of rest to Sunday. He was the first Christian Roman emperor, but he also respected the pagan solar god. It helped set the precedent for the Christian day of worship. You see, most people have no clue they celebrate pagan gods and rituals seven days a week."

Cori raised an eyebrow. "*Celebrate* is a strong word."

"Maybe when it comes to days of the week," he admitted. "But pagan traditions had a huge impact on Christmas celebrations. Early Germans believed that Wotan rode around on Christmas Eve giving fruit and nuts to good children. You can see how that influenced later ideas about Santa Claus. Then, there's the Tree of Life."

"Hey, Edgar. Let's stay focused on the—"

"Wotan plucked out his eye to gain the wisdom of the ages. He hung for nine days on the World Tree to learn the secrets of the magic runes. Later, Wotan's followers commemorated their December holiday by hanging ornaments on *Tannenbäume*. When you hang an ornament on your Christmas tree, you're actually paying homage to Wotan. It has little to do with Jesus, that's for sure."

"What does Wotan have to do with Carl Jung?"

"He had an interest in the Wotan legend." Wurm gave a hard look. "He found inspiration in many places. Jung had mystical experiences that revealed forgotten truths to him. During one episode in December 1913, he perceived a snake coiling around his body. While sweating in the viper's grip, Jung envisioned himself transforming into a pagan god."

"Let me get this straight. This famous psychiatrist thought he was a pagan deity?"

"Some might claim that, but that's not the way I see it. Whatever the truth, we do know that Jung had a powerful mystical experience. During a visionary journey, he joined an ancient mystery religion, one that flourished in Greco-Roman times."

Wurm explained that ancient mystery cults were secret

societies dedicated to a deity, such as the Persian sun god, Mithras. The cult of Mithras arose around the same time as Christianity and shared similar traditions. Mystery cults even celebrated Mithras's birth on December 25, paralleling the Christian holiday of Christmas.

He added that the Mithraic brotherhoods practiced the *unio mystica*, a union of humans with a god. It was this kind of self-deification that Jung experienced during his 1913 altered state of consciousness. Wurm explained that during the trancelike vision, Jung perceived himself transforming into a lion-headed god.

"Wow," she remarked. "Pretty trippy."

He sipped coffee. "A published account of Jung's self-deification based on a closed seminar he gave in 1925 appeared in 1989. Psychologist Richard Noll claimed that Jung's deification was withheld from most followers for more than sixty years. Prior to that, the only way you could read about Jung's transformation was to undergo at least one hundred hours of 'approved' analysis, and only then after you secured permission from your analyst."

He pulled at his beard. "Jung exerted a significant influence on the people in his circle. Several called him a new light. Around 1916, when he delivered the *Seven Sermons to the Dead*, his interest shifted from the Mithras cult to Gnosticism. In later years, he incorporated these interests into his study of alchemy."

Almost unconsciously, Cori stood and began pacing, absorbing the fabric of the conversation. Wurm studied her.

"Your mother interviewed one of Jung's closest followers, a woman who was the daughter of European royalty. She claimed that Jung believed his spiritual destiny would be fulfilled if he found the Radix. She compared him to Wotan, who sought knowledge by hanging from the World Tree."

"That's the same as the Tree of Life?" Cori asked, brushing away bangs.

He nodded. "The tree is mentioned in every culture from Greek to Russian to Indian to European to the Indonesian islands. Like Christmas celebrations, the Church was careful with Wotan's tree. Pope Gregory the Great advised a missionary in England to exercise care with pagan communities who worshiped a sacred tree. To avoid offending the pagans, he instructed the abbot to not cut down the tree. Instead, they attributed the tree's mystical power to Christ."

"Is there a connection with the tree in the Garden of Eden?"

"Genesis 2:9 describes two trees. The Tree of Life and the Tree of Knowledge of Good and Evil. Adam and Eve sampled fruit from the latter one. They were expelled from Eden so they wouldn't eat from the Tree of Life. Cherubs and a flaming sword guarded the path to the Tree of Life in the center of the garden."

"What would have happened if they had eaten from the Tree of Life?"

"Immortality," he answered. "Adam and Eve would have lived forever."

She returned to her chair. "Did Jung believe the Radix was the last remaining piece of the Tree of Life?"

"Whatever he believed about the Radix, he shrouded it in secrecy." He unwrapped a stick of gum and popped it into his mouth. "Jung knew the Scintilla was worth little without the Radix. I think he waited to reveal the Scintilla's hiding place until the Radix was discovered. That didn't happen in his lifetime. Careful to the end, he gave clues to finding the Scintilla. As far as we know, none of his followers discovered it."

"We know he never found the Radix. John Brynstone did." She held the vial under the table, sensing the Radix's power. "You think Jung found the Scintilla?"

"I suspect he concealed it at Bollingen Tower. That's why we're flying to Switzerland."

* * *

Airborne over Kansas
2:22 P.M.

The private jet blasted over lonely prairie farmland. Brynstone leaned back in a leather club chair, working on a computer. He was watching real-time surveillance of a home, broken into a matrix of small windows. Jordan bent down, staring at his screen. She pointed to a window that displayed an office with the NSA emblem on the wall behind the desk.

"Is that DIRNSA's office?" she asked.

"Yeah. When I was at Delgado's home, I broke into his computer and created an operating system backdoor so I can monitor his activity. Didn't get time to establish audio, but I can access the closed-circuit television cameras around his house. Even the camera inside his computer." He frowned. "I admit. That part is a little creepy."

"Isn't that a violation of his civil liberties?"

"Yeah," he answered. "Ask me if I care."

"It's sort of funny," she said. "Eavesdropping on the director of the National Security Agency. It's like interrupting a telemarketer's dinner with a sales call."

"Did you learn anything about Metzger? Any physical description?"

"He's like a phantom. An Egyptian journalist described Metzger as five-five, pale complexion, and heavy, with long brown hair. Then I found another description from a few years ago when he assassinated the leader of Yamaguchi Gumi, one of the biggest Yakuza groups."

"Wait a minute. Metzger killed a Japanese Mafia boss?"

"Guy's got balls. The Yakuza boss's wife spotted Metzger in Kobe. The *ane-san* said he was about six-one, dark, and one hundred forty pounds, wearing short blond hair. I found three more eyewitness descriptions, all contradicting each other. I even called an old boyfriend who worked CIA. When I asked about Metzger's physical ID, he just laughed."

"The CIA didn't give you anything on him?"

"He did tell me that the Company refers to Metzger as the Poet."

"Yeah?" he asked. "Why do they call him that?"

"The poet Dante used *contrapasso* to describe the punishments of different sinners in his *Inferno*. Metzger kills using a *contrapasso* theme, the idea that punishments reflect the crime. He has a reputation for assassinating people in the same manner they use to kill their own victims. As sick as it sounds, they say he has the heart of a poet. I'm sorry, John. That's all I know about him."

Brynstone turned away, thinking about Metzger pulling a hit on a Yakuza boss. Then, he thought about his wife and baby girl in the hands of that monster.

Chapter Thirty-four

Potomac
3:52 P.M.

In the studio at the back of his spacious house, the Knight studied the canvas on his easel. Something wasn't right. He wasn't capturing the strain in the abdominal muscles.

Since childhood, he had been obsessed with the crucifixion of Saint Andrew. The apostle's fate had been sealed when a Roman governor named Aegeates sentenced him to death. To prolong Andrew's suffering, Aegeates had the disciple bound—not nailed—on an X-shaped cross. Like his crucified brother Peter, Andrew was posed in an upside-down position.

The Knight dabbed his brush into a swirl of Payne's-gray

paint. He glanced at the canvas, then ran a gray line beneath the rib cage, giving shadow to the apostle's stomach. He had perfected it now. Although far from complete, his painting of a man crucified on an X-shaped cross was already remarkable.

He turned from his canvas. He spoke to his subject for the first time in hours. "This is a great honor, you know," he called to the homeless man ten feet away. "Andrew was the Protocletus. That means the 'first called.' Jesus summoned Andrew as the first apostle."

Bound with arms and legs spread in opposite directions, Andy's body formed an X. Blood glistened on the ropes encircling the homeless man's wrists and ankles. Every muscle quivered. Blood had rushed to Andy's head, giving his face a scarlet cast.

"Do you know why Saint Andrew was crucified in an inverted position? He thought himself unworthy to be martyred on the same type of cross as Jesus. Nailed in an upside-down position, Andrew could train his gaze not on his executioners nor on the earth, but on the heavens above, where his beloved kingdom awaited."

Andy didn't answer. He couldn't. The laryngectomy prevented him from speaking. Without his voice box, Andy couldn't muster a sound. The Knight insisted on the surgery because screaming distracted him from his painting.

"More blood."

Max Cress came over with a glass syringe. "In the red?"

"Please."

Cress stabbed the syringe's needle into a dab of paint on the Knight's palette. He pushed the plunger, squirting Andy's blood into the red ochre.

"Stop," the Knight said. "Enough."

He twirled his brush, mixing blood with paint. He touched the paintbrush to canvas, dotting blood droplets around the blessed saint's face.

"Blood has iron in it," Cress said. "When it dries, does it change the color of the paint?"

"A little, but it's all about transformation. Andy is more than my model. His blood and soul are poured into this painting."

Cress tapped his touch-screen PDA. "Your guest from Italy arrived. Who is he?"

"Gabriel Bitonti. He heads the Vatican's Consulta Medica, a medical board of one hundred doctors who investigate miracles. He is also a consultant to the Pontifical Institute of Christian Archeology."

"I read about him. They call him the Miracle Detective. When are you meeting him?"

"I need more time with Andy." The Knight examined his paint-flecked fingers. "Dr. Bitonti must be exhausted from his long flight. A nap and a shower might refresh him. Tell the doctor he has time for such an indulgence if he wishes. Then I'll clean up and meet with him."

Washington, D.C.
4:12 P.M.

Founded in 1824, the George Washington University Hospital had a long history of treating presidents and other world leaders with crippling illnesses and medical emergencies. After arriving at the hospital, Deena had learned that Dillon remained in critical condition. Still comatose, he had been moved into the GW Surgery Center for additional treatment. Dillon's story dominated the holiday news cycle. Reporters circled the hospital like sharks. She had sent an e-mail to the Taft-Ryder stockholders, reporting on his condition. Her back ached from the explosion, so she had consulted a nurse, who gave her painkillers.

She glanced around the hospital's private VIP suite, watching Beltway insiders mingle with business people. Despite the tragic circumstances, the power games were in overdrive. Almost everyone here was a high-ranking business or political figure.

Inside a cluster of friends and family, Brooke Armstrong looked composed as she sat on a sofa. It was awkward seeing her here. Of course, Brooke had no idea about Deena's tryst with her husband. Deena planned to talk to the woman, but decided to wait. She was headed to the restroom when she saw President Armstrong down the hallway with his Service detail. He had finished meeting with surgeons.

"Anything new on Dillon?"

"Not as promising as before the surgery. Right now, it's touch and go." He pointed to a conference room. "Let's talk."

She followed him. Stepping inside, the president closed the door.

"I didn't want to say this in the hallway, but they might need to amputate Dillon's legs."

She dropped into a chair, stunned by the news.

"Listen, Deena, if the Radix can do what you claimed earlier, we could help Dillon."

"I had the same thought. I think Dillon would want to give the Radix a try. He was interested in purchasing it. The seller is demanding payment later today. If we miss this window, the Radix goes to another buyer."

The president grabbed his neck, working an inflamed muscle. "How much money are we talking?"

"Two billion, if it's authentic." She moved close to the president, taking his hand. "It's called the perfect medicine. If they've found the Radix, it's worth the money."

"I don't get it, Deena. Why would it be worth that kind of money?"

"Because," she said, "the Radix belonged to Jesus Christ."

Part Five
The Eye of God

Death is indeed a fearful piece of brutality; there is no sense pretending otherwise.
—Carl Jung

Chapter Thirty-five

"The Radix belonged to Jesus Christ?" Armstrong asked. He wasn't sure he had heard Deena right.

"According to legend, Jesus used the Radix to create medicine," she explained. "Along with his disciple, Luke. The physician. They consecrated oil for healing. You know the miracles described in the New Testament?"

"Jesus performed them using the Radix?"

She nodded. "At Gethsemane, Jesus handed the root to Luke. Fearing his own arrest, Luke gave it to a wealthy senator from the Sanhedrin, the supreme Jewish council. His name was Joseph of Arimathea. He was meeting with Luke when the Sanhedrin questioned Jesus."

"I've heard of Joseph of Arimathea," Armstrong said, tracing one finger along the handle of his coffee mug. "Can't say I know much about him."

"Some people think he may have been Jesus's maternal uncle. After the crucifixion, he asked Pontius Pilate for Jesus's body to prepare it for burial. Together with Nicodemus, Joseph wrapped Christ's body in linen and consecrated it with spices mixed with the Radix. They entombed him in Joseph's own sepulchre, then rolled a stone into place, blocking the grave. According to legend, the Radix plants withered and vanished from the earth around the time of Jesus's crucifixion. The canonical Gospels don't discuss Arimathea's later life. Apocryphal legend fills in the gaps. Joseph traveled to Gaul in Western

Europe on a preaching mission with Mary Magdalene and Lazarus."

"Western Europe?"

"Southern France. Mary Magdalene and Lazarus remained in Marseilles. The rest headed north. Joseph traveled with twelve followers to establish Christianity on the British Isles. He had made money in the metal trade. The Roman Empire established fertile mining districts in southwestern Britain. Some believe he traveled there on an earlier trip, possibly taking his nephew."

"You're joking," he said, sipping coffee. "Jesus traveled to England?"

"The poet William Blake thought so. Others did too. After the crucifixion, Joseph landed in the Glastonbury Marshes. He climbed a hill with a staff grown from Christ's crown of thorns. He thrust it into the ground, saying he and his companions were 'weary all.' The staff took root, flowering for centuries at Christmastime. Today a thorn bush stands on Wearyall Hill."

"After the crucifixion, did Joseph take the Radix to England?"

"According to legend. In addition to the staff, he brought two cups. He'd used one to catch the blood and the other the sweat of Jesus as he died on the cross."

"The Holy Grail, right? I thought it was one cup."

"Sometimes the Grail is described as twin cruets used at the Last Supper. Some believe Jesus and Luke used one cup to mix the Radix and other ingredients into a medicine known as the White Chrism."

"Why did this one root survive, when all the other plants perished?"

"Good question," she said. "In plant biology, a member of a species can survive even after mass extinction. According to medieval legend, Joseph of Arimathea dipped this last-known piece of the Radix in a cruet containing Christ's blood, preserving it. The truth is, no one knows. It's one of many mysteries surrounding the Radix."

"Joseph of Arimathea was the first Grail Keeper?"

"More importantly, he was the first Keeper of the Radix."

She explained that Joseph hid the Radix near Glastonbury. For ten centuries, it remained buried but never forgotten, as generations of mystery cults kept alive the Radix romance. In 1113, a farmer named Thomas Locke discovered a bag of relics while digging his brother's grave in his Glastonbury field. Sensing its importance, Locke traveled to the Holy Land to have it blessed. During his pilgrimage, thieves assaulted Locke and left him for dead. The Knights of Saint John of Jerusalem found him. At the time of the First Crusade, they were a medical brotherhood known as the Knights Hospitaller. They had founded hospice camps, giving inspiration in later centuries for the word *hospital*. At one hospice, they nursed Locke back to health. Like other grateful patients saved by the Hospitallers, Locke bequeathed his estate to the order. The Knights' leader, a Benedictine named Gerard de Saxo, visited the farmer. In gratitude for saving his life, Locke presented his bag of relics to Brother Gerard. After that, the Knights of Saint John became the Keepers of the Radix.

The Knights of Saint John had a long interest in herbal medicines, including treating the wounds of crusaders with Saint-John's-wort, using an Anglo-Saxon word that referred to a medicinal herb. The Hospitallers studied the Radix, hoping to tap its healing power. They kept their Radix gift a secret, even years later while locked in a bitter rivalry with the military Order of the Knights Templar.

She explained that the Templars had been charged with defending the Holy Land, while the Hospitaller order cared for wounded soldiers and pilgrims during the Crusades. Tension swelled between the two orders over the Templar obsession with finding treasures in the Holy Land. The bad blood continued in 1191 when the Knights Templar moved to Cyprus, leaving the Hospitallers to both protect pilgrims and care for them. For centuries, the Hospitallers were renowned as brilliant healers. One pope described their healing arts as miraculous. The Vatican had no idea the Knights Hospitaller possessed the greatest relic in Christendom.

He studied her. "If the Knights understood its power, how did they lose it?"

"The son of Pope Alexander VI heard a rumor from Leonardo da Vinci. Using Vatican pressure, Cesare Borgia discovered that the Hospitallers—then called the Knights of Rhodes—possessed the Radix. After assaulting the Knights' grand master, Cesare Borgia seized it."

"Now you want it."

Deena's eyes twinkled. "Think I'm crazy?"

"If anyone else told me this," he said, "the answer would be a resounding yes. But you and my brother are hard-nosed businesspeople. You don't believe in superstitions."

"I believe in the Radix. So does your brother. Do you?"

"Maybe," he said. "If it can save Dillon."

Chapter Thirty-six

Los Angeles
1:35 P.M.

Brynstone didn't like sitting on his ass, doing nothing, a bitter holdover from his days in a wheelchair. Right now, he didn't have much choice. During the six-hour nonstop flight from New Jersey to California, his mind drifted from his wife and daughter to the blood inside the Zanchetti mummy to Cori and Wurm in Switzerland to Delgado's lies.

He could barely stay in his seat when the pilot announced their descent. Jordan had recruited three former NSA spec ops and they were waiting at Los Angeles International. He didn't know if they were right for this job, but he had faith in her judgment. He just hoped they could find Kaylyn and Shay in time.

The fugitive sun lingered in seclusion over the smoggy California sky as the private aircraft taxied across the runway. Even on Christmas afternoon, LAX earned its reputation as one of the world's busiest airports. It was more sedate on the airfield's south side, where the Armstrong family jet pulled into a Mercury Air Center FBO hangar.

They hurried off the Gulfstream jetliner and headed toward a black Navigator.

He climbed in front with the driver, an ex-marine sniper who introduced himself as Bob. An Irishman with an unshaved face and stringy long hair, Bob was wearing a black shirt emblazoned with the message "Guns don't kill people. I kill people."

A man of subtlety.

Behind them, Jordan had wedged between a big man named Steven Cloud and an even bigger agent named Spencer Tilton. Both were ex-Delta intel and demo operatives. An assortment of Heckler & Koch firearms occupied space at the rear of the vehicle. They came ready to play.

Metzger was supposed to call at any minute. As they waited, Bob the Driver looked over, seeing the one-eyed cat curled on Brynstone's lap, preening herself.

"That thing belong to you?" he smirked.

"Yeah," Brynstone answered. "You got a problem with my cat?"

"Nope," Bob said, admiring his diamond pinkie ring. "No problem."

Nobody spoke until Brynstone's phone rang. He snapped up the cell. Restricted call. He put it on speaker.

His wife blurted out the words, "John, where are you?"

"In town. You okay?"

Nothing.

"Kaylyn?"

"Welcome home, Herr Doktor." Metzger made no attempt to smother his sharp accent. "You may think I'm beneath you, but you'll find I'm a fearsome challenger."

"Cut the crap and tell me where to find my family."

"The Linda Vista Hospital in Boyle Heights. Be here in twenty."

"Let me talk to my wife."

Metzger hung up. The waiting game was over. Jordan was strapping on her Kevlar. Bob the Driver was already pulling onto La Cienega Boulevard.

"Head for I-105 East," Brynstone ordered. "From there, we'll go to I-110 North. Move."

The Linda Vista Community Hospital had been built in 1937 as an east-LA hospital for Santa Fe Railroad employees. Now the art-deco building was locked behind a wall of chain link and razor-ribbon wire. After medical operations ceased in 1990, Linda Vista had survived the decades—not always with grace—as a set for film crews. Years back, Brynstone had passed through Boyle Heights and recognized the building from TV medical dramas and a low-budget horror movie.

Turning off South Chicago, Bob the Driver pulled up beside a portico with a red Spanish tiled rooftop. A shattered padlock rested in front of a wide gate. Brynstone jumped out before the Lincoln Navigator rolled to a stop, taking a look around. Jordan handed out comm sets as the team joined him. He planned the approach and entry into the hospital as the team locked and loaded their H&K MP5 submachine guns.

"We're moving on a quick and dirty contingency here. If you see Metzger, take him down, no questions. After we enter, we'll break into two teams. Bob, you're

on overwatch." He paused. "Thanks everybody for helping get my family back."

The team gave him a nod, acknowledging the plan and
his gratitude.

Brynstone was running the operation in the mind of
everyone but Bob the Driver. He could tell the guy was
itching to be on the entry team, but he had the most snip-
ing experience in the group, hands down. Bob's eyes revealed he was pissed off about the assignment, but he
grabbed a PSG-1 semiautomatic sniper rifle and posted
up outside the portico, keeping watch for anyone coming out. Brynstone placed Banshee on the floor of the
Navigator, then closed the door. The cat stared at him,
swishing her tail in a wide swath as she made an ex-
haled snort.

He could tell she didn't like her assignment any better
than Bob.

Brynstone moved under the walkway, then kicked
opened the portico gate. He sprinted ahead, leading the
squad in a snake pattern to the ambulance entrance. A
window had been broken near the door. He paused beside it. "Sound suppressors on?"

Everyone nodded. They were decked out in Kevlar and
tactical gear.

"Breech and clear?" Cloud asked.

"Negative," he answered. "My family's inside. There's
no room for error."

He checked the emergency entrance for explosives.
Finding it safe, he went in Linda Vista's admission area as
point. The place surprised him. He'd expected to find
abandoned hospital rooms with boarded-up windows. Although aging, Linda Vista's first floor had been scrubbed
and renovated to attract filmmakers. It seemed like a normal hospital with all the equipment and beds and facilities, but no people. And that, along with the deathly
stillness, made the place chilling. Linda Vista had been associated with supernatural sightings, everything from a

giggling little girl to the ghost of a mental patient locked inside a cage.

The squad spread out and cleared the room, sweeping from left to right, then moving into their respective areas of responsibility. From her AOR, Jordan whispered in her comm set, "Clear." Brynstone joined in with Cloud and Tilton, each reporting the area clear as they proceeded through the first floor. That's when Brynstone's cell vibrated. He answered it.

"Who are your friends?" Metzger asked. "LAPD? FBI?"

"I don't work with cops. Don't like 'em any better than you do."

A faint chuckle. "Why is that, Dr. Brynstone?"

"Long story. Hand over my wife and kid and I'll tell you over a cold beer."

Another chuckle. "I almost like you."

"Terrific. Where's Kaylyn and my daughter?"

"Want to know?" Metzger taunted. "Come find us." He hung up.

Brynstone glanced outside the window. He had ordered Bob the Driver to post up outside the portico. The man wasn't there. He tried to reach him. No answer.

"Where's Bob? Anyone see him?"

"Don't know," Tilton grunted. "Guy's a Section Eight. Always one for tie-ups."

"If that lunatic blows this," Brynstone growled, "my wife and baby pay the price."

Metzger saw a man with long greasy hair in the hospital stairwell. Shame it wasn't Dr. Brynstone, but he sensed this fellow would provide amusement. This one was a rebel. A man ready for action. He had been posted outside the hospital. Metzger had lingered in front of a window, allowing himself to be seen. As expected, the man had deserted his post. Why? He liked the glory that would come from tracking down the world's greatest assassin. The evidence was in his smirk.

Like a specter, Metzger followed him down the stairs. His prey had no clue. He admired the sniper rifle. He had a nice view of the *Präzisionsscharfschützengewehr* as it hung from the man's back. Five months back in Hamburg, he had taken out a *Spezialeinsatzkommando* who packed a PSG-1. A dangerous weapon in the wrong hands.

The man kissed his pinkie ring. His arm, extended as he sighted down his pistol, was decorated with a tattoo: KILL OR BE KILLED. It was his creed, Metzger guessed, spelled in ink across his skin. Leading with his sidearm, a Heckler & Koch USP40, the man stepped off the stairs, then looked around. He sucked in a breath when he saw a woman thirty feet away, tied to a chair. No doubt the man was thinking this would be easy. Time to introduce him to reality.

"Excuse me, are you lost?" Metzger asked with a welcome expression, looking like a neighbor coming over to introduce himself.

The guy raised the pistol. Metzger brought out his gun and fired at the man's wrist, then his bicep on the same arm. The USP40 slid away as he dropped it. Moving to clutch his bleeding right arm, he squeezed his eyes in pain.

"Okay, you surprised me," the man wheezed. "But you should've killed me when you had the chance."

He chuckled, a feigned sympathy on his face. "Why is that, I wonder?"

"'Cause you lost the advantage. I know you're Erich Metzger."

"Then you do have the advantage, because I don't know you."

"Name's Bob Macintyre. And, my friend, you're gonna wish you'd never heard the name." He reached back with his left hand for the sniper rifle.

Metzger fired twice, the bullets making a *thwack* sound as they burst out the suppressor, shattering both of the man's kneecaps. He dropped to the floor, letting out a guttural scream and rolling on his side as his body lapsed into shock. Icy sweat coated his face.

He was fighting the pain. The man was tough.

"You were correct when you said I missed the chance to kill you." Metzger's cold eyes sparkled. "Believe me, there are few things I relish more than killing Irishmen. But why do you assume it was my last chance to murder you?"

Bob's pupils dilated inside his vacant eyes. He groaned, "You like to play games, huh?"

"*Ja*," Metzger winked. "I like games. Know why? Because I always win."

Chapter Thirty-seven

Potomac
5:34 P.M.

The Knight found Gabriel Bitonti waiting near the portico. Despite his age, the Vatican doctor was baby-faced, with ruffled dark hair. His suit was modest, but well tailored.

"How is the Pope?" the Knight asked.

"His Holiness is well. Thank you for asking."

Passing through a glass atrium, Bitonti admired the panoramic view of snow-draped meadows and woods. The Knight directed him into the library.

"It was good of you to come on such short notice," he said, easing into a wingback chair. "I have news that will delight the Pope. Soon, I will have in my hands the Radix."

"How can this be?" Bitonti leaned forward. "The Radix vanished centuries ago."

"It has been recovered."

Thinking it over, the doctor pulled back. "If you are correct, I would need to examine the Radix before the Holy Father sees it."

"Of course," the Knight said, pressing tobacco into his pipe. "That is why I have brought you here. You have a reputation as a skeptic."

"It is true. I have examined countless 'miracles' and found them wanting. I go into each investigation as a pessimist and pray I will emerge an optimist. I seldom authenticate miracles."

"You are the world's expert on such matters," the Knight said, lighting his pipe.

He had long admired Bitonti's work on medical miracles and healing relics. As a consultant to the Pontifical Institute of Christian Archeology, Bitonti had discussed some of Christendom's greatest healing relics, such as the Edessa Cloth. Sometimes known as the Mandylion—an Arabic term meaning "little veil"—it was a cloth Jesus Christ had used to wipe his face, imprinting it with his features. He gave the cloth to Hannan, who presented it to King Abgar of Edessa. After touching the cloth, Abgar's leprosy vanished. Around 525 CE, the cloth had been discovered above an Edessan city gate. It vanished during the Crusades in 1204.

The history of Christianity was littered with mythical healing agents, ranging from the Holy Grail to the shadow of Saint Peter. Even some Marian plants and herbs—symbolizing the Virgin Mother—were said to possess healing powers. Bitonti had been skeptical about them.

"I look forward to your investigation of the Radix. You will not be disappointed."

"I would delight in telling the Holy Father that what you have found is authentic."

"Indeed. But the Radix will come at a price."

"You want money?" Bitonti snorted. "You have more than enough money."

"I want something more precious than money," he said as smoke rolled over his lips. "Tell me, what is the current state of Geoffrey Cuvier's health?"

The question surprised Bitonti. "The grand master of the Sovereign Military Order of Malta is quite ill. Cuvier is not expected to see the new year."

"After Cuvier's death, the Pope will need to approve the election of a new grand master."

Like his father and grandfather, the Knight belonged to the Order of Malta. Better known as the Knights of Malta, the elite Roman Catholic organization could be traced to the First Crusade. Headquartered in Rome, the order was recognized by international law as a landless sovereign nation that issued coins, stamps, license plates, and passports. Some regarded it as the world's smallest country. Since 1994, the order held permanent observer status at the United Nations. Its members honored distinguished Catholics and provided humanitarian and medical assistance to the poor and needy.

The Knight believed that the Order of Malta could succeed at reaching a far greater goal. Two additional knights agreed with him. The other members—all blind fools—had rejected his plan. After the Holy See made him the grand master, he would recast the Order of Malta to achieve more ambitious objectives. First, he needed the Radix.

"Let me understand," Bitonti said. "If you deliver the Radix to the Vatican—"

"I would demand the Pope approve my election as grand master of the Sovereign Military Order of Malta."

"No one can deny the power you hold outside the Church. And your private donations are substantial. Still, the Holy Father would have reservations about approving your election to the top position within the Knights of Malta. A dark shadow haunts your family. Your father tainted the Church with the scandal involving our Institute for Religious Works."

"You're speaking about the alleged laundering of Nazi gold through the Vatican Bank."

"The bank was never involved in anything like that, but I have heard stories that Nazi resources provided the foundation for your family's considerable wealth."

"My father was removed as a Vatican Bank advisor, but the Order of Malta did not revoke his knighthood. They made me a knight in spite of ridiculous rumors."

"Rumors or not, the Holy Father takes them seriously."

"Tell the Pope to ignore such rumors. It is I whom he must take seriously, not my father."

Chapter Thirty-eight

Los Angeles
2:50 P.M.

Brynstone searched the Linda Vista Hospital. On the first floor, he found a cluttered file room. Overturned green bookshelves had collapsed onto strewn papers and boxes. Farther down the wing, Jordan searched the morgue, X-ray facility, and autopsy rooms. On the second floor, Cloud reported in after checking the medical wing and exam rooms. Tilton had looked around a chapel, kitchen, cafeteria, and dayroom.

No sign of his family or the assassin.

Brynstone returned to the admission area on the first floor while Jordan moved to the third floor with Tilton. Cloud searched the fourth. It was clear Metzger liked mind games. His favorite? A sadistic version of cat and mouse. He flashed back to when the assassin had called about Linda Vista. What had he said? He remembered now. *You may think I'm beneath you, but you'll find*

I'm a fearsome challenger. He repeated the words: "I'm beneath you."

Was Metzger giving his location?

Brynstone ran toward a basement door, calling the others to follow. Leading with the MP5, he moved down a corridor opening into a grimy boiler room. Under a canopy of rusted pipes, a desolate brick wall framed a huge red boiler. Gang graffiti decorated the walls. He checked behind an air duct that had been spray-painted to resemble an enormous green snake.

A pipe creaked inside the wall, making an unnerving sound. He paused at a decrepit door. With the barrel of his MP5, he eased it open, moving forward and staying low. His eyes strained as he glanced at stairs leading down to a filthy cement floor. He made it to the landing. Fresh blood spatter down here. He peered around the corner. The basement had been redecorated as a prison set for a low-budget movie.

As he looked down his sights, sweeping through the room, he saw a woman thirty feet away. Kaylyn was seated inside a jail cell, displayed like a trophy behind bars. He couldn't tell if she was alive or dead. Shay was nowhere in sight.

Jordan hurried down the stairs with Tilton and Cloud. They found Brynstone standing in the dank basement. Each moved to one side of the room, taking cover along the wall. With a sharp motion of his hand, he signaled to move forward. They followed his lead, spiraling across the basement. Their boots made light scuffing sounds across the concrete.

He headed to his wife, fighting the urge to sprint toward her. He reached the jail cell and ran his hand up the door, making sure it wasn't rigged. The metal bars creaked open. Inside, she was tied to a chair. Her head drooped. Tangled hair covered her face, reaching to her chest. The ripped blouse hanging off her shoulder was stained with blood. Her gaunt arms trembled.

What had Metzger done to her?

"I'm sorry, Kaylyn," he whispered, kneeling to work on the ropes.

Her head shot up. She blinked with terrified eyes. A strip of electrician's tape covered her mouth. Brynstone jolted backward, staring at her.

Jordan hustled over and began cutting the ropes at her feet.

Cloud patted his back. "Don't see Bob or your baby. At least we found your wife."

He didn't answer. He couldn't take his gaze off her. ·

"Dr. Brynstone? What's wrong?"

Without blinking, he whispered, "She's not my wife."

Tied to the chair, the ravaged teenager looked at him with dazed eyes. A trail of needle marks scored her grimy arm. She wore Bob the Driver's pinkie ring on her finger.

"We're running out of time," Brynstone said. "Find Metzger. Go."

As Jordan and the team sprinted away, he quizzed the girl. Metzger had abducted her from Hollenbeck Park, then dragged her to Linda Vista. The assassin had slipped Bob's ring on her hand before wiping blood across her mouth. After confessing all this, the teenager shuddered. She didn't know anything about Kaylyn or Shay. Brynstone turned away.

The girl darted off like a scared deer, heading up the stairs. He let her go. She'd been through enough. He let her keep the ring. He had a feeling Bob wouldn't miss it. Maybe she'd pawn the ring and use the money for something other than heroin.

Right.

He returned to the emergency entrance, his mind racing. Movement outside caught his eye. In a black blur, Banshee bounded onto the window ledge, then squeezed through the opening in the broken glass. Jumping to the floor, the cat grunted as she stared at him.

He frowned. "How did you get out of the car?"

Following instinct, he darted outside the lobby entrance with the cat chasing him. The SUV was parked in the courtyard. Bob the Driver was nowhere in sight.

"Get to the front," he whispered into his comm.

He could see something inside the Navigator. He had no way of knowing if Metzger had his sights set on the vehicle, but Brynstone knew he had to move. Staying low, he hustled to the car, sliding down beside it. As he opened the driver's-side door, Bob Macintyre's body slumped sideways, collapsing into his arms. He shoved Macintyre back onto the driver's seat. His body showed multiple bullet wounds, including one in the forehead.

The ex-NSA ops team joined him. Jordan scanned the rooftop, searching for Metzger.

"Call someone to get Bob's body."

"I'm on it," Tilton answered.

Brynstone studied the dead man's face. Blood encircled his lips as on the heroin addict's mouth. He thought for a beat, then crammed his fingers between Macintyre's lips.

"What are you doing?" Jordan asked, coming over.

He didn't answer, forcing his fingers deeper inside the man's throat like a kid cramming his hand inside a gumball machine. He removed a ring. He closed the man's mouth, then wiped Kaylyn's wedding band. Metzger had scratched a message into the ring.

"What's it say?" Jordan asked.

He looked at her. "It says, 'Go home.'"

Potomac
6:00 P.M.

"Che bello," Gabriel Bitonti said. "Your gallery is impressive."

The Knight smiled. He enjoyed showing his art collection.

Bitonti admired a Cy Twombly painting. "I saw this at

the Venice Biennale," he said, staring at the twelve-panel piece. "Must be worth ten million."

"About that on the secondary market. Follow me. I would appreciate your opinion."

He directed the doctor to a painting at the end of the gallery. Bitonti took a step back when he saw the painting of Saint Sebastian tied to a tree, his body pierced with arrows.

"I don't recognize the artist. The work is reminiscent of Velázquez, but with greater animation." He moved to the next painting. "And this one. The same artist. The crucifixion of Saint Peter. Who painted this?"

"I did," the Knight said.

"I'm impressed." Bitonti returned his attention to the painting of a curly-haired man nailed upside down on a cross. "The realism astounds me. I feel as if the man is screaming through the paint. I can almost hear his cries of agony."

"I go to great effort to capture emotion. Even as a child, I desired a career as a painter. I took a year from college to study at the Sorbonne, but my father had other ideas. Despite the demands of my career, the artist within me never perished."

Cress emerged from the studio, carrying a large canvas. He brought it to the doctor.

"I am far from finished, but this is my latest work," the Knight said. "As you can see, it is a painting of the crucifixion of Saint Andrew on the cross saltire."

Bitonti clasped his hands. "It is beautiful in a disturbing way. Your fluency with the brush is staggering. I have a great interest in seeing where such creativity is brought to birth. May I see your studio?"

"Another time perhaps." He motioned for Cress to take away the painting. "I'm afraid my studio is in a frightful disarray." The Knight grabbed his arm, then led him to the dining room. "Besides, it's time for our Christmas dinner."

Fifteen minutes later, he sliced into the wild goose on

his plate. Sitting across the table, Bitonti raised his glass of Chardonnay. His phone interrupted the toast. The Vatican doctor lowered his wine glass, then reached for his cell.

After Bitonti excused himself and moved to the next room, the Knight summoned Max Cress. "Have you disposed of Andy's body?" he whispered.

"Yes, sir. And we wiped his blood from your sword."

Cress backed away as Bitonti returned.

"I bring urgent news from the Vatican. A doctor from the Palazzo di Malta called to say last rites have been administered to Grand Master Cuvier."

"It is a sign," the Knight announced. "The Knights of Malta will need a new leader."

"So it seems," Bitonti said, returning to his seat at the long dining table.

"If I presented the Radix to the Vatican, could I be assured of becoming grand master?"

"I do not make such decisions, but the Holy Father will be anxious to name Cuvier's successor. I shall speak to my colleagues at the Consulta Medica. If we authenticate the Radix, it might strengthen your case." Bitonti leaned forward. "I wish to investigate the relic and report to the Vatican. When may I see it?"

"Soon," the Knight assured him. "Perhaps tonight."

Los Angeles
3:29 P.M.

Brynstone parked outside his Tudor home in the Hancock Park neighborhood. No sign of a forced entry. The house looked quiet.

Steve Cloud leaned in from the back seat. "How do you keep your cool? If Metzger kidnapped my wife, I'd lose it."

"Don't allow myself that luxury," he answered. Before opening the Navigator's door, he turned to Jordan, Cloud, and Tilton. "Metzger could be in the house. Cover me as I go in."

Banshee bolted toward the front door. Brynstone sprinted after her and unlocked it.

Inside the house, the team moved from room to room.

He checked the living room, indulging a fantasy about finding Kaylyn and Shay, safe and waiting for him. Metzger wouldn't make it that easy, but reality didn't diminish the hope. His homecoming felt bittersweet when he spotted his daughter's unopened Christmas presents. On a pedestal, Kaylyn's *Eclipse* sculpture reminded him about the day he'd bought it at an LA gallery. The house seemed lifeless without his family.

He was searching his wife's studio when Jordan's call came over the comm.

"John," she said, "I'm in the basement. Get down here."

He raced downstairs, then hurried through the kitchen and took the basement stairs. His heart sank. No sign of his wife or daughter. Jordan and Cloud stood over a man sprawled on the floor. Watching them, Banshee tiptoed around the top of the water heater.

"Your cat squealed. That's what brought me down here." Jordan said. "Know the guy?"

He nodded, staring at the body. "A neighbor."

Bill Adler was a widower and a former CIA spook. Whenever Brynstone was in the field, he kept an eye on Kaylyn and Shay. Adler must've caught Metzger breaking into the house.

"See the blood on the steps? Looks like he was dragged down. Cloud found spatter near your piano. Bet that's where your neighbor was killed."

Dried blood encircled Adler's mouth, just as it had on Bob the Driver. Brynstone parted the dead man's lips. He took a flashlight and shone light inside the exposed mouth. A message was stitched in black thread on Bill Adler's tongue:

Vegas 9p

"Enough games," Brynstone announced. "We're set-tling this in Las Vegas."

Chapter Thirty-nine

Bollingen, Switzerland
12:40 A.M.

Wintry and silent, a lake road known as the Uznacher-strasse invited Cori Cassidy and Edgar Wurm to the sleepy Swiss village of Bollingen. Awaiting them near the shallow upper end of Lake Zurich, Bollingen consisted of scattered buildings, farmhouses, and a commanding white church. She didn't see light in any windows as their chili red MINI Cooper passed through town. After taking a sharp turn, they drove under a railroad overpass and came to a small park with a playground.

The MINI's GPS directed them along a narrow road. Paved at first, the Strandweg turned to gravel, then ran parallel to train tracks. Farther down the Strandweg, they pulled into a parking spot beside a shed. Wurm grabbed a backpack of supplies he had found in an equip-ment cabinet on the jet. The woodland quiet was both tranquil and eerie. They stepped over a wire fence near a grassy triangle, then walked southward into the dark woods. Thorn bushes cut at their legs.

Jung's dream castle loomed ahead. Bollingen Tower was haunting. And haunted.

In his autobiography, Jung described the tower as "con-nected to the dead." One evening in 1924, the sound of strangers prowling around the tower awakened Jung. When he opened the bedroom shutters, he saw nothing. Thinking it a dream, he returned to bed. Before long, laughter, singing, and music flooded the woods. Jung sensed dark figures parading around the tower. He hurried to the window and again found nothing more than a "deathly still moonlit night." He learned later he was not the first to witness the *Sälig Lüt*. Known as the "departed folk," in Swiss legend, the phantoms were said to be Wotan's army of deceased souls.

Approaching the castle, they passed a row of woodpiles. Covered in snow, a deep trench ran straight toward the main structure. Jung had constructed high courtyard walls around Bollingen. Cori directed the flashlight at the vine-crossed wall. Odd dark stains marred the stone. The archways and turrets gave the look of a small medieval castle. They circled around the Bollingen complex, then made their way down to the gray lake. Moving past tall grasses and reeds along the rocky shore of the Obersee, they found the entrance. Above the entryway to Jung's Tower, Wurm pointed to a Latin inscription carved in stone.

PHILEMONIS SACRUM—FAUSTI POENITENTIA

"The Shrine of Philemon—Repentance of Faust," he told her.

Her mother's journal mentioned Jung's fascination with Faust. His grandfather, also Carl Jung, suggested he might be the illegitimate son of Johann Wolfgang Goethe, the renowned German poet who wrote *Faust*. Maybe like his grandfather, Jung had identified with Faust, the necromancer in German literature who sold his soul to Mephistopheles for wisdom and power.

The Jung family had locked the 2,300-square-foot lakeshore facility. Jung would have approved. During his time at Bollingen, he had raised colored "mood flags" that signaled whether he wanted visitors or privacy.

Wurm picked the gate's lock. He pushed open two doors on massive hinges. Twin towers dominated the stone courtyard. Jung had made four revisions to the complex over three decades, beginning in 1923 with his "maternal" tower. He had built it after his mother's death. The fortresslike door to the maternal tower wasn't locked. Cori led the way inside.

In silence, they wandered the timber-framed floor, discovering the tower's primitive charm. Jung had refused the convenience of electricity or running water at Bollingen. He'd insisted on chopping wood and pumping water from a well. Inside the cramped kitchen, an oversized stone mantel crowned the fireplace. Pans and utensils clustered on a shelf. A wall peg displayed the leather apron Jung had used when dressing stone. Burlap swatches covered some wall paintings. She lifted one flap, finding Jung's painting of a moon and stars.

Hanging onto a guide rope, they navigated narrow steps to the second floor. In an upstairs room, they discovered a large blue mandala—a "magic circle" that symbolized selfhood—painted above Jung's bed. An enormous mural of Philemon spread across his bedroom wall. Jung had painted his spiritual guide with a flowing white beard, held aloft by blazing kingfisher wings. Philemon stared right at them.

The creepy part about the image? Philemon looked like Edgar Wurm.

"Let's check the other tower," Cori said, uneasiness seeping into her voice.

Moving outside, she watched as Wurm picked the lock leading to the second tower.

"My childhood fascination with Harry Houdini inspired this skill," he told her. "By the time I was five, there wasn't a lock I couldn't pick."

She frowned at the thought of a five-year-old spending his days picking locks. Wurm must have been as bizarre a child as he was an adult.

"Jung's Number Two personality inspired this tower," he said.

Since childhood, Jung had believed he had competing sides to his personality. His "Number One" personality, as he called it, was grounded in logic and science. This side inspired Jung to become a man of science and the founder of a famous school of psychotherapy. His "Number Two" personality, by contrast, was drawn to mysticism and pagan spirituality. Moving away from psychoanalysis, his Number Two explored a psychology grounded in things like alchemy and Gnosticism. Like Jung's father, Sigmund Freud adored the Number One personality, but detested Number Two. As Jung aged, he plunged into the mystical side of his Number Two personality.

Jung had built the first tower as a maternal structure, a tribute to his mother and his wife, Emma. In 1931, Jung began construction on a second tower. More slender than the original, the second tower became Jung's "place of spiritual concentration." Centered between the two towers, he constructed a second-story bedroom and office that he called the chapel. He kept the keys to his spiritual tower and the chapel around his neck at all times. No one entered without his permission.

Wurm waved his hand, inviting her to enter.

Jung's spiritual tower was overwhelming, almost as if they had climbed inside his unconscious mind. Cori didn't believe in ghosts, but a disquieting feeling came over her. She sensed Jung's presence.

Wurm pulled battery-powered halogen lamps from his backpack. He flipped them on, blasting the room with light. Cori turned in a slow circle, taking it in. Jung had described the second tower as "my confession of faith in stone," a confession to his faith in alchemy, Gnosticism, and pagan mythology. He had adorned the interior with graffiti representing his dreams and visions. Symbols and images crammed the curved walls, some painted in vibrant colors, others carved into stone. A wolf devoured a dead king. Mercury straddled the globe with winged feet. Beneath a galaxy, an Egyptian crescent ship sailed into the underworld. Jonah languished inside a whale. A green lion feasted on the sun.

"This place is surreal," she said.

Jung had decorated the tower walls with more mandalas. He'd included geometrical symbols representing selfhood from Navajo Indian sand paintings and the Tibetan Wheel of Life. Inspired by alchemy, a menagerie of creatures prowled the tower walls. Dragons acted as silent sentries along with falcons, bulls, fishes, unicorns, and scarab beetles. Philemon made an appearance too, but rendered in small colorful tiles. The mosaic gallery also featured life-size images of Faust, a Christian saint, and a brown leathery dwarf.

Quotations from Goethe, Paracelsus, Dante, and Milton emblazoned the tower wall. Jung had memorialized their words in Latin, Greek, English, Old Swiss, German, and Sanskrit. Wurm pressed his face against the wall, running fingers into the engraved symbols. He looked like a veteran touching names etched into the granite skin of the Vietnam Memorial wall.

"There are answers in this room," she whispered. "But where do we begin?"

"With the Tree of Life," he answered, pointing. Protruding from the wall, a sculpture of a white oak climbed the tower. Albino serpents coiled up the tree like vines. Beneath a knothole, Jung had carved two words into the trunk: ARBOR PHILOSOPHICA.

"Tree of the Philosophers," he announced. "Another name for the Tree of Life."

She realized her mother's message about the tree of life blossoming in the land of the dead referred to *this* tree. Bollingen was a stone representation of Jung's unconscious, the Land of the Dead. They'd found a tree inside a metaphor of Jung's mind.

"Wotan hung from the World Tree to gain wisdom. Maybe we should try it."

Cori stuck her foot into a knothole, climbing as she reached for the next one. She grabbed a stone serpent, then pulled herself to another foothold. Wurm trained his flashlight beam on her lithe body as she scaled the stone tree. She climbed up twelve feet.

"See anything?" he called.

"Words and images. Nothing jumps out."

A tree branch reached out near the top. Looping her legs around it, she anchored her foot, then hung upside down. She'd executed this move a hundred times in gymnastics class, but not since middle school. Back then, golden hair had hung like a curtain around her face. Blood ran to her head now as she scanned the walls. "Shine the light over there."

Wurm directed the beam higher on the wall. "What do you see?"

She grabbed the branch, tilting her flushed head upright to relieve the pressure. She pointed at four letters carved into the wall.

HSVS

Clinging to the branch, she turned upside down again.

Looking up, Wurm cocked his head, reading the words upside down. "What do you know? If you fill in the V to make it an A, you get s-a-s-h." He chuckled. "Sash."

Cori dangled from the tree carved into Jung's second tower. One stone branch looked more straight and smooth than the others. She managed to unscrew it from the trunk. She studied the branch, then dropped it to Wurm.

"Jung engraved the word *sash* at the top of this tower," she said, climbing down. "Does a sash have anything to do with the Scintilla?"

"Maybe it refers to the Holy Sash. Remember Thomas the apostle? He doubted Christ's resurrection."

"I remember," she said, wiping dusty hands. "Doubting Thomas wasn't there to see it, so he didn't believe."

"Turns out he wasn't around when the Virgin Mother ascended into heaven, either. Interesting things always seemed to happen when the guy was out of the room."

"Did he doubt Mary's ascension?" she asked.

"Thomas needed proof. Know what convinced him? The Virgin tossed her glittering sash to him. That did the trick. For a time, the Church of France was said to have possessed the sash as a relic. Disappeared centuries ago." Wurm's voice trailed off as she walked to the wall.

Jung had portrayed four figures in mosaic. Faust and Philemon stood beside the mosaic saint, a bearded man with a halo. "This guy has a sash," she said, pointing to rows of red tile encircling the saint's waist. "Is he Thomas?"

"Christian iconography portrays saints with certain symbols. Judas is often dressed in yellow. Peter holds keys. Thomas wears a red sash."

She ran her fingers around the border. Placing her hands on the red tiles, she pushed. A shallow drawer slid out.

"Hey," Wurm chuckled. "How'd you know to do that?"

"Good guess." She removed a leather bag from the drawer. A CGJ monogram branded the bag. Untying the drawstrings, she pulled out a black, red, and gold sash. "I read about this on the plane. Jung's grandfather attended an 1817 festival at the Wartburg Castle, near Eisenach. While demonstrating in favor of a national state, scores of university students wore sashes and marched with torches."

He studied it. "Same colors as the German flag."

"I read that later, when the German feudal states united, the black-red-gold scheme of the Wartburg festival sash was adopted for the flag." She unfolded the sash. "Hmm. The Wartburg sash didn't have letters," she said, looking at two rows of faded letters embroidered on the front. "Someone stitched these words on the sash. Maybe Jung. Or maybe his grandfather."

ALKAHEST♃HORUSARGENTUM
NEKYIATYRESYMBOLELIXIR

As if she were looking at tickertape, Cori ran her hands across the sash as Wurm held it. *"Alkahest,"* she said, reading the first word. "That's an alchemical term used to describe a universal solvent. And the next letters spell *Horus*. But what's the symbol between them?"

"It's a symbol for Jupiter, the chief god of the Roman state religion," Wurm answered. "And that last word is *argentum*. That's the Latin name for silver. The alchemists used it. *Argentum* inspired silver's 'Ag' title on the periodic table."

"And *Nekyia*," Cori said, looking at the next line. "It refers to the Greek poem, where Odysseus descended into the underworld. He journeyed into the Land of the Dead."

"That next word doesn't come from alchemy," he said, "but Tyre is important for Freemasons. King Hiram of Tyre sent materials and workers to King Solomon to help build the temple. Freemasonry is called the royal art, because the kings of Israel and Tyre founded it."

"There's also *symbol* and *elixir*. The words on this sash come from alchemy, mythology, and Freemasonry," she observed. "But what do they mean for us?"

She turned the sash, finding two additional rows of cryptic characters. The letters looked brighter. Although matched in style to the words on the opposite side, the characters were embroidered in a heavier thread. Cori guessed a different person had stitched this message.

LIFEHERABEYAORCUS26ISISSAL
EVEWODANREXNIGHTSEATURM

"Life," she started reading. "Hera. Beya, a figure in alchemy. What's *Orcus* mean?"

"Orcus is a figure in Roman mythology," Wurm said. "Like Pluto, he was the god of the underworld. The ruler of the Land of the Dead."

"And maybe 26 refers to Jung's July twenty-sixth birthday," she continued. "After that, the Egyptian goddess Isis. *Sal*, the alchemical name for the ingredient salt. Eve. Wodan, a variation of Wotan. *Rex*, the Latin name for king, used by the alchemists. The night sea journey, same as *Nekyia* on the opposite side of the sash."

"And *Turm* is the German word for 'tower,'" Wurm added. "Der Turm was Jung's name for this place. Perhaps these words can help us find the Scintilla."

"Maybe the first letter of each word spells something." She recited the first two rows as A-ℐ-H-A and N-T-S-E. "No luck. Maybe it's meant to be an acronym."

"It isn't an acronym." Wurm studied the sash. "Ever hear of a scytale?" he asked, pronouncing it like *Italy*.

She shook her head.

"It's a transposition cipher." He wrapped the sash around his arm. "Goes back to the Spartans in the fifth century BCE. According to the Greek historian Thucydides, a general named Lysander created ciphers by wrapping a strip of leather or papyrus around a wooden baton."

"Like a grip on a tennis racket?"

"Exactly. After wrapping it, you cut or burn letters into the belt." He pointed to letters running in a vertical pattern down his arm. "Unwrap it from the baton, and you get a pattern of letters that appear random and meaningless." Wurm unwrapped the sash. "However, the person receiving the scytale must have the same diameter of baton to line up the characters. If it's a different size, it won't make sense."

"But wait. This sash must not form a scytale, because the characters are not random or meaningless. Like *Nekyia*. Jung used that term in his analytical psychology."

Wurm nodded. "And yet, our faithful guide, Dr. Jung, has a history of subterfuge. Perhaps he concealed his scytale message inside the illusion of meaningful words."

"Let's say you're right. Then our sash needs a baton."

"Look for something like a staff, cane, or sword," he said, searching the tower. "I have an idea. Bring the sash. Follow me." He darted out the door.

She joined him outside. Wurm headed to a stone tablet across the courtyard. A crackling sound came from behind. In the pale moonlight, a figure darted past the courtyard door.

"Did you see that?" Wurm asked. "We have company."

She thought about going back inside the tower, but decided to stick with him. Taking it slow, Wurm shone his flashlight across a trench outside the Bollingen complex. Cori shifted her gaze toward the forest and saw the fluttering branches of a Norway spruce. It wasn't the wind.

Wurm darted to the tree, brushing past it. "Stop right there," he shouted. *"Anschlag."*

Staying back, she saw woodland shadows and nothing more.

"Whoever it is, I guess they're gone," he said, heading back. "You know those stone tablets in the courtyard? Let's wrap the sash around the smaller one."

"I have a better idea," she said, heading for the tower.

Chapter Forty

"I can solve the scytale," Cori announced, back inside Jung's tower. She grabbed the stone branch she'd removed from the Tree of the Philosophers.

"You've changed," Wurm said. "You're decisive and in control. So different from the patient I met in Baltimore."

"Thanks," she answered, guessing he was stingy with compliments. She held the branch upright, with hands positioned at top and bottom. Wurm wrapped the sash like a medic winding gauze around a soldier's leg. She studied the embroidered white characters.

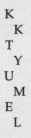

"The scytale characters aren't lining up," he observed. "Not the right diameter."

"Maybe the branch is right, but we have the wrong side of the sash."

He unwrapped it, then flipped the sash. The letters on

this side were sewn closer together. He centered a letter
at top and wrapped the sash around the branch. The letters aligned in a vertical column.

I
V
H
O
A
N
Y

"They line up better," he said. "Still doesn't tell us anything."

"There are two more sets of characters. I'll rotate it."
She turned the branch to read the second sequence.

L
E
E
W
R
A
E

"Could be someone's name," he suggested. "Lee Wrae-
something?"

She rotated the scytale, holding the top and bottom.
"Check out the words on this side."

F
E
E
D
B
R
A

"Feedbra?" he asked. "What's that supposed to mean?"

"Be patient. We haven't finished." She wrapped the last strip of scytale around the branch. She stood back and studied it. "Wish I knew what the message means."

Wurm ran his fingers down the characters.

F
E
E
D
B
R
A
N
C
H
2
E
S
U
S

"Jung missed a letter," he said, pointing below the number two. "See? He missed a *J*."

"Think it should read 'Jesus'? 'Feed branch to Jesus.' What's that supposed to mean?"

"How should I know?" he asked. "Let me rewrap it."

"No need," she said, rotating the scytale. "There's not a *J* anywhere on the sash."

"You're right," he fumed. "We're left feeding a branch to Esus. One problem, though. Who the hell is Esus?"

"Maybe John knows."

"Brynstone?" he snapped. "If he gave a damn, he'd be here."

"He's trying to rescue his wife and child," Cori said with ice coating her voice. "Someone wants to kill Kaylyn Brynstone and her daughter."

He waved his hand. "Fine. Let them do it fast, so Brynstone can get here to help us."

She reached up and slapped his face.

He grabbed her wrist, glaring with that dangerous look
again. "Give it to me," he growled. "Give me the Radix."

"Or you'll do what?" she asked. "You don't trust me
with it?"

"It's better in my hands."

"John gave it to me."

"Bad call on his part. You haven't earned the right. You
don't deserve the Radix."

"Tough. I'm keeping it, Edgar. Now let go of my wrist."

They locked their gaze, neither ready to yield. Wurm
was big and powerful, but she couldn't lose her nerve. He
snorted, then released her arm. He turned for the door. "I
need air."

"Good idea," she answered. "But while you're outside,
keep thinking about 'Feed branch to Esus.' Help me figure out what it means."

Wurm looked back. His right eye made a slight twitch.

She understood why he was acting like this. The Radix
could seduce even the strongest of wills. Her voice softened. "Keep your head together, Edgar. I need you."

He headed out the door.

Wurm breathed cool Swiss air. His mouth was growing
dry. He'd kicked a two-pack-a-day habit, but the nicotine
craving found him at the worst times. He stared at his
hand, sensing a smoldering cigarette between his fingers.
He drew in another cleansing breath. Playing to his ad-
diction, he dropped the phantom cigarette and stamped
it beneath his shoe.

He walked down to the snowy shore outside the Bollingen courtyard.

He respected Cori. That didn't mean Brynstone was
right to entrust the Radix to her. She wasn't fit to serve as
Keeper of the Radix. He had dedicated his life's work to

the holy root. He knew more about it than anyone. It was his destiny. The Radix was in his blood. It was a part of him. He had refused it because he thought he wasn't ready. But now? He hungered to be the Keeper. He glanced back at the tower.

For the moment, she was the Keeper. It was a mistake in need of correction.

Sooner or later, Wurm knew, he would need to take the root from Cori.

Even if it meant killing her.

Cori paced inside Jung's tower, waiting for Brynstone to answer his cell. When he picked up, she felt a giddy thrill hearing his rich voice. "John, where are you?"

"Headed to LAX. Stuck in traffic."

"Have you found Kaylyn and your daughter?"

"We're on a wild-goose chase," he grunted. "The man who kidnapped my family wants to meet in Vegas. He likes to play mind games. Hopefully, we play better than he does."

"Good luck, John," she said. "Real quick question. Esus. Mean anything to you?"

"Druid god to the Gauls," he answered. "Esus was a woodsman god, often portrayed with a hammer. A Celtic version of Hercules. His followers made human sacrifices, sometimes nailing criminals to oak trees in his honor. He's associated with the Green Man. Wurm should know about it. Call back if he doesn't."

"One more thing," she said. "How's Banshee?"

"Dropped her off with the Friedmans next door. She's not making the trip to Vegas."

"Aww. You should have let her come to Europe with us."

"Yeah. Wurm would have loved that."

After Cori ended the phone call, she found herself worrying about him.

"Talking to Brynstone?" Wurm asked, stepping inside Jung's spiritual tower.

"Mm-hmm," she said, whirling around. "He said you'd know about the Green Man."

"He was right." Wurm stretched. "The Green Man legend goes back to Egyptian mythology. Osiris was their god of nature and vegetation. In Egyptian paintings, he's often shown with green skin. Later Celtic legends described a god of tree worship based on Jack-in-the-Green, a creature who roamed the woodlands. Despite the Green Man's pagan background, he's immortalized in medieval churches all across Europe."

"Immortalized how?"

He led her to a relief on Jung's wall. Flowing leaves surrounded a carved face. The eyebrows, hair, cheeks, and beard created a mask of foliage. Curled horns jutted from the creature's forehead.

"John said the Green Man is associated with Esus. Like the scytale says, we need to 'feed branch to Esus.'" She tried to insert the branch in the Green Man's mouth. Didn't work. She flipped the branch, trying the other end. It slid inside the mouth like a key inside a lock. A rumbling sound echoed below. A rectangular hatch opened at the base of the wall.

"You found a passage," Wurm marveled.

They knelt and examined the opening with their flashlights. Six red letters painted inside the passageway jumped into view. "We're on the right track," she said. "See?"

Wurm smiled, reading the word. "Nekyia."

Nekyia was a central theme in Jungian psychology. To achieve psychological wholeness, a person must take a night-sea journey into the unconscious mind. Ancient mythology had inspired Jung's notion. The Egyptians believed that upon death, the soul traveled on a boat through the world of night. During the journey, the soul had to face a series of challenges before reaching the promise of rebirth at dawn. Jung found examples of Nekyia in the legend of Jonah inside the great fish and the story of Odysseus descending into Hades. A person undergoing Jungian analysis must make a similar journey toward "individuation," emerging as a more complete person. The idea fit his notion that therapy—like alchemy—could transform people.

"Think we can squeeze into that hatch?" Wurm asked, scratching his head.

She handed her coat to him. "Jung was a big guy like you. If he did it, you can do it."

He winked. "Ladies first."

A mildew odor tickled Cori's nose as she squeezed headfirst into the Nekyia opening. Without warning, she slid down a metal chute into blackness. She splashed into frigid water. Completely submerged. Desperate for air, she flailed about underwater. She couldn't tell if her body was up or down until her elbow scraped bottom. She panicked, realizing she had nearly hit her head on the watery floor of Jung's subterranean chamber. She rolled, then planted her feet. She lunged upward, bursting above the water. Disoriented and choking, she rubbed her eyes and glanced up at the hatch opening, seeing Wurm's silhouette in the rectangle of light.

"You all right?" he called.

"Flooded down here," she sputtered between coughs.

"No surprise, given the proximity to the lake."

"Can't see a thing. Lost my flashlight." Water swirled around her chest. "Inside the opening, a slide drops down about twelve feet. Find a rope."

"I brought a climber's rig from the jet. Used to be a mountain climber, you know. Years ago, I climbed the Eiger in the Bernese Oberland here in Switzerland."

"*Edgar*," she shouted, "just get a rope. Tie it to the Tree of the Philosophers."

Cori splashed through the dark water. Fumbling, she

found the wall. It was too slick to climb. After wiping bangs off her wet forehead, she plunged her hand back into the water, then patted her jeans. She felt the Radix tucked inside her pocket. Hopefully, the vial was water-tight.

It was dark down here, but she explored the submerged cavern. She drifted to a different wall, trying to make sense of this place. Then something cold slithered past her shoulder.

Chapter Forty-one

Bollingen
1:17 A.M.

Wurm was sliding on a spelunker's headlamp when he heard Cori's scream, harsh and piercing, from down in the watery chamber. He fed the rope's free end into the Nekyia opening. Wiggling to squeeze inside, he followed the rope, easing in feetfirst. He crammed his large frame through the rectangular hole, scraping skin on his back.

Cori wouldn't stop screaming.

"What's wrong?" he yelled. He moved down the slide, clinging to the taut rope. Stopping at the slide's level bottom, he held out his hand in the blackness and pulled her onto the landing. Dripping wet, she scrambled into his arms. Keeping his balance, he hugged her shivering body. He slid spelunker headgear on Cori, positioning the LED lamp on her forehead.

"There's a snake down here," she gasped. "I hate snakes."

"So did Jung." He scanned the black water, then looked

over at the wall. Paintings and symbols covered its surface. He squinted at the water. Something broke the surface. He touched the nape of her neck, wet hair clinging to his fingers as he turned her head.

"That's no snake. Take a look."

A white arm floated on the water with fingers pointing upward.

She shuddered, curling into his chest. He released her, then climbed off the slide's bottom. He eased into the water, lowering himself to the submerged floor.

"Be careful," she warned.

Icy water splashed around his stomach. He couldn't resist the thought of Gilgamesh, the ancient Mesopotamian hero, plunging to the bottom of the sea to find a plant that offered the elixir of life. As he moved to the wall, something grazed his waist. He fished around, then caught it. A leg. He followed it to the hip, then ran his fingers across the corpse's stomach. Finding the shoulders, he raised it above water. A woman. With wet clothes clinging to her body, her flesh was blue and swollen. Wurm cringed. He recognized her.

"Her name is Lucrezia Borgia," he called. "Named after Cesare Borgia's sister."

He stared into the woman's blank eyes. Distended lips had curled open as if about to speak. Her hair covered a wide gash.

"What happened to her?"

"Struck her head, I think, then drowned."

"Not surprised," Cori called. "I almost did the same thing."

"I'm sorry," he whispered to the woman in his arms. "Poor Lucrezia."

After crawling up to the hatch, Wurm dug in the backpack. He removed a climbing harness, then lowered it down to Cori. She strapped Lucrezia Borgia in the harness. He hauled her dripping corpse from the Nekyia chamber. After unfastening the harness, he carried Lucrezia to Jung's bedroom in the maternal tower.

He hurried back to the spiritual tower, where Cori waited down in the chamber.

Before joining her, he stuck his head inside the chamber. His caving lamp brightened the area above the hatch door. He saw where Jung had constructed a primitive network of weights, pulleys, and siphons that opened the hatch when the branch was inserted into the mouth of Esus. Once opened, a person's weight on the slide would activate a primitive timer. After clicking off the minutes, the timer would trigger a force pump to close the hatch. Wurm smiled. Jung's design brought to mind the ancient scientist Hero and his studies on hydromechanics.

"Let's not waste time," he advised, making his way down the slide. "This hatch will close again, sealing us in here like it did for Lucrezia."

"How much time do we have?"

"Maybe a half hour." He checked his water-resistant watch. "I'm guessing we opened the hatch around one seventeen, Central European Time."

Standing with him on the slide, she pointed. "Edgar, look over there."

Three papers floated on the surface where he had fished out Lucrezia's body.

He crawled into the water, then drifted over to collect them. Cori coaxed herself into the pool, then joined him. Wurm shone the light on a dripping paper.

"It's a faxed page from my mother's notebook," she told him. "The final words spell out 'Feed branch 2 Esus.'"

"Your mom made it that far. Her notes would have saved us time."

"The Borgias broke into my house to steal this." She looked up. "They assaulted my roommate, Tessa. Then they faxed the pages to Switzerland."

"For Lucrezia. They've tracked you since the publication of your mother's book. If you'd been home, they would have killed you."

She drifted to a wall where Jung had painted a red and white rose. After studying the alchemical symbol, Cori ran her hand along a seam. "I found a hidden room," she announced. "Jung built a maze down here. Follow me." She moved through the water, taking the glare of her headlamp around the bend.

Wurm trailed along the coarse wall, turning the corner. He didn't see her.

"Cori," he said in a halting shiver. "Where are you?"

"Over here," she called in the distance. "Go to the end of the wall. Take a left."

Wurm moved through water and turned the corner. And another and another. He felt lost and confused, foreign feelings to him. Cold water stiffened his weary body. He turned another corner. No sign of Cori. Wurm muttered, "Blast her."

"C'mon." Her voice sounded more remote. "I'm near the center."

"I'm turning back," he called, embracing himself to stay warm. "If someone's not in the tower, the timer will click off, then the hatch will close. We'll be trapped down here."

He turned, confident he could get out, thinking it wouldn't be more difficult than his book maze. As for Cori, she had found her way in. She could bloody well find her way out.

Cori waded to the center of the labyrinth beneath Jung's tower. The water seemed cold at first, but now adrenaline blocked the chill. She moved around a corner and found herself facing a symbol known as the eye of god. Painted in black on the wall, a brow arched over the eye. Two lines, one straight, one curled, emerged beneath the bottom eyelid.

She remembered the first time she'd seen the ancient Egyptian symbol. She'd been eight, visiting her mother's class at Princeton. During the lecture, she'd sat in the front row beside two sorority girls, who smiled and waved at her. While she worked magic with a crayon in her Hello Kitty coloring book, her mother had shown the class a transparency of the Eye of Horus. She had looked up, mesmerized.

Her mother had explained that Horus was the falcon-headed son of the Egyptian gods Osiris and Isis. Osiris's brother, Set, who became king of Egypt, murdered Osiris. Horus avenged his father's death by facing his uncle in an epic battle. Set was captured but escaped. Horus defeated him a second time, but not before Set plucked out Horus's left eye. Horus offered the eye to his father. As Osiris and Isis ascended into heaven, Horus became the king of Egypt. The entire line of Egyptian pharaohs had descended from him.

Known as the udjat eye, the symbol became popular on amulets used to grant health and ward off illness. In her lecture, Ariel Cassidy had shown variations on the Eye of Horus—stripped of falconlike markings beneath it—in the Masonic symbol of an eye nestled inside a pyramid. A similar eye also appeared in the Great Seal on the U.S. dollar bill.

What her mother didn't tell the class was that the Eye of Horus served as a symbol for the Radix. Studying the udjat eye, Cori could see how the iris and the lines beneath it mimicked the basic shape of the letter *R*. Over the centuries, the eye inspired use of the Rx symbol as shorthand for the Radix.

She remembered something else about Horus; it meant "above" in the ancient Egyptian language. She aimed her headlamp above the eye symbol. Near the ceiling, one stone jutted an inch from the wall, forming a ledge. Was something up there?

She clutched the rough-hewn wall, then raised herself out of the water. She ran her fingers along the surface. Nothing on the outer edge. Pushing her hand higher, moving her palm over the stone, she found she couldn't touch the wall behind the ledge. Reaching inside the small alcove was impossible from down here. Cori embraced the wall, climbing until she could peer over the stone. A black metal box waited inside the alcove. She smiled, coaxing the box from its hiding place. Heart pounding, she became lost in the dizzy thrill of discovery. Was the Scintilla inside? Hugging the box, she eased back into the murky water.

A short time later, Cori found Wurm in the maternal tower. He was basking in the glow of a fire in Jung's small kitchen. She caught his gaze as he noticed the box in her hands.

"Good lord, child. What did you find in Jung's labyrinth?"

"I hope it's the Scintilla." She glanced around. "Where's Lucrezia?"

"Vanished." He shrugged, warming his hands. "I laid her on Jung's bed. Someone claimed her body while we were in the maze. Probably the person we saw outside the tower. Probably the Borgias."

That troubled her, knowing the Borgias were near. She tried to dismiss the thought.

Holding her breath, she opened the metal box. Wurm leaned in for a closer look. Cori brought out an old book. The worn leather cover featured a cross growing out of a tree. Embossed in gold, the words *Die heilige Schrift* appeared above the treelike cross.

"It's an old German Bible." He raised a metal clasp on the cover and opened the book, turning to the first page. "It's in good condition. Look at the signature."

In flowing blackletter script, "Prof. Carl Gustav Jung" appeared below "25 Juli 1858."

"Jung wasn't born until July 1875," she said. "This belonged to his grandfather."

They scanned the old book, finding page after yellowed page filled with Fraktur script and woodcut illustrations of biblical dramas. The book was free of any notation, except the last page. At the back of the Bible, obscure symbols spelled out three separate messages. The characters were printed with the same careful handwriting as the signature on the title page.

"How curious," he observed. "The elder Jung wrote in cryptorunes."

"The Scintilla." She shot out a breath. "It has to be. Can you decipher it?"

He interlaced his fingers, then cracked his knuckles. "I'll give it a shot."

Cori felt the buzz of nervous anticipation as Wurm translated the runes. After a couple minutes, he gave her a look, as if she were distracting him. Unable to stand still, she stepped into the courtyard outside Jung's tower. Drying wet hair with her hands, she wandered to a loggia. Pulling back striped curtains, she found that the open-sided room featured a fireplace and small lake-view windows. She raised her headlamp, sweeping light across the ceiling. Divided into squares, the ceiling displayed paintings of different family crests. In one panel, Jung had painted a bearded man wielding a large green plant. She wondered if the plant represented the Radix.

When she returned to the maternal tower, Wurm was hunched over the table, translating runes by candlelight.

He looked up from the Jung family Bible. "The elder Jung printed each message in a different runic script. The first is written in an early Teutonic form used in Northern Europe before eight hundred CE. The second is a Nordic version from Iceland around the thirteenth century. The last is an Anglo-Saxon rune from the eleven hundreds."

"Is it the Scintilla?"

He shook his head. He translated Jung's first message as

Where upon the pagan ground of Jupiter,
Our Lady transformed into the goddess of reason
The Great Secret hides within

"Any idea what it means?" she wondered.

"It means the Scintilla is not here. This message directs us to a new destination."

Before two in the morning, Cori drove the MINI Cooper on the Bellerivestrasse toward Zurich Airport. Wurm had crammed into the seat beside her. He mumbled while translating Jung's final two messages. She gave a quick glance at the mirror, checking if the Borgias were following them. Relieved, she slumped in her seat. She didn't want to face them again.

"Got it," he announced. Taking a breath, he recited the translation. Jung's second message was as cryptic as the first.

Where once dragons rained down,
God with us towers above the zero of paradise

"I know part of it," she said. "I used to date a guy named Emmanuel. The name means 'God with us.' We need to find an Emmanuel towering 'above the zero of paradise.'"

"That should be easy," he said sarcastically. He read the third message.

When one is in doubt, turn away
And the truth shall be revealed

"Know what it means?" she asked.

"Not a clue. But I know the answer lies in Paris."

"In Notre-Dame." She added, "I'm not religious or anything, but I know *notre dame* means 'our lady.'"

"Ah, but Europe has several cathedrals named Notre-Dame. We need the one in Paris. Know why?"

"Bet you're gonna tell me."

"Remember Jung's first clue?" Wurm asked, scratching at his beard. "It said, 'Where upon the pagan ground of Jupiter, Our Lady transformed into the goddess of reason.' Notre-Dame of Paris resides on the same site where centuries before a Roman temple had been built. Long before Notre-Dame, the Romans dedicated their temple to their chief god, Jupiter."

"Notre-Dame was built on pagan ground. That explains the first part. What about the part about transforming 'Our Lady into the goddess of reason'?"

"It refers to the French Revolution. In 1793, the guillotine claimed the heads of King Louis XVI and Marie Antoinette. That November, the French revolutionary government outlawed religion. Christianity was overthrown. Bibles were burned. Notre-Dame was renamed the 'Temple of Reason.' A festival was staged to celebrate the victory of philosophy over religion. The Paris Opéra redecorated the cathedral for the occasion. The Opéra sent singers to celebrate the rechristening. Mademoiselle Aubry, a young star at the time, dressed in a Roman stola, think the Statue of Liberty, but in tricolor. She wore a long white robe and blue mantle with a red Phrygian bonnet."

"A *what* bonnet?" Cori asked.

"A liberty cap." He sketched it. "The French wore them as a symbol of freedom during the revolution." He showed his drawing of a Phrygian bonnet.

She glanced over. "Looks like a Smurf hat."

"Anyway, at the ceremony," he continued, "the corps de ballet escorted Mademoiselle Aubry into the sanctuary. The crowd cheered her as the goddess of reason. After that, over two thousand French churches were renamed 'Temple of Reason.' But Mademoiselle Aubry, as the goddess of reason, graced one temple."

"So, Our Lady transformed into the goddess of reason at the Paris cathedral."

"Feel free to speed, Cori. We need to catch a flight to France."

Chapter Forty-two

Los Angeles
5:05 P.M.

John Brynstone passed rows of palm trees lining La Cienega Boulevard as he drove the team to the Armstrong private jet at LAX's Mercury terminal. He couldn't wait to get to Vegas to find his family and settle things with Metzger. Beside him, Jordan had called to check in with Cori. When she hung up, he asked, "Did I hear you say they're headed to Paris?"

"Notre-Dame."

He hadn't connected the Scintilla with the famed cathedral. "Are they safe?"

"So far. They found Lucrezia Borgia at Jung's tower. She's dead. Can you believe it?"

He shook his head. After Wurm killed her mother years ago, Lucrezia had become the reigning matriarch of the House of Borgia. She had been a powerhouse, pushing her family to find the Radix. The stakes were raised now for Adriana and her clan. As he pulled into the FBO hangar, Brynstone said, "I just hope the Borgias don't track Cori and Wurm to Paris."

Washington, D.C.
8:32 P.M.

Alexander Armstrong saw Isaac Starr walking toward him. "Secret Service cleared you to join me at the hospital?"

Starr nodded. "You wanted an update on Brynstone. He's being treated as a potential threat to national security. Delgado mobilized a DevGroup team to bring him in."

"Big mistake. Brynstone's not a threat."

"With all due respect," Starr responded, "DIRNSA is on the right side of this issue. We need to bring in Brynstone."

"I trust him. The man knows what he's doing."

"It's clear you have faith in Brynstone. Mind telling me why?"

"Our first summer in the White House," he began, "I learned about a plot to kidnap my son while he was on vacation with Helena in Punta Cana."

"I'll never forget that, Alex. Everything turned out fine. The Service stormed into a building in Bávaro and apprehended the kidnappers. I slept a lot better that night."

"Me too. And for that, we can thank John Brynstone. He took point on a clandestine op involving surveillance and penetration of a target facility in Haiti. He helped coordinate the Secret Service operation and the kidnappers were arrested before initiating their mission."

"Brynstone did that?"

Armstrong nodded. "See why I'm willing to give the guy a second chance?"

Airborne over Europe
3:36 A.M.

At the conference table, Cori rested her chin on her hand as Wurm spoke broken French into the phone. Barely twenty-four hours ago, he had dragged her into his book maze. Now she was flying to Paris with him. He fascinated and frightened her, but she sensed a connection.

As the Airbus soared over Zurich, she closed the German Bible, then fastened the leather strap on the cover. He had convinced her to bring the book with them. She pushed aside the aging book, then opened her mother's journals, looking for information on Jung's grandfather. Ariel Cassidy had recorded a visit with a European baroness about a conversation she had had with Jung. At his invitation, the baroness had attended an October 1959 taping as the BBC television program *Face to Face* interviewed Jung at his Swiss home.

That night, they stayed up drinking wine and Jung told a story about his grandfather. In 1845, the elder Jung had welcomed a guest from Paris. The man was a Freemason and the head of the Office of Historic Monuments. He described finding a weathered document while restoring an old building. Hearing the description, Grand Master Jung identified the document as the Scintilla. He offered to buy it on the spot.

The young Freemason told him it was too late.

While restoring the Parisian building, the Freemason had created a new hiding place for the document. "Under different circumstances, my grandfather might have owned the Scintilla on that night," Jung had told the European baroness. "We were that close, my dear. That close."

Was it possible that the old building was Notre-Dame? In her interview with Ariel Cassidy, the baroness didn't mention the cathedral. Cori was digging into another journal when Wurm ended his call. He ambled toward her, shoving his hands inside his pockets.

"It's past three in the morning," she said, standing to stretch. "Who were you calling?"

"Nicolette Bettencourt. I'm her godfather. Nicolette is the concierge at Notre-Dame. It took some arm twisting, but she agreed to unlock the cathedral for us." He noticed Cori's long-sleeve T-shirt and black yoga pants. "You changed clothes."

"I found them here on the jet. My jeans were soaked after Bollingen." She glanced at her watch. "I just realized it's December twenty-sixth. Christmas is over."

"Good," Wurm grumbled.

"Feel like I missed it."

"We're heading to Paris on a luxury jet owned by the president and his billionaire brother. Beats celebrating the holiday in a mental hospital."

"Good point."

"You called someone before I talked to Nicolette."

"My roommate. She's in the hospital. Tessa didn't answer. I left a message. Since I'm not family, the nurse wouldn't give me a report." She studied him. "Forgive me for getting personal, but you seemed to know that woman we found beneath Wurm's Tower."

"Lucrezia Borgia?" He looked down. "Maybe Brynstone told you I'm a cryptanalyst. Twenty-eight years ago, I attended a cryptology symposium in Tokyo. I met Lucrezia in the hotel bar. She started flirting with me over drinks."

"Did you know she was a Borgia?"

"Not at the time. Lucrezia fueled my interest in the Radix. I thought our meeting was a chance encounter. Turns out, she'd been tracking me for months. The Borgias are a ranting bunch of psychopaths, and I fell into a race to find the Radix before them. When I checked into Amherst, I gave it my full attention." He noticed Ariel Cassidy's journal. "Find anything interesting?"

Cori explained how a Parisian Freemason had visited Jung's grandfather thirty years before Carl Jung's birth. The man stashed the Scintilla in the same building in which he had discovered it.

"You think the Freemason meant Notre-Dame?"

"It's quite possible." Wurm tapped his chin. "I discovered something about della Rovere in the Voynich manuscript. I was working on decoding it before we met at Amherst yesterday. We know the priest smuggled the Radix and Scintilla out of the Vatican. He rode on horseback to the Italian village of Navelli. A friend at the Church of San Sebastiano warned that Cesare Borgia and his militia were hunting for della Rovere. The desperate priest concealed the Radix inside the Zanchetti mummy, then fled the village before the Holy Guard captured him. History records that Borgia marched back to Cesena with della Rovere's head on a pike."

"Where did Borgia find him?"

"It's unclear. Borgia reported to his father, the Pope, that della Rovere didn't have the Radix or the Scintilla. I concluded from the Voynich manuscript that della Rovere fled Italy with the Scintilla and planned to stash it in a separate country. Now we learn that a Freemason found the Scintilla in an old Parisian building during the 1840s. Perhaps it was Notre-Dame."

"He told Grand Master Jung the location. Jung's grandfather recorded it in cryptorunes in the back of his Bible." She looked down. "Maybe Cesare Borgia tracked della Rovere to Notre-Dame. Before Borgia arrived, the priest concealed the Scintilla inside the Paris cathedral."

"I hope we're right about this." He moved behind a computer on the jet's conference table. He stared at the monitor. "Come here, Cori. I want you to see something remarkable."

She pulled up a chair beside him. The computer screen showed a medieval mansion flanked by an octagonal tower. "This is the National Museum of the Middle Ages in Paris," he explained. "Formerly the Cluny Museum."

"My mom visited this place."

"It houses ancient relics taken from the site where Notre-Dame was built. I found something interesting on the virtual tour." Navigating an online room, he zoomed in on square column fragments. "These tablets are the oldest man-made things in Paris. They were discovered beneath Notre-Dame in 1711."

"From the Temple of Jupiter?"

"Exactly," he whispered, before reciting the rune he'd translated. " 'Where upon the pagan ground of Jupiter, Our Lady transformed into the goddess of reason.' " He brought up an image of a stone block. "Look at this."

Known as the Pillar of the Nautes, it was a four-foot altar dedicated to the boatmen who sailed the River Seine a century after Jesus. Wurm rotated the virtual image, showing Jupiter. The Roman god Vulcan and his hammer appeared on another side. On the next, she saw Taurus the bull, an icon to early Gauls. The pillar's fourth side shocked her. Carved in bas-relief, a muscular man wielded a hatchet in his raised hand. In a show of determination, he cleaved a bush with leafy branches. Above his head, the Druid god's name was carved in Roman letters: ESVS. The altar carving resembled the bearded man with the plant on Jung's loggia ceiling.

"Esus," she said. "The woodland god."

"In all his glory. This relic belonged to the Parisii, the Celtic tribe who worshipped Esus and gave their name to the city of Paris. Take a look at the branch he's chopping," Wurm said, his eyes crinkling at the corners. "The museum hired paleobotanists to examine the stalk. Scientists can't identify it because they've never seen a plant like it."

"We've seen it," Cori whispered. "It's the Radix."

Chapter Forty-three

The Gulfstream jetliner cut across darkened western skies. Clouds assembled like clumps of torn feather pillows, concealing sparse city lights below.

Consumed with thoughts about his family, Brynstone was lousy company on the flight to Vegas. Before leaving the house, he'd grabbed a change of clothes and his favorite photograph of his daughter. He stared at the picture now, of the delicate child curled on Kaylyn's lap. A straw hat shaded her eyes. Shay's lips puffed on a dandelion. A mist of downy seeds scattered around her bright face. A small moment of happiness. He slumped in his chair, thinking about his lost family. To find them, he had to find Metzger. He had to gamble.

As Spencer Tilton and Steve Cloud snoozed in the front row, he moved behind a computer. He worked for a few minutes, when Jordan Rayne came up behind him.

"You monitoring DIRNSA again?" she asked, staring at the grid of small windows on his computer's desktop.

"I'm going to call him. I accessed CCTV surveillance to see if Delgado's at home."

"He has cameras everywhere. And his house is huge."

"He came into a big inheritance. His sister died a year before his father. Everything went to Delgado."

She squinted at several windows open on the computer monitor. "Where is he now?"

"The billiard room." He pointed to a window on the screen showing Delgado behind his bar, pouring a drink.

She pointed to a blackened window. "Why is that dark?"

"The camera in that room has been disabled, so I haven't been able to access it. I'm working on a way to override the master control. It'll take some time, but I'm pretty sure I can activate that surveillance cam."

"When are you calling Delgado?"

"Now." He grabbed the phone, then walked to the back of the jet. He kept his cool as he waited for Delgado to pick up.

"John, how nice of you to call."

"You've pushed it too far," he said. "It's one thing to attack me. But you crossed the line when you ordered the kidnapping of Kaylyn and Shay."

"I don't know what you're talking about, John," he said in his tranquil monotone. "Enlighten me."

"Leave my wife and child alone," he demanded. "Call off Metzger."

Silence for a beat until Delgado said, "Are you talking about Erich Metzger? The assassin? He kidnapped your family?"

"Stop playing games."

"I'm serious, John. I had no idea. You know I adore Kaylyn. I would never—"

Brynstone cut in. "I used to believe your lies. Not anymore. If anything happens to my wife and daughter, you'll never get the Radix."

"Oh, I'll get it," Delgado vowed, his voice revealing a fracture in his composure. He growled, "If you don't give it to me, I'll send a team to apprehend you."

"I'll take out anyone you send my way. Then I'll come for you."

"Is that a threat, John?"

"It's a guarantee, Jim."

He closed the phone and returned to his seat, grabbing his computer. He didn't like to bluff with his family on the line. He didn't have the Radix with him anymore, but he was willing to try anything. The stakes were too high.

Jordan walked up. "You okay?"

"I will be after we find my family. First, we need to find Metzger."

Brynstone felt as though he could trust no one except Jordan and Wurm and Cori. Chances were good he wouldn't come out of this alive. No matter what, he had to make sure Kaylyn and Shay survived.

Paris, France
3:57 A.M.

The jet made a final approach toward Charles de Gaulle Airport. Cori closed an alchemy book and searched for the Eiffel Tower. Green lights strung across the tower formed the image of a Christmas tree.

"First time in Paris?" Wurm asked.

She nodded. "Mom came here all the time, but always alone. Dad joked she had a French lover."

He gave a sly grin. "Did she?"

She blinked. "Of course not."

"Did your mother ever speak of a 1926 book called *The Mystery of the Cathedrals*?"

"Yeah. By a mysterious figure writing under the name of Fulcanelli. He claimed the great secrets of alchemy are revealed on the walls of Notre-Dame. The so-called *parole perdue*, or lost word."

"Fulcanelli believed the most famous alchemists of the Middle Ages held secret conferences at Notre-Dame. He claimed they spoke in a secret language Jesus taught to his apostles. The Freemasons called it the green language, which Fulcanelli says 'teaches the mystery of things.' Did your mother believe in his ideas?"

"She was interested in Fulcanelli's discussion of the cabalistic Tree of Life. She did find alchemical symbols on Notre-Dame, like a salamander enveloped in flames.

You don't see symbols like that in Christian iconography. Fulcanelli claimed he decoded the cathedral's alchemical messages but never revealed what great mysteries he discovered."

"Does that surprise you? Alchemists seldom reveal their secrets."

"True, but there are many shady things about Fulcanelli. I'm not even sure he was a real person."

"I think he was real. Like Fulcanelli, your mother was secretive because she understood that powerful people want the Radix. The root was at the heart of alchemy, but the alchemists weren't the only ones who hungered for it. Over the centuries, the Radix was seen as an elusive, almost ephemeral relic in Western society. To this day, people are out there who will do anything to possess it."

She grabbed a bouclé pillow from the sofa. "You mean other than the Borgias?"

He nodded. "My psychiatrist back at Amherst was a man named Albert Usher."

"Mack Shaw pointed him out. Usher knew about the Radix?"

"He's a knight in the Sovereign Military Order of Malta. It's the world's oldest order of chivalry, founded in Jerusalem in 1099. Originally called the Knights Hospitaller, they have over ten thousand members, and fifty-four priories, including the Federal Association in Washington, D.C."

"How is the Order of Malta involved?"

"They have a long interest in the Radix," Wurm said. He explained that their more famous rivals, the Knights Templar, had succumbed to greed and power, inciting the Vatican's wrath. In 1314, Jaques de Molay, the grand master of the Templar order, was executed at Notre-Dame. After the Templar order was crushed, the Knights Hospitaller flourished.

"The Hospitallers, or Knights of Malta, have flown under the radar," he said. "Not glory hogs like the Templars."

Whereas the Templars were sometimes perceived as greedy, the Hospitallers enjoyed a more heroic reputation. Legends told of their bravery during the Crusades. When their enemies tossed glass bombs containing naphtha and other flammable chemicals, the Hospitallers put out the fires. To this day, numerous American firefighters used the Hospitaller's Maltese cross in their eight-point insignia.

He mentioned that the Hospitallers moved to the island of Malta in 1530, taking with them sacred relics, like the hand of John the Baptist. But they mourned their most prized possession. Twenty-eight years earlier, the Pope's son, Cesare Borgia, had stolen the Radix from their grand master, Pierre d'Aubusson.

"A handful of knights and dames of Malta know about the Radix," he continued. "But Usher belongs to a small contingent obsessed with finding it. They plan to strengthen the Order of Malta's power base by delivering the Radix to the Pope."

"Makes sense," she said. "Using the Radix, the Vatican could heal millions, but they'd need to keep it secret. If someone—say, John Brynstone—used it to cure blindness or cancer, the credit would go to the Radix, not Brynstone. People would worship it as the perfect drug. But if the Pope secretly used the Radix to heal, then he would get credit for the miracles."

"In the eyes of millions, the notion of papal infallibility would be restored," Wurm added. "It would be the supreme triumph of religion over science."

She nodded. "At the same time, new followers would flood the Catholic Church."

"If you turned on the television and saw the Pope walk through an ICU healing people or watched him raise a man from his deathbed, wouldn't you be the next convert?"

Cori frowned. "Maybe we're being paranoid about the Church's motives."

"Don't get me wrong. The Order of Malta is a benevolent organization that helps countless poor and sick people. Believe me, they've come a long way from the Hospitallers of old. The order has power and influence. Not to mention ties to the CIA."

"The CIA?"

"Two founding members of the Central Intelligence Agency were Knights of Malta," he said. "William 'Wild Bill' Donovan and Allen Dulles. A guy named John McCone was Kennedy's CIA director. He was a Knight of Malta. So was William Casey, Ronald Reagan's director. Then there's the current administration. You know about Mark McKibbon?"

She thought for a beat. "The CIA director. The one President Armstrong appointed?"

"McKibbon's a Malta knight," Wurm said as the jet touched down on the rain-streaked runway outside the airport's remote T-9 terminal. "Like I said, you have no idea how many powerful people want the Radix."

Part Six
Archetype

Formerly, when religion was strong and science weak, men mistook magic for medicine; now, when science is strong and religion weak, men mistake medicine for magic.
—Thomas Szasz

Chapter Forty-four

The Charles de Gaulle Airport seemed stark and lonely at this hour. Feeling out of place, Cori watched as Wurm embraced Nicolette Bettencourt. In her early thirties, the woman was dressed in a wool coat with a knit cap pulled over sweeping raven hair. Her complexion accented high cheekbones and soft brown eyes. Her boots were gorgeous. Seemed like all the French women Cori saw wore amazing shoes.

Wurm shared that Bettencourt had been a French kickboxing champion in her teens. Somehow, she didn't seem like a caretaker for a cathedral.

Cori patted her coat pocket. Since her borrowed yoga pants didn't have pockets, she had transferred the vial containing the Radix to a pocket inside her peacoat.

Raising an eyebrow, Bettencourt pinched Cori's chin in her gloved hand. "Beautiful, but so young. Are you his lover?"

"A friend," Cori stuttered. "We're friends."

"Good. You are far too young for Edgar." She gave a disgusted look at Cori's running shoes, still damp from Bollingen. She glanced back at Wurm. "When you called this morning, Edgar, it was shocking. It has been almost two years since I've heard from you."

"I had to drop out of society for a while," he answered. "I was working on something important. That's why I need you to open the cathedral."

Nicolette Bettencourt gave a Gallic shrug, raising her shoulders and holding up her hands, palms out. Sticking out her bottom lip, she said, "I could lose my job as concierge. You know the Préfecture de Police is across from Notre-Dame." She removed a Gauloises cigarette from a flat blue box, but didn't light it. "But for you, dear Edgar, I will do it."

4:23 A.M.

First time in Paris. Nighttime deepened the lamp-lit romance of the city. Riding in the back of the Peugeot sedan, Cori paused for a moment, imagining Édith Piaf singing "Sous le ciel de Paris." She drifted back as Nicolette Bettencourt chatted with Wurm up front.

"Still live in the Marais?" he asked her.

"Sold my house," Bettencourt said, punching the Pug's V-6 engine. "As concierge, I now live on the Notre-Dame grounds."

Wurm leaned back, bringing Cori into the conversation. "Her father owns several Left Bank properties, including the Hotel Montalembert. Nicolette had this amazing mansion overlooking the Seine's Right Bank."

"Enough distraction." Bettencourt looked into the rearview mirror. "I insist you explain your little adventure now."

"Where should I begin?" Wurm said. "For the past few decades, I've—"

"Just a minute, Edgar," Cori blurted, cutting him off. She was thinking about Jung's second cryptic message. "Nicolette, you know Notre-Dame. Maybe you can help. Do you know how we can find 'paradise'?"

Chapter Forty-five

After the jet landed, Brynstone was happy to leave the chaos of ringing slots in McCarran Airport. The lights of the Strip flashed across their windshield as they navigated congestion on Las Vegas Boulevard. Cloud and Tilton complained about how the desert shouldn't feel this cold, even in December. Jordan quieted them when Metzger called.

"Welcome to town," the German assassin greeted. "Bring your friends? I like the redhead. More pleasing to the eye than your thugs."

"Do you have my wife and daughter?"

"They're here. Kaylyn is anxious to see you, and your baby is here in a safe place. We'll meet at nine."

"We meet now."

"You must understand, Dr. Brynstone, I am a man who enjoys control." He paused. "But you have earned my respect, as strange as it feels to confess that. Meet me at the Helios Tower." He hung up.

"Where do we go?" Tilton asked.

"Place called Helios Tower," Brynstone said. "Check GPS."

"Already on it," Jordan replied, tapping keys on her notebook computer. "Got it. Stay on the Strip and go to Harmon Avenue. Helios Tower is a condominium-hotel tower under construction. It's part of the MGM CityCenter complex. Behind the Monte Carlo."

* * *

Erich Metzger stood inside a maze of exposed steel girders that formed the Helios Tower skeleton. The unfinished condominium hotel reigned as the tallest building
on the Las Vegas skyline. Peering out from the sixty-fifth
floor, he studied the dazzling vulgarity below him.

The tower stood behind the southwest end of the City-
Center. Like a city within a city, the complex spread out
over sixty-plus acres sandwiched between the Bellagio
and Monte Carlo casinos. Back in 2006, MGM Mirage had
razed the aging Boardwalk Hotel and started construction on a hotel casino, two nongaming boutique hotels,
and two glass towers surrounded by a retail district.

While purchasing the Mandalay Resort Group in April
2005, MGM Mirage had acquired underdeveloped property behind the Monte Carlo and New York-New York
casinos. The Helios Tower was designed as a third tower
to capitalize on the Strip's demand for luxury residential
units. Management had halted construction for the holiday. Work would resume in the morning. On this Christmas night, however, the tower was abandoned. Metzger
tapped his fingers on a red steel girder. A perfect place to
meet Brynstone.

Metzger turned, then walked across the floor, cluttered
with sawdust and orphaned nails. People like John and
Kaylyn Brynstone gave meaning to his work. They made
life worthwhile. Their deaths would bring even greater
fulfillment.

Chapter Forty-six

Victor Hugo had once called Notre-Dame the "aged queen of French cathedrals." Crafted from two centuries of sweat and labor, it was a breathtaking archetype for Gothic architecture. Cast in amber light, the western facade reached into the night with majesty. Twin bell towers framed the limestone cathedral. A rose window on the western face sprayed out in a bouquet of reds and blues, forming an enormous halo behind a statue of the Madonna. Above the rose window, gargoyles lurked in spotlights around the towers.

Cori knew it could guard a million secrets. Where would they look for answers?

A brilliant Christmas tree greeted them on a plaza known as the Place du Parvis.

"Our Lady is magnificent, *non*?" Nicolette Bettencourt asked.

"*Très magnifique,*" Cori answered, attempting French. "She shames all other cathedrals."

Bettencourt shrugged. "You will find many who do not agree. Our Lady has beautiful sisters around Europe. But for me? They do not compare. That's my view."

"Tell us," Wurm interrupted. "How can we find paradise?"

"You're standing on it." She waved her arms. "This is paradise."

"The parvis?"

"*Oui. Parvis* is a medieval French word for 'paradise.'"

Remembering Jung's message, Wurm asked, "Know anything about dragons raining down on the parvis?"

"Hang on, I'm thinking," Bettencourt said. "Perhaps this is it. A seventh-century legend claims that a dragon named La Gargouille crawled from a cave near the Seine. He destroyed livestock and attacked villages in Paris. The dragon also capsized ships and devoured sailors. Each year, villagers sacrificed a criminal to appease him. A brave priest named Saint Romanis slew La Gargouille and hauled him back to Paris. He set the dragon ablaze, but the head and neck would not burn. Romanis pulled it from the fire and nailed the head to a church wall."

"Making La Gargouille the first gargoyle," Cori said.

"*Non*," she corrected. "The first grotesque."

"What's the difference between a gargoyle and a grotesque?"

"Gargoyles serve as rain spouts," Bettencourt explained, "directing water away from the cathedral on nights like tonight. So, we have the inspiration for the old French word *gargouille*, meaning 'throat.' It refers to the sound water makes passing through the gullet."

"Like *gurgle* in English," he said, "or *gargle*."

"Grotesques don't have waterspouts?" Cori asked.

Bettencourt shook her head. She pointed to the cathedral walls. "See up there? Grotesques have lined the cathedral walls since the Middle Ages. Some crumbled after centuries of watching the city. After deterioration, they dropped from their perches onto the parvis. In the olden days, the stone creatures crashed down, killing the citizens of Paris. The stories inspired a dread of gargoyles and grotesques. Can you imagine?"

"The dragons raining down on paradise refer to those grotesques outside the cathedral towers." Wurm stared at them. "They don't seem primed to fall."

"They are not original. Viollet-le-Duc added the ones

you see. He was the architect who supervised Notre-Dame's restoration."

"Let's see," Cori said, "*parvis* means 'paradise,' and those grotesques are the dragons. Do you have any idea where we find something called the zero of paradise?"

"Hmm? Oh, you mean the *kilomètre zéro*? Come on, then."

Bettencourt led them to a worn bronze marker embedded near the parvis's northeastern corner. A sun symbol filled an octagon, its eight sharp tips pointing out. Like a Jungian mandala representing the center of the self, this plaque represented the center of Paris. The Notre-Dame marker—known as Point Zero—was the spot from where distances were measured in France, even to its most remote boundaries.

Cori remembered the words from Jung's Bible: *Where once dragons rained down, God with us towers above the zero of paradise.* A smile traced her lips. They had found Point Zero on paradise, where stone dragons had once rained down. She looked at the cathedral's twin towers stretching into the night sky. "Any chance you have an Emmanuel up there?"

Bettencourt nodded. "Follow me."

They climbed more than two hundred and fifty steps of aged stone inside Notre-Dame's north tower. Cori followed Bettencourt up the spiral staircase as Wurm trailed behind. Moving past the darkened bookshop, they took more stairs to a small doorway. Emerging from the tower, they were treated to a breathtaking view of the Paris skyline. On boulevard after boulevard below, monumental architecture and freestone buildings with gray slate roofs boasted the old Second Empire style. But beyond the Île de la Cité, skyscrapers crowded the aging architecture, threatening with their brand of Parisian urbanism.

They walked across a colonnaded gallery featuring an army of grotesques. Cori remembered Bettencourt saying that an architect had replaced older deteriorating grotesques with the current ones. She joined the others inside the south tower, where they climbed a creaking wooden staircase to the belfry. Even with flashlights, the place was creepy.

"At first, only the north tower had bells. They all had names. The bell Guillaume was installed around 1248. Later, his brothers Pugnaise, Chambellan, Pasquier, Jean, Nicolas, Gabriel, and Claude joined Guillaume. Among the ladies were the sisters Marie and Jacqueline in the south tower along with Françoise, Catherine, Anne, and Barbara."

"You didn't mention Emmanuel," Wurm said as they moved inside the belfry.

"I haven't finished." Annoyance crept into her voice. "Jacqueline was recast in 1681. She underwent a sex change, so to speak, and was renamed Emmanuel. This bell is Emmanuel."

Cori imagined Quasimodo swinging from the enormous bell.

"At almost thirty thousand pounds, Emmanuel possessed the deepest voice," Bettencourt continued. "During the revolution, the bells were seized from their towers. Insurgents planned to melt them into cannon at the foundry. The great bell Emmanuel was the one to return home. The others are lost in the mists of time."

"Why would Jung want us to visit a bell?" Wurm asked, looking around the south belfry.

Cori remembered her mother's notes. "You mentioned the architect who oversaw the restoration. Do you know if he headed the Office of Historic Monuments here in Paris?"

"As a matter of fact, he did," Bettencourt answered. "How did you know?"

"A Freemason in charge of the Office of Historic Monuments visited Jung's grandfather. Must be the same man. What was the name of the architect who restored Notre-Dame?"

"Eugène-Emmanuel Viollet-le-Duc."

"*Emmanuel?*" Wurm asked.

"Maybe the 'God with us' refers to him and not the bell," Cori said. "Can we find Viollet-le-Duc's name around here? Like on a plaque?"

Bettencourt thought about it. "His name appears on that statue." She pointed to the cathedral spire east of the bell towers. Surrounded by floodlights, the steeple cut into the night sky like a barbed spearhead. Twelve statues surrounded the spire's base, three on each side. "During the restoration in the 1840s, Geoffroy-Dechaume sculpted twelve apostles for outside the spire. He carved a likeness of Viollet-le-Duc's face on one. The name Emmanuel is engraved on the staff in that apostle's hand."

"Which apostle?"

"Eleven apostles face the city," Bettencourt explained. "Only the Viollet-le-Duc statue looks away. He is turned toward the spire, admiring it. Geoffroy-Dechaume thought it fitting to put Viollet-le-Duc's face on the patron saint of architects."

"Which apostle is the patron saint of architects?"

"Thomas. Viollet-le-Duc's face appears on the Saint Thomas statue."

"When one is in doubt, turn away." Cori repeated Jung's rune as she gazed at the statue. "The doubting apostle is turned away."

"Doubting Thomas?" Wurm's eyes brightened. "The saint with the sash." He slammed his fist into his hand. "Nicolette, take us to him at once."

Like many Gothic cathedrals, Notre-Dame was rendered in a cross-shaped design. Heading down the tower staircase, Cori listened as Nicolette Bettencourt explained that twelve apostles were positioned outside the cathedral spire on the roof where the transept intersected with the apse. The spire rose above the center of the cross.

"Tell us about your security," Wurm said.

"You are fortunate," Bettencourt answered. "Our Christmas Mass concluded last night. Because of funding cutbacks and the holiday season, we have one security man tonight. I will keep Anton Vaden busy. He is an unrepentant flirt, so please do not take long."

When they reached the nave, she directed them to hide behind a pillar. She gave directions. "There are no security devices in the spire," Bettencourt whispered, handing Wurm a key. "This unlocks the door. After I lure Vaden into my office, you may go up. Text me when you are finished." She headed across the nave.

At the altar, a guard with thinning black hair lit a votive candle. Bettencourt ran her hand across his back. Their conversation spiraled into flirtation. They walked the aisle, turning toward her office.

"She's good," Cori admitted. "But how long can her flirting keep him busy?"

"You'd be surprised," Wurm answered. "Let's go."

Notre-Dame's spire soared to a height of 295 feet. Halfway up, a ring of metal barbs curled out from the spire, giving the look of a crown of thorns. Cori rushed to the spire's arched opening. Twelve apostles were stationed around its base. On each of the four sides of the spire, a staircase-shaped flèche supported three disciples, with each statue posed on a different step. From below, floodlights illuminated each figure.

"They're green men," Wurm marveled. "Not like Esus, but green men nonetheless."

Cori leaned out, seeing a disciple's mint green head. Dressed in a robe, the statue embraced a cross-shaped staff. On the step below, a second apostle clutched an open book. The third was positioned in a twisted pose, with his left arm outstretched and his right reaching down. Bent at the knees with his feet sideways on the step, the third apostle looked as though he were trying to regain his balance before toppling off the flèche. Either that, or he was posing as a biblical surfer dude, cracking open a gnarly wave. On the bottom step, a little winged bull craned up his green neck as if worried the surfer apostle would fall and knock them from the roof.

"I found him," Wurm announced. "On this side."

She peeked out the archway above the southeast flèche. Wurm shone the flashlight at Saint Thomas's green face. The statue's left hand seemed to shield his eyes as he peered into the light. In his right hand, he held a flat staff that resembled an oversized yardstick.

Saint Thomas faced the spire, admiring it with his back turned away from the city and the two disciples behind him. *When one is in doubt, turn away.* Among the twelve figures mounted around the spire, only the doubting apostle turned away.

"We're on the right track. Now what?"

"See the sash around his waist?" he asked. "Remind you of anything?"

"Jung's scytale."

"And the staff in his hand?"

"We need to wrap the scytale around Saint Thomas's staff. Jung's sash had characters sewn on both sides. One side was meant for Bollingen. Maybe the other side was intended for Notre-Dame. But there's one problem." Her voice moved from excitement to disappointment. "The sash is back in Switzerland."

"Wanna bet?" Wurm raised his shirt, revealing Jung's sash around his waist. "After we argued about taking Jung's Bible, I decided it was a waste of time debating the sash. I took it."

"Okay, maybe it's a good thing you're a klepto."

As he brought out the sash, she added, "You know how the letters on this side look less faded? I bet Jung added the words here after his grandfather embroidered the other side."

"His grandfather created a scytale on his cherished Wartburg sash, intending it for Notre-Dame. Decades later, Jung made a scytale keyed to Bollingen on the same sash."

She nodded, then leaned out the spire opening, looking down. "We'll need to climb onto the roof to reach Saint Thomas. There's not room on the flèche for both of us. I'll go."

"Nonsense." He pulled the climbing rope from his backpack. He tied the rope in a figure-eight knot around the spire opening. "I'm the experienced climber. I'll go."

"See your bandaged fingers? After Adriana's manicure, you shouldn't hang onto ropes."

"I didn't have a problem climbing down into Jung's Nekyia chamber."

"There's one impartial way to decide," she smiled. "Rock, paper, scissors. Ready?"

He cocked his head. After a three count, he balled his hand into a fist. He looked at Cori's hand. Flat like paper. His eyes lowered to slits. "Best of three."

"No time," she answered, taking the sash. Sliding out the arched trefoil window, she grabbed the rope and lowered herself out the opening. She moved onto the wooden flèche. It was narrower than she had expected. She glanced east at the city lights reflecting off the River Seine. With floodlights projected at Notre-Dame, she realized they might be spotted from the Île Saint-Louis or the Left Bank. Holding the rope, she balanced on the flèche while hugging Thomas's waist with one arm, looking small beside the oversized green sculpture.

"What are those letters on Thomas's staff?" Wurm called down.

"The architect's name is engraved in abbreviated Roman text," she answered, reading the words EVG-EMMAN VIOLLET. Below the apostle's thumb, Viollet-le-Duc's name continued with LE DVC, followed by his title as architect. She pressed the sash against the top of the staff as she wrapped it. A raindrop splashed on her cheek. She looked up at the overcast sky, hoping it wouldn't rain. She coached herself to focus on the sash. "The scytale spells a French word. This staff is thicker than the Bollingen branch. The sash ends right at his thumb."

"What does it spell?"

"L-E-S-T-R-Y-G-E," she called. "A French word, I guess. *Le stryge.*"

"Any idea what it means?"

"My French is awful," she admitted. Raindrops pounded as she unwrapped the sash from the green apostle's staff. "Let's ask Nicolette."

She wrapped the sash around her waist, then took the rope and climbed from the flèche to the spire. Wurm hauled in Cori as if she were a rag doll. Catching her breath, she texted a message to Nicolette. After sending it, she saw a call coming in. She couldn't believe it when she saw Tessa's number. She answered her roommate's call as she joined Wurm on the stairs.

"Where are you?" her roommate asked, sounding weak.

"Never mind, it's not important," she replied, unsure if the police were listening to their call. "How are you? I've been worried."

"I'll be okay."

"I'm so sorry. I feel terrible that Adriana hurt you."

"Um," Tessa said in a dreamy voice. "Who's Adriana?"

"She almost killed you. You know, tall and spooky, and strong. Black hair."

"Wait, Cori. That's not who attacked me."

Chapter Forty-seven

Brynstone and his team searched the Helios Tower lobby, circling the vast room in their search for Metzger. Looking around the unfinished condominium hotel, he pointed to an elevator. Large and scrawled in blood, the number sixty-five marked the elevator doors. Was it Shay's blood or Kaylyn's? He hated the thought, but couldn't stop it from entering his mind.

"This place is under construction," he said, punching the button. "Assuming there's power, we'll take the elevator."

"Elevator could be rigged," Cloud replied. "Stairs might be safer."

"Metzger likes control. We'll play the game his way. Let him feel in power. For now."

"Good point," Jordan added. "If he wanted to kill us, he would have done it already."

The elevator doors opened. He started to step inside, but stopped.

Jordan touched his arm. "John, what's wrong?"

A stuffed bunny rested on the elevator floor. Blood speckled the pink fur. He remembered buying the Christmas gift for his daughter. His face tightened with anger. *Metzger, you're a dead man.* He stepped into the glass-encased elevator, checking the ceiling as he entered. He picked up the stuffed animal. "Let's go," he said, tucking it inside his coat pocket.

Jordan came in, then patted his shoulder. Tilton and Cloud fell in behind.

During the ride up to the sixty-fifth floor, he stared at the city glittering in the desert night. He felt his phone vibrate. He answered the call from Cori.

"John, this is important," she said, sounding worried. "Have you found Kaylyn?"

"Not yet. Where are you, Cori?"

"Paris. Where's Jordan Rayne?"

"She's right here," he said, looking at her. "Why?"

Jordan cocked her head, listening.

"I talked to Tessa," Cori rasped. "Remember her?"

"Your roommate. Look, this isn't a good time to talk."

"Listen to me. Tessa described the woman who attacked her at my home in Baltimore."

"Adriana Borgia."

"No, John. It wasn't Adriana. Tessa's description fits Jordan Rayne. The red hair. Even the beauty mark. I think Jordan tried to kill Tessa. She faxed pages from my mother's journal to Lucrezia Borgia in Switzerland."

Can't be, Brynstone thought as the elevator shivered to a halt. He flinched, glancing at Jordan, then looking away. He couldn't believe it. He closed his phone, then began to swing around with his sidearm. Jordan understood what was happening. In a quick motion, she shoved Spencer Tilton into Brynstone, forcing them against the back wall of the elevator.

The doors opened and she darted out.

Tilton's eyes widened. "What's going on?"

Brynstone pushed him aside. "We can't trust her."

He saw it all now. She was working with the Borgias. That's how they knew about Wurm's hospital ward. Jordan told them. She had shown up at Cori's house and assaulted Tessa to get Ariel Cassidy's notebook. She'd known where to find the slaughterhouse all along. She met the Borgias there and gave them the notebook before he had arrived. Jordan let them torture Wurm.

Why didn't I see it before? But why would she work with the Borgias? Because she wanted the Radix, that's why. Jordan hadn't seen him give the Radix to Cori. A thought burned in his mind. *She thinks I have it. That's why Jordan didn't go to Europe.*

He emerged from the elevator with a steady gun. He wasn't just watching for Metzger now. He had to keep an eye open for Jordan Rayne as well. Individual suites were framed, but sheets of drywall waited in stacks. The open walls gave the sixty-fifth floor the look of a cavernous maze. He searched the high-rise with Tilton and Cloud close behind. Clinging to support beams, ghostly plastic sheets flapped in the breeze. The exterior walls weren't up yet on the bare top floors, giving a panoramic view of Las Vegas. Peering through the forest of girders, he searched for Kaylyn.

"There," Steve Cloud said, pointing over Brynstone's shoulder.

Tied to a beam, a woman struggled to get free. Another drug addict? They hurried across the sawdust-littered floor. A bullet sizzled through the darkness, cutting down Cloud.

"Don't take another step," Metzger barked.

They stopped. Brynstone listened, trying to track the direction of the voice. Tilton bent over the fallen man, checking Cloud's pulse. He shook his head and whispered, "Dead."

They crouched in the dark, taking refuge behind exposed steel girders. He glanced at the woman tied to the beam. Couldn't tell if she was Kaylyn.

"At last, we meet," Metzger's voice echoed from the blackness.

"Easy now," Brynstone said, searching for him. "Tell me what you want."

"Are we pretending?" Metzger asked. "You know why I'm here."

"You were sent to kill me."

"But first—"

"You want the Radix. Delgado sent you to get it."

"You are mistaken," Metzger said. "I was hired by a man who calls himself the Knight."

"How do you know you can trust this knight?" Brynstone asked, wanting him to talk. "Huh, Metzger? How do you know he won't put a bullet in your head as soon as you deliver?"

"Tell me, Herr Doktor. Do you take me for such a simple man?"

That's it. Keep talking. He followed the voice. The assassin was moving.

"There is a danger in trusting the Knight," Metzger stated. "He is a psychopath."

And you're not? Brynstone thought. He tried to track Metzger's voice as he moved around the unfinished highrise tower. He couldn't get a bead on the assassin.

"I think I see him," Spencer Tilton called as he took aim.

Dumb thing to say. Gunfire blasted through the night. Tilton's body convulsed as bullets ripped through his flesh, trapping him in midair and refusing to let him fall. Brynstone hit the floor, rolling. He returned fire as Metzger darted for cover. Gunshots echoed against the steel girders. In the back of his mind, he never stopped thinking, *Where is Jordan?*

The woman tied to the beam was caught in the middle. He didn't want to draw fire to her, but he had to know if she was Kaylyn. He started to move in her direction, but stopped when he heard a helicopter roar thirty feet away.

Hovering outside the Helios Tower's exposed skeleton, the MH-6 "Little Bird" blasted a spotlight on Brynstone. Painted black for nighttime ops, the helicopter carried three commandos on each outboard bench. Tasked for counterterrorism ops, each team member was armed with an M4A1 carbine. Delgado hadn't sent Metzger. True to his word, he had sent a commando team.

"John Brynstone," the pilot called over the aerial loudspeaker. "Drop your weapon and raise both hands in the air. I repeat: drop your weapon. This is your sole warning."

He cursed. He had nowhere to run in the blinding light.

From the periphery, a figure moved near an exterior beam. Metzger raised an assault rifle and took aim at the bird. Before Brynstone could react, Metzger fired his G36, taking out both men in the cockpit. The pilot slumped forward, forcing the yoke to one side. As the commandos struggled to hang on, the chopper whirled away from sight.

Brynstone aimed his gun in Metzger's direction, but his eyes were adjusting after the spotlight's glare. He needed cover. He ran toward the exterior girder, still too blind to get a bead on the assassin.

One commando managed to scramble inside the cockpit. He took the controls as the chopper plunged toward the Strip. He avoided crashing into another CityCenter high-rise tower. Even with a new pilot, the bird seemed ready to crash into the traffic clogging Las Vegas Boulevard. The helicopter swerved, missing cars and a crowd lingering on the sidewalk. The chopper dove toward the eight-acre lake facing the Bellagio hotel. It splashed into the dancing fountains, blasting up a wall of water. The chopper flipped, then rolled twice before landing on its side in the lake. The long blades of the main rotor shattered against the concrete floor of the pool and burst up, spinning in every direction.

Brynstone turned back, looking for the assassin. Not far away, moonlight glinted off a black boot. Was Metzger getting careless? Not taking a chance, Brynstone fired the Glock, which kicked back against his hand. The spent casing burst from the side, tinkling on the ground. He heard a grunt, followed by heavy footfalls. Had he hit the assassin?

* * *

Diving behind a pillar, Metzger rolled over and clutched his leg. As warm blood gushed into his sock, he hissed, *"Verdammte Scheisse."* He couldn't stop the next words from escaping his lips. Words he'd never said in his life. "You shot me."

Brynstone pulled a knife from his belt, then charged toward the woman. Relief flooded him when he looked into Kaylyn's eyes. Even with tape across her mouth, she seemed to speak a thousand words. He wanted to kiss and hug her, but couldn't take time. After slicing the ropes, he sheathed the knife as she crumpled into his arms.

He scooped up Kaylyn, then hurried past Tilton on the floor. As he headed for the stairwell, Metzger fired a handgun. A bullet grazed Brynstone's shoulder. Another split his calf. He spun away. Pushing through blistering pain, he staggered to an alcove near the stairwell. Bending on shaky legs, he lowered Kaylyn to the floor before he toppled over her.

Metzger couldn't believe it. *Brynstone shot me.* He ripped his shirt, then tied off his right leg. He'd trained himself to ignore pain. He wasn't angry, only determined. Closing his eyes, he thought about his mother. He'd had no trouble killing Truda Metzger. Why couldn't he neutralize John Brynstone?

Metzger's eyes snapped open. Someone was behind him. Before he could stand, a boot slammed into his shoulder, toppling him. Catching himself on his hands, he started to push off the floor. Before he could, the person landed another hit, this one on his skull. The second blow came faster than the first. Dizzy red spots danced before his eyes. The pain was beautiful. It inspired Metzger. This is what he had been missing. This would help him kill Brynstone.

He sensed the next move before it happened. He could

hear Brynstone's boot, inches away. Rolling over, Metzger found the calf and chomped his teeth into flesh. Something didn't feel right. Despite the swift attack, there was tenderness in the leg muscle. He wasn't fighting Brynstone. He was fighting the redheaded woman. The one Brynstone called Jordan.

Metzger pounced on her, flipping Jordan on her back. His good knee rammed into her stomach. He grabbed her delicate throat and squeezed. She gurgled. Her eyes glowed with terror. Metzger forced pressure on her windpipe. She tried to fight him. No contest.

He loved killing beautiful things.

Huddled behind a wall, Kaylyn hugged her husband. "He took Shay. She's here somewhere. I heard her cry, but it's been several minutes."

"See that stairwell?" Brynstone said. "Get out of here."

"What about Shay?"

"I'll find her," he answered. "Promise you'll hit the stairs as fast as you can?"

She nodded, tears standing in her eyes. She touched tender skin where John had ripped tape from her mouth.

"I love you," he said, kissing her. "Now go."

A faint cry. Her head snapped around. "That's Shay."

As John hurried away, she noticed blood soaking through his shirt. After he ducked around a concrete pillar, she checked for the assassin. Couldn't see him. She sprinted to the stairwell and pushed open the door. She heard the German not far away in the darkness.

"Do not fight death," he told his victim. "Embrace it."

Does he have John? She couldn't leave. Not now.

Chapter Forty-eight

Notre-Dame's scale and grandeur overpowered Cori the moment she stepped inside. Oversized pillars sheltered a scattered collection of relics and statues. Prayer candles flickered inside the vast sanctuary, casting it in a medieval glow. Lightning crackled outside the rose window, brightening the stained glass. Everything went black inside the cathedral, except for rows of votive candles clustered around the altar.

"We lost power," Wurm said.

"The Île de la Cité gets hit hard," Bettencourt sighed. "The island goes black, except for the Préfecture de Police." The woman had stolen away from the security guard, Vaden, to meet with them.

"Does the name Le Stryge mean anything to you?" Wurm asked.

Bettencourt frowned at his mispronunciation. "It comes from a Greek word meaning 'night bird.' For centuries, people described winged demons that preyed on children, sucking them dry of blood. As you might suspect, these night spirits were associated with vampires."

Cori and Wurm glanced at each other, wondering why Jung's sash hinted at a vampire.

"Come, let me introduce you to Notre-Dame's most celebrated grotesque," Bettencourt said, as rain splashed against the rose window. "His name is Le Stryge."

Chapter Forty-nine

Las Vegas
8:16 P.M.

Brynstone searched the sixty-fifth floor of the Helios Tower. Individual suites were framed, but with open walls, the floor was a cavernous room. No sign of Shay. A woman's scream froze him. Jordan had found Metzger. More likely, Metzger had found Jordan. Should he help Jordan or keep searching for Shay? No question. Find the baby.

He tried to stifle a bitter thought. *I want to kill Metzger.*

Kaylyn peeked around a pillar. The German kidnapper straddled a woman, choking her.

"You should be dead." His glassy eyes blazed as he spoke to his prey. "I've grown careless on this assignment. You must pay for my mediocrity."

Kaylyn saw a stack of two-by-fours. She grabbed one, then sprinted toward the man. Picturing her child, she put everything she had into her swing. The board blasted into his head, vibrating so hard it made her arms ache. He fumbled to his knees, trying to keep balance. She took it to him again and connected. The blow flipped the man. He collapsed face-first.

She bent over the woman. Red hair flowed around her delicate face.

"Are you okay?"

"Thanks to you," she wheezed. "My name's Jordan. I work with your husband."

Kaylyn scooped her arm around the taller woman, then struggled to help her stand. Jordan's head rolled back and she winced. Blood dribbled from her nose. Kaylyn looked back at the German. He was holding his head. He tried to roll onto his hands and knees.

"We have to go, Jordan."

The woman was bigger and more athletic than Kaylyn, making it hard to support her weight. Straining, she glanced up at her face. Jordan was smiling.

It was chilling.

Brynstone sensed the pain, bright and deep inside his body. He had been shot in the shoulder and leg, Metzger's bullets grazing him both times. *Fight through it.* He reminded himself he'd been shot before, back when he was a Ranger.

Where is Shay? he wondered. *What did that monster do to her?* He'd heard her cry, but he couldn't track the sound. He turned. *Wait a minute.* He flipped on the flashlight, sweeping it across a wall safe the size of a dorm-room refrigerator.

Oh God, no.

Chapter Fifty

Paris
5:19 A.M.

For the second time this morning, Cori and Wurm followed as Nicolette Bettencourt led the way up the worn spiral staircase inside Notre-Dame's north tower. Moving out into the rainy night, Cori noticed that most of Paris still had power, including the Latin Quarter. The Louvre and the Arc de Triomphe glowed in the distance beyond the Île de la Cité.

A bitter chill cut through her body as she shared an umbrella with Bettencourt. "Careful," the French woman warned. "It is slippery."

They returned to the narrow walkway known as the Galerie de Chimières, where haunting grotesques surrounded them. The rain and power outage cast the gallery in an eerie atmosphere. In the murky morning, the cathedral's stone citizens possessed an unnatural animation. Crouching dragons and dogs and demons seemed poised to attack. Cori peeked over the ledge for a glimpse of the Christmas tree below. The parvis glistened with rain. It was a straight drop of two hundred feet.

The gallery was encased in a security cage, a web of steel-reinforced cables separating them from the grotesques perched on the cathedral walls. Bettencourt grabbed the security fence. "Some people come to Notre-Dame with the motive of ending their lives. In 1989, a suicidal man dove off the tower and landed on a thirteen-year-old girl waiting in line near the entrance. A year later, this security retainer was installed to prevent further tragedies."

"Still, it's a shame they had to close it in like this," Wurm said, tipping back his umbrella to inspect the retainer trusses stretching overhead.

"It can't be helped," Bettencourt yelled over the roar of the raindrops pounding on the umbrella. "But now to other things. Permit me to introduce Le Stryge." She pointed to a winged grotesque perched on the ledge, his head crowned with horns.

Cupping his jaw in his hands, the creature had stabbed his tongue at the Paris skyline for more than a century and a half. On the way up the tower stairs, Bettencourt had explained that the grotesque had guarded Notre-Dame for less than a decade when illustrator Charles Meryon christened him Le Stryge in 1854. Later, American artist John

Taylor Arms playfully named him Le Penseur, or the
Thinker. Memorialized in sepia-washed postcards, he was
better known as the Spitting Gargoyle.

Created during the cathedral's restoration, the grotesque was rumored to be spitting at the site that would
host the Eiffel Tower in 1889. Nicolette Bettencourt
seemed to relish the symbolism of stone taunting steel, a
blithe gesture of the old world mocking the new.

"I was thinking about della Rovere coming up the
stairs," Cori said. "I'm guessing, but maybe the priest hid
the Scintilla inside a gargoyle in 1502, before Cesare Borgia found him. Over the centuries, gargoyles crumbled
and crashed onto the parvis. Cut to Viollet-le-Duc's reconstruction during the 1840s. The architect removes any
gargoyles posing a safety risk. During the reconstruction, he discovers the Scintilla inside a deteriorating gargoyle."

"What are you driving at?" Bettencourt asked.

"Maybe the architect finds this thing and decides to
conceal it inside a new grotesque. Around that time, he
tells Carl Jung's grandfather, the grand master of the
Swiss Masons."

"Viollet-le-Duc traveled often to Switzerland," Bettencourt said. "He lived his final years in Lausanne. He died
there in 1879."

"It is plausible he might have known Jung's grandfather," Cori added. She tugged on the network of security cables that separated them from Le Stryge and other
grotesques mounted around the gallery. "Can we go out
there to see him?"

"Promise to be careful. It is dark and quite dangerous,"
Bettencourt said, handing over the umbrella. She unlocked a black door composed of metal bars, like on a jail
cell. "Go, but I must see Vaden before he becomes suspicious." She headed for the tower.

Cori maneuvered her umbrella through the security
door to visit Le Stryge. She popped it open again as Wurm

joined her. The grotesque looked more sinister up close. Her mind flashed to a childhood memory of watching *The Wizard of Oz*. The Spitting Gargoyle reminded her of those creepy flying monkeys that raised hell with Dorothy and her pals.

Wurm leaned close. The slick black skin of their umbrellas pressed together. "You think the Scintilla is inside this thing?"

"Hope so." She found herself wondering why Viollet-le-Duc had chosen the cathedral's most famous grotesque to guard the Scintilla. Why draw attention to the hiding place? Then she realized the architect had had no conception of the fame that awaited Le Stryge.

Power returned to the cathedral, bathing the western facade in light. She jumped, then caught her breath. Hugging herself, she looked at the clearing sky. The rain stopped, but the air had turned bitter. She leaned her umbrella against the railing.

To the grotesque's left was a shrieking owl sculpture, its tongue also sticking out. Beneath Le Stryge, two leaf-shaped decorations known as crockets curved out from the gallery railing, the top projecting farther than the one beneath it. Near the crockets, poles with miniature spotlights protruded beyond the railing. Lights cast an amber glow on the grotesque.

With damp hair plastered against her face, Cori closed her eyes. Reaching around Le Stryge's wing, her hand glided along his pitted hide. Like a blind person exploring an unfamiliar face, she moved her fingers from the horns down to the ridged forehead and around to his deep ear cavities. She touched the sunken cheekbones and flaring nostrils of his hooknose. Nearly two centuries of unforgiving Parisian weather had dulled the grotesque's features. Once sharp and curved like a saber-toothed cat fang, the horns were now shorter and flattened on top. The crown on his forehead had eroded. So had his nose, and even the tip of his notorious tongue.

"There's one sure way to see if the Scintilla is inside," Wurm said, staring at Le Stryge. "Let's break open this thing."

"We can't destroy this grotesque. It's an important artifact."

"It's nothing more than a bloody rock."

Hearing footsteps from behind, Cori and Wurm turned. A man stepped from the northern tower. He was tall and brawny, cords framing his muscular neck. He fumed as he stepped through the door, joining them on the small balcony.

"Santo Borgia," Wurm said. "Haven't seen you since the slaughterhouse."

"We found our mother's body at Bollingen," Santo said, balling his fist. "How many of us have you killed over the years, Dr. Wurm?"

"How many Borgias?" he asked. "Must be three or four. I'm a decent fighter. It always surprises people when they get their butt kicked by a mathematician. But I didn't kill your mother. Lucrezia struck her head in the watery chamber beneath Jung's tower."

"Expect me to believe that? Just shut up and hand over the relic."

Wurm shook his head. "It is lost to history."

Santo lunged, then snapped his arms around Cori. Wurm jumped on him, but Santo Borgia flung him off. Screaming, Cori wriggled enough to bite his hand. It didn't faze him. With a sweeping motion, Santo hoisted her body above his head, then pitched her over Le Stryge. She felt weightless as her body cut through the air. Flying over the grotesque, Cori saw the parvis far below. She couldn't breathe, terror freezing her lungs.

On Notre-Dame's tower gallery, Wurm watched as Santo Borgia heaved Cori over Le Stryge. Wurm burst into a rage, then rammed into the man. Borgia was a powerhouse, all force and muscle, but he was no match for

Wurm's fury. He swung the metal flashlight, shattering Santo's collarbone before clubbing his skull. He heard bone crack in Borgia's nose. Dropping the flashlight, Wurm grabbed the man's arm and neck, driving his body as he slammed Borgia's head into the stone balustrade.

"You shouldn't have thrown Cori off the tower," he snarled.

Wurm stepped over the unconscious man, then rushed to the ledge.

Cori dangled on the bottom crocket a few feet beneath Le Stryge. As Santo had flipped her over the grotesque, she had twisted toward the gallery wall. Jerking sideways, she'd missed Le Stryge but slammed into the top crocket. It had busted apart as pain roared in her left arm. The bottom crocket jabbed her rib cage, slowing her fall before she grabbed the curved stone.

Straining to pull herself up, she realized how close she had come to dying. Hanging from the crocket, she thought about how it could still happen if she lost her hold and dropped two hundred feet to the parvis. Finding a desperate breath, she wrapped her arm around the crocket. She swung her leg over the metal pole holding the spotlight. Bracing against the parapet, she glanced at the highest crocket below Le Stryge, the one broken by her fall. A wooden handle stuck out of busted masonry. She guessed Viollet-le-Duc had stashed the object inside the crocket beneath the grotesque's ledge during his restoration.

Her arm burning as she climbed, Cori grasped the meaning behind Le Stryge's famous spitting tongue. Never intended as a mocking gesture at the Eiffel Tower's future home, the grotesque's tongue instead pointed at the crocket a few feet below. The Scintilla wasn't concealed inside the grotesque, but beneath him. Her muscles protested as she reached for Le Stryge. Wurm appeared from behind the grotesque. He pulled her onto the balustrade.

Cori saw Santo Borgia facedown on the gallery floor. She panted, "Nice work."

Wurm brought her into his big arms. "I thought I'd lost you."

The affection surprised her. He pulled away, acting like the moment had never happened. He pointed at Le Stryge. "We need to tear apart this brute."

"No need," she answered, straddling the ledge. "Take a look."

He looped his arm around Le Stryge. Leaning over the balustrade, he studied the crocket beneath the grotesque.

"Crumbled when I fell on it." She clawed at a handle sticking out of the broken crocket. Masonry chunks crumbled away as she tugged on the handle.

He handed the umbrella to her. "Jam the sharp end of this into the stone."

Cori chiseled away at the eroded stone. A minute later, she wiggled the handle from the fractured crocket. "A hammer. An ancient one."

"Probably belonged to one of Viollet-le-Duc's workers," Wurm said, sliding back to the gallery. He sighed, "We need the Scintilla, not a hammer."

Chapter Fifty-one

Las Vegas
8:22 P.M.

Brynstone was reeling. He remembered his phone call with Metzger, when they'd first hit town. The assassin had said that Shay was in a "safe place." He meant it. The sick son of a bitch had locked her inside a wall safe. How long could she survive in there?

Although the Vegas high-rise was far from finished, contractors had already installed safes in the luxury suites. The safe featured an LED display and an electronic push-button lock like the one on the door to Zaki's mummy chamber. He figured Metzger had used an audit trail module unit to override the original password-protected combination. After that, he could program in a new combination.

His daughter's muffled cry rose from inside.

"Baby girl?" he called. "Daddy's here. I'll get you out."

Brynstone needed to think like Metzger. He tapped the alphanumeric keypad, punching in the code 7-2-3-4-9, a number sequence spelling out *Radix*. Didn't work. He tried 3-7-4-2-4 for Metzger's first name. No success. He tried Metzger's birth date. Then he punched in the sequence 8-7-8-3-2 for Truda, the assassin's mother. No luck. *Be systematic*, he coached himself. Five-letter German words passed through his mind. None unlocked the safe.

He was running out of time to save Shay. Her cries sounded weaker. He kept talking as he punched digits. "Hang on, baby girl."

Shay whimpered. He had to break this combination. He didn't think about another thing until he heard his wife's voice.

"John? Where are you?"

"Kaylyn, get out," he called. "Metzger's around here somewhere."

"*Ja*, I am."

He spun around. Metzger was twelve feet away, bare-chested and unarmed. His face was swollen. His leg a bloody mess. His shirt served as a tourniquet.

"Give me the combination," Brynstone growled, training the Glock on him.

Metzger limped closer. "Let's trade. The Radix for the combination."

He was unarmed. Didn't matter. He would be a threat even on his deathbed.

He purred through a reptilian smile, "Do you wish to kill me? Or do you wish to save Shayna?"

"Both. Now stay where you are."

Metzger came closer. "I understand you, Dr. Brynstone. I thought that like me, you were a man without fear. But that's not true, is it? There is one thing that terrifies you. Something that scares you to death. And that's losing your family."

He was eight feet away. Brynstone aimed lower. "Want me to take out your other leg?"

Metzger stopped.

Brynstone caught movement to his right. Jordan stepped from the shadows. She pressed the SIG's barrel against Kaylyn's temple. Fear washed over his wife's face.

Erich Metzger and Jordan Rayne were competing for the Radix. Metzger could kill Shay. Jordan could kill Kaylyn. Ugly choices. Brynstone took his aim off Metzger, then pointed the gun at Jordan. Could he take her out without hitting Kaylyn? His wife's terrified eyes made him hesitate.

Jordan snarled, "Give me the Radix or I'll kill Kaylyn."

"I expected more from you," Brynstone said between gritted teeth. "I never thought you would work for the Borgias."

"The Borgias work for me," she boasted. "I'm using them. Tell you what, John. Give me the Radix and we'll sell it to my buyer. I'll cut you in for half."

"You're holding a gun to my wife's head, Jordan. You double-crossed Delgado and the Borgias. You expect me to trust you?"

"Do you realize," Metzger asked in a hushed voice, "that your baby has stopped crying?"

Brynstone held his breath and listened.

"Tell me," Metzger said, "have you seen a baby die of asphyxiation? As cyanosis sets in, her face changes to a bluish purple color. Blood vessels pop as her eyes begin to bulge."

"Give him the Radix," Kaylyn screamed.

"Shut up," Jordan demanded. She shook her powerful arm, jerking Kaylyn's head. She pressed the barrel beneath Kaylyn's eye. Brynstone swallowed. Jordan had betrayed him. How far would she go? He looked at Metzger. "I'm getting the Radix." He reached into his pocket, then removed the *cista mystica*. He lifted the lid, then held up the vial containing Wurm's replica of the Radix. "Tell me the combination."

"Think about your wife, John," Jordan growled.

Metzger smiled. "I'll give you three numbers. Give me the Radix. I'll give the last two."

Sweat breaking on his forehead, Brynstone dropped the *cista mystica*, then said, "Do it."

"*Drei-drei-zwei.*" Metzger paused.

"You're making a big mistake," Jordan called. "Forget about Shayna. Save your wife, John. You and Kaylyn can have another kid."

Keeping the gun steady, he bent down, then rolled the vial across the floor. He cocked his head, making a quick glance at the safe as he punched in 3-3-2. The vial rolled across the floor before stopping at Metzger's blood-speckled boot. The assassin grabbed the vial, then studied the small root inside. Would Metzger know it was a decoy? Brynstone had no choice but to chance it. "The last two numbers?" he demanded.

Metzger's eyes gleamed. His lips parted; then he answered in a raspy voice, "*Acht—*"

Brynstone knew the last number, saying "*vier*" at the same time as Metzger, realizing the 3-3-2-8-4 combination spelled D-E-A-T-H. He turned away, knowing the man might charge. He couldn't deprive his daughter of air a second longer. He punched the final two numbers. The bolt inside the safe released. As he opened the door, he looked back to shoot Metzger.

He was gone.

Brynstone aimed the gun at Jordan. Kaylyn was on the floor, rubbing her head. Jordan Rayne was nowhere in sight. He holstered his gun, then reached inside the safe for his daughter.

Chapter Fifty-two

Las Vegas
8:26 P.M.

Erich Metzger slipped out of the Helios Tower. In the darkness of the construction site, he brought out his phone, then headed for his vehicle. The Knight answered after the first ring.

"I have the Radix," Metzger told him.

"Excellent. My contact is waiting to meet you. Take the Radix—"

"I must call back," he whispered. "Someone is coming." He ended the call.

A figure ducked around a yellow backhoe loader, as if stalking prey. He knew who it was and the realization warmed him. Kaylyn had been a curiosity and an amusement. But this American woman named Jordan? She was pure fascination. He watched her glide in the shadows. Jordan found his van. If he waited, she would find him. There was no time for that.

Ignoring the pain in his leg, he limped toward her. "Ms. Rayne, may I congratulate you?"

She gasped in surprise, bringing her gun around in one fluid motion.

"You impress me. You engineered some lovely tricks on Brynstone, that nasty Borgia family, the National Security Agency, and God knows who else. Beautifully played."

"Give me the Radix," she demanded.

"That can be arranged. I understand you intend to make money from this little root. May I inquire about your buyer?"

"Taft-Ryder Pharmaceuticals."

"A drug company. The Radix would appeal to them. How much money?"

"Two billion placed in a numbered account in Luxembourg. I'm meeting a contact in the desert in one hour. I get the first billion tonight. The second after they authenticate it."

"A man who calls himself the Knight hired me. Your drug lords are offering a great deal more than my knight. Perhaps we could work together." He locked his hands on his hips. "Although you are armed and I am not, we both know I can kill you. Are we agreed on that?"

She didn't answer.

"You can die here now or make me a partner and give me a fifty-fifty cut."

She studied him, thinking it over.

"Do you hear the sirens?" he asked. "The Brynstones have called an ambulance. Las Vegas's finest will be here any moment. Don't take long deciding your fate."

"One question. Why cut a deal with me?"

"I'm willing to gamble on you," he purred. "Isn't that what Vegas is all about?"

Chapter Fifty-three

At the bottom of Notre-Dame's north-tower stairs, Cori heard a distant voice. She grabbed Wurm's arm. "Adriana's here. Coming this way."

They ducked behind a marble column.

Adriana hustled up the spiral staircase, calling her brother's name.

"I don't want to mess with the Borgias," Cori said. "Let's go."

"Not without the Scintilla. We've come too far. Sacrificed too much. And all we have is this blasted hammer. It's not fit to pound a proper nail." Wurm struck the weathered hammer against a pillar. The head broke off before spiraling to the floor. "See what I mean?"

Tilting her head, she stared at the wooden handle in Wurm's hand. She studied it. Rolled vellum peeked from the center of the headless hammer. "There's something inside."

He shone his flashlight on the straight-grained ash handle. "Looks like Viollet-le-Duc hollowed out the hammer to conceal something in here. Then he placed it inside the crocket under Le Stryge during his cathedral reconstruction."

She removed the curled strip of vellum from the hammer. Two columns, written in some ancient Semitic script. Unable to read it, she handed the vellum to Wurm.

"Is it the Scintilla?" she asked, unable to suppress her excitement.

Wurm looked up with twinkling eyes. "It's the formula for the White Chrism."

He flipped it over.

"What's wrong?"

His brows furrowed. "Nothing here about the Black Chrism. It looks like the bottom portion has been torn off. I wonder—"

"Edgar, just tell me what it says."

As he translated the Aramaic and Hebraic text, she brought out her cell phone, then typed each ingredient into an e-mail message.

"What are you doing?"

"Keep going," she said, tapping keys with both thumbs. "I'm sending this to John."

Wurm finished the list of ingredients. "How curious. Add these items to the prime material—the Radix—and it creates the spark."

She slid the rolled vellum inside the hammer's hollow base. She placed it inside her coat with the Radix. "Let's find Nicolette. Then we can go."

She called Bettencourt. The woman answered in a wavering voice.

"Help me, Cori. I am in the spire."

"What's wrong?"

"You must come now. Hurry." She ended the call.

"Let's go, Edgar. I think Nicolette is in trouble."

They rushed down the cavernous nave, then darted toward the stairs leading to the spire.

At the top of the stairs, they found Nicolette leaning against the doorway, making the sign of the cross. Cori came over, running her arm across the woman's shoulder.

"Nicolette, what's wrong?"

"Dear God," Wurm said, shining his flashlight into the spire.

She moved beside him.

From high inside the spire, a thick rope rocked Anton Vaden in midair. A slipknot squeezed the guard's broken neck. The man's glazed eyes stared at her.

Cori steadied Vaden's body as Wurm tried to free him from the rope. Nicolette Bettencourt wiped away tears, unable to look at the dead man.

Footfalls sounded on the stairs behind them.

Adriana Borgia appeared in the spire doorway with her brother. After Wurm's beating, Santo's nose was bloody. One arm dangled at his side.

"Leave him hanging. I like him better that way." She pointed a gun. "Hand over the relic from the gargoyle's crocket."

"Forget it," Cori answered, aware of the hammer handle in her coat pocket.

Bettencourt came over. "*Putain!*" she cursed at Adriana. "You monsters killed my friend. Are you out of your minds?" The French woman lunged, wrestling the gun from Adriana. Without hesitation, she flipped around, kicking the weapon from Bettencourt's hand.

Santo Borgia dove for the gun. Wurm got there first, kicking it down the stairs. Santo threw a cross-body block on Wurm, then tore into him with punch after punch.

Cori backed away.

Bettencourt leveled a decent hit on Adriana's chin. She shrugged, then wiped blood from her mouth before blasting her fist into Bettencourt's gut. Adriana followed with a jumping kick to her neck. Bettencourt went down, but grabbed Adriana's ankle, toppling her.

As Wurm struggled to get free, Cori threw herself on Santo's back, clawing his face. He dropped Wurm, then reached over his shoulder. Santo grabbed her arm, then yanked, flipping Cori into the wall. Santo shoved aside Anton Vaden's twirling body as he stalked her. She saw his fist coming and blocked it with her forearm. The collision felt like she had jarred every bone in her body. He grabbed her wrist, twisting hard. Rage boiled in his eyes, hungry and unpredictable. She broke away, but he caught her wool coat. Santo Borgia ripped it from her body and tossed the coat out the spire window.

Her eyes brightened with horror. *"No!"* she cried.

She needed to climb out there to get the Radix and Scintilla from her coat pocket. Reaching for the window, she felt Santo grab her neck. He twisted her arm and flung her to the ground. She collapsed, breath paralyzed in her throat.

"She wants something in that coat," Santo called to his sister.

"Must be the relic," Adriana answered before Bettencourt pinned her to the wall.

Catching his breath, Wurm attacked Santo from behind. As he tried to stand, Wurm kicked, driving his size-fourteen shoe into Santo's face. Borgia hit the wall and slumped.

"That's payback for the slaughterhouse."

Wurm scrambled to the window and climbed out the spire.

Adriana shoved aside Bettencourt, then grabbed the rope and slid out the opening after Wurm. Instead of chasing her, Bettencourt hustled down the stairs outside the spire door. Cori struggled to her feet. The pain seemed hotter now, searing deep inside.

Bettencourt returned, holding Vaden's gun.

Cori peered down the southeastern side, where they had wrapped Jung's sash around Saint Thomas's staff less than an hour ago. It wasn't a straight drop off the roof. Instead, a narrow catwalk separated the roof from the flying buttresses. With the coat in hand, Wurm was almost to the edge, gripping the rope as he eased down the shingles. She felt helpless, watching as Wurm made it to the catwalk. Adriana wasn't far behind, easing down the slick roof.

"She's gaining on him."

"Enough is enough. We must stop that terrible woman," Bettencourt muttered, aiming Vaden's gun. "I have one shot. Better make it count."

Cori spun, hearing a sound. Santo Borgia had climbed to his feet. Bettencourt turned, pointing the gun. Santo ducked behind Vaden's hanging body.

"Shoot me and you shoot him," he warned, before taunting, "We had fun stringing up this loser."

"Ta gueule!" Bettencourt yelled.

Santo moved out from behind Vaden. "I'm gonna have fun playing with you two girls."

He started to charge. Bettencourt squeezed off the final shot, the bullet ripping through his upper chest. Borgia staggered to his knees. The big man looked in amazement as smoke rolled from the hole in his shirt. He forced a shallow cough before collapsing on the spire floor.

Police sirens wailed in the distance.

Cori looked west beyond Notre-Dame's twin towers toward the Préfecture de Police. She turned and looked back out the spire. Holding her coat, Wurm headed east along the balcony. Adriana was gaining, about twenty feet behind him.

Grabbing the rope, Cori climbed out the window. Bettencourt followed.

Edgar Wurm removed the Radix from the coat pocket. Adriana hadn't noticed as she stepped onto the catwalk above the flying buttresses. This time, he wasn't giving it back to Cori.

"We've come a long way together," Adriana purred. "Haven't we?"

"You're smarter than your half brothers. But like your mother, you've gone too far. Lucrezia was a good woman, but her obsession with the Radix blinded her."

"Isn't the same true of you, Father?"

"I told you to never call me that." Wurm raised his bandaged fingers. "Especially after what you did to me back at the slaughterhouse."

"I've never revealed our little secret," Adriana laughed, strutting as she moved closer. "My half brothers don't know about you and mother."

"They never will. That was your late mother's wish as well as my own. If you respect Lucrezia, you'll remain silent about my relationship with her."

"Throw me the coat," Adriana demanded, walking toward him on the catwalk.

"What's in it for me?"

"Your life."

He shrugged, then tossed Cori's coat to Adriana. She dug in the pocket and removed the hammer. She saw the vellum peeking out. Her face brightened. "At last, the Scintilla." She dropped the coat between the buttresses surrounding the cathedral.

Behind her, Cori and Nicolette reached the catwalk.

Sirens cried over the soft rush of the River Seine. Wurm looked down. With lights blazing, white police cars raced across the sidewalk of the Square Jean XXIII, a park bordering the cathedral. French police flooded the grounds with weapons raised.

"Edgar!" Cori screamed. "Get down. Police want you down."

Three officers leaned out the spire. A policewoman dressed in a dark blue uniform barked orders. Cori and Nicolette crouched on their knees, hands behind their heads.

Wurm opened the vial.

"What's that?" Adriana squinted. "It's the Radix, isn't it? Jordan told us Brynstone took it to Vegas."

"Thought you had it all figured out, didn't you? Your people will never learn."

She extended her hand. "Give me the Radix. I have Cesare Borgia's blood flowing inside me. The Radix is my birthright."

"I am destined to be the Keeper." The root slid onto his palm. He held up the Radix, pinched between his thumb and forefinger. "This is my salvation for a broken life."

Adriana sprinted toward him. An officer started firing. A shot ricocheted off the ledge and grazed her hip. Another ripped through her arm but didn't slow her.

Wurm popped the Radix into his mouth.

Seeing her father swallow the root, Adriana's face registered fury in the midair sweep of a jumping kick. Her black boot slammed into his chest, thrusting him backward. As he teetered on the catwalk, she grabbed his throat, digging fingers into his flesh.

"Cough up the Radix," she barked.

A bullet pierced his leg. Adriana shuddered as gunfire ripped through her neck. Her powerful hand was still gripping Wurm's throat as they plummeted. Locked together, their bodies glanced off an arching buttress before hitting the hard wet surface.

Cori screamed as Edgar Wurm and Adriana Borgia fell from the cathedral. Officers climbed down to the catwalk, shouting in French. Behind her, Bettencourt yelled back at them.

Reeling from the sight of Wurm's death, Cori buried her head in her hands. She pulled back, teary eyed, then stared down at his broken body draped over Adriana. She bit her lip, then tried to stand. She hadn't always understood Wurm, but Cori knew she would never forget him.

Chapter Fifty-four

Las Vegas
8:39 P.M.

John and Kaylyn Brynstone had resuscitated their daughter back at the Helios Tower. Had it been enough? Huddled over Shay's limp body, they rode in a blaring blue and white ambulance. His soul felt numb, holding her tiny blue hand as a female EMT used a laryngoscope to place a tube in Shay's windpipe. Unable to watch, Kaylyn glanced out the back window, looking toward the Paris and Bally's resorts as the ambulance headed east on Flamingo.

"Hospital's three miles from the Strip," the EMT said. "Been a crazy night. A military helicopter crashed into the Bellagio fountains. Both pilots died. Thank God no one else did."

Brynstone nodded, staring with weary eyes but not seeing the woman. Not seeing anything.

Washington, D.C.
11:40 P.M.

"Pantera has the Radix," Deena Riverside said into her cell. "Are you ready to make the exchange as we discussed?"

"You got it," Kirby Faulkner said. His voice sounded gruff, but professional.

He had been a private detective for years. A decade back, the state of Indiana's Private Detective Licensing

Board had revoked his license. After that, he joined
Omara Associates, a risk-consulting company that provided security services to major corporations. He was a
perfect contact to make the exchange with Pantera.

"Same place we agreed on?"

"El Dorado Canyon," she said, pacing in the hospital
hallway. "You're in Vegas now?"

"Correct. I have the account information for the exchange," Faulkner said. "I'll meet with Pantera. Then I'll
call when I have the Radix."

Deena slid the phone in her purse, then searched the
hospital for President Armstrong. She couldn't wait to
tell him the news.

Las Vegas
8:44 P.M.

Brynstone glanced out the window as the ambulance
turned off East Flamingo onto South Bruce. Dressed in
curving brown-and-tan-checked brick, the Desert Springs
Hospital featured an oversized green glass window set
behind six palm trees. As the ambulance turned off Bruce,
he saw a red emergency sign.

In their time at the Las Vegas hospital, the emergency
staff had treated drunken gamblers, messed-up prosti-
tutes, and assorted celebrities. They'd seen about everything, so no one registered surprise when the Brynstones
hurried in with their daughter.

Kaylyn followed as they spirited away Shay. Staff per-
mitted one visitor at a time. They didn't argue over the
choice.

Outside Henderson, Nevada
8:58 P.M.

Metzger turned the Chevrolet Starcraft onto Highway 95,
heading south. He always preferred nondescript vehicles,

not caring to draw attention to himself. A van such as this one had been perfect for transporting a kidnapped woman and her mewling infant. He supposed it was less suitable for driving around with a beautiful woman.

He rolled down the window, inviting in a refreshing desert breeze. "How much farther to El Dorado Canyon?"

"Less than thirty miles," Jordan said, in the seat beside him. "I'm meeting a man named Kirby Faulkner. He's a representative for Taft-Ryder. I've confirmed it with Deena Riverside, the Taft-Ryder CEO. She's the one I called when we left Vegas."

"How much does she know about the Radix?"

"Enough to pay dearly for it."

"Might I ask how you came to work with Taft-Ryder?"

"After I learned about the Radix, I began profiling big pharmaceutical companies. Taft-Ryder had fallen on hard times and needed a 'miracle drug' boost. Their CEO is willing to take big risks and play dirty. These big pharmaceuticals like to sabotage each other. Faulkner did some behind-the-scenes corporate warfare stuff for Taft-Ryder. Even better, her company has a connection with Dillon Armstrong. He brought in the big-time cash."

"How much does Riverside know about you?"

"She's never seen me. We only communicate via text message."

"You identified yourself as Pantera when you spoke to her," he said. "The Italian word for 'panther.' It fits."

"I thought so."

His phone chimed. He grabbed it, then gave a cold smile when he saw the number.

"Who is it?" Jordan asked.

"The Knight."

"Put him on speaker."

"I'd rather not."

"Jeez, cowboy, what are you afraid of?"

In an amused voice, he said, "You're playing with me. Aren't you, Jordan?"

"C'mon. We're partners now. Besides, I want to hear what your knight sounds like. Hurry before he hangs up."

"He won't hang up. He's relentless." Keeping one hand on the steering wheel, he punched the speaker button. Metzger sensed that the Knight was furious. He disguised his voice with indifference.

"Before you hung up on me, you said you had the Radix. Do you?"

"*Ja.*"

"You ended your call because someone was approaching."

"A woman. Some redhead Brynstone brought with him. Beautiful but annoying."

"Did you talk to her?"

"*Nein.* I killed her." He was having fun now. Metzger glanced over at Jordan. Her green eyes grew wide and blank. Her striking face had drained of color.

"Good," the Knight answered.

"Now, leave me alone or you will not ever see the Radix. The next time we talk will be when I call you."

Metzger ended the call before the Knight could protest. He glanced at the woman. "Did I frighten you?"

"That was the Knight?" she asked. "That's the guy who hired you to kill Brynstone and get the Radix?"

Metzger nodded. "Why?"

"I know the guy. I'd recognize that voice in my sleep."

"Are you certain?"

"Bet my life on it." Jordan ran her fingers through her red hair. "The Knight? The man who called you? He's my boss. His name is Lieutenant General James Delgado."

Las Vegas
9:04 P.M.

After a Desert Springs Hospital ER nurse treated the gunshot wounds in Brynstone's shoulder and leg, Las Vegas cops quizzed him about events at the Helios Tower.

The conversation didn't last long after he showed his government credentials. They made a phone call, then let him go.

A few minutes later, Kaylyn emerged from ICU with a report. She was distraught and inconsolable, hugging herself. Lost in shock, she muttered a few words to Brynstone. He tried to talk to her. She wasn't interested. He understood, watching her return to ICU.

A family in the waiting room called some relatives, explaining that their father had suffered multiple seizures after neurosurgery for a brain tumor. Brynstone left the room, giving them privacy. Walking down the hallway, he found himself thinking about Jordan. She had betrayed him by working with the Borgias. Jordan must've told them to follow Wurm and Cori to Bollingen. She may have told the Borgias to head to Notre-Dame after Jordan called Cori from LA. He guessed Jordan's plan was to bide her time until the Borgias had the Scintilla.

He didn't like hospitals, but he'd do whatever he could to help Shay. After that, he'd find Erich Metzger. Then he'd track down Jordan Rayne.

As he bought a bottle of Propel water from a vending machine, he overheard two docs discussing his daughter. They didn't recognize him. Their story sounded grim compared with the version Kaylyn had heard. One doctor predicted Shay would last a few hours at most.

Shaken by the news, he walked past the nurses' station on his way to the chapel. He went inside and sat down in a pew, staring at the blood-spattered bunny. His gaze drifted to a stained-glass picture. Sunshine illuminated a lakeside mountain. Two trees sheltered red and orange flowers. The idyllic scene brought to mind a passage from Ezekiel 47:12, describing a tree that grew alongside a river outside the Temple. Ezekiel claimed the tree's leaf never faded and was used as medicine. It was the first description of the Radix in the Old Testament.

He hadn't thought about the Radix in hours. He tucked the stuffed animal back in his coat, then pulled out the *cista mystica*. He removed the stone lid, then stared at the empty box. Then he grabbed his cell and called Cori.

Paris
6:05 A.M.

Standing on the parvis, Cori watched French SAMU paramedics wheel out the bodies of Edgar Wurm, Anton Vaden, and Adriana Borgia. They loaded the corpses into white cars that resembled station wagons more than American ambulances. The Paris police had seized the hammer and the Scintilla vellum. An officer discussed the relics on a conference call with a Louvre curator and an agent from the Art and Antique Squad at Scotland Yard.

As Cori was escorted by a policewoman, her phone rang. The petite officer held it in her white-gloved hand. Cori struggled to say "That's my phone" in French, then added, *"s'il vous plaît?"*

The woman glanced at another officer before handing over the phone.

She grabbed it, offering a quick *"Merci."*

Chapter Fifty-five

Brynstone paced the Desert Springs chapel, ear pressed against the phone. It rang forever before Cori picked up. Her voice was fragile and weary.

"John, how's your family?"

"Not good. I'll explain later. Where are you?"

"Paris. They're taking me to the police station."

"Did you find the Scintilla?"

"Yeah. I sent you an e-mail with the ingredients. Did you get it?"

"Let me look." He found Cori's message with ingredients for the White Chrism. Balsam. Figs. Salt. A few other ingredients. And of course, the Radix.

"Yeah, I got it," he said, his voice cracking. "Cori, um, my daughter is dying."

"Oh, John. I'm sorry."

"I need the Radix. Now."

She paused. "I can't do that."

"Wh-why not?"

"Edgar Wurm swallowed it. Right before he died."

"Wurm's dead?" Brynstone slumped against a wall. He couldn't believe it.

"John? *John*, are you there? I have to hang up."

"Never should've happened this way," he muttered.

Her voice went low. "You know that locket I gave you?"

He was dazed. "What?"

"The locket I gave you at Teterboro Airport. Back in Jersey. You know, the one from my mother. Still have it?"

He fished inside his pocket. "Yeah."

"Give it to your daughter."

"Give it to Shay?"

"I have to go," she said, careful about her words. "Give the locket to your daughter. Trust me and do it. *Now*. It'll help her feel better."

"Cori?"

She was gone.

He studied the ornate locket. He pressed on the delicate golden clasp, then opened it. His eyes widened. The locket held a green sliver with a blackish purple bloom. Before flying to Switzerland, Cori must've stripped a piece from the Radix, then placed it inside the locket.

Jumping up, Brynstone sprinted down the corridor, catching a nurse.

"If my wife comes out," he said, "tell her I'll be right back."

El Dorado Canyon, Nevada
9:12 P.M.

At one time, El Dorado Canyon had hosted one of the biggest silver booms in Nevada history. Now, on an eerie Christmas night, the same desert would witness an exchange that Jordan predicted would rock the pharmaceutical industry.

"Where is your man?" Metzger asked.

"Kirby Faulkner? He'll be here."

"Why aren't you meeting him inside the canyon?"

"There's one way in and one way out. Road dead-ends at the Colorado River. Not a good place for an exchange." She flashed a seductive smile. "Mind giving me the Radix?"

"First, give me the Luxembourg account number and your passwords."

Jordan brought out her smartphone, then showed him. Metzger pursed his lips. He held out his hand, revealing a vial. She snatched it.

"I see headlights," he said, before climbing in the backseat.

Seventy feet away, a Mercedes slowed to a stop in a cloud of dust.

Jordan cursed. She had opened the vial and was examining the stalk.

"Is there a problem?"

"John let me see the Radix when we were flying from Aspen. It was inside a small stone box. He removed it, but—"

"But what, Ms. Rayne?"

"This is not the Radix. Bastard switched it on us," she muttered to herself. "This is a replica of the Radix. Not bad, but it's nothing like the real thing."

"Does it matter?" he asked. "From what you said, no one but you and Brynstone have seen it in over five hundred years." He peered through the windshield. Kirby Faulkner stepped from the Mercedes. "He won't know it's fake until after we have the money."

"We'll only get half now. We won't get the rest if they realize it's a fake."

"One billion isn't bad for a counterfeit miracle plant." He patted her shoulder. "*Go.*"

Metzger admired Jordan Rayne's body as she walked out to meet Faulkner in the Nevada desert. She was tough and beautiful, a rare combination. Jordan could be a worthy asset.

He glanced out the passenger window. The sandstone formations looked eerie in the moonlight. Like some German boys of his generation, he'd grown up watching American cowboy movies. El Dorado Canyon appealed to that childhood romance. Unlike his boyhood friends, however, Metzger identified with vigilantes more than the men with badges. He brought night-vision binoculars to his eyes. Jordan was talking to Kirby Faulkner. She was taller, blocking the man's face. She held out the vial. He took the root and inspected it with a flashlight. Faulkner was visible now. Middle-aged, dressed in a suit. He resembled an accountant.

Faulkner nodded. He made a phone call.

Jordan used her smartphone to confirm the transfer to a numbered Luxembourg account. She said something. Faulkner laughed. Satisfied, she turned away. Walking toward the van, she wore an enormous smile. Red hair drifted around her face, almost in slow motion.

"That was easy," Metzger said aloud.

Only it wasn't. Faulkner reached inside his coat, then pulled out a gun. Metzger bolted from his seat as the man shot Jordan in the back. She dropped. Faulkner shot her again.

Such a waste. Metzger sighed as he tossed aside the binoculars. He brought out his gun.

The night was clear as he emerged from the van. Faulkner had grabbed Jordan's smartphone. He headed to his Mercedes with the counterfeit Radix.

Metzger called out, "Excuse me."

The man turned, surprise blanking his features.

"Have you no dignity?" he asked, limping toward him. "You shot her in the back. You are a coward."

Faulkner reached into his coat. Metzger paused until the man brought out his weapon. Metzger raised his handgun and fired. The bullet sliced through two of Faulkner's fingers. The gun spiraled out of his hand. Metzger smiled. It was like something in a Western.

"Stay away," Faulkner cried, stumbling toward his car.

Metzger passed Jordan's body without looking down. "I will not shoot you in the back, coward," he called. "But I will kill you. Have no illusions about that."

Keeping his back to Metzger, Faulkner opened the car door, then started to crawl inside. The man looked back for a single second. His final mistake. Metzger's bullet

THE RADIX 323

shattered the window and pierced Faulkner's right eye. He dropped to the desert floor. Metzger came over and rolled the dead man. He reached inside the coat, then removed the smartphone with the Luxembourg account information. He kicked dirt on the man's bloody face.

He walked back to Jordan. He nudged her limp body, beautiful even in death. Such a waste. He held up the vial and studied it in the moonlight.

"My, my, my," Metzger said to the little root. "You have caused a great many problems for a great many people."

Las Vegas
9:14 P.M.

Las Vegas never slept. Unless you were off the Strip. And if you were, getting a taxi at night was close to impossible. Desperate for a ride, Brynstone glanced around the hospital parking lot, looking for an older car. Many vehicles from the eighties had a carbureted engine and a single ignition coil and distributor that made for an easy hot-wire.

He spied a teenager who had delivered pizza to the hospital. He stopped the kid and offered him a thousand to use his car. He insisted on driving, asking the pizza guy for directions to a grocery store. They stopped at a Sunflower Market on Tropicana, then made another stop. A nearby Walgreen's was closed. They drove to a Rite Aid on Spencer and Flamingo.

Darting into the store with a Sunflower grocery bag, he ripped a box from a shelf, then tore it open. Plastic spoons sprayed in every direction as he grabbed one. Dropping the box, he blasted past a customer, almost knocking him over as he sprinted down another aisle.

A clerk called for the manager.

After finding pharmaceutical items and a meat tenderizer, he took a plastic bowl, then peeled off the lid. He dropped to his knees in aisle four, then emptied the bag from the health-food store. He added balsam and fever-few in the bowl, then sprinkled in salt, wood sage, aloe, figs, and other ingredients. He grabbed the meat tenderizer and crushed everything together. He stirred the ingredients, then closed his eyes. Pausing for a deep breath, he opened Cori's locket. He dropped the Radix sliver into the bowl. He knew he'd better be right about this. Visualizing Shay's face, he mashed the root with the mixture, then grabbed a spoon and stirred.

The paste transformed into an iridescent liquid.

As he poured it into his empty Propel bottle, an Arab-American man in a white shirt and striped tie walked up to him. "Mister, you need to pay for that."

Brynstone handed the manager a hundred-dollar bill. "Sorry for the mess."

He sprinted toward the door. He had the White Chrism.

Paris
6:15 A.M.

The morning sky was bitter and still as a police car bearing Cori parked outside the Préfecture de Police. A French officer opened her door, while another extended his gloved hand to help her out. He was dressed in dark pants and a light blue shirt with a red epaulette curling over his shoulder.

She saw a young man standing in a circle of officers. Dressed in a black suit, he was lean and commanding, with a precision haircut. He argued with the chief inspector. The man pointed at Cori and said something in French. The inspector nodded to the officer beside her. The policewoman unlocked Cori's handcuffs. The man came over to her, squeezing past officers.

"Don't worry, Ms. Cassidy. I'm taking you home."

She was stunned. "Who are you?"

"My name is Stephen Angelilli. I'm with the Central Intelligence Agency. Give me a couple minutes more with the inspector; then we'll be on our way to the airport. I'll give you a briefing when we fly back to the States."

She thanked Agent Angelilli before remembering Wurm's claim that the CIA director was a Knight of Malta. Did the CIA know about everything that had happened at Notre-Dame?

She didn't ask.

Chapter Fifty-six

Washington, D.C.
12:17 A.M.

After his latest surgery, Dillon Armstrong had been transferred to a private ICU room at the George Washington University Hospital. It looked inevitable that he would lose both legs. To complicate things, he had developed a septic reaction where a blood infection had caused low blood pressure and increased heart rate. His wife, Brooke, had returned to a nearby hotel to rest.

The president invited Deena to join him and the First Lady as they held vigil at Dillon's bedside. Deena was apprehensive, but Helena Armstrong was cordial. It was difficult to see Dillon attached to tubes and medical equipment. He looked helpless. The minutes slowed, blurring into an indistinguishable haze. She wanted to call Faulkner, but resisted the urge. She hoped Pantera would deliver.

After the First Lady left the ICU to find a restroom, the president said, "Any news on the Radix?"

She shook her head, but detected urgency in his voice. "I'll call my contact person. It's been enough time." Falling back into a chair, she called Faulkner. It rang until his voice mail picked up. She left a brief message. "Call as soon as possible," she urged, then hung up.

The president had moved into the hallway to talk with a doctor. She ran her fingers through Dillon's hair, then walked to the window. She stared down at a statue of George Washington on horseback in Washington Circle.

"Al." Soft and drowsy, the word seemed to come from nowhere. She turned. Eyes open now, Dillon stared at the ceiling. His lips parted. "Al." He swallowed, then whispered, "ex."

"Alex," she yelled, heading for the bed. "Come here."

President Armstrong bolted in with a Latina nurse behind him. They hurried to Dillon's bed. The nurse took a look, then hurried to find a doctor. The president leaned over his brother.

"Alex." Dillon swallowed, forcing out another few words. "You win." He closed his eyes. His body slumped. A flood of doctors and nurses burst into the room, shoving aside President Armstrong and Deena. First to the bed, a nurse yelled, "We got V-tach."

"He's crashing," a doctor yelled. "Get the paddles."

A man rolled a cart to the bed. Panicked, Deena tried to get to Dillon. Too many people in the way. Alex grabbed her shoulder, pulling her back as she reached for the doctors.

"Charge two fifty. Clear."

She fought, trying to break away. President Armstrong was stronger. As Secret Service joined them, they hustled her out of the room. As they made it to the door, Deena heard a doctor say, "He's not responding. Charge three hundred."

Outside Fort Meade
12:21 A.M.

Riding in his limousine, the Knight was furious. Metzger wasn't returning his calls. His mood changed when he saw a call coming in from Gabriel Bitonti.

"Good news," the Knight said, answering it. "The Radix will soon be in our hands."

The Vatican doctor paused. "I am returning to Rome."

"Did you not hear? I will have the blessed Radix."

"Enough with your fantasies," Bitonti countered. "You are a madman."

His right eye twitched. In a measured voice, he said, "No one calls me that. Not even an official of the Mother Church."

"But you are mad. I say it as a doctor. I am demanding an investigation. You will be excommunicated. With God's blessing, you will find yourself in prison."

"What inspired this nonsense?"

"Your assistant, Max Cress, drove me around Washington, D.C."

"It was my idea."

"I asked to see the National Cathedral. After twenty minutes inside, a homeless man approached me. He had seen me talking to Cress before I entered the cathedral. The man had seen Cress kidnap his friend. He showed a picture of a man named Andy. I recognized the face."

The Knight held his breath.

"You are a fine artist," Bitonti continued. "And a madman."

"I am a knight," he shouted. "You would accept a homeless man's word over mine?"

"You will not be a knight for long. I contacted the Federal Association of the Order of Malta. They told me about you and the CIA director, Mr. McKibbon."

"What did they say?"

"They said you discussed finding the fabled Radix after an induction ceremony at Saint Patrick's Cathedral. No one believed you except McKibbon. They regard you as a fanatic. After I spoke with them, they now know you are a dangerous fanatic."

"Nothing but lies."

"You have brought dishonor to the Sovereign Order of

Malta. They will strip you of your knighthood. Of course, I can prove nothing until the police find Andy's body."

"Won't happen."

"I'm confident it will. You will lose your knighthood and your NSA directorship."

"Listen and fear me. I am a knight of the Lord. I am greater than your blind church. Run to the Vatican and hide. I will find you. And I will destroy you."

Bitonti hung up.

Delgado wrapped his fingers around the phone, snapping the cover shut.

Washington, D.C.
12:25 A.M.

President Armstrong waited outside the ICU. Deena buried her face in his shoulder, sobbing. Good thing Helena wasn't here to witness the moment.

"He'll pull through. Dillon always pulls through."

He couldn't escape the thought of his brother in a wheelchair. He was active and still a decent athlete for a man his age. It would be a blow for Dillon to lose his legs.

A doctor walked up, a small man with a pinched face and dark crescents under his eyes. "Mr. President. Can I speak with you?"

He nodded. Deena pulled back, wiping her eyes.

"It's about your brother. I'm sorry to tell you . . ."

The words faded into a deadened silence, the man still moving his lips, but the words not making their way to Armstrong. He glanced at Deena, looking into her reddened eyes. And he knew. He knew that she and his brother had shared something that went far beyond business. And he knew that he had lost Dillon forever.

Chapter Fifty-seven

Brynstone had not come into this assignment as a believer. Everything changed after he saw blood ooze from Friar Zanchetti's mummy. Now more than ever, he believed in the power of the Radix. Was skepticism even a choice right now? Not if he wanted to save his daughter.

It seemed like forever before they made it back to the hospital. He skidded to a stop in the pizza guy's car, then darted across the parking lot to Desert Springs. He sprinted toward the ICU. Coming around the corner, he saw a man in a white coat. Tanned and balding, the doctor stopped him. Despite smile lines carved into his angular face, the man's eyes looked haunted.

"We were about to call you, Mr. Brynstone. We tried everything. She was a courageous little fighter. I'm sorry."

Brynstone stared at him.

"We lost her about fifteen minutes ago. We moved your daughter to a private room. Nurse Gradishar will take you. Go say good-bye to Shayna."

Brynstone opened his mouth to speak. Nothing came out.

Brynstone walked into the hospital room as Kaylyn finished praying. She knelt beside the bed, holding Shay's little hand. She always blew a kiss at the end of her prayers. He'd never seen her eyes so red. As they embraced, he glanced over at Shay. He thought his daughter would have a peaceful appearance. She didn't—only fragile and pale.

"I can't lose you too," Kaylyn said through soft tears. "I'm so confused about so many things. But I know I want you in my life, John."

The words lingered like a melody in his ear.

"We'll build our life back together again."

Kaylyn nodded. "I already miss her." She hugged tighter. He couldn't bear to let go, but he had to do it.

"Can I"—he swallowed hard—"be with her a minute?"

She pulled away, but didn't leave the room. He stood beside the bed. He felt empty inside looking at Shay's little face. He leaned in, his fingers gliding through fine curls and down her soft cheek, moving toward her parched lips. He pushed down, opening her mouth. When he pulled away his finger, her lips stayed open.

Kaylyn stepped closer. "What are you doing?"

He shut his eyes. Bit his lip. "I have to try something."

She saw the Propel bottle in his hand.

"This is the White Chrism," he explained. "The perfect medicine. It contains the Radix. The thing I've been searching for."

"Oh, John," she said in a weary voice. "Haven't you put us through enough?"

"It can save Shay. I believe in the Radix. You have to believe too."

"John, I wanted to believe in you again." Her face tightened. "I did."

"Honey, please. Trust me. I can save her. I can bring her back."

"You're crazy. You know it?" she said, wiping tears from her swollen eyes.

"Kay, trust me."

"John, stop it," she cried. "Just stop it."

She collapsed against the wall, sliding down before coming to a rest on the floor. She cupped her face in her hands. Lost in grief, she folded herself up, drawing her legs into her chest, melting into uncontrollable tears.

He wanted to comfort his wife, but time was running out. He was back in game mode, fixated on saving his daughter. In this solitary moment, saving Shay was the only thing that mattered. Metzger had been right, after all. He was terrified of losing his family.

This was Shay's only shot.

Twisting open the blue lid, he touched it to her lip. He tipped the bottle, watching the liquid chrism pour over her tongue. He eased his hand behind her neck, tilting Shay's head. When her little mouth filled up with purplish white medicine, he closed her lips.

John Brynstone kissed his daughter on the forehead, then whispered a prayer. Scripture drifted into his mind, where Jesus took a dead child by the hand and said, *"Talitha, kum,"* meaning, "Little girl, get up."

Aftermath

There is no light without shadow.
—Carl Jung

Chapter Fifty-eight

With a confident stride, the Knight followed a Secret Service agent into the vice president's ceremonial office on the second floor of the Eisenhower Executive Office Building. Globe chandeliers brightened the ornamented room, hinting at the Victorian gasoliers that had hung overhead when Teddy Roosevelt had been vice president. At that time, the room had served as the navy secretary's office. More than a century later, maritime themes and symbols remained in the oil paintings and wall stenciling. Dressed in his three-star army uniform, the Knight greeted Vice President Starr with a power handshake.

"Good to see you, General Delgado."

Following Starr's encouragement, President Armstrong had appointed both the Knight as National Security Agency director and Mark McKibbon as the CIA director. As the Knight settled on a sofa opposite McKibbon, Vice President Starr brought out Cuban Cohiba cigars, offering them to the Knight and McKibbon.

"I joined President Armstrong at his brother's funeral." Starr held a match to the cigar as he toasted the foot. "Will anyone find out you hired people to take care of Dillon Armstrong?"

The Knight wadded the cigar's brown-stained cellophane. "Not if I can help it."

"The president is unhappy with you. I'm running

damage control. Dillon's death pulled the focus off you. Otherwise, you'd be fired."

The Knight shrugged off the news. He wasn't worried. "Remember, Isaac, you're the one who called me about Dillon."

"The president was watching a movie when he mentioned his brother's interest in the Radix. I stepped out of the theater and called, but I never said to kill him. That was your doing."

"As long as I don't get fired, no one will know you called about Dillon."

McKibbon changed the subject. "Dillon Armstrong's death rocked market confidence in Taft-Ryder Pharmaceuticals. Did you see what it was trading at?"

Starr nodded. "Shareholders want Deena Riverside's head."

"Word is she'll step aside as CEO," the Knight added.

"Speaking of stepping down, is the Order of Malta stripping your title as knight?"

"That Vatican doctor is making life difficult. I intend to make life difficult for him."

"Gabriel Bitonti didn't implicate me or McKibbon, did he?" Starr asked.

"No." The Knight smiled. "You mustn't worry, Mr. Vice President. I'm traveling to Italy tomorrow. I'll handle Bitonti."

"Be discreet." Starr pulled out his cigar, exhaling. "On another matter, Mark, thanks for getting Cori Cassidy out of France. When is Dr. Wurm's funeral?"

"Today at three," McKibbon reported. "We'll have men posted."

"Wurm and Brynstone were our best shot at finding the Radix," Starr said. "Guess it was worth paying for Wurm's stay in that Baltimore hospital."

The Knight agreed. "Amherst was a good choice. We kept a close eye on Wurm, even arranged for a psychiatrist named Albert Usher to monitor him."

"Usher's not NSA or CIA, is he?" Starr asked.

"We picked him because of his association with the Order of Malta."

"Does Brynstone know what happened to Jordan Rayne?"

"Vanished." McKibbon shook his head. "Brynstone is as baffled as us. I sense he'd like to find her. For personal reasons."

"Man's been through hell. Wouldn't blame Brynstone for being angry."

"Oh, he's angry," the Knight said. "I had to triple my security. And Brynstone won't ever find Rayne. Metzger claimed he killed her."

"Brynstone found the Radix, but Wurm was last sighted with it. So where is it?"

"Don't know, sir," McKibbon confessed. "We searched Notre-Dame in case he'd dropped it. No sign of the Radix. There's no evidence Adriana Borgia had it before her death. I'm interviewing Brynstone later today. We'll find out what happened."

Starr walked to his desk. He crushed the smoldering cigar and grabbed a newspaper. "Fascinating story in the *Las Vegas Review-Journal*. A baby girl was pronounced dead on Christmas night. To the surprise of her doctors, she was alive and well twenty minutes later." The vice president brought over the paper. "The 'miracle baby' is John Brynstone's daughter."

"Brynstone says he gave the Radix to Wurm and Cassidy before they went to Europe. Claims he didn't see it after that."

"General, if this newspaper story is right, Brynstone is a liar." Starr tossed the newspaper at him. "I want both agencies watching Shayna Brynstone for the rest of her life."

"Already in the works, sir."

"Someday, when I become president, we'll have a unique opportunity, gentlemen." Vice President Starr crossed his arms. "Never before have the Knights of Malta held positions as president, CIA Director, and NSA Director at the same time. With our high-ranking positions, we can strengthen the order's influence. The Radix is out there. We just need to find it."

"We have not been this close to possessing it in over five hundred years," the Knight agreed.

"As brothers in the order"—Starr clamped his hands on McKibbon's shoulder—"we must use every resource to regain it. The Knights will once again possess the Radix."

3:15 P.M.

Afternoon shadows stretched across the rolling lawns of Mount Olivet Cemetery as Cori Cassidy slipped into a huddle of mourners. She found John Brynstone, running her hand along his back as he embraced her. Holding their toddler, Kaylyn gave a one-armed hug. Nicolette Bettencourt stood beside her father. She nodded at Cori. That chilling night at Notre-Dame last week had forged an unlikely friendship between her and the French woman.

Gnarled oaks framed the Wurm mausoleum. Edgar Wurm's coffin rested inside the crypt, but the priest—a stern-looking man in his fifties—officiated the closed-casket service outside. The sun made an uncharacteristic appearance, cutting the winter gloom. Cori reached for her sunglasses, feeling numb. After Mack Shaw's, this was the second funeral this week. His death haunted her with guilt. After a visit from CIA agents, Baltimore police stopped investigating her role in the homicides of Mack and Perez. The best news was that Tessa would make a full recovery.

After heated negotiation, French officials released Wurm's body for burial in his family's mausoleum. Wurm could be intimidating and moody, but she'd walked away respecting his passion and intelligence. The thing that troubled her about that night at Notre-Dame? Nicolette had shot Adriana's brother, but his body had disappeared. She had seen blood spatter on the floor when Paris police dragged her into the spire, but there was no sign of him. She couldn't duck the thought of Santo Borgia out there in the world.

Nearby, a grieving couple adorned a child's grave site with decorations. The woman arranged flowers as her husband planted colorful pinwheels. A fuzzy duckling and a sad-faced bear cuddled against the heart-shaped monument, stuffed companions sharing time with a lost child. Crumbling in sorrow, the couple dropped to their knees in the snow.

A tear emerged from beneath Cori's sunglasses and crawled down her cheek. She opened her purse and unfolded a handkerchief that had belonged to her mother. Seemed like a handful of yesterdays since Ariel Cassidy's passing. Cori wept as bittersweet memories flooded back.

Shay Brynstone reached for her father. Leaning on John's shoulder now, the toddler stared at her reflection in Cori's sunglasses. She was a beautiful child, dressed in white tights and a velvet dress under a black winter coat. John had quit his government job, hoping to patch up his marriage. Kaylyn had agreed to attend today after John explained how Wurm had saved Shay's life by finding the Scintilla. Shay gurgled and gave a funny smile. Cori grinned as the child nuzzled her freshly scrubbed pink rabbit.

Knowing Shay had died was creepy. John confided that his daughter had been dead at least twenty minutes before he brought her back. What would that do to a person? Shay looked beautiful now, but what changes did the Radix produce inside her tiny body? Cori's mind flashed to middle school, when she'd read W. W. Jacob's chilling story, "The Monkey's Paw." Was it like that? Sure, you get your child back from the dead. Only problem? It's not the same child.

As she tucked the handkerchief in her purse, she noticed a lanky African-American man dressed in a dark turtleneck, pants, and a tattered coat. Wearing a dingy Nationals baseball cap, the homeless man stood beside an angel monument. He was staring at John and Shay. Cori's gaze dropped to the man's leather shoes. Black and polished, like the kind she'd noticed on CIA agents. The disquieting figure caught her eyes. They stared, locked in wary curiosity.

Brynstone had worked for a government agency. Would he recognize the stranger? She tugged on his arm, whispering in his ear. He looked over, lowering Shay to the ground.

"What guy?" he asked.

She turned back, pointing at the angel monument. The stranger was nowhere in sight.

Shay tottered away from the mourners. John reached for her, but Cori grabbed his arm. "I'll get her," she whispered. Kaylyn nodded and thanked her.

Shay was unsteady on her feet, but she maneuvered around patches of snow clumped on the brown grass. Looking adorable in her black coat and matching wool beret, she headed for the heart-shaped monument. After arranging colorful pinwheels and flowers and stuffed animals, the parents had returned to their car.

All at once, Cori had a terrible sense that the stranger from behind the angel monument was hiding somewhere out here, waiting to snatch the toddler.

As Shay hurried to the little girl's grave, her ankle boot slipped on the snow, forcing her leg into an awkward twist. The child toppled, striking her knee on the headstone. She crumpled on her back, collecting snow on her dark coat.

Cori sprinted after her. "Shay, are you all right?"

The toddler made a face, her mouth tight. Her blonde, almost invisible eyebrows furrowed. A single tear clutched her eyelash. Shay didn't make a whimper as she grabbed at her shiny black boot. Cori glanced at the mourners. Kaylyn and John were listening to the priest. They hadn't seen their daughter's accident.

Cori bent down and curled Shay against her, examining the child's leg. Mud smeared her white tights. Blood ran bright from a gash beneath her torn knee. Beneath a flap of skin, the jagged cut ran a couple inches in length. She guessed the child would need stitches.

"Sorry I didn't catch you, sweetie." Raising Shay's knee, she dabbed at the blood with her mother's handkerchief. The pressure made the child wince. "You're such a brave girl."

Hoping for distraction, Cori pointed at stuffed animals braced against the monument. The child trained her gaze on the bear and duckling. She held out her bunny, dancing it in a jumble of floppy ears as she shared a bubbling conversation with the other creatures.

While using the handkerchief as a compress, Cori dusted snow off the beret. She pulled it atop the toddler's head. "Bet your mommy has a bandage we can put on your owie."

Balancing Shay on her leg, Cori noticed a tuft of gray fur resting behind the monument. A bushy-tailed squirrel curled on a crust of snow, the flat look of death in its eye. It was unsettling. She hoped Shay hadn't seen the dead creature.

Cori turned her attention to the handkerchief, raising it for a look at the wound. She blinked, staring at the child's knee.

The jagged cut had vanished.

Doubting her eyes, she glanced at Shay's other knee. The tights stretching over her left leg were pristine and white. She studied the bloodstained handkerchief in her hand, then looked at the ripped hose beneath the child's right knee. The tights were flecked with dirt and blood. Even the underside of Shay's dress showed a smear of blood. But there was no sign of the gash that had marred her soft skin.

Shay looked up with clear blue eyes. A serene look crossed her face. Her small lips parted as she said, "Auw gone." The little girl giggled.

Heart drumming in her ears, she scooped up Shay, her chin riding on Cori's shoulder. She returned to the mourners, unable to believe what she had witnessed. With the White Chrism inside of her, Shay Brynstone had become the ultimate realization of the alchemical dream.

Chapter Fifty-nine

Potomac
10:57 P.M.

The Knight awakened with a coughing spasm, blood spilling down his chin. He didn't want to black out again. Both wrists were pulled tight behind his back. He couldn't budge. The tall metal stake braced his body in an upright position.

His left eye wouldn't open. Too swollen. His head burned with a fever. He coughed more blood. He glanced around the room and recognized the walls. The studio. He was home. He squinted. A man was seated behind the easel, his legs visible beneath an oversized linen canvas on the crossbar. Small flames darted across the frame.

He knew that Brynstone would return someday for his revenge.

The Knight's voice rasped, "John?"

Hard laughter erupted from behind the fiery canvas.

"Answer me, John. Answer, damn you."

"Were you expecting Dr. Brynstone?" the man asked, a metallic German accent coloring his words. He stepped from behind the burning canvas. His small, terrible eyes fixed on the Knight. Erich Metzger was a contradiction. Slight but powerful. Tranquil but fierce.

The assassin crossed his arms. "I warned you about becoming my enemy."

"Where are my security personnel?"

"Now? In hell, perhaps." He smiled. "Look at your feet."

The Knight rolled his head, blinking his swollen eye. He was perched atop a mound composed of smashed antique tables and chairs, draperies, and rare volumes from his library. Five canvases were scattered around his feet. His cherished paintings. Saint Peter. Saint James the Greater. Saint Sebastian. Saint George. And Saint Andrew.

"How dare you touch my work?"

"You are now my work," Metzger answered. "You adore martyrs. Don't you wish to become one?"

"You can't do this."

"When I kill a killer, I utilize his methodology. Your victims died recreating martyrdom. But your saints hold no fascination for me."

"And a miscreant like you would hold no fascination for my saints."

"Have you heard about a Dominican friar named Giordano Bruno?" Metzger asked. "He claimed the universe held innumerable suns. For him, living beings inhabited worlds beyond our own. He believed Jesus was not divine, but a clever magician. The Church imprisoned Bruno in a dungeon. The Inquisition branded him a heretic. In 1600, he was burned at the stake."

"I suppose a lunatic like Bruno is your kind of saint. A scientific martyr."

"Bruno wasn't much of a scientist," Metzger admitted. He grabbed the burning canvas, then pitched it onto the pyre. "I respect him because he was radical. He died for an idea."

"So did my saints."

"Hardly. They died for salvation. Then learned there is no salvation. Certainly not for you."

Delgado glowered as fire crawled toward his beloved painting of Saint James. Metzger snatched the canvas from the pyre. He studied the painting. A king slashing a martyr.

"An early work," Metzger observed. "Different style. Not as controlled or defined."

"My first in the series," he said. "King Herod Agrippa stabbing Saint James the Greater. He was the first apostle to be martyred."

"Before I killed your man Cress, he told me you painted your models as they were dying," Metzger said. "But I recognize this man. He is still alive."

"You are wrong. He is long dead. He is the only saint whose face I painted from memory."

"I'll hang onto this one. I have a friend who might find it compelling."

The Knight sensed warmth on his bare feet. Between gritted teeth, he said, "I have a safe in my library. Free me and I'll pay—"

"I don't need money," Metzger interrupted. "Because of Jordan Rayne, I am quite wealthy. Besides, your library will not survive to see the new year."

The Knight looked out the studio door. A woman appeared in the doorway. Behind her, flickering light danced across the walls near the atrium. "You're burning my home?"

"No, that responsibility rests with Franka. I've never had an appetite for arson."

"My possessions," he pleaded. "Will they burn?"

"It all dies with you." Metzger raised a vial. Removing the lid, he slid a greenish stock onto his palm. "This is the Radix. Or at least, Brynstone claimed so when he surrendered it."

"Give it to me."

The assassin kicked aside a burning canvas and climbed

on the pyre. The Knight opened his mouth. Metzger placed the root on his tongue. The Knight swallowed it.

Metzger leaped from the pyre. "Tonight, we'll pit my blaze against your little plant," he smiled. "Herr Delgado, how strong is your faith in Dr. Brynstone's root?"

11:15 P.M.

In a fury, Brynstone turned off the Beltway and raced his rental Lexus onto Maryland's River Road. After Kaylyn and Shayna had drifted to sleep back at their Washington, D.C., hotel, he had pulled up the closed-circuit television at Delgado's Potomac home. After some tinkering, he had accessed security cams, including one mounted in the studio. Back at the hotel, he had tuned in as a man strapped an unconscious James Delgado to a tall metal stake. Brynstone had grabbed a visual on the intruder. He had jumped up when he saw Metzger's face. He had grabbed the computer along with his Glock before hurrying out of the hotel. Metzger and Delgado were in the same room at the same time. He had to get there. Fast.

While in the car, he had overheard Metzger's conversation with Delgado, listening to the feed streaming in from Delgado's studio. Now minutes away, he gave a quick glance at the computer on the seat. Metzger fed the counterfeit Radix to Delgado. Jumping off the pyre, Metzger spotted the studio surveillance cam. The assassin raised a gun and fired.

The screen went black.

Brynstone cursed as he slapped down the cover of the notebook computer. He was close. Turning into the Bradley Farms neighborhood, he punched the accelerator. He wanted to kill Delgado. Then he'd make Metzger pay.

The isolated studio was located at the rear of Delgado's mansion. Brynstone had visited the house countless times, but had seen the studio only once. Like Delgado,

Kaylyn was an artist, and he had given them a tour a few years ago. All other times, he kept the studio locked.

He swerved the black Lexus off the driveway, then tore across the vast lawn, spinning dead grass and snow as he pulled behind Delgado's mansion. Smoke boiled from a window on the three-level Colonial. Although situated on secluded land, neighbors would notice and make an emergency call soon.

Bringing out his Glock, he rushed into the fiery building. He knew the home, knew the fastest way to find the general. The sweltering blaze overpowered the atrium.

He had the sense someone was watching him. Swinging around with his handgun, he aimed at a figure standing behind crisscrossed burning timber. Dressed all in black, a ghostly woman studied him. Her gaunt face was lined by chin-length hair, disheveled and purple. She darted away from the main hall, moving back toward the fire.

Ignoring her, he sprinted to the studio. He kept watch for Metzger as he headed into the room. Delgado was positioned in the center of the studio, fire crawling the wall behind him. The man squirmed as flames seethed at the base around his bare feet. He wheezed, taking in smoke as Brynstone hurried to him. Delgado's head snapped up.

"I know you're the Knight. I know you hired Metzger. Why'd you try to kill me?"

"You knew too much, John. I had ambitious plans. It was only a matter of time before you ruined things. I knew that sooner or later, you would stand in my way." His eyes narrowed. "Last week wasn't the first time I tried to kill you."

"What are you talking about?"

"Think back twenty years. At your summer cottage. Remember when you found me on the floor of your father's study?"

"A man broke into our home. You warned me to get out before he found me."

"There was no one else, John. I acted like I had been attacked. When you wheeled down the hallway, I came after you. I planned to stab you with the dagger I'd used to kill your father."

"You killed my dad?"

"Jayson was my friend, but he wanted to pull Wurm off his Voynich work. I tried talking him out of it. He was too stubborn. Murder was a consequence he brought on himself."

Brynstone growled, "That means you pushed me down the stairs."

Delgado strained to rise on his toes as flames licked his feet. The metal stake was drawing in heat, blistering his back. "You can thank Wurm for that. He interrupted everything."

"What about the lacerations? You had multiple stab wounds."

"What's the best way to avoid suspicion, John? Self-inflicted injuries. A facial gash can be quite convincing." Delgado choked, his face bright from the firelight. "I bled that evening for the grace of God, but it was worth the pain. That night, I transformed into the Knight." Perspiration rolled down his face. "I'm the Knight and you're a pawn. So was your father. Pawns are easy to kill. I loved killing your father."

Brynstone raised the handgun, aiming it at the general. His finger quivered on the trigger. Then it hit him. He knew what the man was doing. Delgado wanted to bait him into firing the weapon. He wanted to die before the flames consumed him.

"What's wrong?" Delgado asked, wincing as fire burned his flesh. "Lose your nerve?"

Brynstone lowered the Glock. "Told you before. I don't believe in wasting bullets."

As fire curled around Delgado, he screamed, "I am the Knight!"

An explosion rocked the north wing of the mansion,

cutting off his words. Sirens accompanied the roar. A column of flame engulfed Lieutenant General James Delgado. His face contorted in agony, making a death mask more haunting than the martyred souls in his paintings.

Brynstone had minutes—maybe seconds—to escape the inferno. He raced out of the studio, leaping through flames spreading across the atrium. Glancing out the window, he saw three fire teams arrive. An exterior crew of firefighters ran hose lines around the front, responding to the structure fire. They were preparing to execute rescue ops, but it was too late. The fire had progressed and the main hall collapsed along with the studio.

Brynstone darted out the back of the burning structure, staying away from police and firefighters. He had a documented record of conflict with Delgado, making him an immediate suspect. Overhead, a news helicopter blasted a searchlight across Delgado's estate. Ducking into the shadows, he glanced around, hoping to find Metzger. The searchlight blurred past, running a sweep of the area. This was turning bad. He wanted Metzger, but now wasn't the time. Fighting instinct, Brynstone rushed for the Lexus.

Getting closer, he saw a shadowy image in the front seat. His mind flashed to the Linda Vista Hospital, when he had found Bob the Driver's body. Keeping his gun steady, he moved into a crouch beside the car. Taking a hard look, he saw a rectangular canvas. It didn't look rigged. He opened the door. A small card was attached near the upper corner of the blackened painting. A few lines were written in small, precise penmanship:

How good of you to let the Knight burn. You now have one less enemy in the world.

You might find the artwork intriguing. Please accept it with my compliments.

Perhaps we'll meet in the new year?
—M

Brynstone's heart beat a little faster. The painting was in Delgado's style. More crude than his later work, it showed a king stabbing a saint. As with his other paintings, the look of terror on the martyr's face was haunting in its realism. A wave of nausea rolled inside his stomach. Brynstone knew the inspiration for this painting. He recognized the saint's face. He studied the ice blue eyes, captured forever in torment. His father's eyes.

Chapter Sixty

Washington, D.C.
11:57 P.M.

Brynstone parked near the Mount Olivet Cemetery. He had been driving in a stupor since leaving Delgado's home. Climbing over the fence, he found himself alone in a cemetery at midnight. James Delgado, Erich Metzger, and Jordan Rayne. One down. Two to go. Learning the truth about his father's murder dampened any satisfaction. Would he feel closure after tracking down Metzger and Rayne?

In the distance, the Washington Memorial glowed like a phantom obelisk. Distant fireworks crackled and burst, spraying the night with twinkling color. New Year's Eve. He wasn't in the mood for celebration as he headed for the Wurm mausoleum.

A figure darted past a darkened oak tree. He brought out his gun.

"Stop right there," he barked.

The woman screamed, then backed against the tree. He holstered the Glock. Cori Cassidy stared at him, shock blanking her features. "John," she gasped. "Why are you here?"

"Long story," he said. "What about you?"

"Left a friend's party at the Wyndom Hotel. Not in a party mood." She embraced him, then pulled back. "I was going to call. You met with the CIA director today, right? Everything go okay?"

"It was strange," he confessed. "Edgar Wurm always claimed the Knights of Malta wanted the Radix. Before I met with McKibbon, I contacted the president of the Federal Association of the Order of Malta. He confirmed that the order did not play a role in the search for the Radix. A couple people on the fringes of the order were looking for it. Director McKibbon was one. General Delgado was another."

"Your boss? He was involved with the Order of Malta?"

"Doesn't matter now. He's dead."

"What happened?"

"Later."

Taking the hint, she changed the subject. "John, I need to tell you something. At Edgar's funeral today, Shay fell down and cut her knee. Bad enough to—"

He raised his hand to silence her. He listened. Had he heard footsteps? Or maybe wind rustling a tree. He wasn't in the mood to take a chance. He pulled Cori inside the Wurm mausoleum. No one else in here. He turned toward the door, shielding her against the wall.

He didn't hear anything outside.

In the center of the mausoleum, a raised oblong coffin stone supported the Belgian marble tomb where Edgar Wurm had been laid to rest. The lid had been moved to the mausoleum floor. Brynstone rushed over, gliding his hand along the polished black marble. He peered down with a flashlight.

Wurm's body was not inside. The tomb was empty.

He glanced at Cori. "Did you tell the CIA that Edgar swallowed the Radix?"

"Agent Angelilli talked to Nicolette Bettencourt. She saw Wurm pop something in his mouth. Flying back from Paris, Angelilli asked if Edgar swallowed the Radix. He was suspicious, but I covered it." She glanced inside the tomb. "The noise we heard. Was that the CIA? Did they take Edgar's body?"

Brynstone didn't answer. He darted outside, running to where they had heard the sound. The night was still. No sign of another person.

Moving behind a massive oak tree, he inspected the ground. She stepped behind him, then peered over his shoulder. Footprints carved in fresh snow. Leading from the mausoleum's door, the prints curled past the tree and disappeared at the wet road.

Cori stepped alongside one footprint, measuring it against her boot. "These prints are huge."

"About size fourteen, I'd guess."

She studied him. "That footprint could belong to Santo Borgia."

Brynstone nodded. "Or Edgar Wurm."

Author's Note

Napoleon Bonaparte may have said it best: "What is history but a fable agreed upon?" Embellishment is a vice for historians, but a virtue for novelists. My ultimate goal in writing *The Radix* was to craft an entertaining story. Along the way, I committed a few historical transgressions in the name of fiction. So, let me set the record straight on a few topics.

Let's begin with the Borgias. People from Alexandre Dumas, pére, to Mario Puzo have suggested that Cesare Borgia's face inspired the depiction of Jesus Christ in Italian Renaissance paintings. In turn, the idea goes, paintings that emulated Borgia's look continued to shape the portrayal of Christ. As mentioned in Chapter Twenty-eight, Borgia did contract syphilis and he was reputed to have worn a mask to conceal his scarred features. His father, Rodrigo Borgia, better known as the controversial Pope Alexander VI, was also syphilitic. A Raffaele della Rovere did exist and was murdered in 1502 by Oliverotto da Fermo, an acquaintance of Cesare Borgia, but he bears little resemblance to Raphael della Rovere, the character in my book.

As depicted in the prologue, Niccolò Machiavelli was in the service of Borgia during Christmas 1502, although there is no record that they traveled to Paris at that time. Machiavelli drew upon Borgia's commanding style while writing *The Prince*, his 1532 book on leadership and the psychology of power. We learn in Chapter Forty-two that Cesare Borgia displayed an enemy's head on a pike in Cesena on December 26, 1502. That's true, but the decapitated head belonged to a governor named Ramiro de

Lorqua. So, do the tales of Borgia's brutal exploits represent a fable agreed upon? Maybe, but it is clear you didn't want to make the guy angry.

Unequaled as a book of puzzles, the Voynich manuscript is an authentic document with distinct Voynichese "languages." It contains drawings of 113 unidentified plant species and over 100 species of medicinal herbs and roots. Housed at the Beinecke Rare Book and Manuscript Library at Yale University, it has frustrated a legion of amateur and professional cryptanalysts hoping to unlock its centuries-old mystery. Either a book of secret codes or one of the most sophisticated hoaxes in history, the origin and meaning of the Voynich manuscript remain unknown. My speculation in Chapter Fifteen about the Voynich author is pure fiction.

What about the Rx symbol? Familiar to anyone who has been in an American pharmacy, this symbol's origin offers its own mystery. As Cori notes in Chapter Forty-one, some are convinced that its origins can be found in the symbol for the Egyptian god Horus. Another popular idea suggests that the symbol is derived from the Latin *recipere* or *recipe*, meaning "take thus," while other variations insist the origin came from *fiat mistura*, or "let a mixture be made." There are still more theories. In truth, there is a great deal of speculation, but no real consensus.

In his 1944 book *Psychology and Alchemy*, Carl Jung used the term *radix ipsius* while discussing the prime material. The Scintilla receives broader coverage in his last major work, *Mysterium Coniunctionis*. I took liberties in my interpretation of the Radix and Scintilla that bear little resemblance to alchemical concepts that fascinated Jung. As mentioned in Chapter Thirty-one, Jung did build the Bollingen Tower complex, but the descriptions inside his spiritual tower (Chapter Thirty-nine) are the product of my imagination. I should add that Jung's paintings as well as imagery from his writings inspired the images that I described on the Bollingen walls.

From as far back as 1949, the accusation that Jungian psychology inspired a cult and secret society has arisen in several books and private interviews (Chapter Thirty-three). In the most aggressive charge, Richard Noll wrote *The Jung Cult: Origins of a Charismatic Movement* and *The Aryan Christ: The Secret Life of Carl Jung*, with the assertion that Jung was the "most influential liar of the twentieth century." In Noll's version, Jung found inspiration in polygamy and Aryan sun worship and served as a self-appointed cult leader. Jung did experience a trance-like vision of himself transforming into a lion-headed deity, a practice arising from the Mithraic *unio mystica*, a fusion of a human with a god. For Noll, the transformation into the Deus Leontocephalus was a dramatic experience that was forbidden knowledge to all but a few in Jung's inner circle. Sonu Shamdasani countered Noll's accusations in his book, *Cult Fictions: C. G. Jung and the Founding of Analytical Psychology*. Shamdasani argues that Jung had no appetite to serve as a cult leader—regardless of what a few followers may have believed—nor did he use his analytical psychology to shroud a quasi-religious sect.

Jung's grandfather did serve as grand master of the Swiss Freemasons. Although Eugène Emmanuel Viollet-le-Duc spent his final years in Switzerland, there is no evidence that the architect interacted with the elder Jung. As the driving force behind Notre-Dame's restoration, Viollet-le-Duc's likeness does appear on the cathedral statue of Saint Thomas, with the architect's name on the staff (Chapter Forty-six). The information concerning the Pillar of the Nautes (Chapter Forty-two), Fulcanelli (Chapter Forty-three), and the grotesque, Le Stryge (Chapter Fifty), are based in fact. Although Friar Zanchetti is fictional, the "catacomb mummies" from central Italy are real. In Navelli, a floor collapsed in the Church of San Sebastiano, revealing the mummified remains of two hundred bodies. And let me be clear that the Sovereign

Military Order of Malta, in its long and storied history, has never expressed interest in the mythical Radix.

To see the *cista mystica* or to learn more about the fact behind the fiction in this novel, please visit my website: authorbrettking.com. You can also find me on Facebook and Twitter. Thanks for reading *The Radix*!

"Wood writes like a dark, demented angel."
—Ken Bruen, Bestselling Author
of *Once Were Cops*

TERMINATED

Gwen crossed the wrong coworker when she gave Stephen Tarbell a poor performance evaluation. That was all it took to push Tarbell over the edge. He already believed Gwen stole the promotion that was rightfully his. He won't let her take anything else from him. Now it's his turn to take . . . and take. By the time he's finished with her, Tarbell plans to take her job, her family—even her life.

"Wood's got the goods to craft thriller scenarios."
—Bookgasm

SIMON WOOD

"Simon Wood knows how to create tension, he knows how to build three-dimensional characters, and he has proven he can tie everything together in a high-octane climax."
—Book Browser

ISBN 13: 978-0-8439-6367-0

GREGG LOOMIS

Author of *The Sinai Secret*

It was a gala evening to celebrate the find of the century—previously unknown Gospels containing startling revelations. But before the parchments could be revealed, shots rang out in the British Museum and the Gospels—along with Lang Reilly's friend—were taken. An ancient and mysterious organization will gladly kill anyone who comes close to the parchments, but Lang can't be intimidated. The more his life is threatened, the more determined he is to find the truth behind…

THE COPTIC SECRET

"Dan Brown fans will find *The Julian Secret* a delight."
—I Love a Mystery

ISBN 13: 978-0-8439-6274-1

STACY DITTRICH

Stacy Dittrich is a police officer and former detective specializing in sexual crimes, with over seventeen years of law enforcement experience. She has appeared as a commentator on CNN, *Geraldo at Large*, *The O'Reilly Factor* and *The Nancy Grace Show*. Now she's used her experience to create a thrillingly realistic detective, in cases that are both gripping and authentic!

THE BODY MAFIA

When the bodies of local homeless men begin turning up missing major organs, Detective CeeCee Gallagher is hot on the trail of a killer. Only after her husband, FBI Agent Michael Hagerman, is the target of a car bomb, does CeeCee realize what she's really dealing with. This is no mere madman. These killers are organized—and more dangerous than any CeeCee's seen before.

"A book to send true chills down the spine. Four and a half stars!"
—*RT Book Reviews* on *Mary Jane's Grave*

ISBN 13: 978-0-8439-6289-5

SANDRA RUTTAN

Her body was found in a Dumpster. But one look at the victim told Hart and Tain that this would be no ordinary investigation. There were details eerily similar to the first case that they had worked on together, a search for a terrifying murderer called the Missing Killer. And when they saw the victim's face they realized something else—this woman was the only one to escape the Missing Killer with her life. But Hart, Tain and Nolan solved that case almost two years ago. The killer is dead. Isn't he? Is someone out to finish what the Missing Killer started? Or did they get the wrong man?

LULLABY FOR THE NAMELESS

ISBN 13: 978-0-8439-6286-4

INTERACT WITH DORCHESTER ONLINE!

Want to learn more about your favorite books and authors?
Want to talk with other readers that like to read the same books as you?
Want to see up-to-the-minute Dorchester news?

VISIT DORCHESTER AT:
DorchesterPub.com
Twitter.com/DorchesterPub
Facebook.com (Search Pages)

DISCUSS DORCHESTER'S NOVELS AT:
Dorchester Forums at DorchesterPub.com
GoodReads.com
LibraryThing.com
Myspace.com/books
Shelfari.com
WeRead.com

☐ **YES!**

Sign me up for the Leisure Thriller Book Club and send my FREE BOOKS! If I choose to stay in the club, I will pay only $4.25* each month, a savings of $3.74!

NAME: _____

ADDRESS: _____

TELEPHONE: _____

EMAIL: _____

☐ I want to pay by credit card.

☐ **VISA**   ☐ **MasterCard**   ☐ **DISCOVER**

ACCOUNT #: _____

EXPIRATION DATE: _____

SIGNATURE: _____

Mail this page along with $2.00 shipping and handling to:
Leisure Thriller Book Club
PO Box 6640
Wayne, PA 19087
Or fax (must include credit card information) to:
610-995-9274

You can also sign up online at **www.dorchesterpub.com**.
*Plus $2.00 for shipping. Offer open to residents of the U.S. and Canada only.
Canadian residents please call 1-800-481-9191 for pricing information.
If under 18, a parent or guardian must sign. Terms, prices and conditions subject to change. Subscription subject to acceptance. Dorchester Publishing reserves the right to reject any order or cancel any subscription.